When We Were Rich is Tim Lott ⎯ ⎯ ⎯ ⎯ ⎯ ⎯ ⎯ ⎯ ⎯ ⎯
Scent of Dried Roses, is a Penguin Mode⎯ ⎯ ⎯ ⎯ ⎯ ⎯ es in Lond⎯ ⎯.
He teaches writing both for *Guardian* M⎯ ⎯ ⎯ ⎯ ses and through
personal tutoring.

www.thenovelry.com/findamentor

Praise for *When We Were Rich*

'A sharp and very funny portrait of a brash era which is also a surprisingly tender take on flawed masculinity' Sarah Hughes, *i paper*

'What a terrific novel — wickedly sharp, wildly entertaining — I was gripped from start to finish. With its twisty plots and interwoven characters it paints a vivid portrait of a crucial decade. It's laugh-out-loud funny, too' Deborah Moggach

'Wickedly funny and deeply humane. I loved this book' Sadie Jones

'Tim Lott revisits the years between millennium fever and the financial crisis, and brings this already long-lost era back to life in a novel every bit as evocative and compelling as we would expect from this prodigiously gifted author' Jonathan Coe

'Lott delivers many hilarious and sad scenes of life in a long-term relationship. He also explores the poignancy and fragility of male friendships, in a manner reminiscent of Graham Swift's *Last Orders* . . . [He is,] crucially, careful to linger over moral difficulty and vulnerability rather than evading it' *TLS*

WHEN WE WERE RICH

TIM LOTT

SCRIBNER

LONDON NEW YORK SYDNEY TORONTO NEW DELHI

First published in Great Britain by Scribner, an imprint of
Simon & Schuster UK Ltd, 2019
This paperback edition published by Scribner, an imprint of
Simon & Schuster UK Ltd, 2020
A CBS COMPANY

SCRIBNER and design are registered trademarks of The Gale Group, Inc.,
used under licence by Simon & Schuster Inc.

1 3 5 7 9 10 8 6 4 2

Simon & Schuster UK Ltd
1st Floor
222 Gray's Inn Road
London WC1X 8HB

Simon & Schuster Australia, Sydney
Simon & Schuster India, New Delhi

www.simonandschuster.co.uk
www.simonandschuster.com.au
www.simonandschuster.co.in

A CIP catalogue record for this book
is available from the British Library

Paperback ISBN: 978-1-4711-6158-2
eBook ISBN: 978-1-4711-6157-5

Typeset by M Rules
Printed and bound by CPI Group (UK) Ltd, Croydon, CR0 4YY

For Tamara Gray

Millennium

Veronica Tree turns the key in the latch of the faux Victorian slate-grey front door and hurls herself inward, out of the murk of a chill December evening. She is met with a sultry barrier of convected air. Her husband has turned the thermostat higher than she can stand, both in terms of her comfort and her anxiety about the impact on global warming.

She sheds her denim jacket onto the reclaimed 1950s school cloakroom hook in the hall then removes her chunky orange sweater and drapes it over the jacket. Underneath, she is wearing her blue hospital scrubs. She turns the thermostat down five degrees, knowing that Frankie will turn it up again the moment he becomes aware of the drop in temperature. He is cold-blooded, he says. He also says – to her irritation – that the planet can take care of itself, or we're all doomed anyway, depending on whether he is feeling optimistic or pessimistic.

Divested of outer layers but still overheated and flushed, Veronica strides into the living room of the two-bedroom terraced house in Brackenbury Village, Hammersmith. Or perhaps *slides* is a better word. She is slim, flat-chested, long-legged, limber. Her slightly snaggled front teeth do nothing to diminish her husband's persistent desire for her, which, after only four months of marriage, is becoming as much an irritation as it is flattery.

There are cardboard boxes scattered on the floor at the bottom of the stairs that lead up to the two small bedrooms on the first floor. The couple are moving to a new house soon, to a larger place on the St Quintin Estate in North Kensington. Completion comes at the end of January. Veronica idly inspects the open boxes which contain practically everything Frankie owns. Visible at the moment are board games (Risk, Trivial Pursuit, Monopoly), a set of golf clubs, a pair of football shorts and a bottle of Acqua di Parma aftershave. She is astonished at how little he possesses. Her stuff, taken out of her flat (now sold), nearly fills the substantial shed at the back of the house. That's without the furniture, which languishes expensively in storage.

Veronica sees Frankie is sitting on the sofa, still in his office suit, immersed in cathode rays from the TV, holding the remote in one hand and a bottle of chilled Peroni in the other. Veronica leans over and pecks him on the cheek. He makes a moue without putting it anywhere. The television barks the headlines.

Yeltsin resigns while Vladimir Putin takes over in Russia . . . The prime minister Tony Blair will get ready to welcome in the new century at the Millennium Dome . . .

Veronica kicks off her flat hospital shoes and pads her way towards the open-plan kitchen. On the way she stops at the telephone answering machine, which is showing one message. She hits the button and pauses to listen.

Hi, Frankie. It's Ralph. Sorry I didn't see you at the office Christmas party. I've been a bit off colour. Nothing serious. I hope. (Chuckles). So. Anyway. Thanks for your all your hard work over the past year. Have a happy new millennium. Love to Veronica. And I'll see you in the office, you know, whenever. Much to talk about. Oh, and Polly sends her love. Pip pip.

A click and a burr as the machine shuts itself off.

Did you hear that?

Uh, says Frankie.

She goes to the kitchen, fills and switches on the Braun kettle.

Hot beverage?

Nah, says Frankie, eyes still magnetized by the television.

Veronica picks a carrot out of the monumental American-style fridge and nibbles on it with her small incisors. She draws a large glass of filtered water from the front panel of the fridge and downs it in one. She can't remember when it became common sense to drink large quantities of water, but she has become convinced by the weight of peer opinion that the practice makes you live longer and keeps you pure. She feels the maintenance of purity to be a pressing concern, although this sits uneasily with her medical awareness that the body is an irremediable and necessary jungle of prowling bacteria and rampaging microorganisms.

The narrow end of the carrot is rotten – organic veg goes off almost as soon as you get them from the shop – so she flips the food waste bin lid to throw it in, and on impulse checks the other two bins, one for landfill, the other for recycling paper and plastics. She grimaces.

There's food in the paper bin. Again. What is it, yoghurt?

She is weary and resigned rather than angry.

It all goes in landfill, anyway, says Frankie.

She extracts yesterday's *Guardian* from under the goo.

The yoghurt is all over it.

Sour milk. Seems appropriate.

I asked you to save that issue. There's a recipe I want. I never throw away your comics before you've finished with them.

She picks up the copy of *Estate Agent Today* that is on the kitchen table and flicks through the pages.

Oh look! The results of the 'Estate Agent of the Year' awards. I'm surprised that one didn't make the evening news.

You may laugh.

No sign of Farley, Ratchett and Gwynne.

We didn't enter.

Veronica studies the transparent window in the kettle behind which the water will shortly start to effervesce. Frankie stretches out on the white leather sofa, trying unsuccessfully to get comfortable.

How long have we got, Frankie?

You were right about this settee. It looks good in here alright. But you can't find a spot on it.

Did you hear me? And it's a sofa.

Frankie puts down the Peroni bottle, picks up his Psion Organiser from the Swedish-style pine coffee table in front of him and checks it.

You'll have time to get changed.

He wriggles on the sofa again.

I don't know why we couldn't get the brown leather one.

Because it was like something out of Acorn Antiques.

Comfortable, though.

Frankie picks at his teeth with a matchstick he has produced from somewhere, and makes a face as he digs at his gums.

You still want to go out tonight? says Veronica. *Okay if you don't. We can stay home and watch Jools on the TV.*

This is your way of saying you don't want to go. Right?

He digs deeper, right at the back of the mouth, wrenching his face into a distended grimace.

I was thinking of you.

He takes the toothpick out, smacks his lips, and throws the soggy stick into the waste paper bin.

Millennium night isn't every day. So to speak. Celebration is not optional. Anyway, Nodge and Fraser and Colin are relying on me to sign them into the club.

Colin who?

Colin who do you think?

Colin Burden?

No, Colin Firth. Of course Colin Burden.

You didn't tell me he was coming.

I didn't tell you he wasn't coming.

Veronica pulls a mug out of the cupboard, making enough superfluous noise to ensure that Frankie registers her dissatisfaction.

Is Nodge definitely bringing Fraser?

She sprinkles her voice with vinegar, but Frankie's mood is antacid, oblivious.

Last I heard.

Veronica propels the mug down onto the worktop with what now registers with Frankie as unnecessary force. He finally summons the wherewithal to look up from the TV.

They'll probably peel off soon enough, he says. *To do something, you know, gay.*

5

Veronica shovels coffee into the Bodum tetchily.

Fraser doesn't like me. Or you. Or anyone in particular. You know what I think of Colin. I'd be just as happy watching the Hootennany here.

Too late to change plans now. Who's on Jools anyway?

Jamiroquai. Travis. Skin from Skunk Anansie.

Not a lineup really worth staying in for, is it? Also, a river of fire on the Thames just isn't going to have the same effect on the box. We've made the arrangements. They're relying on us.

Veronica pours boiling water over the coffee, enjoying the agitation and steam and swirl. She fetches soya milk from the fridge. She decided she had a gluten intolerance some months earlier, around the time her water intake swelled to several litres a day.

Is Tony coming too? Did that slip your mind as well?

Tony who?

Tony Diamonte. Sex addict, coke snorter, bully, racist. That Tony.

Persona non grata. As you well know.

Yeh. But then I thought Colin was persona non grata.

Tony's different. Tony's in rehab somewhere. Again. As for Colin — well. Nodge said it would be good. A nice gesture. He sort of shamed me into it. He's good at that.

Colin's baggage.

He got us a nice wedding present.

He bought you a nice wedding present. I had nothing to do with it.

He's not such a bad guy.

He's weak.

So?

Weak people are dangerous.

How's he weak?

People who turn to Jesus halfway through life are always weak.

He's not religious anymore, says Frankie, now channel surfing pointlessly between UK Gold and Sky One.

Not very much anyway. That lasted about three months. Colin never really could commit himself to anything.

You can stand a few hours with an old friend, says Frankie. *Can't you?*

Not much I can do about it now.

It's only once every thousand years. Anyway, he's bringing a date. That should keep him occupied.

Veronica stops the plunger of the cafetière half-depressed.

Colin's got a date?

Couldn't suppress his excitement. Someone from his office who got blown out by someone else at the last moment. So he got lucky.

More than you can say for her.

She finishes depressing the plunger and stands back to wait. It will be exactly three minutes, Frankie knows. Veronica is precise about such matters.

After Veronica pours the coffee, she emerges from the kitchen, gazing around the room critically. Since their marriage she has made an effort to gussy up the space – atomizer, a few colourful cushions, scented candles and fresh flowers. It's a pleasant space here, but very obviously, until quite recently, the home of a single man, a man who works as an estate agent and therefore values and advises anonymity in design.

Veronica makes her way to the bedroom, with its super king-size bed, ornate retro iron bedstead – the sole import from her recently sold flat – and single erotic Modigliani print on the wall. There is another large television under the sash window that bulks out behind with a pregnant swell of tubes and wires.

We need to invest in a flat screen, says Frankie, who, following her into the room, glances critically at the TV.

Too expensive.

I'm an early adopter.

Not anymore you're not. Not now we're moving. We won't be able to afford it. So you'd better get used to being a late adopter. Or a non-adopter.

She starts to remove her hospital scrubs, mandatory workwear for her job as a pathologist at St Mary's Hospital in Paddington. She has a couple of outfits crammed in next to Frankie's selection of suits. Most of her clothes are in the garden shed. Frankie picks up the remote, but she holds up her hand.

I need to do my twenty minutes, says Veronica.

Do we have the time? Frankie checks his watch.

There's always time. Time is all we have.

Cool, man, he says softly, but loud enough for her to hear.

Why don't you join me? she says, preparing her little brass gong and lighting an incense stick.

Same reason I didn't join you last time. And the time before that.

Remind me.

Because. I. Fucking. Hate. Meditation.

Mindfulness.

New way of flogging gongs and candles.

Frankie has tried, under Veronica's encouragement, to watch his own thoughts, but he cannot catch them long enough to let them go, however hard he tries or tries not to try. He is unable to remove himself sufficiently in order to isolate and observe the ghostly rumour of ego and the river of thought. The contents of his mind are all of a piece for him, a barely manageable chaos of chattering, random, desire-driven agitation. A snowstorm of cascading impressions in a globe of self that sits on his shoulders invisibly, a spectral Janus looking, puzzlingly, both outward and inward.

It's very calming, says Veronica, closing her eyes, putting her thumbs and forefingers together and crossing her legs.

I'll be calm enough when I'm dead, Frankie says, scratching himself under the arm with fingernails manicured, clean and sharp.

* * *

By eight o clock, Frankie and Veronica have showered and dressed. Frankie is wearing boot-cut jeans, Rockport boots with Argyle socks and an off-white Von Dutch T-shirt with a Vintage Lacoste fine-knit cardigan in umber. He covers up with a designer puffa jacket by Armani. Veronica is wearing a halter top and sequined trousers. The addition of a lurid red sweater reminds Frankie momentarily of an elongated pillar-box, but he dismisses the unkind thought promptly. They are sinking a final glass of Chardonnay in the kitchen before they leave.

So what's your New Millennium's resolution? Frankie asks, tidying his hair with his fingers rather than a comb, to achieve a carelessly rumpled look.

Resolutions are pointless.

You have to have one. At least this year.

Not if you believe in fate.

Whatever that might be.

All you really want is for me to ask you what yours is.

Am I so predictable?

So what is it, then?

Frankie stands up, checks himself in the mirror, and teases up the front of his waxed fringe.

I've got two. A New Year's one and a Millennium one. The New Year's one is to become a partner at the firm. Ralph as good as promised it to me when the New Year comes. He wants to retire. Since his heart attack, he's been getting very tired. I've seen it. Can hardly get himself up from the desk sometimes.

He looked fine last time I saw him.

He'll be fine if he looks after himself. Keeping on a healthy diet and so on. Polly's looking out for him. The doctors say he's good for at least another decade. But anyway. He's looking to the future. And I'm part of it.

Ratchett won't like that.

Ratchett won't have anything to do with it.

That's great, Frankie. Really great. I'm so happy for you.

Thank you.

But it's not exactly a resolution. More something you already know about that you're waiting to happen.

You're just nitpicking.

What's the Millennium resolution then?

It's not for this year. It's for Eventually. One day.

Frankie picks up the magazine that Veronica cast on the worktop. It is still open at the photos from the awards ceremony.

I'm going to win Estate Agent of the Year.

Veronica stares at him.

You're being serious, aren't you?

Frankie's attention is on the page, the shiny photographs of the winners illuminated by spotlights.

What's wrong with wanting to be the best? You're such a snob. Just because they don't hold a Pathologist of the Year. Or do they? Category: Trocar-ing. Category: Skull stripping. Category—

Anything else?

Veronica takes both of his hands in hers. Frankie stares back blankly.

Not that I can think of.

Veronica holds his gaze. He feels a tiny dent of understanding, as if a penny has fallen onto a pillow.

Start a family maybe? Eventually? says Frankie.

Veronica doesn't respond. One eyebrow rises very slightly.

As soon as we've got enough behind us. Because I'm going to be working myself into the ground for the next couple of years at least. So much to do. It's not going to be easy.

The other eyebrow rises.

Frankie checks his watch.

I guess we'd better be going. They won't be able to get in without me.

Veronica lets go of his hands and turns sharply away.

So you said. Are you even allowed four guests?

Her voice is flatter than before, uninterested, her words mere prop and foundation for the profounder message of the tone, the look, the defensive cast of her shoulders.

I know Maurice, the owner. We're old muckers. And it's five guests. Colin's bringing someone, I told you, Frankie continues, cheerfully, oblivious.

Veronica gives up, switches off the central heating, checks her three-year-old Mulberry bag, now beginning to look tired. She resolves to buy a fresh one in the January sales.

* * *

11

When they get to the Embankment Club, Fraser and Nodge are standing in the reception area. Fraser Pike is picking at his fingernails, and barely glances up when Frankie and Veronica arrive. Dark, vaguely Semitic, he is four inches taller than Nodge, a muscle Mary in a ripped white T-shirt and a faded pair of extremely well cut APC jeans. He has six-inch tattoos of coiling snakes insinuating their way along each of his forearms. But he falls short of good-looking, face off kilter with squinty eyes, and is maybe twenty years older than Nodge. He has furrowed skin, a close-cropped head and deep canals on the back of his hands and neck. Frankie has met him twice before, and has liked him less on each occasion.

Here they are, says Nodge, dourly. He is slightly overweight, and dressed in fresh jeans with turn-ups, a check work shirt and Timberlands.

Sitting on a cushioned bench to his left is Colin, who looks up eagerly as if grateful for the distraction. Next to him sits a woman who appears to be in her late thirties. She has ironed and dyed yellow hair, ski pants and a tight halter top. Crimson lipstick makes a gash on white pancake make-up. Without getting up, she smiles, broadly, in the direction of Frankie and Veronica. Frankie worries that the make-up might crack and slide. He sees her shift a couple of inches away from Colin, so that she is not accidentally touching legs with him.

Sorry we're late. Roads were murder, says Frankie.

The over-made-up woman stands up and holds out her hand. Frankie notices a tattoo on the inside of her wrist, a tiny four-petalled flower.

Sorry to gatecrash. It's embarrassing. I'm Roxanne Peacock. Roxy. I'm a sort of friend of a friend of Colin's. Sort of.

Veronica ignores the hand and embraces Roxy.

Happy Millennium, Roxanne Peacock. I'm Veronica Tree. Vronky.

Frankie gives Nodge an affectionate punch on the shoulder. Nodge grabs Frankie's hand in both of his and squeezes.

Don't worry about us. We're just chopped liver, pet.

Fraser is speaking in a booming Northern accent – Geordie, according to Nodge, but it sounds more like Brummie to Frankie.

Shut up, Fraser, says Nodge. He says it tenderly, without reproof. *Actually we only just got here five minutes ago ourselves. We dropped down the Admiral Duncan for a couple of shots. Sort of a pilgrimage.*

Bad year for those of your persuasion, says Frankie.

Always is, says Fraser. *Your neo-Nazi with a nail bomb can put quite a damper on things. For those of our 'persuasion'.*

The old-style ones weren't much better, says Nodge. *The ones with the swastikas and torches.*

Do you know how many gays died in the camps? says Fraser. *Do you?* But he seems to be addressing no one in particular.

Can we talk about something cheerful? says Frankie.

Sorry, says Nodge. *Fraser is very passionate.*

It's always with the politics when it comes to you. It's meant to be party time.

Don't apologize for me, says Fraser.

Sorry, says Nodge.

Fraser, apparently mollified, sidles up to Frankie and stage-whispers.

I love your friend, Frankie, says Fraser, nodding towards Colin. *He's like a funny little Toby jug, yeh?*

Hi, Frankie, says Colin, rising from the bench and briefly shaking Frankie's hand. He pretends not to hear Fraser.

13

Hi, Colin. Glad you could make it. Nice to meet you Roxy. Shall we all go in? Without waiting for an answer, Frankie turns to the reception desk and announces his name, showing his card. He feels a flash of joy at the fact of his membership and silently repeats to himself that the two-year wait for membership and the exorbitant four-figure joining fee are worth the kudos that the silver card bestows.

Happy Millennium, says the receptionist, without looking up, as Frankie signs them all in. Roxy totters and stumbles on three-inch heels. It appears to Frankie that she is already slightly drunk. Colin leans in as if to support her, but she pulls back.

Once inside, they head straight for the bar. Stacks of glittering, spectroscopic, backlit bottles of liquor adorn the mirrored wall behind the two spry and immaculate bar staff, dressed in white shirts and black waistcoats. After a few minutes of jostling, Frankie manages to order a round of drinks. He looks over his shoulder, noticing that Roxy and Colin are sitting together in silence, staring straight ahead.

Frankie has a whisky sour, Fraser a large glass of Pinot Noir, Nodge a G&T and both Roxy and Veronica order Cosmopolitans. Colin has asked – more in hope than expectation – for a Hofmeister, the lager he drinks without fail, but the brand is in serious decline and the Embankment Club is not the sort of place to stock it. He settles reluctantly for a bottle of Budvar.

Then they drink. And drink and drink, one round chasing another with hysteric rapidity. Within an hour, everyone is merry or slurred, unloosened and unbuttoned.

This is how Frankie wants it to be. The end of a thousand years, an unforgettable night – celebrated with the oldest and most reliable extinguisher of memory.

* * *

As the hour of eleven is breached, Frankie and Colin perch next to one another on bar stools, while Nodge, Fraser and Veronica sit together at a low smoked-glass table five feet behind them. Roxy has gone to the cloakroom to work on her face, after disapprovingly catching sight of it in one of the mirrored columns that punctuate the room.

You two don't seem to be exactly hitting it off, says Frankie.

I barely know her, says Colin, glumly. *She was meant to be going out tonight with her boyfriend. Got dumped at the last minute. So I invited her. She was impressed that I had an invite to the Embankment Club. I didn't see the harm.*

You never do.

Nodge gets up from the table and walks over to Colin and Frankie at the bar. Fraser, from his low seat, watches him carefully.

That little Toby jug, says Fraser, who is elegantly drunk. Veronica rolls her eyes.

Shhh, she says. *Be nice.*

He just looks like someone is going to eat him up, says Fraser. *He looks like he wants someone to eat him up, in fact.*

As a matter of fact, his mother pretty much consumed him for most of his life. Didn't stop till she died last year.

That must have been a relief.

Be nice, Fraser. Please.

My mother was a bitch.

Excuse me, Fraser. I need another drink.

Suit yourself.

Fraser shrugs and Veronica makes her way towards the bar,

where Frankie is holding forth. This is his empire, his domain. His largesse feels unlimited.

We can watch the fireworks from the roof, he says, gesturing vaguely upwards. *There's a garden up there. More drinks?*

Where's Roxy? says Colin.

They look around. Roxy is nowhere to be seen.

In the loo, says Veronica. *I'll see if she's alright. Cosmopolitan for me, Frankie.*

What about Fraser?

I didn't ask. Something bitter would probably do.

* * *

Veronica makes her way into the elegant toilets – a single, long marble sink, low hush-hush lighting, blue and white microtiles and mock-sandstone pillars.

The bathroom is empty except for Roxy, who, Veronica sees immediately, is silently weeping. She looks up in alarm when Veronica enters.

Shit, says Roxy.

She takes a tissue from a box on the ledge in front of her and starts furiously scrubbing at her eyes with her knuckles. Veronica stands next to her and rests her hand lightly on her back.

What's the matter?

Roxy shakes her head, starts to sob again, this time making no attempt to mute the choking sounds.

Veronica takes another tissue from a dispenser on the sink surface and hands it to Roxy, who attempts a weak laugh.

Thank kew.

She takes the tissue and finishes the job.

I'm sorry. Sorry. Veronica. Is it Veronica?

Vronky. What's the matter?

What's the matter? What do you think? It's Millennium night and I'm in a club where I don't know anybody with a man who I've only met once before and who I don't fancy or particularly like. I'm thirty-six years old. How did I get here?

She reaches into her bag, pulls out a small pencil and starts applying eyeliner. She is stretching her eyelid and grimacing. She turns to Veronica pleadingly.

Also, just to cap everything off, I'm bleeding like a stuck bloody pig. You got any tammies?

I might have something.

Veronica feels inside her bag, then failing to find what she is looking for, unloads the bag onto the marble surface. First out is a pack of three condoms.

Only three? says Roxy, cackling now. Veronica says nothing.

A tube of moisturizer. Keys on a keyring with an enamel tag attached. A battery and a mini flashlight. A collapsible umbrella. A tangerine, half peeled. Hospital ID card. A small camera. Then there, right at the bottom, two tampons loose in their fitted cellophane jackets.

Got some. Veronica places one triumphantly on the edge of the sink. Roxy reaches unsteadily over, slips and knocks the pile of Veronica's possessions onto the floor. The camera falls in a puddle of water.

Fuck!

Don't worry about it.

They scrabble to pick up the contents. Some has fallen under the sinks, and behind the upright, but most of it is in plain sight. Veronica herself is feeling the effects of her four cocktails, and isn't too concerned. Roxy takes one tampon and puts the other in her bag.

Thanks Veronica. Vronky.

Nice bag, says Veronica. She takes some lipstick and starts touching up her own make-up.

Balenciaga, says Roxy. *I like to splash out now and then.*

It really is *a nice bag. How much did it cost?*

I'm too embarrassed to say.

Go on.

Seven hundred pounds.

For real?

Little Christmas present to myself. And an investment. You got to make an impression, isn't it? If you want to get anywhere. I love a bit of shopping therapy. One of the few things I'm good at.

I'm sure that's not true.

Oh, it is though. What do you do then, Veronica? She has noticed the medical card. *You a nurse?*

I'm a . . .

She hesitates, reframes the thought.

Medical technician.

I'm none the wiser. Still.

You?

In management.

Which company?

I'm a shop manager. For Top Shop. In Brent Cross Shopping Centre. Assistant manager, anyway.

Veronica finishes applying her lipstick, dabs her mouth with a paper towel. Roxy is working on her eyelashes with a spoolie brush.

How do you know Colin?

Who?

The bloke you came with.

Oh, him. I don't hardly know him at all. I got stood up. My so-called boyfriend of two months. Dumps me on Millennium night. Says he wants a new start. More like a new tart. A mate of mine who works for Sony tipped me the wink when I swallowed enough pride to ask if she knew any single men free and available at short notice. She trawled the depths and came up with Colin. He's apparently wedged and nearly always single. So I thought, it's better than sitting at home alone. Anything for a laugh.

Veronica applies her blusher. Roxy is finishing up.

She reaches in her bag and takes out a business card which she offers to Veronica, who takes it.

That's me. If you're ever in Brent Cross. Which I wouldn't necessarily recommend.

Thanks.

So how do you know Colin then?

One of my husband's oldest friends.

Weird little guy.

They were very close once. As children. Then Frankie worked out that he was only sticking with him out of pity.

I know the feeling.

Roxy tidies up her mascara.

What else? Important to do some research on a blind date.

He's a Christian, says Veronica.

Roxy's mouth opens, exposing a slightly crooked 'O'.

This just gets better and better.

When his mother died about a year ago he embraced the Lord. To be fair, I think he's backed down a bit nowadays. Sort of over it, Frankie says. But he still goes to church now and then. Frankie invited him tonight, I think, for old times' sake. Him and Nodge and Colin go back a long way. All the way to school days. He's some sort of computer genius. An 'idiot savant', Frankie says. All the companies are trying to get him to work for them. Designs computer games. For Sony. But you know that already.

Veronica takes out her phone and checks the time.

They're going out on the roof in a moment. Better get back out there.

She sees Veronica putting her wedding ring back on.

That looks fresh.

Four months.

What's being married like?

Veronica flinches slightly at the question.

We're still getting to know each other.

Uh oh.

Relationships are difficult.

Right.

Worth the effort, though.

If you say so. 'Spose anything's got to be better than sitting watching Wife Swap *reruns every night with a bottle of Lambrini and a joint.*

They both clip their bags closed, in perfect synchronicity, and head back to the bar.

Look, says Veronica, who is surprised at how much she likes this woman. *Let me know how it goes. Ring me.*

She takes out a pen and scribbles her number on the back of Roxy's hand.

A hundred per cent, says Roxy.

* * *

Ten minutes to go, announces Frankie. *Let's move.*

He leads them to a small lift, finished with brushed steel interior, which they squeeze into. Colin, the shortest of them — since both Roxy and Veronica are wearing heels — looks the most uncomfortable. He is wearing a black hoodie and a pair of shapeless fawn-coloured chinos.

The lift travels up ten storeys, then they tumble out onto the roof. A mist of garbled sound is floating up from street level. Down on the Embankment the crowd behaves as a single organism, throbbing, pulsing then simultaneously waving like a windswept field of fat, dark grass.

There's Big Ben, says Colin, rapturously. Frankie over the years has noticed how Colin only seems to have two forms of expression — flat and disinterested, or overexcited.

Fraser is gossiping animatedly about shopping with Roxy. Nodge, bored, joins Frankie, who is peering over the edge at the thrumming crowds below.

Do you know where it's all going to start, Frankie? says Nodge. *The first place to see the new millennium?*

Dunno.

Think. Way down south.

Battersea?

Guess proper.

Australia?

Fiji, Frankie. Fiji. Down there it's been the Millennium for two hours already.

Frankie regards Nodge affectionately.

You never did go, did you?

One day I will.

Nodge stares down at the crowd.

What a ringside seat. Thanks for getting us in.

I'm surprised you're here. I thought you'd be out at Greenwich with your friend Tony.

Diamond Tony?

Not Tony Diamonte. Tony Blair. At the Dome.

Roxy turns to Veronica.

Why are they talking about Fiji? she says.

Nodge always wanted to go there. Ever since he was a kid. It's a kind of standing thing between Frankie and him.

Now there are fifty members of the club craning their necks towards the river. Down below is a clear view of the crowd standing at least ten deep. There is the constant iteration of flashbulbs.

Frankie takes a bulky Polaroid camera out of the dun-coloured canvas man bag he has recently begun to favour over pockets. Seeing Roxy and Veronica standing together, he motions for them to come closer to one another.

Let's get a shot.

They put their arms awkwardly around one another and vamp for the camera. Frankie clicks, and a small square of glossy paper slips out of the front. A picture begins to emerge, a memory forging itself from chemicals and light.

What's that? An antique? says Colin, while Frankie holds the photo up to the night air and waves it back and forth like a tiny flag to dry the emulsion. Colin takes a shiny silver object out of his pocket, flips it open, looks through an aperture and points the object at Frankie. It seems he has been waiting for this moment. He clicks and lowers the gadget.

What is that thing? says Nodge.

Camera phone. I got it from a friend in Japan. Prototype. Take a look.

Nodge takes the phone and examines it. The rest of the group gather. They see the image of Frankie captured on the screen.

Hmmm, says Nodge, non-commitally.

It's like — a camera. And — a phone, says Fraser.

The Sharp J-SH04, says Colin, proudly. *The J-phone. 256-colour STN display on the front side.*

Lousy quality. says Fraser, trying not to show how impressed he is. *What is it, about fifteen pixels?*

A hundred and ten thousand. It'll get better. Look. It has a tiny mirror next to the lens to help you do self-portraits.

What's a pixel? asks Veronica.

I don't know what the fuck you're talking about but I want one! says Roxy. For the first time, she seems to be making voluntary body contact with Colin.

The best thing is, you can send the picture to anyone else who has got one of these phones, says Colin.

What do you mean, 'send'?

Electronically. Via text messages. You know.

The group look bewildered.

That's useful, says Fraser. *Given that no one else has one.*

Probably cost a fortune, says Nodge.

About five hundred pounds.

It's a gimmick, says Nodge.

Don't you see the potential? says Colin, excited to be the centre of attention. *Once it catches on — well you could for instance go shopping, take pictures of some piece of clothing and text it back to a friend while you were in the shop. Or you could set friends up on dates. Or anything. It's an obvious move. It's just the beginning.*

What's the end? says Frankie.

Who knows? says Colin.

I love it, says Roxy.

I might be able to get you one, says Colin slyly.

You couldn't! she replies, delighted.

I might.

What would be the price of that then, whispers Fraser into Roxy's ear. *Hand job, blow job or the full Monty?*

You're disgusting, says Veronica.

Roxy, however, looks both unoffended and thoughtful.

The group continue to stare at the image on the camera phone, but look up as the chimes of Big Ben begin to sound. Attention falls away from Colin. A rolling wave of noise is rising from the Embankment below as the crowd begins to count down to midnight.

Everyone starts to clap and cheer. The group on the roof join in.

Bong

Ten

Bong

Nine

Bong

Now the cheering gathers momentum, a great wave of sound surging up from below, and at the same time over the Thames, clusters of fireworks ignite and as the chimes continue, the ignitions multiply, a collective orgasm. Rockets fly and phosphate flowers, a thousand foot across, bloom in the sky. A million cameras flash, trying to capture this end to a thousand years of chaos, conflict, love, misery, confusion, struggle, sex, death, beauty, hurt.

Frankie looks at Big Ben and feels something he almost never feels. *Pride.* Although he is not sure what he is proud of. But he is drunk and happy, and newly married and still almost young.

24

Veronica steps in front of him and kisses him as the fireworks continue to flare. Fraser and Nodge meanwhile have their tongues down each other's throats and are writhing against the skyline.

Colin and Roxy stand awkwardly next to one another, Colin still fidgeting with his phone, occasionally pointing it at the display and pressing a button. Roxy can barely take her eyes off it.

So shiny, so new, she thinks.

She stares at Colin with eyes that glitter with reflected light from the pyrotechnics. The sounds of firecrackers popping and missiles launching continues to punctuate the deepening night.

It's going to be a wonderful new time, Vronky, says Frankie, leaning over and whispering in her ear.

I know, says Vronky. *So much good is going to happen.*

White spotlights pester the night sky while the fireworks continue to multiply, an impasto of coloured light along the Thames.

Can I try? says Roxy to Colin, swaying slightly on her feet.

How much have you drunk?

Cosmopolitan, Negroni, two Moscow Mules . . . fuck knows.

How are you feeling?

I'm feeling that I want your phone.

Colin hands it to her and she stares at it with a lover's gaze.

Will you take a picture of me?

He takes the camera phone out of her hands and tells her to pose. She pouts, and bends to reveal her cleavage. Colin clicks and shows her the result. She whoops.

Can we take one of us together?

Now Colin holds the camera at arm's length, while he and Roxy gurn for the lens.

Showers of fire are falling from the heavens, launched from a line of barges and a solid, steady roar rises from below. Screeches and unintelligible calls of elation float in the air, like fireworks drawn in sound instead of light. Whistles sound continuously as if part of one long exhalation of breath.

Frankie thinks he can see in the far distance Tower Bridge where the whole performance seems to have started. He imagines the drawbridge raised in salute. Foghorns and car horns join in the glorious cacophony. Explosions in the sky remind him of war zones he has glimpsed on news broadcasts, but there is no atmosphere of threat, only unconstrained joy ringing out, for human survival, for simply being here. For remaining alive, as a species, against all odds.

Before the chimes have even finished marking out the end of the old millennium, the sky is more light than dark, more colour than white. There is beauty everywhere, imposed like a spectroscopic screen over the grey spread of the city. Starbursts fizzle and sizzle. The colours glitter on the River Thames and bounce off the spray of new, bright glass buildings that sprout along the riverside. Big Ben is enveloped in an eerie green fog.

The fireworks build in intensity until it seems they can build no further, then just become louder, and brighter, and wilder, and more beautiful. The barely visible moon blankly invigilates this display of exuberant human imagination, which has been so often cramped, dark and malevolent during the preceding centuries. All the individual pops of firecrackers merge into a single burst of sound, a continuous crackling. Crests of smoke proceed down the Thames, penetrated by aureoles of chemical lightning. The screams of girls sound to Frankie, in his imagination, like a thousand women climaxing.

He takes his phone to check if there are any messages. There is just one.

Happy Milennium, mate. Auld acquaintance be forgot and never brought to mind? Beer sometime?

The text is signed 'Tony D.'

Frankie stares at it for a moment then deletes it.

They look molecular, thinks Colin, staring at the cresting fireworks. *Like what lies at the centre of everything. Atoms. Molecules. Matter in motion.*

I love you, Fraser, says Nodge.

It's a giant sky fuck, says Fraser.

Now the night is painted with smoke and drenched in the odour of cordite and gunpowder. The group on the roof of the club are no different from the dots below, screaming and whooping and wowing. The biggest fireball of all explodes, apparently right above their heads, white and silver. Frankie and Veronica and Colin and Fraser and Roxy and Nodge all gasp as one.

Not exactly a river of fire though, was it? says Nodge, as the fireworks finish and the flare begins to fade.

* * *

The Embankment Club closes at 2 a.m. Colin, Roxy, Veronica and Frankie are disgorged, tumbling and stumbling out into the street. Nodge and Fraser, with drunken kisses and goodnights, have headed off together to the night club Heaven, a few hundred yards away under Charing Cross Station.

The crowds are still vast, and at one point sweep the

27

group apart, leaving Colin and Roxy abruptly separated from Veronica and Frankie. They cannot reclaim them – the push of the crowd is too wild. Colin and Roxy break away into a small, dark empty alley.

Where do you live? asks Colin.

Finchley, says Roxy, looking behind her, trying to relocate Veronica and Frankie.

Shall we share a cab? says Colin. His mouth, she notices, is wet and loose. *I'm in Shepherd's Bush.*

We're not going to find a cab. I'll get the tube. It's been, um, nice . . .

Just then Roxy notices a taxi with a light on and runs towards it waving. But another couple – a big shovel-faced man and a tall stringy woman – notice her gesture and chase her, trying to snag the cab for themselves. Colin follows, pushing through the crowd.

The cab, miraculously, pulls over. But the big man pushes Roxy to one side and jumps in.

Hey! says Roxy *That's mine!*

His partner, the stringy woman, is still making her way through the crowd, some twenty feet behind, staggering on a pair of heels even higher than Roxy's. Roxy sees Colin appears beside the heeled woman, then overtake her. As he does, the woman seems to disappear from sight. A few seconds later Colin joins Roxy on the kerbside.

This monkey stole the cab, yells Roxy over the noise of the crowd.

Colin nods, then gets into the back of the cab with the big man who looks solid and unrepentant. Colin whispers something in his ear. The man, at first bridling, looks over Colin's

shoulder, then mysteriously gets out. Colin beckons Roxy
to follow.

Come on.

With some trepidation, Roxy climbs in.

What did you say to him?

His wife or whatever she was fell over and hurt herself.

Roxy throws a glance over her shoulder and catches sight of
the big man cradling the woman against his shoulder. There is
blood on her forehead.

Running in high heels can be dangerous.

Roxy stares at Colin, puzzled. She turns again and sees the
woman through the window, pointing towards the cab. The
big man is looking up and beginning to rise from his crouching position. Then Roxy notices Veronica, flanked by Frankie.
She is waving to Roxy furiously. Roxy waves back. This is her
chance to make her escape.

Go go go, says Colin to the cab driver, urgently, who on
cue pulls away just in time, as the big man has risen from his
crouching position and is sprinting towards the kerb. Only the
press of people stops him making it to the cab in time. He is
shouting something, but Roxy cannot hear him. Then the cab
pulls away and out of sight of Veronica and Frankie.

Where to? says the cabbie in leaden cockney tones.

Shepherd's Bush, then . . .

Colin looks across at Roxy.

Finchley.

I'm not going to Finchley, says the cabbie, firmly. *I'll do the Bush
and that's your lot.*

* * *

TIM LOTT

Nodge stands by himself leaning against the wall of Heaven. The music is thudding, violent, relentless. The night comes at him in a series of flashes. Balloons that were released from the ceiling at midnight are scattered on the floor like carnival landmines, popping repeatedly as someone or other steps on one. A man with a flashing '2000' bow tie. Another man dressed in silver lamé with silver feathers in his hair. A lot of bleached crops. One man with green hair and painted thick red lips and three sets of heavily painted eyebrows, a red polo neck with red spandex, with two nipple ring piercings through the spandex and a thick gold necklace. He has no shoes and toenails painted green. A glamorous black woman with piled-up hair in a pure white dress, smoking a fat cigar. Nodge feels plain and boring.

Fraser has disappeared into a dark area at the back with someone he apparently once had a fling with and now wants to repeat the experience. Nodge, who has only been on the scene for a few months, has to assume that this is normal. But he doesn't like it. It seems impolite and it hurts his feelings. He thinks he needs to get over this sensibility. His wish, since he came out, is simply to fit in.

No one is making eye contact with him. Neither does he want them to. He feels foolish, out of place, as if the fact that he has only just come out after thirty years of living a lie is tattooed across his forehead. He wants to cuddle up in bed with Fraser, who, he knows, can be tender, despite the acidity of his tongue.

He never imagined himself with a boyfriend not much younger than his dad, but Fraser had picked him out at a Labour Party branch meeting and taken him for a drink after the endless, torturous and possibly pointless debates had finished.

Six weeks after that meeting, Fraser had taken him back to his flat in Hammersmith, and seduced him with wine and E. Nodge had been excited, flattered and – he had to confess – the sex had been high voltage, spellbinding. Fraser had been exactly what he had been looking for, someone to show him the ropes. He was beginning to learn that coming to terms with your sexual orientation wasn't as straightforward as simply changing the gender of the person you slept with.

They got on well too, well enough, anyway, although Fraser was well to the left of the Party, which Nodge was nowadays semi-detached from. Labour's power in government had become entrenched and inevitable, and this had the effect of lessening Nodge's commitment, which remained at a level just high enough to turn up to every other meeting, if that, although he rarely spoke at them.

He shifts from foot to foot and checks his watch. He is tired and wants to go home. He'd expected and hoped that he would spend the night with Fraser, in the ornate hand-wrought Brazilian iron bed at his stripped-bare minimalist converted warehouse space, but he is losing patience. He has no interest in spending what's left of the night in a meat rack.

Finally Fraser emerges from the back of the club, flushed and looking self-satisfied. He smiles at Nodge and nods. Nodge tries not to feel jealous – this, he assumes, is just the way things are – but taps his watch face with his finger. Fraser responds by starting to dance, lazily, pairing himself with any satellite body which comes within his orbit. Fraser moves easily, his muscular body pumping in perfect time with the music. Nodge cannot dance or at any rate, cannot dance well. He suspects that this is going to be even more of a disadvantage on the gay scene than it had been when he had convinced himself that he was straight. It is, he decides, going to be a long night.

Half the men have no shirts on, with shaven chests and shaven heads, something that Nodge couldn't contemplate for himself. The music is like buzz saws and hammers, hard house and techno. Nodge tries to synchronize his body with the rhythm but feels awkward, self-conscious.

After a few minutes, Fraser ambles up, catlike, and tells him straight out, over the racket, that he dances *like a heifer*. Nodge knows it's true, but is hurt all the same. The lighting is bright and monochrome, casting too many shadows.

Bullet heads, Fred Perrys, Doc Martens. Nodge the newbie is both overweight and hairy, something between an otter and a bear and a chub (Nodge is still struggling to master the argot). Fraser, though, was close to having a perfect hard-body – he was ripped but not particularly bulked up. That body fills him with intense desire.

What Fraser sees in Nodge, Nodge isn't sure, except that Nodge is safe and naïve and loyal – and young, by Fraser's standards. But there is a gulf between them. Nodge doesn't want to suck some anonymous punter off in the toilets. He wants to be with Fraser.

He is tempted to walk out of the club alone, but resists, out of fear as much as determination.

* * *

Frankie and Veronica arrive home close to 3 a.m. They are drunk, exultant, aroused.

Did you see what Colin did to that woman? says Veronica, kicking off her shoes.

What woman?

When they were trying to get a cab. He tripped her up. She really went flying.

I'm sure it was an accident.

I'm not. Colin isn't always as meek as he looks.

Now they both strip off their clothes, scattering them behind them, like a trail of breadcrumbs marking their path into the woods, waiting to be blown by the draught from under the bedroom door.

Veronica reaches out to Frankie and kisses him. The kiss lasts for longer than Frankie can remember a kiss lasting before.

When they pull apart, breathless, Frankie reaches in his pocket and produces a small package. He holds it out in front of him.

Something for you. A millennium present.

Frankie! You only just gave me a Christmas present.

This is something else.

She pulls the paper off the gift, leaving it to drop on the floor. Inside is a matchbox.

Bryant & May's! You shouldn't have.

Look inside.

She pulls open the box. Inside there is a key, an ordinary Yale, which, she can see even in the dark, is a strangely deep yellow rather than the normal brass or nickel silver.

What's this?

Do you remember the first flat I took you to see? When we met for the first time.

You told me not to buy it.

This is the key. To that flat.

Veronica looks confused.

It looks brand new.

It is brand new.

But why would you . . . ?

It's made of gold. Because my life turned to gold the day I met you.

Veronica stares at the key in astonishment. She feels herself suddenly helpless, overflowing.

You're so soppy.

She turns and kisses Frankie again.

Thank you, is all she can manage. *Thank you, Frankie. This makes me very happy.*

That's all I want to do, Vronky.

I know. I know you do.

Frankie is drunkenly ecstatic. Bringing Veronica joy fills him with a sense of potency. Staggering slightly now, he almost falls, steadies himself on the mantelpiece. A white embossed card with a clamshell border is balanced there. Grazed by Frankie's elbow, it falls to the floor.

He picks it up and reads it unsteadily even though he knows what it says.

You are invited to lunch
at
Cordelia and Michael's
on the occasion of the new Millennium.
1pm, January 1 2000

RSVP

Naked now, apart from her underwear, Veronica stumbles over to Frankie and stands next to him.

I don't know if I'm going to be able to face this shit, says Frankie. And why did they even send an invite? There's only us and Floss going.

They thought they were going to have a big event then changed their mind. Didn't want to waste the printing bill.

Her arm snakes past his hip and cradles his groin.

Where is it? I can't find my li'l friend.

He drops his hand and covers hers.

The prospect of social crucifixion is having a paralysing effect.

I can fix that.

Veronica slowly removes her hand, dragging her fingernails across his sternum.

Where are the condoms?

Where they always are.

She turns and goes to the bathroom and searches in the cabinet. When she returns, Frankie has finished undressing and is lying on his back in bed, the covers off, his eyes almost closed. He has very visibly recovered his erection.

She staggers slightly as she makes her way towards him. She removes her bra and pants and collapses on top of him.

No condoms, slurs Veronica.

Sure?

Frankie extricates himself from the dead weight of Veronica and makes his way into the bathroom. She can hear him clattering past the Benylin, the aspirin, the embarrassment of the Lanacane. He returns and starts searching through his man bag.

As you say. No condoms.

Hold on. Some in my bag, I think.

Why carry them around? On the off chance?

On the off chance you will get adventurous and get nasty with me in the woods or halfway up a mountain.

I'm not a trees and mountain guy. I'm a fully sprung mattress guy.

Veronica gets out of bed and rummages in her bag but finds nothing.

Must have fallen out in the bathroom when I was helping out Roxy.

We can just fool around, says Frankie

I liked Roxy. She made me laugh. No bullshit.

Common as muck.

Listen to you. You can talk.

Veronica falls across him woozily and, almost immediately, instead of the usual five to six minutes of foreplay, he pushes her over on her back and tries to mount her.

We should stop, Veronica says.

We should, says Frankie. *Absolutely.*

They look at one another. Veronica parts her legs slightly.

I'm yours, Frankie, says Veronica. *Always.*

But . . . says Frankie

I should be safe this time of the month.

Then they cannot be stopped, although Frankie pulls out at the last moment, leaving a wide oval damp mark on the 200 thread-count Egyptian cotton sheets. It is the year 2000, christened now, with a million potential new human beings, wasted.

Minutes later they are both asleep, holding one another loosely, face to face, each faintly smiling.

* * *

The cab driver drops Colin and Roxy outside Colin's flat. Colin pays him, does not tip.

Happy New Year, says the cabbie, sourly.

Yeh, says Colin. *And you.*

Then, turning to Roxy: *Come on up to the flat. I can call a minicab from there.*

Why don't you use your mobile phone from here?

Out of charge. Taking all those photos. Anyway, the number is upstairs.

They take a lift up to the top floor and emerge into a clinical white hallway. There are two identical doors on the landing and Colin unlocks the one to the left. The smell of fresh pine washes through Roxy's nostrils. She blinks as her eyes adjust to the harsh overhead lighting. No lightshade.

Very new in here.

Only moved in a month ago, says Colin. *Do you like it?*

Bit on the Spartan side, isn't it?

To Roxy's surprise, Colin immediately goes to the landline and to his address book. He phones three numbers one after the other. Roxy meanwhile, removes her coat and flops onto the grey, geometric, utilitarian sofa, apparently brand new, but already stained on the left armrest with what look likes coffee, tea, or curry sauce.

No cabs available from any of them. He seems genuinely disappointed on her behalf.

There is a pinboard with cards and leaflets from various local services – plumbers, electricians, cleaners – pinned to it. Roxy drags herself up and inspects it.

What about this? 'Executive Limo Service – Best Rates'.

I'll see how much it is. If they've got anything.

She hands over the card and Colin rings the number.

They have one available.

How much?

A hundred pounds.

I'll get the night bus.

I've got a spare room.

Don't get any ideas.

Roxy sits back down on the sofa and scans the room. It is all very standard. White plaster, oatmeal carpet, PVC-framed double-glazed windows, painted radiators. There are glass doors overlooking a wrought-iron balcony. Not much on the walls except the pinboard and a poster of St George and the Dragon stuck on with Blu Tack.

Nice poster.

It's sort of research. For the video game I'm designing.

What's that then?

It's called Dragon Bane. *I'm a big fan of dragons.*

The room is dominated by an outsize TV connected to a DVD player, an NTL satellite box and a PlayStation games console. There are two cheap-looking red beanbags in front of it.

Tidy.

I pay a cleaning lady to come in every other day when I'm not here.

How can you afford it?

Same way as I can afford the flat. I work hard.

Me too. But I get paid jack shit. Hey, have you heard this one? 'My boss told me to have a nice day. So I went home.'

Right. Oh yeh. I get it.

Roxy walks over to a bookshelf next to the TV. It is entirely free of books. There are simply video games and DVDs, mainly horror, and collections of QPR games from the past few seasons.

Show me the spare room, she says.

Colin leads her to the second bedroom, which contains a single bed covered with a white duvet and waffle cotton pillowcases. There is nothing else in there whatsoever – not a clock, or a painting, or a chair. Roxy notes that there is a lock on the door and a key in the lock.

I'll think about it. Got anything to drink?

Lager.

That's it?

I'm a man of simple tastes.

I'll fetch.

Roxy goes into the kitchen area, finds a couple of murky glasses. In the fridge, she sees a small pack of Kraft cheese slices, half a bottle of milk, yellowing on the surface, an open can of baked beans and a wrap of half-used Kerrygold butter. There is also a Marks & Spencer's Roast Chicken and Roast Potatoes for One. The only other contents are fifteen cans of Hofmeister lager, beaded with condensation.

She returns to the living room, hands him the beer, and knocks back half of her glass on the spot, then lights herself a mentholated cigarette. She starts to pace around the room, examining the television, then checking the video games. There are at least twenty of them. *Diablo II. GoldenEye 007. Call of Duty. Mortal Kombat.*

This is Moral Kombat: Special Forces, *right? I thought that wasn't out until the end of the year.*

I'm on the inside corridor.

Got any PVP games?

A few. Mainly I play PVE.

You play with yourself?

She winks.

It's a bit of an obsession, says Colin, smiling shyly. *It's what I do for a living. It's what paid for all this.*

Roxy casts her eyes around the room, thinking how welcoming it could be if it had even some hint of adornment or decoration.

You sell video games?

I design them.

He takes an unmarked box from the shelf.

This one is called Death Smash. *I did it. Mainly me, anyway. It never went into production, but Sony liked it enough to give me a job.*

Sounds like fun.

You're just saying that, right? You've got no interest whatsoever.

I'm interested.

Roxy continues scanning the shelves.

You've got Wipeout.

Of course.

I love Wipeout.

You've played it?

I'm a wiz.

Okay.

You sound doubtful.

I don't want to come across as, you know, a big head. I was office Wipeout *champion at the Sony Christmas Party. And there's a lot of pretty handy players at Sony.*

You played computer games at your office Christmas party. No snogging?

All men. Desk warriors. Fancy a game?

One hundred per cent. Anything for a laugh.

They boot up *Wipeout* and each take a PS controller. The music starts, surging through Colin's powerful audio system – 'Firestarter' by The Prodigy. The cresta run of lights and images, the thudding electronic music, the swerving and swaying of the virtual spaceship pumps up Colin's adrenaline, as the number counters climb at the bottom of the screen. Girders and virtual fences frame the action. Billboards over the causeway advertise Red Bull. The soft gasping of an electronic voice speaking unintelligible words, the tapping of a drum synthesizer. Lap speeds after lap.

Colin is surprised at how adept Roxy is. Although he wins easily she scores 200 points in the first game, and 220 in the next. She is still knocking back lager, has helped herself to a second glass. An ashtray half full of menthol stubs sits on the oatmeal carpet.

I haven't had this much fun in ages, Colin says, truthfully. He cannot quite believe that he has a woman alone with him in his flat. Maybe the new century is going to work out well for him after all.

I definitely have, says Roxy, but she has to admit that she is enjoying herself. The flat is lovely, smells brand new, smells of money, in fact, and Colin, she thinks now, isn't so bad looking really, although his acne scars are a turnoff.

She spots an old Nintendo N64 player gathering dust behind the PS.

You've got GoldenEye, right?
I think so, yeh.
I used muck around a bit with that with my kid sister.
Do you want a game of that then?
Yeh, why not?

41

I'm pretty good at this one too.

Colin plugs it in. After a few seconds of fiddling with the connections and controls, the James Bond theme pumps out of the speakers. Colin selects multiplay. Roxy chooses 'Natalya' as an avatar. Colin is Bond himself, and the screen splits horizontally into two.

There's a 'slappers only' setting, says Roxy, mock outraged.

That means no weapons.

Yeh, I know, Colin. What did you think I thought? says Roxy, now speaking in a poor Russian accent, blood rushing to her head, making her giddy. *Tell you what. If you beat me you can shag me.*

What did you just say?

That's the liveliest I've seen you look all night.

I don't think I heard you.

I said, 'If. You. Beat. Me. You. Can. Have. A. Shag.'

Colin says nothing. A swirl of embarrassment and excitement stirs in his gut.

Aren't you going to ask what I want if you lose?

I won't lose.

Ask me anyway.

What do you want then?

You have to pay for the limo to take me home.

This isn't fair.

The risk of losing a hundred pounds is too much for the chance of having sex with me?

I don't mean that. You're not going to win. Honestly. I'm really really good at this game. Anyway, that would be paying you to have sex. I don't want to do that.

I don't intend to have sex with you, Colin. I intend to beat you. I just want to get home. And something else.

What?

If I win, I want that phone. For keeps.

Colin laughs.

I design these games for a living.

You could always let me win.

Definitely not if it's going to cost my J-phone. Forget the bet. Just stay in the spare room. It locks, so you'll be safe.

I'm not scared of you, Colin. I could probably beat you up quite easily if you tried anything. Okay, I'm ready to play. Set it up. I want to earn my limo and my phone. Come on. Anything for a laugh.

Still, Colin hesitates.

You're drunk. You're going to lose. Let me pay for the limo. I can afford it.

He reaches for the phone.

Scared? slurs Roxy. *Come on, let's have a go.*

They settle back into the beanbags, grasping their controllers. Colin, true to his boast, is good, fast to react and intuitive, but Roxy is faster, picking up weapons, sniper rifles, ammo, donning armour and moving from location to location with such pace Colin is unable to match her. Colin swears, his face turns red, his tongue protrudes between his teeth as it always does when he concentrates.

They chase one another across bridges, through lakes, inside military bases and out of manholes, up and down ladders, down endless narrow corridors. But within minutes, Bond is dead, Natalya continuing to casually pepper him with bullets as he lies prostrate on a warehouse floor in Leningrad. The screen blurs with a curtain of blood.

Resurrection duly occurs and the game continues. The sounds of bullets, ricochets, slamming steel doors and guttural noises of fear and exertion. You get ten lives. Colin sweats behind the sight of his virtual sniper rifle, but Natalya's KGB pistol, karate technique and knife work is too much time and time again. She wipes him out, 10–0.

I guess your dinner jacket was slowing you down, Mr Bond.

Roxy puts down the control and turns to Colin. She puts out her hand.

J-phone.

He is astonished, decides that he must have subconsciously been giving her an easy ride.

Trial run. Best of three.

Roxy seems unperturbed.

Fine. But then you'll give me the phone, right?

Yeh. Alright.

She beats him again, albeit by a smaller margin, 10–3. She cackles and whoops each time as she takes him down.

You're a useless twat, Mr Bond.

I never lose this game. Never. Colin seems puzzled and sad.

I played it almost non-stop with my sister for the whole of 1998. And I haven't lost my touch.

You're quite the gamer.

Not as good as my sister.

They play one more game, which Colin loses again, going pale with the effort. Then Roxy begins to yawn. Colin looks resigned, but also faintly awestruck.

Come on, I'll get your coat and phone for your limo. You're tired.

Give me the phone then.

He wearily takes it out of his pocket and hands it to her. Roxy laughs.

I was only joking. I'm not going to take it.

You're not?

I just enjoyed seeing you sweat.

A deal is a deal. It's fine. Have it. I can get another one easily enough. You can send me a picture of you when you get home.

She takes it, stares at it for a moment, then hands the phone back to him.

I was never going to take it, Colin.

Colin nods, put down the phone, picks up the landline and starts to dial the number for the limo. Roxy sees his disappointment, so plainly etched on his pale face, and feels a rush of unexpected tenderness.

You know what. I can't be bothered to go all the way back to Finchley.

Really?

Really.

Okay. Great.

Colin doesn't know what to do or say next. Roxy is leaving him beached with her changes of direction. He settles for, *Well then. You know where your room is. Sweet dreams.*

He smiles at her weakly, then starts to move towards his own room, shoulders slightly slumped.

Aren't you going to give me a goodnight kiss?

Colin leans in to kiss her on the cheek. She grabs him round the neck and slides her tongue into his mouth, then pulls away.

You know what? I can't even be bothered to slog all the way to the spare room. Yours is closer.

For the second time that night, Colin is under enchantment by fire, this time burning deep and invisible within.

* * *

In the morning Colin awakes beside Roxy. She is still asleep. He gazes at her, luxuriating in the opportunity to watch a woman's face unobserved. At the age of thirty-one he had slept with only three women in his life. This is the fourth.

He is suddenly astonished that only three months before, he had found it necessary to take refuge and solace in church and prayer. Now – right at this moment – he is willing to believe that his good fortune is the result of his own efforts. No divine intervention has been necessary. Jesus sits on his shoulders lightly now, like a flimsy cloak that can be slipped on and off according to changes in the weather.

Roxy shifts between the white sheets. There is a slight acidic smell. The covers are half off her upper body. She is overweight, and pale, and has skin that, like Colin's, bears the residue of acne, although much more faintly. This is revealed by her face powder having rubbed off during the night. Her lipstick is smeared, her mascara has run. Underneath the foundation he sees a faint universe of freckles.

She is the most beautiful thing he has ever seen.

Her eyelids flicker and Colin flinches and averts his gaze, worried that he might be branded a voyeur. Her eyes open, and he risks a glance. The white is marked with veins. The cornea is a mishmash of brown and blue, like a million others, but somehow her own. She sees Colin looking at her.

Her face contorts into a mask of horror and astonishment.

Who the FUCK are YOU?

Colin starts and his face takes on a fierce blush. He begins to stutter apologies.

I . . . I . . . I . . .

Her face morphs into soft mockery.

Got you, she says.

Colin risks a smile. Roxy puts her hands over her eyes. Colin sees she is wearing a heavy silver ring with an inlaid jade stone on her left index finger, and two plain lighter hoops on the same finger on her right. He thinks of her momentarily as exotic.

My fucking head hurts like a cunting bitch.

She says nothing else, but instead quickly pushes the sheets off her and bolts towards the bathroom. Naked, her flesh shakes and wobbles. She reaches the bathroom without closing the door. Colin hears the sound of retching.

Out of embarrassment, and for want of anything constructive to do, he retreats to the kitchen and puts the kettle on. Sounds of retching from the bathroom continue for several minutes. He brews two cups of tea, then tentatively pushes open the bedroom door to see Roxy sitting on the edge of the bed, holding her head. She looks up.

I've brought you a cup of tea.

She takes it, sips it and frowns.

More sugar. Three. Heaped.

Colin goes back to the kitchen and shovels in white Tate & Lyle from its stained paper bag. He returns and she is hiding under the bedclothes.

Are you feeling better?

Better out than in. She emerges blearily. Colin hands her the mug of tea again. It is inscribed with the legend 'Y2K – The End of the World Is Nigh'.

He sits on the bed a foot away, holding his own mug, blue and white hoops. He stares out of the window at nothing in particular. He is wearing blue boxer shorts. The only decoration in the bedroom is a QPR poster and a small photo-graph of his mother, black and white, taken thirty years before she lost her mind, and another poster of a dragon, this time with Bruce Lee superimposed.

This is what you might call a real bachelor flat, says Roxy, scanning the room and making a loud slurping sound as she sucks on the tea.

I'm not very good at decoration. Furniture and pictures and stuff like that. Knick-knacks.

Where were you living before you moved here?

With my mum on the White City Estate.

She still living there?

She died.

Roxy looks up.

Oh yeh, that's right. Veronica told me. I'm sorry.

That's okay. She was old. Been ill for a long time. To be honest . . . I mean I was sorry when she went. But after the initial shock, I've felt much better about myself somehow. Olive — her name was Olive — was, you know . . . difficult.

I know how that goes.

Do you?

My mother's a bitch too.

Colin stiffens.

Olive wasn't a bitch. She just ended up confused. Didn't know what she was saying half the time.

Sorry. I didn't mean . . .

It's okay.

What about your dad?

Dead years ago. Yours?

A drunk. Never see him.

Mine was too. Billy. Billy Burden.

At least he's dead. I suppose that's something. Mine's still out there, in a gutter somewhere.

Colin looks away.

You shouldn't talk that way about your parents.

Why not?

Now Colin is chewing on his fingernails. Roxy pats the space on the bed next to her.

Come and sit next to me.

He shifts over, still holding his mug. His hands tremble slightly.

So you're an orphan then.

Never thought of it that way, says Colin.

Roxy puts her mug down, still naked, and wraps her arm round his waist. She smells faintly of vomit, but Colin does not recoil.

That was nice last night. So far as I can remember.

Yes.

I'm talking about beating you at GoldenEye, *of course.*

I don't remember that.

Three times.

Still escaping me. Did we play video games?

Roxy strokes Colin's stomach gently with her palm.

Can I tell you something?

Yes.

You might not like it.

Go ahead.

When I first saw you I thought you were a bit of a freak.

Oh.

Your shoes were wrong for your trousers. Your hair looked like you'd cut it yourself. Without a mirror. Your face looked scared. The way you stood — it was stooped. And you're a tall enough guy. Why are you trying to make yourself small?

I never realized I did that.

Tell you the truth? Veronica warned me against you. She said you were a bit damaged.

Colin feels a *ping* of hurt in his chest, which registers in his face. Roxy sees it, and regrets what she has said.

But she said you were nice in your own way, she lies.

Colin suddenly meets her gaze.

I don't know anything about you, he says.

Roxy picks up her discarded pair of knickers and examines them critically. There is blood on them. She now looks down at the sheets. They are heavily stained.

Oh shit. I'm really sorry.

Colin smiles shyly.

It was worth it.

I'm so fucking embarrassed. No, I really am now.

It doesn't matter.

Why is it that girls in tampon commercials are always laughing and dancing? Shouldn't they be burning things down? I don't suppose you have an old pair of boxers I could borrow?

I'll have a look.

Colin roots around in the pine chest of drawers next to the bed.

I haven't been to the laundry for a while.

His eyes dart guiltily towards a wicker basket at the foot of the bed with a lid on but a shirtsleeve spilling from the top of it.

I've only got these.

He produces a pair of boxer shorts with the logo of QPR emblazoned on them, three interlinked blue capitals enclosed in two blue circles.

I can't wear those.

They're clean.

I'm sure they are. But I'm a Chelsea supporter.

Oh. Okay. I'll see if I can . . .

Roxy reaches out and takes the boxers from his hand.

You're quite gullible, aren't you? I like that.

She pulls them on. Then she takes a fold of fat on her stomach in her hands.

I should stop eating so many cakes.

She wobbles the fold of flesh back and forth.

Why don't you, then?

Because I like cakes.

Colin's last girlfriend – four years ago – had been pale, skeletal and terrified of food. He smiles at the sight of Roxy jiggling her belly. She pulls on her bra, then her ski pants and halter top, and glances at herself in the mirror that is attached to the inside of the wardrobe.

I've looked better, to be honest.

You look pretty.

I don't know about that. At least I look like I've had sex. We did have sex, didn't we?

Colin looks startled.

Got you again. You were okay last night. Good even. I didn't expect it, to tell you the truth.

Thanks for the five-star review.

Actually I was too drunk to expect anything much.

She pauses.

In fact to be even more honest, I wasn't entirely sure who you were at one point . . . Mind if I smoke?

I'd rather you didn't.

Oh well. You'll get over it.

She finds the packet of Marlboro menthols in her handbag and lights one.

We didn't, says Colin.

What? she says, inhaling and coughing.

We didn't have sex.

We didn't?

You would have. But you were too drunk, I thought.

Roxy pulls on the cigarette thoughtfully.

That's very gentlemanly of you. If it's true.

It is true. And it's not all that gentlemanly.

Why not?

You gave me a blow job just before you passed out.

She bursts out laughing.

Did I? How was it?

A bit rubbish if I'm honest.

Never been my speciality. Even worse when I'm sober.

* * *

Nodge wakes up alone in his council flat. His final argument with Fraser at Heaven was a bad one. It came to a head when he told Fraser that his Dalmatian, Harvey Milk, was a cliché. He said it out of pique, after having been ignored for so long, but he is remorseful now.

'*A fucking cliché*' is the phrase he used. '*A poof with a Dalmatian. What a joke.*'

This was after Fraser told him he was a crappy dancer and

that he should go and sit down, after which Fraser started dancing with someone else again.

Fraser was furious. Fraser loved Harvey Milk. Nodge, in fact, didn't like dogs at all, although he tried to keep the fact hidden from Fraser. Any dogs. The way they licked your crotch. When he had complained about it, just before they left his flat for the Embankment, Fraser had said something silly like, *If you won't let Harvey lick your crotch, I don't see why I should bother.* Nodge had sulked, even though he knew Fraser was joking. Or at least he thought he was joking.

Since he's come out, Nodge hasn't quite known how to behave. Is there some stance he should adopt, some covert body language? Some particular attitude? Nodge still doesn't know and he isn't sure he is learning very fast. He had watched *Queer as Folk* that year as an education as much as anything else, but Fraser said that it was a load of shit and queers weren't anything like that, in fact they weren't anything like anything in particular. But Fraser said that at the same time he acted up the whole gay thing. He bitched, his voice lilted, he camped it up. Even to Nodge, a newcomer, this performance seemed old-fashioned, but who was he to judge? He didn't have a clue.

Nodge isn't interested in becoming a clone and joining any of the various sub-groups that seem to comprise the Scene. He just wants to feel at ease. To feel, ironically, normal. Or perhaps ironically normal. But he rapidly realized that the gay scene, although it could be fun and it could be friendly, was also scary, wracked, frenetic, particular, codified, strangely formalized.

He just wanted a boyfriend. And when Fraser laughed at him for dancing badly and they had had the argument, he walked out and got himself a minicab home, not back to Fraser's flat as they had planned, but his own place in Shepherd's Bush. A black cab driver himself, he usually avoids minicabs on principle, but on Millennium night he had little choice. He took the minicab home, bullying the Somali driver all the way about the best route. When Fraser phoned his Nokia at 3.30 a.m., Nodge ignored the call and went back to sleep.

Now it is 9 a.m. and he is getting ready to go out on a shift in his cab. None of the other drivers whom he meets in the cab shelters and taxi drivers' cafés know his secret. He feels no urgent need to tell them.

The phone rings. Fraser again. He ignores it. He feels lonely, and needy, and angry. Next time, he knows, he will pick up the phone and make it up with Fraser. He is too scared of loneliness to do anything else.

* * *

Frankie and Veronica do not wake the next morning until gone eleven. Frankie pulls himself out of bed first.

Come on. We'd better get our skates on. We're meant to be at your parents' house at one. We have to pick up Flossie as well. And she won't be ready.

How do you know?

She's never ready.

Why did we agree to this? sighs Veronica, pushing her face into the pillow.

Guilt. The reason you mainly do things when it comes to your mother.

What's your excuse then?

Duty.

Do you think Flossie will be alright with my mum and dad?

No. It's going to be a car crash. But we'll get through it.

Although they have been married four months, Frankie's mother, Flossie, and Veronica's parents, Michael and Cordelia, have never formally met except for exchanging a few greetings at the wedding ceremony. They had avoided one another at the reception entirely, despite sitting at the same table, albeit at different ends.

Frankie showers. When he emerges from the bathroom, Veronica is sitting on the side of the bed, still naked. To his eyes, she is stripped now of last night's sexuality, and seems forlorn. She looks up at him as if she's about to cry.

Should I go and get a morning after pill?

I thought you said you were, you know, not at that time of month. Where you going to get one, anyway?

I've got a friend with a prescription pad. A doctor. Mind you, she lives in Clapham.

Clapham? There and back's going to take two hours at least. We're already running late. That's going to ruin the lunch. Although obviously it's ruined already. Just by virtue of it happening. You know what your mother is like. She's bad enough as it is without us putting her precious schedule out.

I don't know, Frankie. Minty, my friend, she's going away on holiday tonight.

You'll be alright. I pulled out at the last moment.

He indicates the broad stain on the sheet.

Do you know who texted me last night? he says, trying to change the subject.

He turns away, pulls on his trousers, fiddles with his belt, checks his watch.

Veronica, seemingly preoccupied, doesn't provide the necessary follow-up question.

Tony Diamonte. He's got some front.

She continues to ignore him, instead fidgeting nervously with her wedding ring.

We have to go, Vronky. If we don't leave now your mother is going to be a total bitch all afternoon.

She nods, silently rises and presses her lips together as if for safety, to stop wrong words escaping.

* * *

Frankie draws the car up in front of Flossie Blue's un-renovated workman's cottage in the grubby terrace behind Shepherd's Bush Green. She and Frankie's father, Joe, bought it for £2,000 in 1963 and, a century old, it looks its age. Frankie's urgings for his mother to modernize have fallen, always, on deaf ears.

There are hanging baskets on either side of the door, now stripped of their blooms by the punishment of winter. There is a bunch of vivid, unnaturally upright red plastic tulips which, as far as Frankie can remember, have always been there.

He lets himself into the house with the latchkey.

Mum!

Yoo-hoo! comes the answering song from upstairs. *Be down in a mo.*

Skates on. We're running late.

Walking through to the kitchen, he flops into one of the four chairs, the same ones he remembers from childhood, with the splayed backs, now patchy with worn varnish. There's a cellophane-wrapped bunch of orange carnations in a plastic jug of water on the table. He notices, to his surprise, holiday brochures spread on the Fablon-covered surface. 'Morocco – Land of Dreams'. 'The Nile and the World of the Pharaohs'. 'Beach Life in Malaga', 'Cruises in the Mediterranean'.

Veronica appears in the doorway.

Flossie's planning a trip, looks like.

Good for her.

Did you lock the car? There's some right herberts around here. Don't know why she doesn't move to Eastbourne like a normal old duck. Free up some capital.

Veronica tosses him the car keys, which he catches deftly. Now Flossie bustles into the room. Her hair is lank on her shoulders and the buttons at the top of her blouse are undone, showing an inch of yellowy bra. Her face is like serrated dough, her lips are dry. But she has made an effort, Frankie notices. She is wearing her best skirt, midnight blue serge from John Lewis, and a good pair of polished flat black shoes.

Hello, Frankie love. Happy New Year. Hello, Veronica.

Hello, Mrs Blue.

She embraces first Veronica, then Frankie, kissing his cheek wetly.

You had a big night last night? says Flossie, recoiling slightly. *Smells like you did.*

What's all this? Frankie ignores her, vaguely indicating the glossies on the table.

I made some resolutions. About time I had some fun.

Flossie is all bustle, her solid bulk moving with the grace and purpose of a linebacker. She hauls on a coat that looks like it has been cut out of winter curtains, heavy and dusk-blue with a mangy fur collar.

Resolutions to get a suntan?

To spend some money. Have a nice time.

What money?

Your dad left me a bit of a nest egg. You know that. I told you that. Money he'd saved. Life insurance. Not much, but better than a poke in the eye with a burned stick.

You don't want to go mad, Mum.

Don't be daft. I don't need much to get by. Anyway there's ekerty in this house. I could always top up. Downsize or whatever the word is nowadays. You're always telling me. Thought I might spend some of the savings on a bit of fun in the sun. Just what the doctor ordered.

Frankie picks up a cruise brochure – 'The Wonders of the Far East' – and flicks through it.

You've never been further than Southend on Sea. What's come over you?

That's what I'm saying. I've never really done much in my life. We never had the money when your father was alive. And Joe didn't like to go places. I'm sixty years old this year. Not so long left when you think about it.

Don't be silly. You've got thirty years yet.

I've not made old bones just yet. Not quite in my prime – but still. You know what I'm talking about, don't you, Veronica? You're only as young as you feel.

Wouldn't you get lonely? On a cruise by yourself?

What makes you think I'd be going by myself?

Frankie notices a slight preen in her stance. He glances at the bunch of carnations and notices that there is a small card attached. He picks it up and reads it.

'To Fab Floss, Love and Hugs, G x.'

What's this then? Who's G?

To his surprise, Flossie blushes deeply.

It stands for Gordon. He's a gentleman friend.

Who's he when he's at home?

None of your beeswax.

Oh, come on, Mum, why don't you come clean. 'Gordon'. Sounds like a real stud-muffin.

Stop it, Frankie! You're embarrassing me in front of Veronica. But she looks pleased with herself all the same.

Good for you, Mrs Blue, says Veronica. *You've only got one life.*

I thought you believed we had shedloads of them, snaps back Frankie, obscurely irritated. Veronica's belief in reincarnation has always chafed with him. She ignores the jibe and picks up one of the brochures, one for the 'Marvellous Mediterranean'.

This one looks nice, says Veronica.

I do fancy Spain. I've got a cousin with a place out there. Do you remember your Aunt Betty, Frankie? Lizbet?

Not really.

Thinking I might retire there myself one day. You can pick up houses for buttons, Gordon told me.

He's all over the international property markets then. Quite the catch.

Frankie tries to square this new vision of his mother as a pleasure-seeking adventurer and coy lover with his accustomed picture of her. Flossie has always been a home bird. A shy woman, with a strong sense of pride. She still scrubs her doorstep from time to time and keeps her small house, with its Ercol furniture and G-plan sofa and rubber plants in the hallway, clean and tidy. But the swirl of the carpet is distressed, and the wooden chairs around the kitchen table are scratched and rickety. On one of them, a chair leg is held together with crudely knocked-in nails.

Perhaps the travel fever will pass. A fad. 'Gordon' likewise.

Frankie checks his watch, becoming increasingly anxious about the time and so he clucks at Flossie until she is ready. After ten minutes, they leave, Flossie triple-locking the door behind her. She is grasping the bunch of orange carnations, still wrapped in cellophane.

What are they for?

You're meant to bring something, aren't you? Gordon wouldn't mind me . . . what is it? Re-gifting them.

It's not necessary, says Veronica.

All the same.

Carnations, though, Frankie mutters.

What's wrong with carnations?

Orange ones.

Veronica touches him firmly on the sleeve.

Nothing's wrong with carnations, he says.

Just before she gets in the car, as if by reflex, he hugs his mother. She smells of Eucryl and lavender. She lowers herself down into the cream-coloured leather seat and immediately, and loudly, breaks wind.

I do beg your pardon, Veronica. I had some baked beans for break-fast. Sometimes I never learn.

Don't worry, says Veronica, although the stench is foul, like burning rubber and compost.

Frankie winds down the windows and frowns. He is not looking forward to the lunch. He knows that Flossie is going to be uncomfortable. He knows because the moment he enters through the ancient oak door of Veronica's parents' cottage in

Chalfont St Peter he will also feel discomfort, however much he tries to feel nonchalant, relaxed and worldy-wise.

But Michael and Cordelia have invited him, Veronica and his mother – the reverse, with Flossie entertaining them at her old terraced workman's cottage would be unthinkable – and they must all suffer the ceremony. This is the meaning of family, thinks Frankie. Mutually agreed suffering.

The drive takes less than an hour, after the muddle of West London gives way to the primped greenery of Buckinghamshire. Veronica's parents' cottage lies down a short gravel driveway. The tyres crunch as they approach.

Very chocolate-box, isn't it? Did you grow up here, love? Flossie asks Veronica.

Top right-hand bedroom. That was mine.

Her eyes go up to a sash window, the frame surrounded by tendrils of green ivy.

Very old, isn't it? Must be quite a bit of upkeep. Looks dead posh.

Posh people don't actually say 'posh', Mum. They say 'smart'.

Well, you would know all about it, wouldn't you? says Flossie, an edge creeping into her voice.

I wasn't saying that you—

Oh, don't worry, love. You're probably a bit nervous.

I'm not nervous.

She turns to Veronica.

When he was a little boy and he got nervous he used to get ulcers. Didn't you, Frankie? And piles. Those piles were a trial.

Frankie brings the car to a halt. He helps Flossie out, and they all cluster together around the beautifully aged, red stone doorstep. The front door is painted a deep glossy English green, which looks about ten layers thick, with a worn, heavy brass knocker. Veronica raises it, then lets it drop. After maybe thirty seconds, the door can be heard to unlatch. Veronica's mother, around the same age as Flossie, but skinny, stretched and dressed in black, performs a welcoming smile. Her smile is wide enough to span the contrasting emotions it both advertises and conceals.

Lovely. Lovely, is all she says.

She ushers them in, kissing Frankie and then Veronica, but merely shaking hands with Flossie, who seems confused.

Can I take your coat, Mrs Blue?

It's Flossie, love.

She hands Cordelia the orange carnations. Taking them, Cordelia doesn't miss a beat.

How lovely. And how unusual!

They're carnations.

Really? That's lovely. I'll put them in water later. For the moment, I'll just put them . . . here.

Cordelia locates a small litter bin by the side of the telephone table, and places them carefully into it, stalks first.

I hope I'm not being rude. I just need my hands to take the coats.

Flossie is unperturbed.

This is a nice place. Looks about a hundred-and-odd year old.

Built in 1800 originally. Been substantially rebuilt a few times since though.

You've kept it very nice.

We haven't been here for the whole *two hundred years, of course.*

Flossie hands Cordelia, who is waiting for her to laugh, her coat. Realizing that Flossie doesn't understand what is expected of her, Cordelia turns her attention to the coat instead.

What a lovely . . . thing

My late husband, Joseph, bought it for me as an anniversary present. Way back in 1975. Real fox fur collar. Careful, it's a bit lively.

What?

I had it cleaned, but it might still have a few fleas.

Cordelia reflexively holds the coat at arm's length.

Just joking, dear.

Cordelia's smile stays firm as she gingerly hangs up the coat on one of six solid brass hooks fixed to the left of the doorway. Michael appears at the living room door. He is wearing red corduroy trousers and a white shirt tucked in, which emphasizes his pot belly.

Flossie. How lovely to see you. You're looking fantastic. Just fantastic.

I smell lamb, says Veronica, turning in the direction of the kitchen, which lies on the far side of the sitting room.

Well, says Michael, avuncular and glowing. *Well.*

He notices the carnations in the litter bin and thinks to speak, but a glance from Cordelia silences him.

Shall we go through, then? says Michael.

He plants a kiss on the edge of Flossie's mouth. She blushes and looks puzzled, then he raises his eyes to the mistletoe suspended above the doorframe and she relaxes. They move into the living room, where there is a hefty log fire burning. Sparks ascend, fading and dying as they climb the chimney breast.

What a lot of books! says Flossie, scanning the laden shelves.

Do you like reading? asks Michael, his red flushed cheeks taking on still more colour from the fire.

Historical romances are about my limit. I like Georgette Heyer.

Why don't you take a seat? He gestures towards a beautifully distressed sofa.

That's right, Mum, take a load off, says Frankie.

That's a lovely settee.

She sits down, grunting as she does so, then automatically slips off her shoes. There is a hole in the toe of her tights. She looks up and sees Cordelia's expression, then begins to try and put them on again.

It's fine, Flossie, says Veronica, glancing reproachfully at her mother, who raises an eyebrow in return.

They're brand new, just a bit tight. Pinching my feet.

Just leave them off.

She is struggling to put them back on, but because of their newness and tightness is finding it difficult.

I'd better check on the meat, says Cordelia, brightly.

Veronica, with an anxious backward glance, follows her mother into the kitchen.

Can I get you a drink, Flossie? Michael says, mildly.

But she is still preoccupied with the shoes and does not respond.

What about you, Frankie? Thirsty?

What have you got, Michael?

I've got a twelve-year-old Ardbegh. Very peaty if you like that kind of thing.

I'll take it straight. Maybe just a splash of water, says Frankie, automatically feeling his jacket buttons, checking that they are done and undone in the right places.

Flossie, flustered, looks up. She has managed one shoe, but not the other.

What about you, Flossie? says Michael, trying again. *Do you want something to drink? An aperitif? Perhaps a spritzer. Or an Aperol.*

I'd love a glass of plonk. Large. Red if you've got it.

Michael nods and smiles.

Or white, I'm not fussy.

Flossie has finally got both shoes back on and inspects, them, satisfied. Michael disappears into the kitchen. There he finds Cordelia and Veronica together, immersed in sinister silence. Cordelia is theatrically checking on the lamb. Veronica is fidgeting morosely in the cutlery drawer.

Drink, anyone? says Michael.

The silence persists.

Am I interrupting something?

Veronica turns sharply.

Mummy has just been telling me – in that underhand way only she knows how to – what a mistake I made when I married Frankie. That's all.

I wasn't saying that at all. *I was simply saying . . .*

Veronica lowers her voice, but hisses plainly.

You were simply saying that Frankie's mother was 'a bit rough at the edges'. Which is simply a continuance of a conversation we have had about a hundred times that Frankie is 'a bit rough at the edges' too.

You're being ridiculous. That was months ago. Way before the wedding. I'm amazed you're even bringing it up. I apologized at the time.

When you realized that you weren't going to get your way and talk me out of it. And you didn't apologize exactly. You just said, 'I'm sorry if I offended you.'

Why don't you both calm it down a bit? says Michael. *I'll make you a nice gin and it.*

He reaches for the bottle of Tanqueray from the drinks cabinet and pours out a good slug in each of three glasses.

You always take her side, hisses Cordelia, closing the oven door on the meat.

How's that taking her side?

He tops up the gin with a few splashes of tonic and slices of cucumber.

You're not taking mine, anyway. And you think exactly the same as I do about . . . you know . . .

That's not true. I think who Veronica chooses is up to her.

Daddy, it's a little bit true, says Veronica.

No, it isn't.

Daddy.

Well — a little bit, perhaps. At first. But I think he's a pretty decent chap, actually. Hard working. Done it all with the sweat of his brow. I admire anyone who can claw his way up. I admit a graduate of Staines Technical College was not the candidate we had in mind, but . . . no need to look like that, yes, yes, I admit it, we were being horrid snobs. I was entirely wrong and I do apologize. Now, can we smooth all this over and have a lovely lunch together?

You'll see, says Cordelia, attending to the steaming vegetables on the hob.

What now? says Veronica.

Nothing.

What? Spit it out.

Your mother claimed that sooner or later Frankie would ask us for money for something or other.

I never said that! says Cordelia, outraged.

Oh, for God's sake. Veronica grabs the glass out of Michael's hand and swigs it down in one.

* * *

They sit down at the dinner table twenty minutes later. Cordelia brings in the crown roast of lamb, greeted by mutters of appreciation from Veronica, Frankie and Michael. The vegetables are already on the table – carrots, parsnips, roast potatoes, kale and butternut squash.

Help yourself, she says grandly, and Flossie does, enthusiastically, covering her plate with everything from the vegetable plates except the kale and the butternut squash. Michael takes the carving knife and begins to cut the crown roast into portions. Inside the meat is pink, almost red. It oozes juices and blood. Notes of rosemary and oregano drift across the table. He begins to distribute the portions amongst each of the sitters, but when he gets to Flossie, she holds her hand up to stop him.

No, thank you, she says.

Frankie looks up from his plate in bewilderment.

Mum . . .

Flossie shifts in her seat.

I can't, she says.

Why on earth not?

Her eyes dart from side to side, then upwards into defiance.

I've gone vegetarian.

Frankie bursts out laughing.

You're not a vegetarian.

Florence's face is set in a stubborn rictus.

It was one of my new year's resolutions.

Never mind, says Michael.

If you'd let me know, I would have sorted something out for you, says Cordelia crisply.

Well, I couldn't, could I? says Flossie. *I only decided yesterday.*

Cordelia stares resentfully at the half a crown roast, £25 a kilo from the organic butcher in the village, that remains on the serving platter.

Flossie finally breaks the ensuing silence.

The plumber came round the other day. I've had a problem with my washer.

Flossie's voice, Frankie notices with alarm, has become louder and slightly slurred. He has rarely seen his mother drunk, she largely abstains, and for good reason as Frankie recalls. Flossie takes another swig of her wine. Now the others at the table begin to attend to their food, starting to eat.

What kind of a problem? says Michael, politely. His soft brown eyes look at her with something like tenderness.

So he comes in. A black chap. Built like a brick . . . outhouse. Six feet tall if he's an inch. Dreadlocks and everything. About my age though. Maybe a bit younger. He says, what's the problem? I says, I think it's the washer. He says, I'll take a look at that, shall I? I say, do you want a cup of coffee? He says, yes I'd love a cup of coffee. And then I says, black or white? And he says, how you having yours. And I said, I like mine black and strong. He says, you cheeky devil. I said, no, I didn't mean that, and I didn't, I really didn't. I say, I'm not joking, honest, I wasn't being racially prejudiced. He says, I don't mind what I have to drink so long as it's sweet, wet and hot. Then he starts laughing, and I laugh too. You should have seen us. He was nice. I wouldn't have minded.

Flossie cackles. Throughout this Cordelia has been nodding politely, her eyes somehow both flat and unreflective and glittering simultaneously.

So did he fix it? says Cordelia, voice like dust.

What? says Florence.

The washer?

Florence stares at her.

Who cares?

Mum, says Frankie.

It was just a story. A funny story, says Florence, taking the gravy jug and pouring another quarter pint on to her plate. *I thought it was funny, anyway.*

Would you like another glass of wine? says Michael, drawing a fierce look from Cordelia.

Lovely, says Flossie. She has already had two large ones.

Do you think you should? says Frankie.

Go on with you. Flossie holds her glass up for Michael to fill. Her white parchment hand shakes slightly, liver spots a faint, emerging constellation. Frankie notices a wine stain on her lips, and smudged lipstick. *It's a nice drop, what is it?*

Just something from Waitrose.

She squints at the label, grunts, then takes an urgent swig.

Quite punchy. What proof is it?

Proof?

You know, like, beer has about five per cent. Vodka seventy. Proof.

I'm not quite sure.

Kicks like a donkey.

* * *

After the lunch has been finished, and they have eaten a dessert of passion fruit panna cotta, followed by a plate of expensive and pungent cheese, Frankie and Veronica clean up the kitchen. Flossie made the mistake of putting eggs, then tomatoes, then soft cheese in the fridge, each time having them pointedly fished out again by Cordelia, who has now given up and started knocking back the Poire William. Veronica, against Flossie's stubbornly vocal protests, has sent Flossie back to the sitting room to 'relax'. Cordelia announces she is going upstairs to 'fix herself' — what this constitutes is not clear. Michael is sitting in the living room doing the *Times* crossword, while Flossie has now dozed off on the sofa.

Since when has your mum been a vegetarian? says Veronica, as she loads the brushed steel Miele dishwasher, silent as a Rolls-Royce.

She's not, says Frankie.

Veronica puts another handful of soiled knives into the cutlery holder.

So what was that about?

Frankie hands Veronica Flossie's untouched Americano.

She doesn't like the sight of blood. Not on her meat.

Veronica momentarily stops loading the dishwasher.

Why didn't she say something?

Because she was embarrassed — obviously.

Why?

Because she knew your mother would think she was a pikey for not wanting to eat raw meat. Perhaps she thought being a vegetarian would give her a bit of class.

Cordelia doesn't think . . .

Don't waste your breath. She thinks I'm beneath her too. And beneath you as well, since you mention it.

Veronica carefully places a cut crystal glass into the dishwasher. Frankie sees the redness of her fingernail against the transparency and finds it obscurely exciting.

No point in denying it, I suppose, she says, flatly.

And what do you think?

I think she's awful.

Who? Flossie?

Veronica stares at Frankie full in the face.

Not Flossie, she says. *Cordelia.*

None of us can help our upbringing, I suppose, says Frankie, touching her gently on the forearm.

He looks around the room.

Nice place this. What's your dad do in the City again?

He's retired now.

Did in the City, then.

Something to do with Futures. Whatever they are.

And now?

He's vague about it. Invests in this and that. A hobby as much as anything else. Bit of speculation here and there. Keeps his mind sharp.

Interesting.

Why is it interesting?

Well. You know I want to set up my own agency one day.

Veronica twists around. Frankie is terrified by the expression on her face. It is one he has never seen before. When she speaks it is through clenched teeth.

Frankie. Listen to me.

What is it? What's the matter?

Don't even think about it. Ever.

Think about what?

Getting my dad to invest in some . . . project of yours.

I was just saying . . .

Well, don't say. Or think.

She is hissing. There are small flecks of spittle at the edges of her mouth.

Vronky! Why are you so upset?

She looks into the living room to make sure that Cordelia and Michael are out of earshot.

71

My mum thinks you're on the make. She has said, quite openly to me, that sooner or later you're going to ask to borrow money.

No, I would never . . .

What do you mean, you would never? You were just talking about it! Don't say you weren't.

Well, I didn't know—

Promise, Frankie, here and now. Promise me you'll never take money from my parents. I couldn't bear to see the expression on my mother's face.

Alright. Christ!

Say it then.

Say what?

'I promise.'

I promise.

You promise what?

That I'll never borrow money from your parents.

On the grave of your dead father.

On the grave of my dead father.

This seems to satisfy Veronica, and her face softens.

Okay then. Agreed.

Agreed.

* * *

Colin and Roxy are walking together in the local park, a few hundred yards from Colin's flat. Roxy is fighting back a headache. Their elbows touch from time to time. Each time, to Colin, is an electric shock. Then, to his amazement, after a few minutes' walk, she takes his hand.

I could murder a full English, says Roxy.

Could you keep it down?

Kill or cure.

There's a café near here. We might be lucky even if it is New Year's Day.

As they walk, a distant bell chimes. Roxy looks up and notices a spire looming over the hedges that surround the park.

Veronica told me you're a born-again Christian. She was having a laugh, right?

No, says Colin, simply. *Though not so much born again anymore. In the way the phrase is used.*

For real? says Roxy, loosening her hand from his but not quite withdrawing it.

He reels her fingers back in.

Not anymore. Not in that sense. I went through a weird time after my mum died. I think I needed something. Someone. Her passing — it scrambled my mind a bit. I sort of depended on her. So I started to go to church. Read the Bible and that. But it's passed now, pretty much. Don't get me wrong, I still have a sort of faith. But not in a weird way. I just think there's a higher power. Lots of people do. You can call it what you want. But there's more than . . .

He gestures around the park with his hand.

. . . just this grass and rocks and trees and water. More than just . . . stuff.

He regards her steadily, his watery eyes under flickering lids. She looks puzzled.

Do you understand?

Perhaps, she says. *When I was seventeen I went through something like that. Joined a church group. Lasted until the vicar tried to feel me up. Sort of lost my faith after that.*

I was always a bit late in my development, says Colin. *When I was seventeen all I cared about was QPR. That was my religion then, I suppose.*

A duck walks past, head in the air, cheerful, in full command of his environment. Colin envies his confidence, feels a lurch in his stomach. Then he reaches in his pocket and pulls out a small transparent plastic bag full of white mulch.

Wonderloaf, he says.

Wonderloaf?

I don't like fancy bread.

He throws some to the ducks. They ignore it.

Ducks are fussy, says Roxy. *Let me have a go.*

She takes the bag and scatters some of the bread on the ground. It falls in an almost perfect semicircle. The ducks wheel and start to peck at it.

It's all about presentation, says Roxy.

They leave the ducks and head for the café on the adjacent road which is small, shabby and deserted but open. Roxy orders a fry-up with everything, Colin a bacon sandwich.

Do you still go to church, then?

I'm not religious about it. So to speak.

I believe only about 12.5 per cent of what the Bible says.

Do you?

Yeh. I'm an eightheist.

Oh right. Yeh. I've heard it, says Colin.

Roxy looks over at the church.

I sometimes think it would be nice to go again. I used to go when I was a kid. I used to like the quiet.

It can be a bit boring, to be honest, says Colin. *Takes a lot of sticking with. Some of the hymns nowadays are dire.*

I don't mind boring anymore. I've had enough of exciting. You know when I was a teenager I always wanted to have adventure. But when you think about it, adventures are just moments when things can go wrong. And they usually do. Then you think adventures aren't so much fun anymore.

The food arrives and Roxy immediately starts gulping it down, having drenched it with tomato ketchup. Colin doesn't touch his.

What's the matter? she says, chewing on a sausage as she talks, spraying small particles onto the table.

It's not Heinz ketchup. You have to have a bacon sandwich with Heinz ketchup or it's not right.

He picks at the edges of the bacon all the same, tiny scraps which he chews one by one.

After they have finished, Roxy takes what's left of his sandwich and eats that too. Then she checks her watch. Colin notices that it looks expensive.

What is that?

An Omega Deville.

Aren't they pricey?

Not if you buy them in Koh Samui from a market stall. I suppose I should be getting off, says Roxy. *I've got a shift at one. The sales are starting. It's going to be murder.*

Shall I call you a limousine?

That's sweet.

I was joking.

I know. Anyway, it's fine. I can get a train.

She waves her hand in the direction of the railway arches a few hundred yards away.

I'll walk you up there.

They walk to the station more or less in silence, each preparing, in their own way, for the farewell ritual, making decisions, considering options.

75

Just as they reach the first arch Colin, taking a gulp of air first, his heart pounding, asks:

Can I have another chance to beat you at GoldenEye?

I expect you were just too drunk to be at your best.

I suppose there's always the chance you were better than me.

A girl? Beat you? Office champion?

It wasn't only the drink. The pressure got to me.

Given what you thought might be at stake.

Yes.

There is a pause. Colin feels his stomach turn. She isn't interested, he is sure of it now. He feels himself flush with regret and embarrassment for having even suggested another date.

Okay.

Okay what?

I'm up for another game.

Colin grins, his face sparking to life from its usual tugged-down heaviness.

When?

You're keen.

Well . . .

Don't worry. I've been round the block too many times to play hard to get. We can have a rematch as soon as you like.

Tonight?

You're really not very good at this, are you? Leave a girl a little pride. I'm probably busy. Bound to be.

Sorry.

I finish work at eight. I'll come round after that.

Without quite knowing who makes the first move, they kiss, as the District Line train to Upminster thunders overhead.

It's like that film, isn't it, says Roxy, as she breaks off the kiss, smiling as if heartbroken.

What film?

What's it called?

I don't know.

Briefing something. Counter. Briefing Counter.

* * *

Three weeks later

Frankie climbs into the green Mini Cooper emblazoned with the pale cream insignia of Farley, Ratchett and Gwynne which is parked in the port outside his house. Each side of the car has 'FR&G' emblazoned in giant, italic script. Also it's inscribed on the roof. Nick Ratchett is responsible for this branding effort. Frankie likes to tease him about the possibility of the roof sign accessing a niche market in police helicopter pilots.

The interior of the car had been valeted the day before, so it is spruce and tidy, although there is a half-empty pack of Camels on the floor of the passenger seat dropped carelessly by Frankie that morning. Frankie still treats himself to one or two a day, but he's been trying to kick it ever since Ralph Gwynne had his heart attack. Ralph was a thirty-a-day man. Frankie takes one out of the pack and lights it anyway.

Also on the kill list: pork scratchings, stuffed crust pizza and more than two pints of beer in a night. He wants to keep in shape now that he's hit his thirties, although he's not sure for whose benefit – Veronica, his own, or both.

Frankie eases the car into gear and steers onto the furious tumult of the Goldhawk Road, sandwiching himself between a battered white van and a massive, growling HGV haphazardly piled with rubble and scrap metal.

He checks his phone. He realizes that he has had the ringer switched off. There are four messages from Nick Ratchett. As soon as he puts the ringer back on, the phone sounds. He switches to hands free. Sure enough, it's Ratchett.

I'm just on my way in, Nick.

Never mind that.

What's come over you?

It's Ralph.

What about Ralph?

He's had another attack.

What kind of attack?

The heart kind, what do you think?

Shit.

Yeh. Shit is about size of it.

Is he okay?

He's not okay. He's in intensive care.

Frankie's attention has wandered from the road and he has to swerve to avoid a woman on a zebra crossing. He put his hand up in apology.

If you want to see him, you'd better get a move on.

What does that mean?

There's an ominous silence.

He's not in great shape. Polly was in a bad way when she rang to tell me.

Where is he?

St Mary's.

Pause.

How did the sale go yesterday?

Fuck off, Nick.

Frankie hangs up. He finds it hard to concentrate on driving and stalls when the lights change. The white van pulls past him impatiently. The driver stares at him violently as he motors past and opens his mouth to shout something, presumably abuse, but then closes it again. The driver's face configures itself in a way Frankie doesn't understand, then he shifts the van up a gear and drives ahead without further remark or gesture. Frankie engages the motor of the Mini, and checks his mirror before pulling out. It is then that he notices the still-wet tear tracks on his face and his red, swollen eyes. He scrubs at his cheek with the sleeve of his suit.

His Nokia rings again. This time the display shows it to be Veronica. He hits the speaker button.

Ratchett's been ringing me on my mobile. Wanted to speak to you. He sounded weird.

Ralph's had another heart attack.

Ralph who?

Ralph. Ralph. My boss Ralph Gwynne.

Oh, Frankie.

On my way to the hospital now. Yours.

Shall I come and meet you?

Aren't you working?

I can get away. My clients aren't going anywhere.

Yes. Thank you.

I'll be waiting for you.

* * *

Frankie manages to find a parking space just outside the entrance to St Mary's in Paddington.

My lucky day, he thinks, bitterly.

He sees Veronica waiting under the awning that leads into the maw of the building. He parks, feeds the meter and crosses the road to meet her.

Suddenly his legs feel shaky. Veronica supports him as he half-collapses.

Frankie?

I'll be okay.

He straightens himself up.

You've gone grey.

Have I?

He inadvertently touches his hair.

Your skin. Idiot.

She smiles and Frankie manages a weak smile in response.

I don't feel too good.

There's a coffee bar inside. Let's have a sit down for a moment.

Frankie manages to make it through to a seat while Veronica fetches him a double espresso, which he knocks back in one shot. She touches his cheek tenderly with one finger.

Colour's coming back a bit.

Have you found out which ward Ralph is in?

I went to see him already. Didn't know how long you would take to get here. I bumped into Polly. She said I should.

Polly is Ralph's wife of thirty-five years. She and Frankie always got along. He and Veronica would have dinner at their house in Baron's Court once or twice a year. She was a terrible cook, Frankie remembers, randomly.

How's he looking?

Veronica swallows, tries to find Frankie's eyes. Locks onto them.

He's gone. He went before you got here.

Gone where?

He's dead, Frankie.

Frankie feels flat, blank for several seconds. Then a wave of something passes across him. He can't at first identify it, but eventually finds a label for it.

He thinks it might be relief but that makes no sense.

Then, like a seventh wave after the sixth, comes grief, a giant black cloud of nausea and sharp edges.

Frankie? Are you okay?

Frankie nods but says, *No.*

Polly said when you got here . . . to come and see him. Say goodbye. He's still in the bed.

Frankie stares at her. She stands up and holds out her hand for him.

It's on the third floor. Polly's waiting.

Frankie remains seated.

I can't.

She specifically asked . . . she said . . . that you should . . .

I can't, Vronky.

She's in pieces. We're her friends.

He bursts into tears. Veronica strokes his hand.

She lets it rest. His tears dry. Minutes later, Frankie gathers himself, lets go of her hand, leaves the reception area and returns to his car, twenty minutes still left on the meter.

* * *

Two weeks later

In the office bathroom mirror, Frankie uses the polished edge of a manicured fingernail to explore his mulberry-coloured birthmark, the size of a hefty cornflake and the shape of Australia. It stains the hairline along his right temple. It seems to him, as he examines it, larger than it was, but it may be simply that his hair has begun to recede. Since Ralph's death he is sure it has thinned out.

He's at the same age the fallout started with his father, Joe, who was completely bald by the age of forty. Or so his mother, Flossie, has always told him, with a strange kind of triumph. *Bald as a billiard ball he went. The reflection was enough to blind you on a sunny day. Not that there were many of those in those days.*

Having located the imperfection, Frankie finds himself violently sawing at it with the tip of the nail, as if trying to obliterate the blemish altogether. Almost immediately, he gives up, defeated. The birthmark, now carrying a faint purple weal, is more noticeable than before.

He shifts the examination from fingernail to fingertip. Is it just in his imagination that the texture of the mark feels slightly different from the rest of his skin, giving out a shade more friction to the touch, like the finest grade of sandpaper? Odd that he should even notice something novel about it, after thirty years of anxious examination. No – perhaps more like twenty-five years, since there must have been a time, before self-consciousness, when it did not press down on him, marking out his difference, announcing his disfigurement.

Shortly after their wedding, he had allowed Veronica to touch it. It was possibly the most intimate thing he had ever experienced – to allow another human being to inspect his mark, to maul and explore it. She was gentle, but he had flinched, felt himself bunch up within. She tried to reassure him, insisting it was an inseparable part of an integrated whole. *No perfection without flaws*, she said.

One day he wants to be rid of it. A gift to himself for the new millennium, perhaps. Over the last five years several female friends have had cosmetic surgery, for tightening, reducing, stretching or plumping up. But none, he knows, has tried to erase a part of themselves in this way, to this extent.

He applies his hand to the hot air dryer, enjoying the pressure of invisible force. Shaking them free of stubborn germs, he returns to the shop floor, to his functional but expensive desk which sits beneath a large hand-painted sign in italic script

Farley, Ratchett and Gwynne
Estate Agents and Valuers
Est. 1973

The walls are covered with immense fluorescent orange maps of the local area, as if these particular postcodes have become lurid and bloated. There are five other desks in the room, all of which face forward towards the plate-glass window that fronts FR&G. The office is new: the old one, just to the east of the roundabout leading to Holland Park Avenue, had its rent hiked beyond what was possible. So they have lost their fashionable W11 postcode. But so far, trade has been unaffected.

Furthest from the property displays, at the back of the

room, sit Nicholas Ratchett and Simon Farley, the two remaining partners in the firm. Closer to the front, Frankie's own desk is flanked to the right by Victor Strudwick, the lugubrious, rubbery-lipped mortgage broker, his thick curly hair bursting from his head like an unwelcome thought.

At the front of the room, at the coal face, neat in business suits, are the office junior, Jane (thick, posh, fat, Alice band) and Maree, who specializes in rentals and is Ratchett's idea of glamorous (highlighted brunette hair, expensive cosmetics), hence her position close to the plate-glass window. As Ratchett never quite tires of telling Maree – and Jane, in a rather more openly critical tone of voice – appearance and presentation are going to be the keys to success in the new millennium.

Frankie continues to chew over the thought of plastic surgery, but the sound of the phone ringing on his desk tugs at the edges of his distraction. It joins the chorus of three others in the room, as if each is calling for a mate. The property market is irrepressible even this early in the new year. Two of the receivers are immediately picked up, but Frankie ignores the insistent *dring* of his own, earning himself a dark sideways glance from Nick Ratchett who is, as usual, dressed in a black-blue Prada suit – he owns three, all identical – slightly tight across the shoulders, a white tailored-fit satin striped shirt and a grey silk tie, loosened at the neck and releasing a tiny burst of springy, oily chest hair that makes Frankie think of mattress filling escaping under pressure. Sometimes the colour of Ratchett's tie changes – perhaps emerald green or duck-egg blue. Sometimes he even sports a straight knitted version, with a squared-off tip, usually maroon. But the tie is the only variable. Even his socks are uniformly, perpetually, doggedly charcoal.

The suit, despite its label, would have been bought at a knock-down price from someone, or from somewhere, possibly in a pub. Ratchett never paid full price for anything if he could possibly help it, either in his behaviour – in which he was adept at avoiding responsibility – or in his shopping habits. Those habits themselves were purely functional. At his Fulham home, which Frankie had only once or twice visited in his seven years at FR&G, Ratchett had worn cheap saggy T-shirts and fraying sweat pants, while he draped himself over expensive but anonymous-looking, hard-wearing furniture, watching undemanding programmes on a cheap TV. Style in clothing was not a pleasure for Ratchett, but an unavoidable business tool.

Aware of Ratchett's critical gaze but indifferent to it, Frankie checks his Tag Heuer. It was Veronica's wedding present to him. On receiving it, he couldn't resist looking it up in the catalogue, finding himself slightly disappointed that it hadn't been more top of the range. After all, £750 wasn't so much for a watch nowadays, not one which sealed marital vows, anyway. He had spent five times as much on her, technically at least, since he kicked up for the honeymoon and, of course, the engagement ring. Then, clinical pathologists like Veronica didn't earn that much, he supposed, especially in the NHS.

The exasperated jangle of the phone cuts off. Ratchett takes a three-and-a-half inch disc out of his PC, examines it idly, shoots him another glance, replaces it with another disc, then rolls his eyes at Simon Farley. Farley, fat and self-satisfied, but sweet in his way, although weak and pliable as far as Frankie is concerned, gives a half-smile in acknowledgement before politically distracting himself by rustling papers on his desk.

Frankie turns to Ratchett, his face arranged into a conscious evocation of profound weariness.

Stop eyeballing me, Nick.

Instead of responding, Ratchett pointedly surveys the office with bloodshot eyes that customarily look both dismayed and irritated. This at-rest expression disappears under the necessity of supplication when he is selling property. White shows above the grungy, cardboard-brown iris, giving him a slightly crazed look.

Frankie notes a sizeable crumb lodged in Ratchett's carefully clipped and groomed salt-and-pepper stubble, close to the left edge of his sharp, violent mouth. Quarter pounder with cheese, Frankie guesses – not so much because he can infer this from the shape and texture of the residue but because this is pretty much what Ratchett lives on during the daytime. Ratchett's diet only seems to vary when dining out with clients, in which case he always chooses steak, game or some form of expensive offal. As a child, he once told Frankie, his favourite food was ox hearts. Ratchett's failure to die of a heart attack is a surprise to Frankie as well as an enduring disappointment. Why is it always the good that go first? Poor Ralphie.

Frankie dials up the internet on his Apple iBook Clamshell, with 56K dial-up modem, listening to the dialling tone and the ensuing agonized squeal. The screen, as was so often the case, is struggling to load.

Jane, get me a cup of coffee will you? says Ratchett, loudly.

Jane, employed by Farley largely for her submissive nature, starts to rise from her chair.

Frankie glances across at her.

She's not your secretary, Nick. She's an intern on a training programme.

Two sugars. Just a splash of milk.

Don't let him bully you, Jane.

Jane shrugs helplessly and gets up to fetch the coffee. Probably the right move, thinks Frankie. Ratchett would have his revenge on her swiftly enough otherwise.

Ratchett, now further provoked, rises, comes and stands over Frankie's shoulder, staring at his computer screen. The search engine, Ask Jeeves, is still refusing to load. Ratchett owns a bog-standard Lenovo, about the size of a pizza box. Frankie hears the insidious whisper of Ratchett's rounded vowels in his ear. He smells his breath – fries and cigarettes. Bad enough in themselves, they noxiously mingle with Burberry Weekend for Men aftershave that gives out his location like a tart in a fog.

Watching porn on your pretentious piece of hardware again?

It's not pretentious. It's elegant. You're the only one who watches porn in the office. And you've got cheese on your beard.

An extra K is a lot extra to pay for something to look fancy. You're not a graphic designer. You flog bricks and mortar to mugs.

Ratchett explores the perimeter of his mouth with his tongue and locates the food morsel, then places it on the tip of his finger. He holds it out to Frankie.

Want it? It's today's.

I've already eaten, thanks.

Does a salad really qualify?

Does no harm to watch your waistline, says Frankie, casting his eyes over the soft spill that protrudes over Ratchett's trouser belt. Ratchett pushes the finger a few centimetres closer to

87

Frankie's face. Then, feigning boredom, he flicks the scrap of food from his beard towards Frankie's wastepaper basket. It misses, and lands close to Frankie's foot.

Are you going to pick your food scraps up?

Ratchett continues to stand over Frankie's shoulder.

What do you want, Nick?

I was hoping, Francis, for a little tête-à-tête before we finish for the day. An event which you seem to be longing for.

His voice has now produced an increased rounding of his public school vowels, to complement the roseate flush on his cheek that Frankie presumes comes from long country walks at his parents' pile in Gloucestershire. This always has a sinister effect on the tone of his voice. Ratchett, one of three brothers, is the disappointment of the family, Frankie was once told by Ralph. The two others are in Law and the City. Ratchett got a third-class degree from a redbrick in the Midlands before being parachuted into the firm by his father, an old Oxford mucker of Ralph's who was owed a favour. Ralph had spent the ensuing period of Ratchett's appointment regretting it, but there was no easy way back. Ratchett was good enough at his job to avoid being sacked and since he'd been made partner he was almost impossible to get rid of, anyway.

I'm listening, Nicholas.

It would be better if we talked in private.

Frankie raises his head to look at Ratchett directly, but can't read his expression.

I've already had my bonus, Nicholas. No further gesture of gratitude is necessary.

This isn't about your bonus, Francis.

The biggest bonus of last year. By far, if you recall correctly,

Nicholas. Because I certainly do. Recall correctly. Because I sold more houses than anyone else. Including you. And Simon. Combined.

Farley throws him a look, then puts his eyes firmly back down to his desk. Ratchett hesitates. Frankie assumes, correctly, that he is summoning malice. His eyes dart to the top of Frankie's head, where his birthmark is still red and weeping from the scuffing done by Frankie's fingernail.

You should get that birthmark seen to. Might put off the customers.

Fuck off, Nick. You've already seen off Rupert and Giles. You can't afford to lose another employee.

Rupert and Giles were predecessors to Jane and Maree. They quit at the end of the previous year to join rival firms. Ratchett's boorishness was never explicitly named as the cause, but no one in the office doubted it.

Now Ratchett has got the rise he was looking for. Frankie's body language has gone stiff. His arms are crossed defensively.

Shall we go out back?

Must we?

It might be for the best.

The other employees in the office are starting to stare, most notably Jane. A vaguely predatory expression sometimes penetrates her otherwise bland, gormless features, but now it is simply curious. Maree, whom, to Ratchett's annoyance, Frankie has always got on well with, looks concerned. He gives her a wink, and she smiles with frosted baby-pink, thickly painted lips.

Frankie sighs, just loud enough for Ratchett to register it. He is weary of being treated as just another employee at FR&G. His sales record has long been better than anyone else in the agency.

He follows Ratchett into the small office that lies behind the main reception. In contrast to the sales area – all polished surfaces, uncluttered desks and shining pens stacked neatly – the rear office has a tatty, lived-in feel. There is a half drunk cup of coffee on the battered wooden desk and a detritus of paper, brochures, Post-it notes and letters, opened and unopened, strewn across the surface.

Ratchett makes for the seat behind the desk – pole position. The chair is larger, more expensive and positioned at a higher level. He lowers himself onto the seat and begins to fiddle idly with the small, chewed pencil that was resting on a glossy brochure for rental properties. He lights a Marlboro Red and takes a slug on it.

Have a seat.

I'll stand.

Suit yourself.

Ratchett does not speak again, doodling instead on a notepad with the chewed pencil. Frankie matches him, refusing to capitulate by instigating a conversation. He understands that silence, like chair height, is a power ploy. He's used it often enough with customers himself, to tempt them into an offer they only partially wanted to make. His matching silence seems to have the desired effect. Ratchett's fidgeting with the pencil intensifies, and his eyes look more pained and irritable than before.

You might want to make yourself more comfortable.

I'm comfortable standing up. What do you want, Nick? Spit it out. Don't let it choke you.

Ratchett mumbles something into his lap. Frankie understands this to be yet another attempt to assert his – technically – senior position. Having to lean in, having to request that a question be repeated suggested the listener was deficient.

I might as well get back to work if we're just going to hang around here like a couple of mugs.

You're in a hurry, Frankie. Why? Are you busy?

I'm always busy.

You didn't look very busy just now.

Always. That's why . . .

That's why you're 'the best performing salesman at Farley, Ratchett and Gwynne'. I know, I know. You had a lucky year.

The edge of mockery in Ratchett's voice is only just discernible, so as to keep it deniable. Ratchett excels in maintaining deniability. Frankie continues to look at him steadily.

Luck had nothing to do with it.

Don't rest on your laurels.

What's this about, Nick? Why the secrecy?

No secret.

Frankie feels his irritation level rise another notch. Clearly Ratchett is out to rattle him, and is beginning to succeed.

The thing is this, Frankie. And I know this might seem clinical. But business is business. You know me. Heart on my sleeve. Colours to the mast. It's no longer Farley, Ratchett and Gwynne. It's Farley and Ratchett.

Frankie thinks for a moment that he can guess the significance of this remark, but then dismisses the thought. For Ratchett to get into this territory when Ralph is still fresh in his grave. To dishonour his legacy. No. Not even Ratchett would dredge the depths like that.

Why are you bringing this up?

I don't know what Ralph said to you.

Frankie stares back blankly, giving nothing away.

What do you mean, 'what he said to me'?

Don't force me to spell it out. I don't want to seem hard-hearted. But it's never too soon to be practical. Ralph would have agreed. Cards on the table.

Frankie stares out of the window, straining to avoid solving the puzzle. The pane is dirty, blurred. He hardens his voice. This is business, whether he likes it or not. He can't show weakness, particularly not to Nicholas Ratchett.

Okay, so you've got your heart on your sleeve, you've nailed your colours to the mast and you've put your cards on the table. But you still haven't come to the point.

He pauses. Ratchett doesn't react.

You want me to say it, don't you?

Still Ratchett doesn't speak. At least he has enough shame not to be able to make eye contact with Frankie.

You're talking about the partnership, says Frankie.

Well, I don't know. Am I? says Ratchett, now terse. *What did Ralph say to you about partnership?*

You know perfectly well what he said.

I don't think I do, as a matter of fact.

Frankie nods, his batted-away suspicions finally confirmed.

Do you have anything in writing?

Polly knows all about it, Nick. The partnership will be part of Ralph's estate.

It's just business. Ralph would understand that. I'm trying to be fair to you, Frankie. I don't want you to be under any false impressions. I don't want you to spend any more time than is necessary thinking something that isn't.

What kind of false impressions? What something that isn't?

You've already said it. Rumour has it Ralph offered you a partnership in the new year.

It's not a rumour. It's common knowledge. It's an established fact. Polly—

You're not in Polly's good books at the moment. Apparently you wouldn't even go and say goodbye to Ralph. Even though you were downstairs at the hospital. She might not be the ally you think she is. Not when there's this sort of money at stake. Ralph was a generous man. And he liked you. For some reason which I fail to fathom. Now Polly. I'm not so sure about Polly.

What are you saying?

I don't know how much more plainly I can put it, Frankie. No Ralph, no partnership. You were his baby. You ain't mine. Or Simon's. Simple as.

They stare at one another. The white space at the top of Nicholas Ratchett's cornea extends slightly, giving him a wilder look still.

We should get Simon in here, says Frankie, bleakly aware that Ratchett will have prepared the ground. Farley is the lowest in the hierarchy after Ralph and Nick, with the smallest shareholding in the firm, standing at around 17 per cent. Nick, thanks to a big injection of cash from his wealthy family, had 37 per cent. Ralph had the rest.

Of course.

Ratchett goes to the door and puts his head round it.

Simon!

As if he had just been hovering outside, Simon Farley manifests immediately. He is ill-balanced and ungainly, with a persistent sheen of sweat even in the coldest of weathers.

Despite the fact that he is undoubtedly wealthy by now, having been Ralph's original partner, he continues wearing brown suits from Marks & Spencer. He positions himself awkwardly next to Ratchett, on the other side of the desk to Frankie.

Hi, Frankie.

His smile is bright, but razor thin.

Frankie was under the impression he was going to be made a partner in the new year, says Ratchett, doodling on the ink pad in front of him. Frankie sees that he appears to be playing Hangman with himself.

Really? says Farley, mildly, but with an underlying steeliness that Frankie cannot mistake. Ratchett has clearly primed him.

Frankie turns towards Farley, aware by now that his face must be flushing. He can feel his right hand shaking. He wants to punch Ratchett, wants it badly, but knows that the cards Ratchett holds are too powerful. It will play into his hands.

Farley looks at Frankie. Frankie sees a faint flicker of apology in his eyes. Or, perhaps, shame.

There'll always be a job here for you, Frankie, says Farley, weakly.

Frankie raises two fingers.

Do I take that as a resignation? says Ratchett.

Frankie turns and marches back to his desk. Even as they were in the rear office, the sign above has been removed. A workman in blue overalls is putting up a new one.

It reads, 'Farley and Ratchett. Estate Agents'.

* * *

Back at home Frankie sits on the sofa, squirming. There is nowhere to rest his head – the back is too low – and the cushions seem harder than he remembers when he tried it in the shop.

I hate this fucking settee. Sofa.

He punches the right-hand armrest with the side of his fist.

Frankie, what's wrong?

Veronica is sitting on a sternly designed chair opposite. Her eyes remain fixed on her copy of the *New Statesman*. Gordon Brown stares out from the cover, with beetle brows and power hair.

What makes you think anything is wrong?

He rearranges the cushions violently.

Call it intuition.

There's nothing wrong.

Are you sure?

Stop banging on about it, will you?

Frankie gets up off the sofa, kicks it, and walks into the kitchen. Seconds later, he reappears. Veronica has not moved in her chair. She is still calmly reading the *New Statesman*. When he speaks again, his tone has modulated, is softer, with a vapour trail of shame, shading into the clearer air of defiance.

I'm leaving the agency is what's wrong.

Now she looks up from the magazine.

What?

I'm out. Simple as.

But . . . your partnership!

That's gone.

What do you mean, it's gone?

Ratchett and Farley stiffed me. No partnership.

Veronica throws the magazine to one side, adjusts her position on the chair, straight back, hands on knees, narrowed eyes.

Were you sacked?

He doesn't answer.

We're about to move to a new house. And while I appreciate that you've had a bad day, can I just gently point something out? We're married. Decisions like this need to be taken together. You can't quit without talking it through with me.

Frankie considers this.

You're right. Except.

Except what?

I've already quit.

Oh. Right. Great.

I'm sorry, Veronica. I should have . . . I'm still learning. About being married, I mean.

Veronica picks up the magazine and starts reading again.

Put that down. Come and sit next to me.

No. I've made an executive decision about this magazine. I don't have to consult you.

Veronica remains in her chair, back stiff, staring at the page. Eventually, though, she lowers the magazine.

You can go back. I'm sure they'll take you. You're the best salesman they've got.

Now Frankie begins to pace around the room, eyes everywhere except Veronica.

I'm going to start my own agency. FLB Estates. I was going to do it anyway in maybe five years. I'll just have to move my plans forward.

Frankie. Be realistic. Swallow your pride. Think it through.

Nothing could make me go back to Ratchett. Nothing. Not the way he's treated me. I'm going to borrow some money and start the agency.

That's insane!

Frankie takes no notice, and continues pacing.

There's a lot of credit out there at the moment. I'm going to borrow to the limit. Always borrow to the limit. Basic financial sense. Apart from which, I don't have any choice. From what I know about these things, it's going to be at least a year before a new agency turns any kind of profit. And I don't have a salary. But we do have your salary. No other commitments. We can survive for a year — can't we? I mean, we're partners, you and I.

Veronica says nothing and remains in exactly the same stance on the chair. Then she lowers her eyes to the magazine again.

Frankie sits down again, and resumes trying to vainly locate the sweet spot on the sofa.

* * *

The room in the basement of the Irish pub has about thirty rickety wooden chairs arranged randomly across the scratched, dusty floorboards, which are punctuated with cigarette burns. Furthest from the doors, on the north side of the room, sitting behind a small trellis table are one woman (smart, middle-aged) and one man (scruffy, young). They are the chairman and deputy chairman of the local Labour party.

Most of the seats are full in this subterranean debating chamber — more customarily used for cut-price parties and support-the-IRA piss-ups — and arranged in a series of rough semi-circles in front of the chair and deputy chair.

In front of the seating there are some tables supporting drinks from the bar upstairs. The room is already a fug of cigarette smoke. Ashtrays spill at the brim. Nodge pulls on a stick of Craven A. He's been meaning to give up, but can't quite find the wherewithal, despite Fraser's hectoring. Fraser is not only a non-smoker, but also a vegetarian, lately thinking of going vegan.

Nodge and Fraser sit at a table to the left of the room. Noise from the jukebox upstairs permeates. The strains of 'Bring it All Back' by S Club 7 burrow through the floorboards. The chair of the meeting stands and, after welcoming the members, and dealing with formalities, makes the proposal of the evening.

'This ward opposes the official Labour candidacy of Frank Dobson for Mayor of London'.

Go ahead and make my day, jeers a voice from the back of the room. This is the phrase Dobson has used when it was suggested that Ken Livingstone might stand as an official candidate against him. There is scattered laughter from the floor and a few plaintive boos.

Before the chair has a chance to invite speakers, Fraser is on his feet. Tall, nearly six-two, his grey-cropped head nearly makes contact with the low plasterboard ceiling, almost certainly backed – Nodge anxiously believes – with deadly asbestos.

Mr Chair, can I just . . . ?

Can you wait your turn, brother? I think Ms Frobisher had her hand up first. Formally we take questions in order of the raising of hands.

Looking to his right, he sees Maureen Frobisher, a long-standing rival, frowsty in some thick mud-coloured dress, with her hand imperiously raised.

That's typical, says Fraser. *She's had her hand up since before you were meant to put your hand up. Jumping the queue, yeh?*

Nevertheless, says the chair, firmly.

Fraser sits down all the same leaving his arm limply, contemptuously, raised.

Nodge puts his hand on Fraser's shoulder, as if in consolation, but Fraser shrugs it off.

Frobisher, a chubby yet shrivelled woman in her fifties, stands up brandishing a document which she simply seems to use as a conducting wand for her words. It appears to be the minutes of the last meeting. Fraser looks at her with open resentment.

Thank you, Chair.

Her voice is like a fork scraped on the base of a skillet. She nods towards the trestle table, and, taking her time, calmly addresses the room.

I believe this branch, she says, coolly, stealing a glance at Fraser, who still has his arm up, and his lips pressed together, *must support the official Labour candidate for the post of London Mayor. And therefore I oppose the motion.*

A wave of dissenting boos travels immediately across the room.

Stitch up! yells Fraser, furiously. There are cries of *'hear hear'.*

Frobisher, unabashed, continues.

I understand very clearly that there are those who believe that Ken Livingstone more closely represents the ideals and the objectives of certain parts of the Labour Party.

The real Labour party, interjects Fraser, to a few cheers and a roughly equal number of catcalls.

I emphasise. Certain parts. However, I believe we must all put our weight behind Mr Dobson now to ensure that Stephen Norris is firmly defeated.

Who's he? shouts another wag.

Tory candidate, answers another, apparently missing the irony.

One of the several Tory candidates, says Fraser, pointedly. *Because I can't tell the difference between one side and another anymore.*

Shut up Fraser, shouts an elderly-looking Jewish man from across the other side of the room. *Frank Dobson has served this party for twenty years with loyalty and conviction. All your sort ever does is pick fights.*

It's called principles, spits back Fraser. *And what exactly do you mean by 'your sort'? What about your sort?*

What's that meant to mean? responds the Jewish man, rising to his feet.

Order, please, calls the chair.

Trot, mutters the old man, sitting down again, and looking with hooded eyes towards Fraser, who gives him a moue.

If I could continue, says Ms Frobisher.

If you must, mutters Fraser, bitterly.

I wasn't asking your permission, brother Pike.

All this time Nodge stares at the floor, wriggling on his chair in discomfort.

Frank Dobson, whether we like it or not, is the official Labour candidate, she goes on.

Control freakery, yells a young woman from the other side of the room.

Fraser nods vigorously.

If I could continue, says Ms Frobisher, more firmly this time. She waits for the room to fall silent.

In my view Ken Livingstone has let his own personal ambitions . . .

The room erupts.

Order, order, calls the chair.

Tainted! Tainted! shouts a woman on the other side. *Another Millbank fix!*

Even though, resumes Frobisher, calmly, *there is some doubt as to whether Ken Livingstone will stand as an independent candidate, from what I hear, we must assume this to be the case. So I call today, on behalf of this branch, on Ken Livingstone to withdraw his name from the race, to clear the way for Frank Dobson and make sure that this great party—*

Not much great about it anymore, shouts Fraser.

. . . That this great party can gain a working mandate to govern the greatest city in the world. Thank you, Chair.

Can I speak now? says Fraser, rising to his feet.

You already have, says Frobisher, tartly.

Someone has turned the music system up in the pub upstairs and it is becoming harder and harder to hear what is said. Now it's Cher's 'Believe'.

Fraser raises his voice to make sure that he can be heard. Nodge, looking up from his sitting position, notices small bubbles of spittle emerging from the corner of his mouth.

Can I just say . . .

What?

That I fucking love Cher.

There is laughter. The atmosphere relaxes. Nodge raises his eyes from the floor. Fraser's face hardens once more.

Cher aside – may peace be on her – this ridiculous fit-up by Millbank has got to be resisted.

Cheers and whoops. Heartened by this, Fraser raises his voice still further.

This so-called democratic election included the grotesque phenomenon of the Engineering union dispatching four per cent of the entire electoral college on the whim of just fifty-nine people. Fifty-nine people! Is that democracy? No! As usual. The system is corrupt, because Blair and Brown are scared of anything that might look like REAL politics, REAL socialism, or a move towards a REAL Labour party.

Tony Blair won us the election! interjects Frobisher. *Isn't that real enough for you?*

Order! calls the chair.

At least Ken actually stands for something.

He stands for himself and his ego.

For Gay Rights. For Equality. For Ethnic Minorities.

Don't make speeches. You're not in the pulpit.

Livingstone's not going to stand as an Independent anyway, interrupts a young black woman with a faded T-shirt that reads 'Things Can Only Get Better'. *Even if he did he wouldn't have a chance of winning. He hasn't got the machinery behind him.*

He stands against Islamophobia. Against the nuclear deterrent. Against racism, continues Fraser, almost shouting now against the row coming from above and within the room.

Against, against, against! says Frobisher. *But what is he for?*

Even Unison has said that Ken should stay loyal, says the chair.

You're meant to be neutral, says Fraser, furiously. *Unison are sellouts.*

You can't seriously want the vote to be split, says Frobisher. *Your petty personal concerns should not get in the way of what the party needs. Or we could easily get a Tory victory. Another Horace Cutler is just what this city needs.*

Ken got seventy-five thousand votes of those balloted, says Fraser, furiously. *Dobson got twenty-two thousand. How's that fair?*

It's not about fairness! It's about winning elections! shouts a Rasta in a suit.

He's just a sore loser, mutters Saul. *And he's a Jew-hater. Everyone knows that.*

He's at least promising gay marriage, shouts Fraser. *Though I don't suppose you'd fancy that much would you, Saul? Or his stand on Palestine.*

Outrageous! Anti-Semite! Saul rises to his feet, wagging a finger at Fraser.

Zionist! shouts Fraser back in his face.

Order, shouts the chair, desperately now. He has also risen to his feet.

It's back to the loony left! shouts Frobisher, as angry as Fraser.

The debate rages for another ten minutes before each of the participants seems to be exhausted. Nodge has not said a word.

Finally, the moment comes for the vote to be cast.

All those in favour of the motion opposing Mr Dobson's candidature.

Fraser's hand shoots up. As do the arms of maybe a third of the room. Fraser looks at Nodge. He steadies his gaze on him. But Nodge's arm does not move.

All those against.

Most of the rest of the two-thirds of the room raise their hands. Fraser shakes his head in despair.

Abstentions.

Nodge and one other put their hands up. Fraser stares at him, eyes blazing.

* * *

Later, upstairs in the bar, most of the members have gone home. On a table nearer to the bar, Saul is sitting drinking a vodka. Fraser is buying another round for himself and Nodge. Saul gets up to go to the loo. In a flash, Nodge sees Fraser drop something in Saul's glass.

He returns to the table with the drinks.

What did you put in his drink?

Nothing. What are you talking about?

Don't bullshit me.

It was the tiniest bit of a pork scratching. Won't do him any harm.

Jesus, Fraser.

Come on. Revenge. It's a big Jewish value. 'An eye for an eye'. Saul would understand better than anyone. The hebes never let anyone get away with anything.

Revenge is stupid. And don't talk about hebes.

Zionist neo-Nazis, then. And revenge isn't stupid. Not at all. It makes you feel much better. Makes people respect you. I always take revenge when I get the chance.

I don't agree.

That's because you're weak.

You can't judge me as a person because I have a different set of beliefs to you, Fraser.

Not on revenge perhaps. But what about loyalty?

Meaning?

In the meeting. You were disloyal. You should have stood up for me.

I can have personal disagreements with you.

Haven't you heard the news, Nodge? The personal is the political. Where you stand matters. And you don't stand anywhere. I would have respected you more if you'd have voted against the motion. Yeh?

Hmmm.

Don't hmmm me.

I didn't mean to be disloyal to you.

If you didn't want to be disloyal, you should have voted with me.

But you just said you've got to stand on principles. Those were my principles. And I compromised them, so I wouldn't look like I stood against you.

You made a stand by abstaining!

I'm a pragmatist. You always have to be right.

Just because I know what I believe in.

Do you never doubt anything, Fraze? Can't you keep an open mind?

Not so much that my brains fall out. You're just wishy-washy. Like the rest of the centrist faction.

I'm weak, I'm wishy-washy. All because I don't agree with you. Have I abused you personally?

You've called me a bully.

That's because you won't let me have my own point of view.

You can have your own point of view. But if we don't stand against the Blairite tide, there aren't going to be any individual points of view. Only what the party pages us to instruct us to believe. I for one am not prepared to be on message twenty-four hours a day because of those Millbank Nazis.

They're not Nazis, Fraser. That's a ridiculous use of language. We're in power. For the first time in, what? Thirteen years. All you do is bitch about it.

What's the use of power if we don't have principles?

They are still going at it when the landlord calls time. As he ushers them out Nodge wearily delivers his final salvo.

It's not as if it matters a damn what either of us believe anyway. We're some nowhere branch outfit of a Labour party that only pretends to care what we think. And anyway, whatever you do think, people like you—

People with convictions?

. . . People like you are finished in the movement. That's the simple reality. You're gone, you're defeated, and you ain't coming back.

We'll see, says Fraser, darkly.

I'm scared, says Nodge.

You're funny, says Fraser. *Funny ha ha. But our time will come.*

* * *

Outside, the thermometer has hardly climbed above freezing for five days. Inside the house, with Frankie out at work, Veronica has managed to hold the temperature at a steady 65 degrees. She holds a plastic cup under her as she relaxes her bladder, listens as the cup fills. She is three weeks late for her period and her anxiety is on the cusp of bleeding into panic.

She feels the trickle of her urine ceasing its flow, and reaches for a paper tissue. Without bothering to pull up her skirt, she shuffles next door to the bathroom, holding the cup still. She puts it down, picks up the plastic indicator and dips it in the cup, then removes it.

She waits. Minutes later, the two bars show blue.

She feels nothing at first. Then like multiple shots fired rapidly into her heart – or out of it – she experiences joy, loneliness and terror, each competing for supremacy.

The pull of a new life, the weight of the old. The pull of the old life, the weight of the new.

The phone on the wall rings. She thinks of ignoring it, then, still dazed, picks it up.

Frankie?

Hello? Is that Veronica?

It is a woman's voice, one that she only vaguely recognizes.

Who is this?

It's Roxy. You told me to give you a ring sometime. So that's what I'm doing.

Roxy?

106

Roxanne. Roxanne Peacock.

Veronica tries to remember who Roxanne Peacock is but draws a blank. Her mind is divided by two soft blue lines.

From the Embankment Club. Millennium night.

Finally it clicks.

Roxy! Hello. Sorry. I'm a bit ... I'm a little ... I'm a bit distracted.

Almost before the words are out of her mouth, Veronica bursts into helpless tears.

Hey. Hey, says Roxy.

Sorry. Sorry.

This is like our first meeting in reverse, says Roxy. *Remember? I was bawling my eyes out.*

Veronica forces out a laugh between the tears.

What's the matter then? Roxy asks.

It's nothing.

Doesn't sound like nothing.

Veronica dams both laughter and tears. Now her voice when she speaks again is flat and tired.

Oh, what the hell. I'm pregnant. Just found out. This minute, as it happens.

She is astonished to hear herself say it. It seems to make it more real. Perhaps, she thinks, that is why she has spoken the words to a stranger.

What the fuck?

I feel so bad for telling you. I'm sorry. I don't even know you.

That might be why you've told me.

I haven't even told Frankie yet. I only just found out.

Congratulations! You must be delighted.

Perhaps.

There is a pause.

Are you going to . . . ?

What do you mean?

Are you going to keep it, babes?

Am I going to keep what?

You know.

Veronica gathers herself, tries to take a mental step back.

Roxanne. I appreciate you taking an interest. But it's nothing to do with you, really.

There is a heavy silence.

I should go, says Veronica. *I've said too much.*

She does not put down the receiver.

How did it happen, though? says Roxy. *I mean I know how it happened, but . . .*

Carelessness, I suppose.

Now it all floods back to Veronica.

Remember on Millennium night? We were drunk. Me and Frankie. You remember I knocked all my stuff onto the floor of the bathroom in the Embankment Club? Among all the junk on the floor, I didn't pick up the three-pack I usually have with me. And when we got home there were none there. We sort of got carried away.

There is a long pause.

Roxy? Are you still there?

When Roxy finally speaks her voice has changed, darkened a tone.

It was me who knocked that stuff off, not you.

Was it?

So this is my fault. If I hadn't done that, you wouldn't be in this dilemma. So maybe I do have something to do with it. Maybe this is like . . . karma. You believe in karma, right?

Yes. No. That's crazy. You can't think like that. It was just bad luck.

I can think of something that will help clear things up in your mind. And make you feel a lot better at the same time.

Sleep on it?

Shopping. I finish my shift at one. Meet you then?

Shopping?

You can't beat doing something trivial when something serious happens.

* * *

Three hours later, the two of them are at Brent Cross Shopping Centre. Roxy has ordered a large slice of frosted carrot cake which she is vigorously despatching, while Veronica sips liquorice tea with a small drop of Manuka honey that she carries with her for just this purpose.

So anyway, says Roxy, *a guy is sitting at home when he hears a knock at the door. He opens the door and sees a snail on the porch. He picks up the snail and throws it as far as he can. Three years later there's a knock on the door. He opens it and sees the same snail. The snail says: 'What the fuck was that about?'*

Veronica tries to smile.

I told you I could cheer you up.

Are we going to spend all afternoon with you telling me stupid jokes?

If they make you laugh.

I don't want to laugh at the moment.

We're going to go shopping. Like I said. Like you wanted. Some amazing stuff in Whistles, says Roxy. *They have proper sales. Like, half off. Usually the best stuff is gone by now. But you can get lucky.*

None of it's going to fit me in about three months.

That depends on what you decide.

Veronica stares, grim now, out of the café window.

I don't know what to do. It might be for the best to get rid of it for both of us. Frankie wants to get his agency started. He's just lost his job. This is terrible timing.

Right.

It's not like it's an actual baby, is it? It's a few cells.

Yeh, well, I've had it done, says Roxy briskly, finishing off her cake and dropping crumbs on the wooden table. *Twice. Didn't feel so easy as I thought it was going to, tell you the truth. Fact is, I still feel shit about it. But, women's choice and all that. For me it was different. I got pregnant by these proper fucktards. I didn't think twice about it. Didn't want to spread their genes in any direction what-so-ever. One hundred and ten per cent. See what I'm getting at?*

Roxy calls the waitress over and orders a glass of champagne.

Go on, have a tipple. It's on me. Treat.

I'm pregnant. Remember?

Life's too short. Think of it as a celebration or a commiseration, or whatever you like

When the champagne arrives, Roxy knocks back the glass in one go.

How does an Essex girl turn the light on after sex?

Please. No more.

She opens the car door.

What if I can't get pregnant again? says Veronica, not smiling this time.

Given how easily you got up the duff this time, that seems unlikely. Wait till you get to my age before you start freaking out about that stuff.

Listen, Veronica. Thing is. Do you want it?

I hate making decisions.

So let's go shopping instead.

The waitress brings the bill. Roxy takes her large envelope-size purse out of her bag and flips it open. It is completely filled on one side with credit cards. She registers Veronica's look.

They keep offering them to me. Can't resist packing the plastic. Life's too short, you know what I mean?

How many have you got?

Lost count. Every time I max out on one, I borrow from another to make the monthly payments.

Is that altogether wise? says Veronica.

'Altogether wise'. What are you, Rumpole of the Bailey? No, it's altogether stupid. But it's working for me. So far. Until tomorrow comes, anyway.

She pays the bill and they leave the café together, then head out into the mall.

* * *

An hour later, Roxy is carrying two large shopping bags while Veronica has bought only a pair of woollen gloves printed with tiny yellow daisies, from Jigsaw. Roxy takes a sticky paper bag out of her pocket and offers it to Veronica.

Sherbet lemon?

You eat sweets? Veronica holds her palm out in refusal.

My dad used to run a sweetshop. I never really got out of the habit. Better than smoking, I suppose.

But you smoke as well.

What's your point?

Roxy rummages in the bag.

I haven't had a sherbet lemon since I was about six.

Try one.

Sugar is a poison.

Whatevs, says Roxy, popping the dusty yellow globe in her mouth.

Are we decided, then? says Roxy, sucking cheerfully on the boiled sweet.

You mean about . . . ?

Yes. About.

Veronica sees her knuckles white on her shopping bag.

Not quite. I know which way I'm leaning, though.

Well — what?

Don't take this the wrong way, Roxy, but I think I should tell Frankie what I've decided before I tell you.

Of course. Yes. I get that.

Call me tomorrow. I'll let you know then.

You don't have to.

No, I will. You've helped me, Roxy. Really you have. Thank you.

* * *

The frosty light of the next day's morning wakes Veronica. She surfaces from her sleep slowly, like a diver, rising, fearful of the bends. Blearily, she checks her clock and sees she is forty-five minutes late for work. She stayed up the night before, pacing the kitchen like a feral beast, unable to sleep. Throwing herself out of bed, she gets dressed, as silently as she can, trying not to wake Frankie. She puts on the sweater that Roxy eventually bullied her into buying, a cashmere moss green sleeveless crew neck. It looks good, better than she remembered. Roxy has a knack.

She does not even have time for her accustomed breakfast of

muesli and fruit. She must leave, but to her mounting annoyance, she cannot find her phone.

After five minutes of fruitless searching, and calling it – the ringer is turned off – Frankie appears at the door, thumbs hooked into his boxer shorts.

Lost something?

My phone.

I think I saw it. Hold on a minute.

Frankie heads into the en-suite bathroom, where he locates Veronica's phone poking from a pile of last night's dirty washing, half-protruding from her dress pocket. He yawns, picks it up, and immediately spots a text message.

'How did Frankie take it? Love Roxy x'

Frankie, holding up the phone, tries to make sense of the message. He cannot. There is a set to his jaw, a slight narrowing of his eyes. He walks into the living room. Veronica registers his confusion immediately.

What's the matter?

Strategy, thinks Frankie. *Basic strategy. Give her enough rope.*

He keeps hold of the phone.

Why didn't you tell me, Veronica?

Why didn't I tell you what?

You know what.

She holds her hands out for the phone, but he clings on to it. Now Veronica's face falls in a way that makes him feel faintly ill.

How did you find out?

How do you think I found out?

Did you speak to Roxy?

Does it matter how I found out?

Veronica nods mutely.

So — what do you want to do? Frankie asks.

That's pretty obvious, isn't it? Since I didn't tell you about it.

Spell it out for me.

She supports herself against a wall.

I want to get rid of it.

Get rid of it?

I've already made the appointment at the clinic.

You want to get rid of it.

We're not ready, are we? You said so yourself.

Slowly the information sinks into the core of Frankie's self like lava, hardening as it cools into jagged, brittle knowledge.

Oh.

Yes.

You're pregnant.

What?

Now Veronica, suddenly, realizes she's been gulled. She grabs the phone out of Frankie's hand.

Yes, of course I'm pregnant. You know that. Don't you?

I do now. You just told me.

They stand facing one another, unmoving, as if whoever makes a gesture first is conceding ground. Then Frankie takes her hand. Veronica starts to cry.

Do you want it? Frankie strokes the back of her hand, seeming to feel the slow pump of blood in the snake of blue vein.

She looks back up at him, her eyes shot with desperation and confusion.

Do you?

If you want it, then you should go ahead.

But do you want it?

Of course I want it.

He pauses.

As such.

Veronica feels an invisible hand clutching at her heart.

What does that mean?

It's just that . . .

She pulls her hand away. Frankie now can't meet her eye. She sees that he is ashamed.

I've just quit my job, Vronky. We've got no income. Apart from yours. Which will stop when you . . . you know. Or reduce at least. I'm going to be working like a slave for the next couple of years to set myself up. I won't be able to support you properly. You and the . . . you know.

I can support myself.

Of course you can. Of course.

He tries to take back her hand, but she pulls it away. Instead, he sees she is compulsively fingering the golden key that she now always wears around her neck with the other hand.

And if you want to do that, I'll find another job instead of starting my own agency. Or I'll go back and grovel to Ratchett.

But?

But. You know. Bad timing.

She nods, sadly.

You're right. Of course you're right. Bad timing.

Don't make me feel awful.

I don't want to. That's why I wasn't going to tell you.

There is a silence. Now they sit down on the sofa together, both staring at the floor, a gap of several inches between them.

I've already made an appointment at the clinic, says Veronica.

Another silence.

Okay then, says Frankie. *I'll come with you. We're in this together.*

They sit mutely, trying fiercely to tune their way into the bandwidth of the next moment.

I'll make us a cup of tea, says Frankie, eventually, unable to think of what else to do or say. The air is bruised, stifling.

There's no need to feel guilty about this, says Veronica. *I'm not ready myself to have a kid. Not for a couple of years.*

Okay then.

Okay then. Good.

Good.

* * *

Valentine's Day. Colin and Roxy sit together in a restaurant crowded with couples facing one another over starched white tablecloths. There are single red roses in a glass vase on each one.

Colin is wearing the suit that Roxy has convinced him to buy that day. It is soft, unstructured and forgiving. He is rarely so formal – at the office his uniform is chinos and football shirts – but this outfit somehow lets him feel comfortable, despite the slight starchiness of the surroundings.

He looks across the table at Roxy who is examining the menu. He imagines that this is what it must be like to feel happy. He feels something he has rarely felt before – self-confidence. He feels his new suit on his back like a superhero cape.

Now he, too, examines the menu, all in French. His tongue protrudes as it always does when he is trying to concentrate.

Do you want me to translate? asks Roxy.

I'm not stupid, says Colin.

They have English ones. I only have to ask.

Since when did you learn French?

I've waitressed enough to know my way around a menu.

He stares at the menu a bit longer.

What's perseilles?

Sweetbreads.

He stares a bit longer.

What's sweetbreads?

Lamb's pancreas. Head to tail eating. All the rage.

Why would you want to eat all the crappy bits? I was fed enough of that shit as a kid. Olive would stew it up. Ox hearts. Pig's liver. Gross. I'll have the beef en daube.

That's . . .

I know what it is.

Roxy drinks from her glass of Prosecco, included in the set price. There is lipstick showing on the side of her glass. Her teeth make a clicking noise on the edge as they connect with the rim. This irritates Colin, but he brushes the emotion away.

The waiter approaches and they order. Roxy has bone marrow and Colin the *boeuf en daube.*

What shall we talk about? says Colin.

Tell me about when you were young, says Roxy.

Not much to tell. My dad was a drunk. I already told you. My mum got ill after he died. I spent most of my twenties looking after her. Grew up on the White City Estate. Went to the same school as Frankie and Nodge.

You've done well for yourself then. You all have. Made a few bob.

Don't really care about money, tell you the truth. I just like watching football and playing games. And designing them.

Roxy tears at a bread roll and smears it with a quarter of an inch of butter.

It's not good for you, that much butter.

The sight of the spare flesh dangling off her arms bothers him. Why can't she be slim, like Veronica?

I like it, though, says Roxy, stuffing the bread into her mouth. I just generally fucking love eating. What's your favourite food?

Pizza. Curry. Fish and chips.

Result!

She holds her hand up and Colin weakly high-fives her.

We've got so much in common. Also, you can't beat a Maccie D sometimes. How do you stay so slim?

Nervous energy.

Veronica said you could be nervous.

You been talking to Veronica about me again?

Only in a nice way.

How do you know Veronica anyway? You only bumped into her at the Millennium night thing.

We went shopping together. The other day.

How come?

She wanted some advice.

Shopping advice?

Yeh. Shopping advice.

So what did she say about me?

Roxy finishes the roll. Colin notices the crumbs splayed around her plate. His is spotless.

I told her how you're different from how she and Frankie think you are. They think you're all messed up cos of your mother. But I think you're brave and quiet and shy and hardworking.

Colin stares at her. Crumbs snow her lapels.

I'm lucky to have met you, he says. *I've never ... been with anyone like you.*

What — a fat girl from Theydon Bois?

You're not fat. That's not to say that . . .

I couldn't stand to lose a few pounds?

She laughs.

Well you can fuck right off, she says, not unkindly. *This is what you get when you get me, you lanky streak of piss.*

He looks around at all the other couples in the restaurant. Many of them aren't talking. A few are squabbling.

They ramp up the prices on Valentine's night, he says. *Special Valentine dinner. Yeh, special. Specially more expensive.*

I don't care, says Roxy.

You're not paying, thinks Colin.

At the end of the meal, when Roxy has finished off pudding and cheese — obligatory because included in the bill — they get ready to leave. The bill arrives and Roxy seizes it.

No, says Colin.

It's not the twentieth century anymore, says Roxy. *Thank kew,* she says to the waiter, *that was lovely.*

Thank you. Let me leave the tip then.

He fumbles in his wallet and finds two pound coins and a fifty-pence piece which he places on the plate next to the bill, which, he can now read, amounts to £103.50.

Roxy stares at the change. Colin just smiles.

What do you see in me? he says, softly.

Roxy shifts her gaze from the change to Colin. Finding she is lost for words, she rummages for a response.

Three guys stranded on a desert island find a magic lantern containing a genie, who grants them each one wish, says Roxy. *The first guy wishes he was off the island and back home. The second guy wishes the same. The third guy says: 'I'm lonely. I wish my friends were back here.'*

I wish, says Colin, *you would stop telling stupid jokes every time I try and say something serious.*

Soz, says Roxy.

What's soz?

Don't you text?

Not really.

* * *

Frankie, sitting stiffly in the waiting room of the abortion clinic, looks up from his cushioned seat at the receptionist. She is attractive, he notices, then feels ashamed that he has noticed. She is dressed in a quasi-medical style, almost military, a white blouse with blue trim on the pockets. She wears a telephone headset and is made up palely – pale lipstick, heavily powdered, no eye shadow or liner – to suggest, he presumes, seriousness of purpose. Her hair is hygienically scraped back. She wears reassuringly angular glasses that bestow seriousness and authority. When she turns her head, Frankie notices a tattoo behind her multiply pierced ear, a burning heart. It excites him.

He wonders if he'll ever grow up. He wonders why he cannot take his mind off sex, even at a time like this. His mind summons answers, muddled together, half articulated.

Potential new beginnings.

Gestures towards paradise.

Momentary escapes from the rest of the shit.

Yet he loves Veronica. But he is made of meat and genes and chemicals. How can he help what he feels? Good and bad – it's all relative in the end. Has to be. What you can get away with. Perhaps. Or not. He wishes he were a better man and wrenches his eyes from the receptionist.

The reception area could itself be an estate agent's, not a place to prevent, to cut short, the development and growth of life itself. There are black fake leather sofas with tubular steel frames, wooden Venetian blinds, a low glass coffee table with magazines and a bowl of fruit and a vase of flowers arranged on it. In the corner is a pot plant, looking like a monster's fingers emerging from the loamy depths. Veronica has informed him that this is aloe vera.

Polished dark wood floor. Official-looking certificates on the wall abutting non-committal prints of indeterminate landscapes. Milky light comes through large panel windows. There are leaflets and pamphlets, magical texts to reassure that this is impersonal, normal, clinical, safe, unreal. Explanations about Manual Vacuum Aspiration and Safe Aftercare.

Mr and Mrs Blue? says the receptionist. *We have to take care of the formalities.*

Frankie rises from his seat. Veronica has already filled in the health checks. She has confirmed she has no high blood pressure, no history of heart or kidney or liver disease, that she doesn't take any number of medications and drugs, that she hasn't got asthma, etcetera.

Frankie approaches the desk. The receptionist hands Frankie a piece of paper. He examines it mutely.

Surgical Abortion under local anaesthesia:
£850
Settlement now due.

He looks down at Veronica. She is shrunken into herself, as if half her normal size. Her pre-natal condition is in no manner obvious. Her dress is gingham – a little girl's dress. Is that a slant of light from the window marking her face?

He looks again and sees that they are tear tracks.

We agreed, he thinks, haranguing her in his head. *We talked it through and you agreed.*

He stares back at the bill. It is broken down into discrete parts.

Consultation, ultrasound scan, haemoglobin blood group, chlamydia and gonorrhea tests, surgery, theatre fees, ultrasound during surgery.

It was for the best, you said. Leave it a few years and then. Not ready, you said. And I'm going to be too busy setting up the agency, I said.

We agreed. Didn't we?

Well, didn't we?

He tries to stem the conversation pounding in his skull by examining the other occupants of the waiting room. There is a black woman in a pinafore dress who is idly reading a copy of *Chat*. There is a sad-faced young girl, maybe sixteen, staring at the floor, not moving, with what appears to be her mother sitting stern-faced next to her. There is a middle-aged woman, who seems cheerful and unconcerned, reading a copy of the *New Yorker* with the stain of a coffee mug rim on the cover. Frankie can smell something medical, antiseptic. It reminds him of Veronica's pathology lab. The same smell as of death.

It's the common sense thing to do. They do thousands every day across the world. It's routine. It's not a . . .

He withholds the word from himself, then lets it form.

Baby. It's just a collection of multiplying cells at this stage. It's not real.

He replaces the bill on the desk, takes his wallet out and opens it to expose the flap of credit cards. He looks inadvertently at Veronica and sees that she appears to be staring at his credit cards, then she switches her gaze to his face. She sees that he sees her and her expression which is obscure, unreadable, disappearing even more deeply behind a veil.

He looks back at the woman sitting behind the reception counter at the clinic, her scraped-back hair seeming to produce an artificial and permanent smile. She is holding out her hand to take his credit card. He reaches for his Amex Platinum, his pride and joy, available only to selected customers.

He is paying, on credit, for this thing to happen. That which he uses to pay for beer and food and clothes and toilet paper.

Suddenly shaky, he drops his wallet on the floor. The credit cards scatter and mix with cash, notes and coins. He notices, as he picks up the notes, that the floor is in fact grimy, not as clean as he had previously believed. There is a dirty wad of chewing gum stuck under the desk. One of the coins rolls over to Veronica and she picks it up and holds it out to him without looking at him. As he rises and takes it from her, the coin feels icy in his hand.

Can I help, Mr Blue . . . ?

The receptionist rises but Frankie gestures her back to her desk.

Beer and food and clothes and furniture. Products and services.

He gathers up his wallet and the contents, neatly restores the credit cards and cash.

The receptionist has picked up the bill again. Her pen, presumably poising to inscribe the word 'Paid', hovers above the expensive yellow paper. Her expression, welcoming, granting permission, demanding completion, is unchanged.

He gives a slight shake of the head to the receptionist, turns and holds out his hand to Veronica. She takes it, puzzled. He pulls her to her feet.

What are you doing? says Veronica.

We can't afford it.

You're worrying about money? At a time like this?

Sir? says the receptionist, confused, sensing some obscure failure on her part.

I mean you and me. We can't afford to do this. The price is too high.

Is it high?

We'll never stop paying it. Will we?

But . . . what about your new agency? What about FLB Estates?

We'll work something out. Somehow. We have to. If I can get it set up and running before the baby comes . . . I mean the first six months of a business is the hardest . . . after that I will have some time to help at home . . . if you can let me off the leash until then.

For the first time since she has been in that waiting room, Veronica smiles.

She kisses her husband, full on the lips. Feels the weight of the golden key on her breastbone.

Sir? says the receptionist again, flushing slightly now.

But Frankie is lost in Veronica's kiss and ignores her.

The receptionist gives up, crumples the paper with her hand.

* * *

Frankie is sweating even before Veronica walks into the over-heated Mothercare flagship shop in Marble Arch. It is their first time shopping for the gewgaws and sanctified clutter – the word *reliquary* drifts obscurely into Frankie's mind – that is insisted on both by custom and practicality. It feels a strange universe to both of them, a place in which they are aliens or zombies, bodies waiting to be snatched.

Frankie feels swindled, baffled, tricked, resentful, excited, confused. They are not here to actually buy much – it is still too early for that – but, as it were, to become acclimatized to a new way of being. Veronica wanted to come. Frankie doesn't see the harm.

Veronica takes his hand, which is sweaty and slippery. Frankie's eyes jerk to the source of a sound in front of them.

What the fuck is that? he says more loudly than he had intended.

A heavily pregnant woman, holding the hand of a sullen-looking boy who is perhaps five years old and violently kicking his own shoe, stares at him angrily.

Language, she mutters.

Sorry, mouths Veronica to the woman, who simply looks away at nothing in particular. She glares at Frankie.

What the fuck is *it, though?* he says more quietly, taking into account now the other shoppers, many of them trailing children, most of them women.

In front of them is a large plastic representation of a tree, eight feet high, crowned with a corona of green artificial leaves. What is unusual about the tree – apart from the fact that it is in the middle of a shop and made of lurid plastic – is that it is singing, and it has a face, a grotesque mug from what might have been a German expressionist's night horrors. As it sings, its whorls turn into great sagging wrinkles, surrounding the face, which appears to be wearing green eye shadow and purple lipstick. It is bordered by a brown plastic fence as if it were dangerous. The tree is smiling uncertainly and rolling its vast eyes as if trying to lure children to their doom, but conscience-stricken over the act. It has rouged cheeks.

It's a fucking tranny tree, whispers Frankie. *And it's singing! What is it singing, Vronky? What? What?*

They stop and listen and try and pick out the words of the tree-song.

'Mothercare, Mothercare . . . happy children everywhere.'

Calm down, Frankie.

I urgently need to get away from this creature.

They have decided to look for a cot, although it is many months before the birth. The crib, at this point, is purely symbolic. They have come to the shop to try and bolt down the reality of the unfolding situation they find themselves in. For, ever since they left the abortion clinic together, a sense of unreality and distance has taken hold of Frankie.

Veronica, who already feels her body changing, can allow herself no such luxury. Reality is hardening, closing in with its implacable clamps. But she wants to help Frankie understand. Only she is not sure what it is she wants him to understand. Perhaps that things have changed utterly and forever. This is un-rescindable.

They walk silently past an array of dummies, baby carriers, Tommee Tippee mugs, electric breast milk extractors and Avent feeding bottles. Veronica stops frequently to examine the merchandise while Frankie pretends to take an interest for her sake. In the background, the tree can still be heard singing. Over and over and over again, unstoppable, grinding out the sticky melody, backed by an electronic glockenspiel.

They find the cot department – just past pushchairs and bibs. Frankie stops to examine a few pushchairs.

That one's five hundred sovs! What a racket!

Veronica, who has barely spoken since they entered the store, looks at him with pale, watery eyes.

There's hundreds of the bloody things, says Frankie, trying to take in the range on offer. *How many kinds of pushchair can there be?*

He kicks one of the wheels of a £400 model. Veronica stops and holds his hands, halts him in his tracks and seeks his gaze.

Can you imagine? she says. *A child. Our child.*

The price of these things, says Frankie, his eyes still darting. *They've got to be fucking joking. Look, that one's a grand. I could get a car for that.*

Stop panicking, says Veronica.

Mothercare, Mothercare. Happy children everywhere, the tree sings.

There are other pregnant women in the shop. Dozens of them. Scores, teeming. Children's screams and laughter penetrate the air-conditioned, muzak-dipped air.

Frankie finally accepts Veronica's gaze.

I'm sorry, he says. *I'm being weird, aren't I?*

It will be alright, Frankie. Calm down.

He turns and stares resentfully again at the tree in the middle distance.

I know it will, he says. *Only . . .*

Only? says Veronica.

I'm afraid, he thinks. But does not, in the end, say. And then he allows that moment where it might be said to pass.

They reach the cot department.

What about that one? he says, pointing to a hi-tech model constructed in what looks like some kind of black melamine.

That's literally the first one you've seen.

What about this one, then? says Frankie, waving towards an adjacent model. He checks the tag. *Decent price. Solid pine. Or possibly veneer. But convincing.*

Veronica checks the side panel, to see how it unclips.

It's fiddly. You could catch your finger in that.

Frankie points to the next one in the line of around twenty cots.

This is a good price.

Why don't you have a proper look at it?

Frankie checks the side panel and picks up the mattress inside and drops it, then prods the surface with his finger, leaving a small indent.

Seems okay.

I don't want a white painted one. It's boring.

Well, why did you . . . ?

He checks himself, the brittleness of his tone. He tries to soften his voice, but ends up only lowering it.

Which one do you want, then?

This is meant to be a shared experience.

It is. I'm here. You're here. Therefore, it's shared.

Have you thought about what else we're going to need?

Of course.

What?

Frankie feels his Adam's apple bob.

You know. A buggy. Dummies. Nappies.

You want our child to have a dummy?

Not if you don't.

He pauses.

But they do shut them up sometimes.

Veronica rubs her swelling belly. She does this so often now she has become unconscious of it.

Are you really on board with this?

Of course I am. How can you say that? I had a get-out, didn't I? I didn't take it.

You do know what it's going to involve, don't you?

I have a general idea. It's just that — this place weirds me out.

What are you looking forward to most about having a baby?

Frankie considers this for a moment.

Taking him to the zoo. My mum and dad never took me to the zoo.

Why do you think it's going to be a him?

I don't.

Do you want a boy, then?

It would be nice to have someone to take to the football.

Girls can like football.

Yeh.

Frankie pauses.

They usually don't though. In my experience.

In your extensive experience of children.

Frankie checks his watch.

It's going to be a lot of hard work. For both of us, says Veronica.

Well, yes. But I mean . . .

Frankie tries to drop it. He's not ready for this conversation.

What?

It doesn't matter.

What, Frankie? Say what you think.

Obviously I'm going to have things cut out for me at the office while I get the new agency up and running.

I'm going to have things cut out for me looking after the baby. And you said you'd get the worst of the slog out of the way before the baby actually arrives.

Of course. Yes. But we are going to need money. And I'll be the only one making the money. Until you go back to work. I wish it wasn't that way. But it is.

We have to be equal.

Equality is a relative concept.

What's that meant to mean?

Are you going to make an equal amount of money? Are you going to have to put in an equal number of hours at the office?

Don't do this, Frankie. Just support me. Please.

I'm just saying, aren't I?

Frankie?

Yes, Veronica.

Veronica tries to hold the words back, but for reasons she doesn't understand she blurts them out, even though it seems the worst possible moment.

What if I don't want to go back to the pathology lab?

Frankie is now idly inspecting a bottle sterilizer.

What do you mean?

What if I don't want to go back to work at the hospital after maternity leave?

The words finally sink in. Frankie turns, still holding the sterilizer, a totem against gathering devils.

Why would you even ask that?

I'm not saying that I will feel that way. I don't know how I feel.

What are you saying?

You can't understand.

Try me.

Having a child growing inside you. It starts to change the way you think.

Now Frankie slams the sterilizer back on the shelf.

You can't drop that on me out of thin air!

I'm asking you to consider the possibility. That's all.

Just considered it. Sounds mental.

I'm mental now, am I?

I mean, you know. Impractical. What would you do instead?

Apart from spending my days up to my neck in shit and baby food?

Yes. Apart from that.

Veronica pauses. *In for a penny, in for a pound,* she thinks.

I want to retrain. As a therapist.

Frankie clenches both fists, feels his face drain of blood.

You're having a giraffe, aren't you?

Am I?

Veronica. No. It's not going to happen. Absolutely not. No chance.

Hark at you. The prime minister.

What?

You're not all-powerful, Frankie. Stop issuing edicts.

Other shoppers now are beginning to stare at them. Frankie drops his voice and brings his face closer to Veronica's.

Look. I didn't mean to throw my weight around. I'm sorry. But I can't see how it's going to work. How are we going to survive financially?

I would start to make money again soon enough. I could train while

I was being a mother. By the time the baby was in nursery, I would be pretty much ready to go back to work.

That's, like, three years away. At least. We've got a mortgage. A brand-new, great big mortgage. And I've got to find the money to fund the new agency.

What if you can't find the money?

I will.

What if you can't?

Then I'll go back to Ratchett and beg for my job back. Or join another agency.

You promise?

Yes. I promise.

It'll only be for a while.

I said 'I promise', didn't I?

* * *

After thirty more minutes of consideration, they choose a gunmetal grey crib with the decal of a small yellow duck on the side of it. They also choose a mattress, decorated with blank-eyed Miffys. It is the fourth most expensive crib in the store, but Frankie, sensing already that he has let Veronica down, feels unable to argue the case for something a little cheaper.

Frankie produces their joint bank card – they set up an account together as soon as they were married – and hands it to the glum, perspiring shop assistant.

Don't you find listening to that bloody tree all day a little annoying? he says to the shop assistant. *He'd drive me right up the wall.*

She. It's a female tree, says the assistant flatly. *Jenny the Tree.*

Jenny the Tree?

Frankie stares at the figure on the till display, and hesitates.

Don't you want our baby to have the best? says Veronica.

Yes, says Frankie. *Yes, I do.*

The transaction is cleared.

For the mattress, there are no refunds or returns I'm afraid, says the assistant, mechanically.

You said it, thinks Frankie.

* * *

Frankie has six months to set up his new business before the baby arrives. If he can find the capital. And he has to. That or go crawling to Ratchett for his job back.

He waits furtively outside the FR&G office – or F&R as it is now – until he is sure it is otherwise empty and he can catch Victor Strudwick, the mortgage broker, on his own. When he is sure, he enters and sits down on the opposite side of Victor's bog-standard office desk. Strudwick, as ever, is sucking on a roll-up made with liquorice paper.

Hello, Frankie.

Victor.

You look like you mean business.

Why would you think that?

You've obviously waited until the office is empty to talk to me. I've seen you hovering.

No pulling the wool over your eyes, is there?

Why don't you just come straight to the point? Because I've got a fair amount to do before Ratchett comes back. He's being such a shit at the moment. Even by his standards. You leaving has left a big hole, I can tell you.

133

You won't get me contradicting you.

So what do you want, Frankie? How can I help?

Look, Victor. I'll just come out and say it.

Go on then.

Is there any chance of getting a remortgage on the new house?

Strudwick pulls his head slightly down into his shoulders, a gesture Frankie has seen before when Strudwick is feeling obdurate. He firmly stubs his stub out into the ashtray and hits the stick button on the swivel mechanism to dispose of it.

The new house? The one you just bought in North Ken?

I need fifty K at least.

For what?

Never mind that. Can you get it for me?

Victor leans back, stretches and sighs.

Frankie. When I got you the loan I stretched it to the limit, like you told me to. There's no chance they're going to give you any more. Not at the moment. Not right away. Give it a year, maybe the property's gone up by ten per cent, who knows? Then you're in with a chance. But not now. Not for a while, mate. Not even for you.

Can't you make a few phone calls? You know who to speak to.

Frankie. I've always been fond of you. And if there was anything I could do to help I would. I would. But . . .

Can I talk honestly?

Isn't that what we're doing?

Victor, are you happy here?

Now he has Strudwick's attention. He leans forward across the table and lowers his voice, even though there is no one else in the room.

You know how I feel about Ratchett, obviously.

Victor. I need the money to set up my own agency.

Yeh. We all sort of guessed that might be your plan.

And if you can get the loan top-up for me, you can come in. On a percentage. Honestly, I would make it worth your while. And I would enjoy wiping the smile off of Ratchett's smug face. Wouldn't you?

I knew you wouldn't put up with Ratchett and the way he treats you. You've got too much pride. Old Gwynne knew that — that you had pride.

So. Can you help me?

Strudwick seems to deflate slightly. He exhales, then starts to roll another cigarette.

Look, Frankie. If you ever do set up on your own — well, I'll tell you here and now, I would come with you. I'd support you all the way. But I'm not bullshitting you. There's no way I can get a top-up on the loan, not at the moment. No way.

Come on, Victor.

Give me a year. That's all. A year.

I don't have a year.

Then — I'm sorry, Frankie. I truly am. But I can't help.

Frankie sits silently for such a long time that Strudwick is worried that he's too angry to speak. But when he does talk again it is calmly, and with purpose.

Well. There may be another way.

Good. That's great.

But if I find the money, you'll come in with me? Right, Victor?

A hundred per cent, Frankie. For sure. Shake on it.

They gravely shake hands.

Okay then. Okay. Thanks, Victor. Thanks for everything.

You're welcome, mate. Good luck.

And you won't breathe a word of this?

Not a syllabobble.

* * *

Flossie brews him a cup of tea, and sits lumpily on the white wooden chair on the far side of the table.

You don't usually drop in to see me without calling first, Frankie. Is it an emergency?

Not exactly. But I do sort of need your help.

You know me, Frankie. I'll always help my boy. Always.

I know you will, Mum. I'll get to the point then. You know that money you've got saved up? Your nest egg that Dad left you? I was wondering . . . well, I was wondering if I could borrow some of it.

Borrow it? How much of it do you want to borrow?

I don't know. A hundred K?

Seeing the expression on Flossie's face, Frankie finds himself starting to gabble.

Mum, it would be completely safe. I could give it back to you in three years. With interest.

Don't be silly, Frankie. It wasn't anything like that much.

Fifty K then?

I don't know what to say. He left me thirty . . . And, well, I've spent quite a lot of it.

You've done what?

On cruises and stuff. And other bits and pieces.

Cruises?

Me and Gordon. We're going on a Caribbean cruise together. For a month. First class. Who'd have thought it? Me rubbing shoulders with the quality.

Flossie announces this defiantly. She pauses to take a long draught of tea.

How much of it have you spent?

All of it. More or less.

She puts the tea mug down on the table with an almost-slam.

All of it?

Don't look at me like that, Frankie. You've been looking at me like that all my born days. Like I was a half-wit or something. Now you with all your flash suits and books and everything, it's like I was some kind of burden to you.

No, Flossie. I didn't mean that.

I'm doing this off my own back. I don't even care if I'm wrong. I want to do something by myself for a change. For fun. Just fun. You know? Your father, he never let me do anything. And now you're being the same. Well, I'm sorry, Frankie. But I can't help you. I just can't.

Frankie nods.

What about the house?

What house?

This house.

This house? It's my home.

You could easily raise a loan of a hundred K against it. There's got to be a hundred K of capital in this place.

And what if it all goes down the drain? says Flossie.

I've got the house, there's capital in my house too. So I can always pay you back.

What, so, I'd make you and my grandchild-to-be homeless so you could pay me back?

It wouldn't come to that, Mum.

Starting a business is risky. Even I know that. And you'd take the chance of me losing a hundred thousand pounds?

Frankie feels a rush of shame

I'm sorry, Mum. I shouldn't have asked. You're right. You're right.

I'm sorry, son.

It's okay. I'm sorry I asked.

I mean — I would if I could.

Frankie puts his head in his hands and groans.

Now don't take on so, son. There must be another way, Frankie. Surely?

Frankie slowly brings his head up and exhales heavily.

Perhaps. Perhaps there's another way.

He rubs at his birthmark with the tip of his fingernail.

I just can't think what it is at the moment.

* * *

Frankie drives around the streets of Shepherd's Bush in a daze. Ralph has gone. His partnership has gone. The hope of a new business has gone. All it's going to be now is nappy changing and clock watching and bean counting and grovelling to Ratchett. He'll just be another mug, stumbling endlessly over the world's tripwires.

He decides to go right there and then to the office and cast himself on the mercy of Ratchett. There's nothing else to do. He should never have had a tantrum when he did. He can get the old job back, hack it out for a couple of years and start the agency then. It just takes him to swallow his pride is all. Ratchett will take him back. He makes too much money for the firm to refuse.

He drives towards the shop and passes the brightly lit plate-glass window in the car he bought after he resigned, a second-hand Ford Mondeo. Ratchett at that moment looks up, catches a glimpse of him at the wheel. He seems to smirk — at the humbleness of the car, Frankie presumes.

At that moment Frankie knows he will not go back. Cannot go back.

Then, as that thought dies, another idea occurs to him, a notion that has been swilling around his mind for some time, but that he has pushed back down insistently. Now it breaks through to his consciousness with more force than he can resist, sets up a tent at the front of his mind, unzips the opening.

He pulls over.

Slowly, as if moving through glue, he takes his Nokia out of his pocket and sits staring at it for a full thirty seconds before doing anything. He picks it up. Then puts it down again. Then picks it up again.

Then he runs the contacts, selects and dials.

The phone is answered almost immediately.

Hi, it's me, Frankie. Yes, that Frankie. Are you alone? Good. No, everything's fine. I have something I want to talk to you about. Well, need to talk to you about actually. Can we meet? Great. Great. Sooner the better.

2003: The March

They have all arranged to meet at Embankment station. Veronica and Frankie are the first to arrive. The station is busier than he has ever seen it, even though it is a Saturday and the office workers have gone home for the weekend.

Frankie surreptitiously checks his watch.

I get it, says Veronica, noticing.

Get what? says Frankie, looking up with slow, affected casualness, anxious to emphasize that the time was of no consequence to him whatsoever. He has begun to find Veronica's acute observational gifts increasingly rattling. Her ability to notice tiny gestures or hear significant noises in far-off rooms – even now they have a three-storey house – disconcerts him. Marriage, Frankie has been known to complain – thanks to the perpetual surveillance – is more like living in North Korea than North Kensington.

You don't want to be here, do you? I don't know why you bothered.

I was just checking the time.

I knew you didn't want to come.

I wanted to go to the zoo instead. So did China.

You wouldn't have gone to the zoo, anyway. You would have just gone to work. You're always saying you're going to take her to the zoo.

She's too young for this.

She's too young for the zoo as well. She wouldn't have appreciated anything about it.

Children like zoos more than marches.

It's not about 'liking'.

Veronica is holding a large hand-made banner with 'Make Tea Not War' scrawled in red lipstick on a white linen tea towel, supported by two bamboo sticks uprooted from the garden. It keeps catching in the wind and she struggles to control it. Frankie, to her annoyance, makes no move to help her.

China is in her pushchair, a sand-coloured Dutch Bugaboo Frog 'Concept' stroller. Her hazel eyebrows, almost joined in the middle, have a quizzical cast. She wears a hairband decorated with three consecutive tiny white flowers. It holds in place softly curled brown hair, the same colour as Veronica's. Her nose is a tiny mushroom, her lips like jelly sweets. There is nothing about Frankie's own face that he can recognize in his daughter's.

China is eating a huge slice of red watermelon, and has covered herself in pulp and seeds. She smiles at the mess as if it amounts to a considerable achievement. Frankie makes an attempt at cleaning it with wet wipes and manages to get pulp on his white shirt in the process, leaving a large pink indeterminate stain just below his breastbone.

I'm just not sure all this commotion is good for China, he says.

It's important that she's here. It's her future, after all.

She's two. She doesn't know what's going on. How long's this going to take, do you think?

You don't have to stay the whole time. Peel off once we get to Hyde Park if you want.

Where's the rest of them?

On cue, Nodge and Fraser appear at the top of the escalators and walk towards them, through the ticket barriers. They are, as usual, arguing. Fraser is dragging a large, immaculately groomed dog, a Dalmatian, wearing a yellow tabard with 'Pets Against the War' inscribed on it.

I used to think like you, Nodge is saying. *When I was a teenager.*

Don't patronize me, yeh?

I'm not. I just grew up. Also I've got a vague idea what it actually means to be broke. Politics isn't a game for me.

Or for me either.

Nodge gives up and turns his attention to the small family group.

Hi, Frankie. Vronky. China! Look at you. What a catastrophe.

China giggles and spreads more melon around her mouth.

How do you know the dog is against the war? says Frankie to Fraser, leaning down to pat the Dalmatian on the back. It barks back at him angrily.

Because he's my dog, says Fraser. *And he does what he's told. And so he's against the war.*

Nodge leans over China's stroller and starts cooing. He is wearing a black Thinsulate wool cap and a heavyweight sweater. Fraser has a purple Jack Wills rucksack slung over his back. His T-shirt, under his olive flying jacket, reads 'End Israeli Occupation'.

Nodge puts a kazoo in the side of his mouth and begins blowing. No sound comes out.

This thing is useless.

He throws it in the bin. Fraser takes his own kazoo out and starts playing the 'Internationale'. Nodge takes it from him and hums out the theme from *Loony Tunes*. There is the persistent drone of helicopters overhead. People all around them are mostly laughing and joking, despite the seriousness of intent.

Twenty yards behind them, Frankie sees a Muslim woman in a full hijab being questioned by a reporter while a man, presumably her husband, has fallen to his knees and prays to Mecca behind her. The woman waves the reporter away and he goes in search of another target, almost tripping over the praying man.

Frankie checks his watch again.

Just think of it as a day out, says Veronica, finishing the cleaning-up job on China that Frankie has abandoned.

Nodge straightens up and starts clapping his hands together for warmth.

We can't stand here much longer, says Frankie. *Too crowded. Colin's usually on time.*

Roxy isn't, says Veronica. *Ever.*

I'm surprised he's coming at all, says Nodge. *Politics really isn't his thing.*

He's coming for the same reason Frankie turned up, says Fraser, quiet enough so that only Nodge can hear. *Doing what he's told.*

Give them some credit, replies Nodge. *At least they're here.*

Now Colin and Roxy emerge from the ticket gates. Colin is smartly dressed, as he has been since he has begun living with Roxy. His clothes are clearly expensive and even his expression has changed, going from apologetic and placatory to confident, even arrogant. His shoulders are back, his chin high. Roxy, as usual, is buffed, plucked and over-made-up and walks with a cocky rolling gait that irresistibly reminds Frankie of Harold Shand in *The Long Good Friday.*

Colin shakes hands with Nodge, Frankie and Fraser. Veronica gives him a cautious hug, smells talcum powder and what she thinks she recognizes as Vetiver cologne, doubtless chosen by Roxy. Roxy waves a hand in general greeting.

What's the route? says Colin, awkwardly disentangling himself from Veronica and aligning himself with Roxy, who is lighting a cigarette with fat fingers. She offers the pack around, but nobody else smokes now, Frankie having given up, after lobbying from Veronica, in the wake of China's birth, and Nodge under pressure from Fraser.

Up towards Trafalgar Square and Piccadilly, says Roxy.

If we make it that far, says Nodge. *The streets are jammed.*

She winds her arm around Colin's. He stands slightly stiff and uncomfortable.

Who's speaking again? says Colin. *At the rally in the park?*

Tony Benn. Harold Pinter. George Galloway, says Fraser

Bianca Jagger, says Roxy, excitedly.

All your old heroes, Nodge, says Frankie.

Bianca Jagger was never my hero. George Galloway's a knob.

I have a lot of time for him, says Fraser.

Frankie notices Fraser's 'End Israeli Occupation' T-shirt.

What has Israel got to do with anything? says Frankie.

You wouldn't understand, says Fraser, tickling the Dalmatian under the tummy. *They wouldn't understand, would they, Harvey? Would they?*

What does *it actually have to do with anything?* says Nodge.

All part of a continuum, says Fraser, breezily, standing up to his full height, *of historic Western colonialism.* He vigorously pets the Dalmatian who indifferently stretches his neck. *Harvey understands. Don't you, boy?*

Someone in new age dress – all tie dye and artful rips – with crusty locks is touting balloons from a vast bunch. Nodge goes across to buy one for China. He walks past an American flag with the word 'shame' scrawled in large letters across the horizontal stripes.

I'm hungry, says Colin. *Can we get something to eat? They must be doing hot dogs or something.*

He sniffs the air as if he can track distant fast food by smell alone. But the only thing he can see on sale is hot candied peanuts and he's trying to avoid carbs to support Roxy, who is giving the Atkins Diet a try. Colin expects her attempt to last three days, which is the most she's ever managed on other diets before cheerfully giving up with a consolatory, *'life's too short'.*

Nodge comes back with a pink balloon, which he gives to China, who gurgles happily. Then it immediately slips out of her hand and escapes skywards. China begins to cry, softly at first but the volume quickly escalating to a piercing pitch of despair.

Good one, Nodge, says Frankie as he leans over to try, unsuccessfully, to console China.

Do you know what that crusty who was selling the balloons said to me? asks Nodge, of no one in particular.

Was it, 'Do you want to buy one of these balloons?' says Roxy.

I asked her what she thought about the war. And she said 'everyone should just smoke a spliff, chill the fuck out and stop killing each other'. Not exactly Hanna Arendt, is it? Also the balloon was three quid! Someone's making a killing out of this and it isn't only the arms dealers.

Outside the station, the painfully slow drift of the crowd is through Whitehall towards Trafalgar Square. The party of seven follow. The movement of the stroller seems to soothe China and she quietens down. It takes an hour to get to Piccadilly Circus, where a second march is being joined. A multiplex hoarding down a side street announces *Daredevil*, *The Pianist* and *Final Destination 2*.

'Final Destination 2' was shit, says Roxy, checking her make-up in a small mirror which she has just removed from her Louis Vuitton Monogram Multicolore bag. *Just a stupid gorefest. 'The Pianist' was just depressing. Jews being thrown out of windows 'n' shit. Then I suppose you wouldn't mind that much, Fraser.*

Fraser bares his teeth slightly but does not rise to the bait. Roxy pouts, puts the mirror away, then takes a battered paper bag out of her pocket which is stuffed with Cola Cubes and hands it around. No one accepts apart from Fraser.

Top choice of sweetie, Rocks.

Thank kew. They're a bit icky.

I like a bit of ick, says Fraser archly.

A bit of dick more like, says Roxy, guffawing.

You can talk, love, says Fraser, unoffended. *By the way, I'm not an anti-Semite.*

You just hate Israelis.

That's different.

Veronica has picked up China and is cradling her while Frankie wheels the Bugaboo, in which he has placed four cans of lager and a bag of blue corn chips. The crowd is a seething sea of grey, black, cream and brown, the shades of Britain in winter.

She needs changing, says Veronica, holding her out to Frankie, along with a nappy bag.

Really? says Frankie, unenthusiastically. *Is it my turn?*

You owe me about two thousand changes on the latest count.

Frankie sniffs the air and concludes that Veronica is right about China having soiled herself. He looks around for somewhere to change her, but the crowd is packed close and engaged in an almost imperceptible slow surge west. He spots an empty red telephone box, one of those preserved by the heritage enthusiasts. He pushes his way through the mob and puts China down on the dirty floor. She starts screaming. He grapples with her terry towel nappy which is full of greenish shit. He winces at the terrible smell — when she was a newborn, even her excrement smelt sweet. No longer.

The screaming gets louder and China starts to wriggle and kick. Frankie tries to keep her still with one hand, while manipulating the fresh cloth with another, but it is difficult. Someone is knocking on the door, apparently wanting to use the phone.

Fuck off! snarls Frankie, half to himself.

It is a good five minutes before he finally finishes the process, carrying the soiled nappy in a plastic bag, and a still crying, red-faced China. Eventually he rejoins the group.

The joys of fatherhood, says Fraser, mockingly, as Frankie straps China back into the pushchair, wishing, not for the first time, that he could shrug off heterosexuality and join the scene. Roxy, seeing China's distress, takes a liquorice dip out of her pocket and offers some sherbet to China, but Veronica sees it and gently pushes her hand away.

It's only a bit of sherbet.

You know how I feel about sugar.

Yeh, I know. 'It's a killer'. Least I'll die happy, says Roxy, licking her finger, as China continues to screech above the clamour of the crowd.

There are drums thudding and more tattered and tattooed MDMA casualties, dancing, only this crop are nearing their forties. Every fifty yards seems to produce another man or woman in smart clothes pointing a camera or brandishing a microphone. One of them, dressed in a suit with a brown Parka over the top, approaches Frankie, grinning apologetically but determinedly.

Excuse me, sir, I'm from LBC News. Do you mind if I have a word?

Frankie shrugs.

Why are you here today?

Frankie looks at the microphone suspiciously.

I'm not entirely sure, he says.

What do you think about Tony Blair?

Frankie coughs. Fraser stares at him with unblinking eyes.

I think he's been a good prime minister on the whole.

Do you think he is making the right decision intervening in Iraq?

He was right about Kosovo. And Sierra Leone.

Fraser spits on the floor.

May I ask you — are you a Labour voter?

I'm pretty apolitical on the whole. They're all the same, aren't they?

Fraser seems to cough, but there is word concealed underneath: *Tory.*

Thank you, sir.

The reporter moves on to find more grist. To the left, a clutch of policemen are facing a group of demonstrators from Class War. 'No War But Class War' reads their banner, in white letters on a pale blue background. The anarchists are shouting abuse, which the policemen are good-naturedly ignoring. Fraser regards the police icily.

Fascist arseholes.

What do you know about fascism? says Nodge.

Everything. I'm queer.

That's got nothing to do with it.

Do you know how many queers Hitler snuffed out?

You think that policeman is like someone from the SS, do you?

You've got no convictions, Jon.

Don't get annoyed.

I'm not annoyed.

You always call me Jon when you're annoyed. Anyway, convictions are dangerous. Isn't that what we're here to protest against?

Without convictions, 'Nodge', what are you?

Open-minded?

You've got to make a stand sometimes, says Veronica. *I'm not even a big lefty.*

I'm not even a lefty, mutters Colin.

Me neither, says Roxy. *I'm just against killing and that. Anyway, anything for a laugh.*

It's not meant to be a laugh, says Veronica.

What do you think about the war then, Colin? says Fraser, who is spoiling for a fight with someone and has decided that Colin will do.

There isn't one yet, says Colin.

You know exactly what I mean. You're being evasive.

I don't think it would be the worst thing in the world to get rid of Saddam Hussein.

His moustache is shit, says Nodge, trying to lighten the mood.

It's not about Saddam Hussein, says Fraser. *It's about oil.*

I think it's about democracy, says Nodge.

It's about the Kurds, says Frankie, surprising Nodge. He has read a story about them today in the *Independent*, in a dilatory preparation for the march.

What's a curd? says Roxy, crunching loudly on her Cola Cube.

The group move slowly forward, part of a vast seething mob now, up Northumberland Avenue towards Trafalgar Square. A few of the faces are painted, tribal, and there are snatches of angry cursing, but most people seem normal, quiet, suburban even.

A chant rises up, roughly from the direction of the Class War contingent.

Fuck Blair. Fuck the War. Fuck Blair. Fuck the War.

Fraser joins in enthusiastically, Nodge somewhat more timidly. Frankie, Veronica, Colin and Roxy remain silent, although Colin mouths the words.

Fuck, says China, tentatively and giggles.

Can we stop this now? says Veronica in the direction of Nodge and Fraser, bending down to adjust the blanket over China's pushchair.

I told you this wasn't right for her, says Frankie. Veronica looks needled, and hopelessly puts her hands over China's ears. China wriggles in protest and Veronica almost immediately gives up.

You can't shut out reality, dear, says Fraser. He continues with his chant.

She's only two, snaps back Veronica. *It's a parent's job to shut out reality. Anyway, what would you know about it?*

Breeder, mutters Fraser, sourly, then continues chanting.

What did you say? says Frankie, bristling, half-catching the word.

Fraser glances at Frankie's face, which is now stretched tight over the bones. His birthmark glows. He has shifted into an angry and protective stance, body tensed under his sweatshirt.

Fancy your chances? says Fraser, squaring up to Frankie, showing his ripped torso. He has fought off enough attacks in the past. He examines the bridge of Frankie's nose as the soft spot for a head-butt.

Boys, boys, says Veronica, secretly flattered by Frankie's spirited defence of her honour.

Frankie stands his ground, though he is taken aback by Fraser's aggression. He had always thought gays were a bit soft.

What did you say to my wife? says Frankie, a little uncertainly now.

Nodge puts his hand on Fraser's shoulder, and Fraser, after a moment's hesitation, responds, consciously relaxing, climbing down from battle stations.

Calm down, Sir Galahad.

What did you say then?

I said 'he's a bleeder'.

Who's a bleeder?

Tony Blair.

Frankie looks at him and narrows his eyes, knowing that it's a lie, but grateful for a way out. He says nothing, turns away. To their left, a banner that reads 'Eton College Orwell Society People Not Profit People Not War' is held aloft in the midst of a crowd of maybe sixty schoolboys.

The group of seven – eight including Harvey – carry on slowly walking along Piccadilly toward Hyde Park. Colin finds a stall selling sausage rolls, but doesn't like the texture and offers it to Harvey.

No, says Fraser, grabbing the roll out of his hand. *He's a vegetarian.*

A vegetarian dog?

That's right.

That's stupid.

You're stupid.

When they reach the march's epicentre at Hyde Park, already one speaker, a dour-looking man with a scruffy, greying beard is proselytizing, wearing a green tie and cheap-looking blue jacket. His top button is undone, his voice is cracked and strained with peevishness.

. . . You cannot humiliate the Palestinian people in the way they've been humiliated and not expect some problem in the future.

Like I told you, says Fraser, to no one in particular. *Part of a continuum. Right?*

We want to free ourselves from the scourge of war! shouts the bearded man.

I think we can all sign up to that, says Frankie, checking his watch again.

Ken Livingstone is next on the stage, wearing a blue shirt and yellow tie. Fraser cheers loudly. As Livingstone is beginning his remarks, a man in a black eye mask, a yellow tabard and a black and white polka-dot headband runs up to him, grabs the mike and shouts, *Stop the congestion charge!*

Yeh! says Frankie.

Fucking congestion charge, says Nodge.

You're trivial, says Fraser. *This is life and death.*

You going on the front line, are you? says Nodge. *When's the bus from Hammersmith Broadway to Basra leave then?*

Security guards pick up the protestor and virtually throw

him off the podium. Livingstone smiles indulgently, seemingly enjoying the interruption, and calmly continues addressing the crowd, thanking the Stop the War Coalition, CND and the Muslim Alliance of Britain. After Livingstone has finished, Jesse Jackson takes over the microphone. He is far more polished and inspirational than the nasal Livingstone, or his flat and mechanical predecessor. His voice rises and falls according to some inner music, and captures emotion and fury and determination all at once.

It's cold outside, but our hearts are warm.

It may be winter, but all of you together are generating some serious street heat.

George Bush can feel it.

Tony Blair can feel it.

Turn up the heat!

Turn up the heat!

The crowd roars its approval. China, who has only just stopped crying, starts to whimper again.

What's the matter darling? murmurs Veronica, leaning over her.

Fuck, says China, softly.

* * *

Back home, in the terraced house on the quiet street in the tree-lined St Quintin Estate in North Kensington, China has fallen asleep in the hall, slumped in her pushchair. She has retained a 'Stop the War' balloon, which Nodge bought her to replace the lost one, tied to the frame. It flitters anxiously in draughts from under the door.

Veronica is watching the news bulletins, waiting for reports of the march. Frankie is on his Samsung flip-top phone checking messages. Because of the march, he handed over two important sales that day to Jane – now 'fully qualified' – who, like Victor Strudwick, came over to join him at FLB Estates when Frankie started the new agency – much to Ratchett's implacable fury.

The agency has been running for nearly two years out of a nondescript office on Askew Road and has prospered better than Frankie could possibly have expected, but the work rate is gruelling. Ratchett's hatred for him shows no sign of cooling. He will do anything to sabotage Frankie – to the extent of pulling down his 'For Sale' signs (although Frankie can't prove it) and even on one occasion gluing the lock on the front of his shop front so that Frankie couldn't get in (again, he can't prove it).

The messages show him that Jane has failed to close either of the two sales possibilities that were presented that afternoon. He sees, in his mind's eye, thousands of twenty-pound notes burning, a blue-green flame at the heart of a red and orange flower.

Jane, he decides, is not pulling her weight. She looks okay – better than in her days as a newbie at FR&G – but looking good doesn't butter any parsnips, as he is increasingly fond of telling her lately, and in no uncertain terms.

Pressure, he worries, is turning him into a watered-down version of the man he has sworn never to turn into, Nicholas Ratchett. He has made Jane cry on two separate occasions recently and feels bad about it, but business is tough and business is business. He has China to think of now, and private nursery fees (private on Veronica's insistence). Since she has given up her job as a pathologist to train as a therapist, the burden falls on him.

They're saying there were more than a million there, says Veronica, her eyes fixed on the screen.

Right, says Frankie, still chewing on his disappointment at Jane's failure, a junk meal that keeps repeating on him.

I think they're bound to stop it now. Blair can't ignore a crowd like that.

Right, says Frankie. Then he looks up, tries hard to tune in.

No, he says. *I'm sure he can't.*

Veronica picks idly at her nails.

You don't really care.

Frankie returns his attention to the phone.

I went on the march, didn't I?

Only because I made you. You wanted to work.

There are some things more important than work.

Like keeping me happy?

I want you to be happy, yes. What's wrong with that?

But not trying to actually head off a war. In which thousands of people will die.

You're twisting everything.

He looks for other messages, hitting the button below the keyboard, staring at the green luminescent screen of the Samsung.

Did you actually go to the march because it mattered to you? Or because it mattered to me?

Does it make a difference?

Of course it does.

Can we change the subject?

I really do want to know.

Frankie tears his eyes from the screen of his phone. No more messages anyway, but he finds the screen magnetic.

Bush and Blair will do whatever they want to do. They couldn't care less what me or you or anybody else thinks.

It's important to make a statement.

If you say.

Don't you think so?

I don't think it would have made much difference to the future of the Middle East whether I had attended or not. Tell the truth, I'd have been just as happy to attend the other demonstration if you'd asked me to.

What other demonstration?

He nods towards the screen, which is reporting on a man who demonstrated that day against the march, outside the Jordanian embassy. His placard reads 'War is necessary when evil dictators rule and murder their own people.'

If there had been a million people marching for that, I'd have probably gone on that too. You would have as well, probably. We're herd animals at the end of the day.

Veronica, who suddenly feels very tired, picks up a glass ashtray and starts idly playing with it. Flicking her fingernails against it so it makes a slight ringing sound. She feels the weight of the golden key on her breast.

You don't really believe in anything much, do you?

Frankie considers this seriously.

You didn't marry me for my political convictions.

I assumed that we were approximately like-minded.

I keep my horizons limited.

To what?

You. Me. China. Business.

She stares at the ashtray, scrapes her fingernails along its perimeter.

It's China's future we're talking about. Trying to avoid a war.

Why? Do you think she might get sent to Iraq?

Be serious.

You could also say I would have been thinking about China's future by going to meet these customers and closing the deal. Which I didn't and Jane the Flake busted them all out.

So it was about the money.

It just feels more relevant to our lives than what a bunch of skaggy politicians are doing to a bunch of demented towelheads.

We don't say that anymore, Frankie. They're not 'towelheads'. They have lives. Children. Homes.

It's a joke. An expression.

There's a lot you don't mean seriously that is serious.

Like what?

Like calling me 'darling'.

It's a term of affection!

It's boring. And patronizing. And so is 'love' and so is 'dear'.

Have you been talking to Fraser fucking Pike?

No need to swear.

Veronica nods reprovingly towards China who is still in the hall.

She can't understand, can she? Anyway, she's asleep, says Frankie.

How do you know whether she understands or not? She understood enough to say 'fuck' at the demonstration.

That was funny.

Don't swear, though. Please.

Obscurely this provokes Frankie more than anything she has said so far.

You know what you are, Veronica?

Veronica settles into the chair with a faint, placidly provocative smile.

Why don't you tell me?

An old-fashioned middle-class prude.

Is that the best you can do?

You're really spoiling for this.

Go right ahead.

Don't push me.

Her smile widens maliciously. It is enough.

A guilt-ridden, stuck-up would-be liberal who wouldn't know real life if it crept up on her and stuck a banana up her arse.

What else?

A ball buster and a hypocrite who buys the Guardian *and who's put her daughter down on the waiting list for one of the most expensive nurseries in London.*

Come on. Her eyes glitter. *Keep going. Now you've got the wind in your sails.*

Who's now got a fanny like a shopping bag. Filled with cotton wool. That someone spilled a mug of warm tea into.

Veronica stops fingering the ashtray, draws her arm back and slings it, hard, in Frankie's direction.

It hits the wall a couple of inches to his left and shatters.

Frankie stares at the remnants in astonishment.

You could have killed me.

Veronica shrugs. China, in the hallway, wakened by the noise, begins to cry.

You've woken her up, says Frankie, quietly, his voice still tempered by shock.

So it appears, says Veronica.

I'll go and get her.

Frankie walks through to the corridor. China's face is red and distorted. The mouth stretches wide, a reddish blackness within. Her food-stained onesie, decorated with images of blue sailing boats, is unbuttoned in two places. Frankie picks her up and she cries even louder.

Shhh, says Frankie. *Shhh shhh shhh.*

She wriggles wildly. Frankie tries to keep her still. The volume of the crying increases. Her hair is in wild ringlets. A bedraggled, dirty and much-sucked stuffed rabbit remains on the pushchair seat. Frankie picks it up and begins to waggle it in front of her face. With his other hand he fumbles with the straps that are fastened in front of her.

Say hello to Bertie. Say hello. Say hello!

His phone rings. He lets the rabbit fall, and takes his phone out of his pocket but fumbles and drops the phone. It shatters on the tile floor.

Fuck!

Now Veronica is standing in the doorway, her face dark. China looks at her, pausing momentarily from crying, then at Frankie. Then the crying resumes at an even higher volume. Frankie takes her out of the pushchair, leaving the pieces of the phone on the floor. China holds her arms out to Veronica.

I'll take her.

I'm fine, says Frankie.

I'll take her.

Frankie rocks China back and forward. He moves to get his balance, treads accidentally on one of the remnants of his phone, which makes a crunching noise. China cries and wriggles furiously.

Frankie gives up. He weakly handles over the sobbing bundle, gathers the shards of his phone and tries unsuccessfully to piece them together. Veronica puts her daughter over her shoulder and begins to rub her back, slowly, in a circular motion.

There there, she whispers. *There there.*

China calms, breathes deep once, then twice, and stops crying.

Is Daddy being nasty to you?

Stop fucking winding me up.

Don't swear in front of her!

At least Daddy isn't throwing fucking ashtrays at Daddy's fucking head.

Go and earn some money, why don't you? If it makes you feel like a big man.

You're quite happy to spend it.

Yeh. That's why I've got a room full of Prada bags.

You're living in this house which I paid for. Ever since you've been hanging out with that chav Roxy your shopping bill has gone up and up. And I'm not talking about shopping for Sudocrem. Where do you think that money comes from? If I spent all my time protesting against wars, you'd be pushing her around in a second-hand piece of crap from Primark.

It's very sad that money means so much to you, Frankie.

Yeh, it's so sad, I'm crying. And truth is, he is close to it.

Why is it so important to you? Really. It's so . . .

What? Vulgar?

I didn't say that.

Anyway, that's a stupid question.

Why's it a stupid question?

Because . . . because money is . . . money is . . . money is mean-ing. Whatever meaning means. Christ I'm talking as much rubbish as you now.

Veronica rocks China back and forward and keeps her eyes fixed on the child.

I thought I was marrying a man, she says, without looking up. *Not a boy*

In the end, what's the difference?

The difference is knowing the difference, says Veronica.

She continues clucking into China's ear. China gurgles delightedly.

I work my great big hairy balls off for this family. Not that I get any thanks for it.

Your balls are tiny.

Giving up on the decimated phone, Frankie goes to the cupboard under the stairs, gets out a dustpan and brush and goes into the living room to clean up the glass shards from the ashtray. He treads on one of them: his foot is immediately cut and bleeds into his sock. He sweeps the broken glass into the pan with angry strokes, blood seeping from his heel. Veronica walks into the room from the hallway, still holding China, who is laughing now and sucking on a rusk.

You've missed a bit.

She points to a miniscule fragment of glass by the table leg. Frankie reaches over and picks it up between his fingers.

I've cut my foot, says Frankie.

Don't get blood on the carpet. She leaves the room with China and goes upstairs.

Frankie finishes tidying. Minutes later Veronica comes down again, alone.

We need to have a talk, she says.

We just did.

I need you to get on board.

With what? says Frankie.

With this.

I am on board.

You work twelve hours a day.

I have to work twelve hours a day. To pay all the bills.

But what about me? What about my hopes? What about my career? I'm never going to finish my training if I'm under this kind of pressure. I'm meant to be studying at least four hours a day. I don't even get four minutes.

I'll pay for a child-minder. Anyway, she'll be at nursery soon.

I don't want a child-minder. I want us to bring up China together.

You can't have it all ways.

Why don't you put some of the work onto Jane? She could take up some of the slack.

Jane hasn't got the experience.

That's how she'll get experience.

I don't want to give up my commissions to her.

Even if it means having twice the amount of time with your family?

You make it sound like I've got it cushy.

I'm going insane, Frankie. I need to get on with my studies. Look at us. Look what all the stress is turning me into. I don't want to be that woman. It will take me years to learn to be a counsellor. I need support from you.

Just leave it until China's in nursery. Why can't you do that?

Because I promised myself to bring her up by hand for the first few years. I thought I owed it to her. If you loved me, you would find a way to help me.

Everything I suggest you throw cold water on. I can't take my foot off the pedal at the agency now.

I didn't know how hard it was to be a mother.

You don't understand, Vronky.

You *don't understand, Frankie. You don't understand what it's like. Every day. Being here. With her. I'm lonely. And bored. And tired. And irritable. And I can't study. I'm six months behind on where I'm meant to be.*

What about the other mothers?

All they talk about is their kids. You can't imagine how boring it is. I want to have a job.

Maybe you shouldn't have chosen to have a baby then.

It was us who chose. Us! Why should I be the one who has to make that choice?

Because. Because.

Because what?

Frankie puts her arms round her. She stiffens, then softens and begins to weep.

Come on. We can do this. Once my plans have played out, we're going to be sitting pretty.

Veronica wipes her eyes with the back of her hand.

What plans?

Buy to let. It's the future. I already got a little bedsit I let out. And I've just seen a house on the market on Goldhawk Road that's perfect for it. Dilapidated, but since our friend the warmonger, Mr Blair, opened all the floodgates, all these Poles turn up looking for work at about thirty per cent less than the goons and ponces that English builders have got away with for years. I know this bloke, Woyzek, who's got a whole team. They live in a squat in Barnet, they are top-hole and hungry and if I can close on this house, then I'll do it up and shift it on in a year for a thirty per cent profit. Then I repeat. And repeat. Until we're rich.

But you still haven't paid back the money you borrowed from the bank to start your agency. How are you going to get more to buy this new place and do it up?

I've got some cards up my sleeve.

We need to be careful. I'm not going to be making any money out of my therapy practice for a good few years. And the nursery bills are going to start coming in before the end of the year.

Don't worry about it. I want you to be happy. I want your dreams to come true. I want things to be right for China. Trust me?

Veronica pauses for a second too long before she answers.

Of course I do, Frankie. Of course I do.

And though they are still glaring at one another like fighters, they both find a place within the moment to soften and finally, tentatively, embrace.

* * *

Nodge walks through the polished glass portal into the Soho gym with a ragged towel and kit in a plastic Safeway shopping bag. Fraser has told him – repeatedly, and without mercy – that he is fat. Practising considerable self-restraint, Nodge has avoided making the comeback *and you're old and bald.*

Nodge has asked – begged – Fraser to accept him as he is. Fraser, it seems, is unable to do so. So Nodge, finally, has come to the gym. Up until this moment, the closest he has come to keeping fit for several years is walking up and down the stairs at the Porchester Spa baths in Queensway from the lounging area to the saunas and steam rooms.

The man at the gym counter has a buzz cut with whorls like corn circles cut into the side of the furze, and is dressed in a tight white Red or Dead T-shirt. He is chatting with a heavily built black man with an elaborate gothic tattoo on his forearm that spells out the word 'Pride'.

Nodge is intimidated. He has never been in a place like this. The spa he frequents in Queensway is older, more downmarket and not so, well, queeny, although there is a big gay contingent there along with a weird mixture of cabbies, villains, pensioners and straights.

The man in the T-shirt glances sharply at Nodge's plastic bag, then more pointedly still at his undefined torso with a faint expression of distaste that he doesn't trouble to conceal. He turns away and resumes his conversation with the ripped black man, whose teeth, Nodge thinks, seem to sparkle in the brightness of the almost-fluorescent overhead lights. Or is that a racist thought? Fraser polices him for that sort of misstep. He worries since he met Fraser that he is a racist and a sexist and even a homophobe, the latter of which makes very little sense to him, but Fraser seems to make everything convincing, he is so whip-smart and sure of himself.

For some time the man behind the counter – whose name, according to his badge, is Orson – continues to pay no attention to him. Nodge waits for the black man to finish his long rambling speech about what appears to be an extended longueur in his otherwise apparently vigorous sex life. Eventually the man winks at Orson, guffaws for no reason that Nodge can ascertain, and walks away in the direction of the vast, hyperlit gym space, which is soundtracked with hammering techno beats. But Orson continues to blank Nodge, now directing his attention downwards at a red leather bound register in front of him. Nodge sees him scratch what appear to be a few pointless doodles into the margins with a very sharp pencil.

Nodge stands there for another twenty seconds. He coughs. Finally, he speaks.

I'm a guest of Fraser Pike.

The man gives the faintest of nods, but continues doodling and studying the register.

Could you tell me where the changing rooms are, please?

The man behind the counter doesn't even look up. He just waves vaguely towards Nodge's left. Nodge sighs and makes his way into the changing rooms. The two other men in there have absolutely perfect, sculpted bodies. Nodge removes his shirt to reveal his pale overcoat of hair and flab. He changes into a pair of football shorts and a yellowing T-shirt. One of the men fixes him with a stare.

Alright? says Nodge with a hint, now, of resentment.

The man smiles without warmth and turns back to his companion. They are chatting about a party they went to the night before. The drugs they took. What happened in the half-lit back rooms.

Nodge changes as quickly as he can and drags his heavy body into the main hall. The space is vast. There are mirrors on every wall. There are rows of machines for lifting, running, stretching. The soundtrack of techno music pumps out, it seems, even louder than before. It is 'Harder, Better, Faster, Stronger' by Daft Punk, a track he particularly dislikes. He spots Fraser on one of the running machines and walks over. Fraser briefly makes eye contact, but shows no other sign of recognition.

Sorry I'm late, bellows Nodge over the music.

Fraser carries on running silently apart from his slightly elevated level of breathing.

Something the matter, Fraze?

Why should something be the matter? Fraser doesn't bother to raise his voice, but Nodge still somehow hears him.

I said I was sorry for being late. I had a fare out to Richmond. You're not allowed to turn them down.

No need to yell.

How have you been getting on?

Speak up, I can't hear you.

How have you been getting on? shouts Nodge, trying to pitch his voice exactly right between a bellow and ordinary speech.

I'm nearly finished now.

I'll get a move on then.

Nodge gets on the running machine next to Fraser, switches it on. The treadmill begins to turn. Fraser continues to stare straight ahead.

Who was that stuck-up cunt at reception? The guy with crop circles on the back of his head.

Orson? He's okay.

He looked at me like I was shit on his brand new Dunk Lows.

Attitude queen. You come to a place like this, you have to expect it.

Nodge has started to run now, and is already breathing heavily.

This place is like hell, he says. His face has turned red already and his chest is pumping.

You didn't have to come. There's always Shepherd's Bush sports centre.

You wanted me to.

I didn't say that.

You didn't have to say anything. The way you look at me is enough. Don't bother guilting me. It won't work.

I know. I'm not.

Sorry I don't want a fat boyfriend.

I've already lost half a stone.

I don't care about your body, only your beautiful soul.

Nodge for a moment thinks Fraser is being serious, then redoubles his pushing.

I'm doing this for you, Fraser. I hope you know that.

It'll put ten years on your life.

Fraser says nothing more, just carries on running, smoothly, tirelessly. A light sheen of sweat covers his body. Nodge finds the sight exciting. He switches his gaze and looks straight ahead – at himself in the mirror. He sees a shapeless blob – his head – on top of another shapeless blob, his torso. Since coming out more than three years ago, his definition of himself has matured, become more exact and defined and real. Now he wants the same for his body, his personality.

After five minutes, with bursting lungs, Nodge switches to the rowing machine. He rests there for a while. To his left, one of the men from the changing room is rowing at a brisk pace. Nodge starts, taking it in leisurely strokes. He's feeling exhausted already. He takes a swig out of his plastic water bottle. He glances at himself in the mirror again. There is no escape from the shining surfaces. He is repulsed and depressed by what he sees.

There is another rowing machine to his right. Fraser leaves his treadmill and Nodge gestures towards the available rowing machine, but Fraser goes instead to lift some weights.

After five more minutes of rowing, Nodge lies back and closes his eyes. When he opens them again, a heavy, hairy man with a beard is leaning against the rowing machine to his left, which the previous occupant has now vacated. He is tanned and his nose is peeling.

Enjoying it? he says, mildly. His accent has a faint Welsh tang.

Does it look like I'm enjoying it? says Nodge.

There's got to be more to life, he says, smiling at Nodge.

Couldn't agree with you more.

My boyfriend put me up to this. Otherwise I'd be having a catnap. Mine too.

Nodge pulls himself up into an upright position.

You work around here?

I work everywhere. I'm a taxi driver, says Nodge.

I'm in the transportation business myself. I deliver pizzas. On my bicycle. Well, that's one of the things I do. You've probably nearly run me over once or twice. Trouble is, they give me free pizzas. Murder for the waistline. Hopefully it's just a short-term thing.

Don't tell me. You're trying to break into acting.

I'm training for a job at John Lewis. Soft furnishings. Curtains, mainly.

Fraser walks past, swigging on a bottle of Evian. He finishes, then blows Nodge a kiss, without making eye contact, before tackling a squat rack.

That your boyfriend?

Yes, says Nodge, flatly.

Nice pecs.

Nodge takes another drink of water. He can feel his thinning hair matted soggily on his rosy head.

I have a confession, says the man.

You're not training for John Lewis. You're really after a job in the reclining chair department of World of Leather.

I haven't got a boyfriend, says the man. *I'm just here because I thought it would be a nice place to meet people.*

How's that going? says Nodge.

I've met you.

Not exactly. We don't even know each other's names.

I'm Roger Mycock.

I'm Jon Sadler, but people call me . . . that's not really your name, is it?

Obviously not.

What is it really?

Owen Ambrose. What is it people call you?

Noj. It's—

Jon. Backwards. I get it.

Owen holds out a dry, large, meaty hand. Nodge wipes his own hand carefully on his T-shirt and shakes it.

Why aren't you working out with Charlie Atlas there?

Who's Charlie Atlas?

Ask your boyfriend. He'll be old enough to remember. His generation's answer to Schwarzenegger.

He's a bit out of my league. In terms of physical fitness anyway.

Bit long in the tooth for you, isn't he? He must have twenty years on you.

I'm not in a position to be that choosy, says Nodge. *Anyway Fraser's got a lot of good qualities.*

I can see that.

Other than his torso. He's funny. Well, quite dry. Sometimes.

Sounds like a riot.

He's classy. He's got taste. A lot of taste. And he has standards. Both moral and physical.

Hence the gym for you?

Hence that, yes. He's a nice man, really. Well, not 'nice' exactly. Good. Righteous. All appearances to the contrary.

Owen nods, ruminatively.

Shall we have a go at something together? he says. *We can goad and mock one another mercilessly. Good for the motivation.*

What did you have in mind?

How about the punching bags? I've got a lot of pent-up aggression.

Against anything in particular?

Gyms, mainly. And narcissistic muscle Marys. Like this place is busting with.

They go to the punching bags, where they put on gloves and start attacking the red vinyl sand-filled sheaths. Nodge finds it satisfying, although he can feel the flesh on his upper arms wobbling in a way that he worries must look unattractive.

Now this is my idea of a workout. Beating the shit out of something helpless, says Owen between shortening pants of breath.

Nodge smiles at him.

Are you Welsh?

Why would you think that?

Owen? It's a bit of a giveaway.

I like to play down the Welshness. It's all a bit butch.

I like Welsh cakes, says Nodge.

Nice stereotype, says Owen. *Actually, I make a lovely Welsh cake. That's about the only part of Welsh culture I know about.*

Are there other parts?

Probably not. Singing, isn't it? Poetry. Violence.

Fraser walks up, slow and vaguely disdainful. Although he is nearly fifty, and with a bullet head and a hooked nose and thin, prissy lips, his body is a thing of wonder, all prisms and angles and edgy hard bulges.

I'm finished, he says flatly, looking disinterestedly at Owen then glancing at Nodge.

I'll see you in the coffee bar, says Nodge.

Fraser doesn't answer. He takes a slower, more apprais-ing look at Owen, up and down. Then he walks off without another word.

Nice, says Owen.

Yes. He's in good shape.

No. I mean you, says Owen.

Are you flirting with me?

Nothing wrong with that, is there?

Nodge laughs.

Nothing at all. He won't wait for me, you know. At the coffee bar. Once I've finished and got changed he'll be gone.

You two live together?

I live alone. But we spend a lot of time at one another's flats.

Are you lonely?

Nodge, taken back the directness of the question, finds himself looking straight into Owen's eyes. They are bluey-grey. Owen doesn't flinch from the gaze. For some reason, Nodge finds it easy to answer honestly.

Who isn't?

Why don't you and I have that cup of coffee together then? Once we've honed the hardness of our perfect bodies into bur-nished steel.

Could we just go for the coffee and leave the burnishing bit out?

I can't tell you how much I was hoping you would say that, says Owen.

They stop punching and smile at one another. Both have hardly a sweat up.

I'd rather watch telly, wouldn't you? Even something really shit, says Owen. He has freckles and hair that is flat and straight.

He's not good-looking – his forehead is too large and low and his cheeks are puffy – but there is something in his face that is reassuring, open, solid. *Or have a wank.*

Or both, says Nodge, laughing now.

* * *

Over coffee, Owen consumes an enormous carrot muffin and a latte while Nodge makes do with water and a sliver of Marmite-flavoured rice cake that he has brought with him in the Sainsbury's bag.

Nodge stares longingly towards Owen's muffin, and follows the last chunk as it travels to Owen's soft, generous mouth. His teeth, unlike Fraser's, which have been on the receiving end of thousands of pounds' worth of dental work, are yellowing and rather crooked.

You've got a nice tan, says Nodge. *Been somewhere nice?*

Madrid. Had a month. There's a great scene out there. Just made marriage legal. Had the Pride celebrations.

Do you go to Spain often?

Matter of fact I'm half-Spanish. My mother is from Barcelona. Born there, anyway.

So how long before you get to work at John Lewis? Or World of Leather?

End of next month, hopefully. What kind of a cab driver are you? Minicabs?

I've done the knowledge and everything. Black London. Hackney Carriage.

Nodge reaches in his bag and takes out his gold and green oval London Cab Driver badge that he usually wears on a lanyard round his neck.

You come across like a cab driver, come to think of it.

Fat and ignorant?

Seen it all, done it all. Your basic London cynic.

I'm not a cynic, says Nodge. *I'm a realist.*

All cynics think they're realists. So who have you had in the back of your cab lately?

You're not really going to ask me that, are you?

I've got a very uninteresting mindset. I'm Welsh. Well, Hispano-Welsh.

Me too, actually.

You're Welsh too?

No, uninteresting. That's the problem. I'd have been much better in the closet, maybe in the 1950s. Gays are just meant to be so interesting, or stylish, or special, or . . . something, and I'm not.

I doubt that the 1950s would have really been much better.

I did have someone quite interesting the other day as a matter of fact. William Hague.

William Hague?

The shadow home secretary.

I know who William Hague is. Is he really one of us?

Overweight?

A member of the family.

Couldn't quite say. We talked about politics. I thought it was safer than asking if he was queer.

Are you a Tory then?

Labour party member. Card carrying.

Hard core, is it?

Not really. Long time ago perhaps. Militant and all that. When I was a kid. Not anymore. Fraser though, he's dead appropriate. Full on head-banger. Makes for a lot of friction between us. He hates my opinions more than a Tory's. Like I've betrayed the cause. I'm like: 'To secure for the workers by hand or by brain the full fruits of their industry and the most equitable distribution thereof.'

Old school.

I'm not even that anymore. Met too many trade unionists. Printers. Train drivers. Selfish cunts, the lot them. Soft left, Fraser calls me. Or limp left. Says it's like a disease.

So what did he say?

Who?

Hague.

Wasn't very forthcoming. But he said that Theresa May was right. They did have a problem in being seen as the nasty party. So they're working on that. He was quite a nice bloke actually. I liked him.

I vote Tory myself, says Owen, cheerfully. *Wet variety. Can't bear the bloody Labour party. Now that Section 28's gone I don't need to be grinding that axe anymore. Tatchell and all those self-righteous little poofs.*

Owen finishes his cake and licks his lips. They are short, thick and slightly purplish.

I like you, he says.

That's nice, says Nodge. *I like your tan.*

How long have you been with the Ancient of Days? Or should I say the Ancient of Gays?

A few years.

Never seen you on the scene. Where do you go?

Fridge. G.A.Y. The usual. I'm not really a scene sort of guy though. That's more Fraser. I'm more of a cup of cocoa and a biscuit sort.

Nodge turns his face to the window. He sees Fraser leaving the gym, walking out into the street. He hasn't bothered to say goodbye. Owen follows his eye line.

I'm keener on him than he is on me, I think. Also he's away a lot.

How come?

He's an airline pilot.

Glamorous.

He's with EasyJet. More like being a bus driver.

So how do you keep yourself amused when he's gone?

Work. Telly. Football.

You're a footie fan?

For my sins.

Me too. Unfortunately I support QPR, so it's mainly suffering.

Nodge leans forward.

I'm a Hoops fan too!

You poor, sad little man.

They laugh.

Bit of a shot in the dark this, but I'm going to the game on Saturday.
I've got a spare ticket. Do you want to come? says Owen.

Nodge stares at the space Fraser left behind him as he
marched off down the street.

Why not?

Great.

Just one thing, though.

There's always one thing.

I'm realistic, Owen. Fraser is more ripped, better looking, cooler and
richer than me. I don't have much to offer him, to tell you the truth.

That's not true.

No, it is true. At least on a physical level. So what I offer him,
chiefly, is loyalty. He wanted a steady boyfriend. Someone he could
rely on. I am that for him.

I see.

Nodge pauses while he waits for this to sink in.

So do you still want me to come to the match? says Nodge.

Absolutely. Why wouldn't I?

Just being a realist.

Reality can change, says Owen, finishing his muffin with relish then burping and rubbing his stomach with a big, pink, fleshy hand.

* * *

The Spring Fair on Hampstead Heath is in full swing, with a fanfare of bludgeoning, blaring pop and lights shining in the greasy dark like illuminated boiled sweets, sticky and unhealthy. The night is expanding, suffocating the twilight in its grip, and there is pale mist on the breaths of the families, tourists and lovers who parade through the grassy alleyways splayed with coir mats that separate the glowing, glowering attractions. Colin notices black clouds pressing in on the horizon over Highgate Village. It is damp but free from rain for the time being.

Colin waits by the entrance. He is wearing his new grey North Face fleece, an exact copy of his previous one, which Roxy insisted on him throwing away because it had too many moth holes, and his QPR woolly hat, which his mother bought him on his twenty-third birthday, eleven years ago, and which bears an ancient yellowing sweat stain around the inside brow.

Roxy is late, as usual, but only ten minutes so far. The average is more like twenty. Colin has become used to it over the past few years, but still finds it irritating. He works out how long the journey is from Brent Cross to Hampstead, and decides she has no particular excuse but knows that it makes no difference anyway because she is Roxy and this is what Roxy does and he has given up on trying to change her.

Ten minutes later, sure enough, she arrives, hair ironed blonde now in East European pornstar style. In her pocket, he spots a bottle of WKD Orange protruding from her hip-hop puffa jacket, which makes her look twice her normal size. And one in the other pocket too, he sees, as she totters on three-inch wedge heels that sink into the damp ground.

She has already put away three vodka tonics in the pub before leaving Brent Cross. She has been drinking because today is the day she is thinking of breaking up with Colin but cannot quite make the decision, or believe in herself enough to pluck up the courage, or find the cruelty. Colin is so helpless and she pities him and she is also scared to be on her own again.

Living, as she does now, in Colin's flat is pleasant, much more so than the poky flat-share in Neasden she was suffering before she moved in with him after she was evicted from her own place in Finchley for not paying her rent. Colin has uncomplainingly covered all her debts for several years now, and stood by her without comment as she ran up still more, encouraged by the avalanche of credit card offers that fall through their letterbox every week.

Everyone, it appears, wants her trade – the National Trust, Oxfam, every corporation, charity and chain store is pushing credit cards, crack to unwitting whores. For that's what she is, Roxy says to herself, a credit whore. Colin is now on a titanic salary at Sony – something in six figures he has hinted, though has never given her the exact sum – and has nothing much else to spend his money on. He has no material interests.

It is an arrangement, more than anything else, of reciprocal convenience.

Now close to forty, Roxy feels fewer and fewer eyes on her, and although in some ways it is a boon to be free of the catcalls and wolf whistles, her sense of insecurity has grown along with her relief. Her stock she judges to be falling precipitously. She has failed to get the promotion she expected at Brent Cross, and knows she will be stranded as Assistant Manager for the months or years until they decide to get someone younger in.

Already the new manager, five years her junior, looks upon her with a flinty eye, picking up on her every mistake, punishing every oversight. Time presses hard on her imagination, chastening, reproaching, threatening. Roxy looks at a high-velocity ride in front of her, in which the seats are packed into plastic crocodiles – red neon spells out 'Neverland Express'.

She turns her mind to Colin, for whom she has soft feelings which sometimes she presents to herself as love. His artlessness, his need, speaks to some buried need of her own, to mother him, which she cannot deny. As the party years drift away from her, Colin marks a transition into some kind of adulthood which, she knows now, she cannot put off forever.

She admits it to herself; she finds him uninspiring. He mainly passes his spare time playing video games or watching football. The rest of the time he is working, sometimes seven days a week, sometimes fourteen hours a day. Veronica, her firm friend ever since their day shopping together after her pregnancy test, has urged her to make a decision one way or the other, but she is reluctant – partly, she admits to both

Vronky and herself, out of inertia, and partly because she feels sorry for Colin. He makes few demands on her other than her cooking for him occasionally – always the same things, usually with chips – granting him brief and undemanding sex and letting her spend his money on soft furnishings and accoutrements for the flat.

Both she and Colin are relieved to have left the cold, painful world of mid-life dating, but lately for Roxy the price of security has been feeling too high and she cannot escape the suspicion that she is selling herself short. A manager at the Starbucks coffee concession next door to Top Shop has been flirting with her, an Italian with an oiled quiff and a slight harelip. She has been flirting back, but lately he seems to have lost interest. An old story.

She puts her arm around Colin – under the puffa jacket, she is wearing only a sleeveless Primark blouse matched with a Joseph suede skirt – a gesture that always makes Colin feel uncomfortable since she is half an inch taller than him. He smells the alcohol on her breath and wrinkles his forehead. She has bullied him into coming this evening – he wanted to continue developing a new PVP game for Sony, now close to completion. He still has not beaten her at *GoldenEye*, despite his spending many hours training to do so. This, more than anything else, cements and maintains his desire for her. It bestows on her mystique.

After a few seconds of picking their way through the discarded sweet wrappers and soft drink cans and cartons that litter the walkways, he loosely shrugs her arm off. He doesn't mind so much that she drinks but he finds the reminder of his inferior height faintly galling.

What's up with you, you misery guts? says Roxy, a faint slur in her voice.

Why do you think something's up?

They walk silently past a rollercoaster, a painted Edwardian-style merry-go-round and a spiral slide illuminated by yellow and red lights. There is a tatty Ghost Train with plastic skeletons suspended on lanyards, a merry-go-round for toddlers featuring giant plastic teacups, and bumper cars that shed showers of sparks at their connections with the electrical grid on the roof of the dodgem arena. Most people at the fair seem bored or listless. The brightness of the music seems to contain a note of desperation, of reassurance without conviction.

One ride is called 'Enter the Dragon' and features a single vast red Chinese-style dragon belching artificial smoke and flames. Colin stares at this as if transfixed – the lion eyes, the vulture's wings, the snake's scales. Everything that might eat you. He turns away without even working out what the kick you're meant to get out of it is. Fear chased with relief, he supposes, same as most of the rides.

Roxy stops at a shooting range with an array of enormous stuffed toys behind the counter. Giraffes, monkeys, cows with devil horns, all in colours that jangle the nerves.

I want one of those, says Roxy.

Winnie the Pooh?

She points at a sky-blue, three-foot-high giant My Little Pony with a lurid, mulitcoloured mane and tail.

Love Rainbow Dash. She acts first, asks questions later. Self-obsessed. Irresponsible.

You're a bit old to have a stuffed toy pony.

In the films there's always a scene where the boy shoots a target and wins a toy for his girlfriend.

We're not in a film. Anyway, it's the most fancy thing there. You have to get two hundred points to win it. We'd be here all night.

I'll accept an Eeyore. You only have to get 120 points for that.

Why Eeyore?

Because it will remind me of you.

Better a depressed donkey than a fluorescent pony.

Oh, come on, Colinder.

Don't call me that. You know I don't like pet names.

You call me Rocks.

Rocks is a cool name. A colinder is used for draining vegetables.

Colin takes out his wallet and hands ten pounds over to the feral looking coster with a neckerchief, a thick gold earring and a five o'clock shadow standing behind the rack of toys. The coster unsmilingly hands him an air rifle with a barrel that even Colin can tell is slightly bent.

Can I get a different one?

Looking sour, the coster hands him another one, with a slightly less bent barrel. This time Colin doesn't bother to complain. He shoots twenty-five times and scores a total of 35 points. During this time he changes the rifle twice.

You're shit, says Roxy, cheerfully.

All the barrels are twisted.

He looks accusingly at the coster, who smirks.

I'm hungry, she says, swigging on the WKD drink. *I'm going to get some candyfloss. Want some?*

Candyfloss and alcopops?

Like fish and chips or cheese and pickle. A classic. Come on. You have to have candyfloss at the fair. One hundred and ten per cent.

I might have a Westler's.

No onions. Ketchup only if it's proper Heinz.

That's it.

Roxy totters over towards the candyfloss stand and reaches in her bag for her purse, a Louis Vuitton Multicolore with its childish, lurid monograms. Colin bought it for her last birthday. It hurt him to pay that much for a bit of canvas, but if he knows one thing about Roxy it's that she likes bags.

How much for one of those big pony things? Colin asks the villainous-looking carney who now has a damp, unlit roll-up clenched between his jagged teeth and sputum-flecked lips.

You have to win them, he says, looking past Colin as if for more custom.

If I wanted to buy one off you?

Not that simple. They pull in the punters. Loss of takings. I'll have to be throwing that in the mix.

What if someone wins them anyway?

The carney gives Colin a look to say, *That ain't going to happen.* He slowly lights his roll-up with a battered brass Zippo, screws up his eyes as if considering the conundrum, then abandoning the problem, says:

Fifty quid for the pony.

I'll give you a pony for it. That's seems appropriate. Pony for a pony.

Twenty-five sovs? No, mate.

That's got to be twice what it's worth. How much is the Eeyore?

Same price.

It's half the size.

Better quality.

Better quality what?

Stuffing. Look, do you want one of them or not? I haven't got all night.

You have, though. Haven't you? All night is exactly what you've got. Alright, I'll give you thirty.

Forty.

Thirty-five.

Forty.

Alright.

Colin hands over the money, then mutters under his breath.

Chiseller.

Colin isn't sure whether the carney has heard him or not. The doubt dissolves when he takes down Rainbow Dash and wipes his hands unashamedly on her mane, leaving a grubby mark on the vibrant spectrum. He limply holds it out to Colin. Colin reaches to take it.

Thank you, he mutters.

Instead of handing it over, the carney lets the pony drop on the pile of other soft toys then turns away to serve another customer. Colin reaches over and picks it up.

When Roxy comes back, wielding a burger and a bright pink cloud of candyfloss, he brandishes the pony at her. She squeals and skips in the air.

You won me Rainbow Dash! My hero!

Bought it actually. Cost me forty quid from that shark behind the counter.

Roxy's shoulders drop and she hands the burger to Colin then takes the giant pony with her spare hand. Colin feels the sting of her disappointment.

What's the difference? says Colin.

What are you talking about?

No, tell me, Rocks.

It's fine. It was very sweet of you.

You're bullshitting.

I know I'm being ridiculous.

About what?

You were meant to win it for me. That's what happens in the films.

Fine. If you don't want it.

He takes the pony off her and drops it in an overflowing litter bin, where it perches as if about to take flight on its little rainbow wings. Scowling, she immediately rescues the pony from the bin but it has upended a beaker of some blue sticky drink, and its contents are soaked into the mane.

Look what you've made me do.

Roxy. Stop it. I'll buy you a real pony if you want one.

She laughs, then notices his flat tone.

You're serious, aren't you?

Of course I am.

Why would you do that?

Colin mutters something.

Can't hear you, says Roxy.

Cos I bloody love you, don't I?

Roxy stares at him, then decides to skim over it.

It's not going to be much fun keeping a pony on the balcony of the flat in Hammersmith.

We can move to the country. Clean air. Peace and quiet.

Boredom. Lights out at nine.

They walk on in silence for several minutes until the air heals and no more thunder can be heard. Roxy is still clinging to the sticky Rainbow Dash with one arm, while her bag hangs loosely from the other.

She finds herself to be faintly stunned. It is the first time Colin has ever told her that he loves her. She keeps turning the phrase over in her head like a gewgaw in a flea market that may be junk or precious.

Can we go in here?

She is pointing to a hall of mirrors.

Colin nods, pays the entrance fee, and they press through the narrow entrance.

Roxy stands in front of the first one and sees her body stretch and elevate. She bursts out laughing.

Hey look at me! I'm skinny!

But Colin is standing in front of his own mirror, fascinated. It makes his head huge and his body tiny.

Bighead! calls Roxy.

Colin moves on to the next one. This time it makes his stomach enormous and his mouth tiny. He finds this disturbing, as if it has captured his inner life, and switches his eyes back to Roxy.

Now Roxy is standing in front of a mirror that squashes her outward so she is short and fat.

Now this is what I call fat.

Next to her is a real mirror, which gives her the true image.

Suddenly I feel undernourished.

Next, they go on the merry-go-round. Up and down. Round and round. Going nowhere. When they finally get off, Roxy, still holding the pony, looks like she is going to be sick. She even bends for a moment as if to puke.

As she bends, out of nowhere a hooded figure – a skeletal man with waxy skin and black stubble – materializes from the shadows and makes a grab at Roxy's new handbag. Roxy screams and holds on furiously. Colin, without hesitation, leaps at the figure and they struggle. Then another figure appears from behind the first one, tall and powerful, and punches Colin square in the face.

Colin falls to the ground. Roxy screams again, but still will not let go of the bag. Colin is bleeding heavily from the nose. The thieves, seeing the attention they have drawn from the crowd, finally give up and run back behind the tents. Colin, on the floor, has his legs drawn up into a foetal position.

Roxy feels a rush of tenderness at this display of chivalry. She bends down beside him, takes a make-up cleansing wipe out of the bag, which she keeps clutched tight to her chest, and wipes his face. He looks up at her, winded and helpless. He mutters something which she can't quite hear.

What? Do I want to be carried? It looks like you need carrying more than me.

Do you want to get married, I said, says Colin, faintly.

What?

Do you want to be married? I mean — will you marry me?

The merry-go-round starts up again and the noise increases. Roxy watches a little boy sit and watch them, serenely eating a toffee apple. Everyone else is ignoring Colin on the floor.

What — to you?

Of course to me. You . . . silly tart.

He begins to laugh, which seems to cause him pain, and he stops.

I don't know, says Roxy.

I'm sorry. I'm not doing this right.

He forces himself to sit upright, and blood pours out of his nose down his fleece.

You've ruined your new jacket.

But will you? says Colin, persisting.

I don't know, says Roxy.

Oh. Okay.

The merry-go-round gradually decelerates and grinds to a halt. Roxy sees his disappointment, the crumpling of his face, his struggle to control it.

The lights blur in her mind from the shock of the attempted robbery. The alcohol and candyfloss curdling in her stomach. Everything is whorls and colours. It is all madness and unreason. Swirling, rocking, rising, falling.

Look, says Colin. *I've got something.*

He reaches in the zip pocket of his bloodied fleece and takes out a blue velvet box.

Will you? says Colin.

The carousel music begins to slow, the horses becoming sluggish, weary.

She opens the box, inspects the ring that it contains in astonishment. The diamond on it is large. Very large.

Maybe, says Roxy.

Colin, tasting blood, smiles.

* * *

Leaving the Loftus Road ground with Owen feels strange to Nodge. Fraser is shuttling back and forth to Ibiza for three more days. Nodge doesn't ask him what he gets up to while he's away. He left that morning with nothing more than a peck on the cheek for Nodge, who was staying over at his flat to look after Harvey.

Nodge has said nothing to Fraser about Owen. Not, he tells himself, because there is anything suspicious about him meeting up with Owen but because Fraser, despite being openly promiscuous himself, is also always unreasonably jealous.

He and Owen walk slowly towards the Bush Ranger along the Goldhawk Road. The game against Bristol City was pedestrian, even after Kevin Gallen scored a penalty in the nineteenth minute and sealed a weary victory.

Shall we got and get a drink? says Nodge.

Love to.

Owen leans over and kisses him on the cheek. Nodge turns away.

You heard what I told you before. About loyalty.

Look, it's the only gays in the village!

A knot of lager-can-wielding Bristol City fans, having noticed the kiss, are leering at them and shouting. Nodge and Owen ignore the hooligans and carry on walking.

Nodge takes his Blackberry out to check his messages. Just the normal – Frankie complaining about Veronica giving him a hard time, Fraser wanting to check that he'd fed the dog and taken him for a walk, his sister asking him to babysit his nieces.

His thinking is interrupted by a faintly familiar voice drifting out of the crowd. Even before he consciously realizes who it is, Nodge feels the muscles in his back knit with tension.

Love still blooms, eh, Nodge?

Nodge turns and finds himself face to face with Tony Diamonte, handsome as ever, sinuous, imposing, serpentine. The two of them are rooted to the spot for a moment.

Who's this geeze? says Tony, casually nodding towards Owen, as if he and Nodge had never fallen out, although it has been four years since he last set eyes him.

He contemplates ignoring Tony, cannot find it in himself.

*This is Owen. Owen, this is Diamond Tony. An old ...
acquaintance of mine.*

Nice to meet you, Owen. Tony holds out a hand. Owen takes it and Tony crushes his fingers.

They were crap, weren't they? says Tony.

So what's new? says Owen.

They have their moments, says Tony. *We all have our moments.*

Nodge is still staring at Tony. The money is still on him. He guesses a Margaret Howell shirt. Farhi trousers. And that old Nick Ashley red silk-lined Crombie that he used to wear back in the day. But they all look a bit tatty, a bit tired. The crowd swirls around them, pushing them this way and that.

It's good to see you, Nodge. You're looking well. Fit.

Haven't seen you since the golf game, responds Nodge, at the same time looking around for a means of escape. *That didn't go well.*

No. But at least I won.

You didn't win. Frankie did.

Except that he cheated.

Never proven. The result stands.

Well. Bygones and all that. How was Frankie's wedding?

Few years ago now. Look, Tony . . .

I wasn't invited.

I'm aware of that.

The pressure of the crowd increases.

We should get a drink sometime. You, me and the boys. Colin and Frankie. The old crew.

Nodge says nothing.

You should come along, Taffy. We used to be great friends, me and Nodge.

Owen. My name is Owen.

I'm assuming you're Welsh. Ow-en. He puts on a Welsh singsong.

Things change, says Nodge.

They've certainly changed for me, says Tony, his face set in a mirthless smile which Nodge cannot read.

The weight of the crowd cannot be resisted anymore. They are caught up in two different streams.

Tony reaches in his pocket and produces a card.

Take it, he says, the smile dissolving into something more genuine, something like affection. *And say hello to Frankie for me.*

He passes the card. Then the river of fans takes him and propels him away, swiftly out of sight, while Nodge and Owen are carried in the opposite direction.

They are back on the Uxbridge Road before they are released from the grip of the crowd, passing police horses, stewards in yellow tabards, hot dog stands.

Everyone's wearing one of those fucking tabards nowadays.

EU law, says Nodge, still dazed. *Health and safety. Like a virus. The world is going to turn reflective yellow.*

So who's this 'Diamond Tony'? asks Owen.

Someone I knew once.

What was the golf game?

We all had a game of golf together. It didn't turn out well. In fact it was the end of everything between us. I don't want to talk about it.

He takes Tony's card out of his pocket. It is decorated with a skull and crossbones and reads

ANTHONY DIAMONTE
Pirate Hairdresser

'I'll come to your home and cut you'

Good-looking guy, says Owen.

I haven't really given it much thought.

Is he queer? I can usually tell, but I'm not sure about him.

Standard Alpha male unless he's undergone a conversion.

The crowd is still thinning out. They are now approaching the Bush Ranger on the Goldhawk Road.

I'm sorry, says Owen.

What about?

That I kissed you. It was stupid. Especially in front of that pack of bumpkins.

Doesn't matter.

It was wrong of me. You told me it was off limits. It's just that . . . I find you very attractive.

Nodge grimaces doubtfully.

Sure you do.

But I do.

Shall we get that drink? I'm parched.

They enter the pub and go up to the first floor terrace. The tables outside are packed, but inside, it's reasonably quiet. Owen goes to the bar and orders a pint of Stella and a Diet Coke for Nodge.

I'm starving, he says when he returns with the drinks. *I've ordered us a couple of pepperoni pizzas. You're not a veggie, are you, or anything?*

Nodge shakes his head. He takes a sip of his lager, and checks his watch.

Do you mind if I sit next to you?

Very cosy, says Owen.

The food arrives with surprising rapidity.

I suspect the involvement of a microwave, says Owen, prodding at the soggy crust with his finger.

Nodge begins to pick at the salad on the side of the plate while Owen tucks in.

Not as bad as you'd expect, says Owen.

I'm not that hungry, says Nodge.

You weren't hungry last time we met either.

So?

Now Nodge seems irritated. Minutes later, Owen has nearly finished his food while Nodge's remains more or less untouched.

I used to have a girlfriend, says Owen. *Well, a fag hag really — and for years she would always sit next to me. I thought it was because she liked me. Or was even flirting with me.*

Without even noticing that he's doing it, Nodge pushes the plate half an inch away from him.

So she turned out to have an eating disorder. She couldn't stand people watching her eat. It disgusted her. If she sat next to them, she didn't have to see them watching her.

That's interesting, says Nodge.

Are you sure you're not hungry? says Owen.

Nodge listlessly picks up a sliver of rubbery cheese and chews disinterestedly on it.

I'm really not, as a matter of fact.

Mind if I . . . ?

Not at all.

Owen reaches over and starts to wolf down the food. Nodge sucks joylessly on his Diet Coke.

How long have you not been hungry for then? says Owen, cautiously.

Without warning, Nodge flushes and turns on him.

What the fuck are you talking about?

Don't get angry. What's the matter?

I'm sick of you playing fucking mind games with me. Who are you, anyway? Some bloke I met at the gym for five minutes.

Come on, Nodge . . .

But Nodge is on his feet.

This is stupid. I've got a boyfriend. I don't know what I'm doing out with you. I don't know what I'm doing. Let's just cut our losses, shall we? See you around.

Nodge walks out of the bar, leaving Owen staring into the depths of his lager, as if looking for clues there.

* * *

Nodge heads back to Fraser's, still dressed in his blue and white hoops. He can't let go of the anger, or quite understand where the anger comes from or why it is has surfaced with such force.

The lights, to his surprise, at Fraser's flat are switched on. On the sofa, in his boxer shorts, laid out, his perfect body shining in the half-light, is Fraser, Harvey at his feet.

Surprise, says Fraser, without looking up from the DVD he is watching.

Pretending to be undaunted, Nodge picks up the DVD box and reads the title.

'Charlie's Angels'. Really?

It's a classic.

What are you doing here then?

Flight cancelled. Some kind of terrorist scare apparently. They'll probably blame it on Muslims anyway, even if it's an abandoned sandwich box.

Nodge reaches across and kisses him on the lips. Fraser barely responds.

Get me a drink, would you, love?

What do you want?

A Prosecco would be lovely.

Nodge goes to the fridge, takes his scarf off.

Aren't you going to ask where I've been, says Nodge, as he pops the cork and pours the drink.

No, says Fraser. *Though I'm imagining, from the blue and white hoops you're wearing and the overpowering smell of communal male sweat, that you've been to the ballet.*

It would just be nice if you showed an interest.

Nodge hands him his Prosecco. Fraser takes it without saying thank you. Nodge goes back to the kitchen, and returns with a beer and a small packet of taco chips. Fraser shoots him a look, and Nodge leaves the packet unopened.

Can I watch the football results?

In a minute. So who did you go with?

Nodge takes a sip of the beer which he does not enjoy. He feels the tightness of his belt at his waist. He feels the pull of his shirt on his stomach muscles with their pad of fat.

What makes you think I went with anyone?

Isn't that what football fans do? Bonding over primitive chants of abuse?

I saw an old friend.

Fraser has taken up the remote, Nodge assumes to switch it to the football results. But instead he presses the fast-forward button.

Do you remember me telling you about Tony Diamonte?

Who?

Tony Diamonte. Diamond Tony.

Vaguely.

Me and Frankie and Colin and him were all best friends. You remember. And he turned out to be a homophobe.

Can't remember.

And a racist. And a drug addict.

Is he the one that went bankrupt? The hairdresser?

That's him.

You showed me some photos once, I think. What's wrong with this fucking thing?

Fraser is shaking the remote angrily.

Probably run out of battery.

Very good-looking guy? Horns and the hand round his neck?

That's the one.

Fraser gives up with the remote.

You might as well watch your results.

He lifts himself off the sofa in a single fluid movement. His muscles ripple under his skin. The soft bulge in his boxers. Nodge reaches out a hand and strokes his stomach as he passes.

I'm tired. I've been stuck at the airport all day. Go and have a wank or something.

Fraser drains what is left of his Prosecco, and disappears into his bedroom.

Nodge goes back into the kitchen and silently opens the packet of taco chips. He puts one in his mouth and, very quietly, begins to chew. A minute later the packet is gone.

Ten minutes later he goes to the loo and throws up, closing the door tightly so Fraser will not hear him.

* * *

Later that night, when Fraser is in bed, Nodge picks up the phone and dials Owen's number. Owen picks up immediately.

Hello?

Owen? It's Nodge.

Oh. Hello there. How are you?

Never mind that. I'm ringing to tell you that I'm sorry for the way I behaved today.

It's alright.

I don't know what came over me.

Well — no, I won't say it.

What?

I'd quite like to come over you.

Nodge laughs, then checks himself.

Stop it. Please. Look. Anyway. I just wanted to say that I was sorry. That's all.

Okay then.

Are you angry with me?

I'm not angry with you.

Maybe we'll bump into one another again.

I hope so.

It's probably inevitable anyway.

Goodbye, Nodge.

See you soon, I expect.

They both wait for the other to hang up the phone. It is Nodge who, finally, places the receiver back on the cradle. But even then, he stays by the phone for some time, as if expecting it to ring at any second.

* * *

Sunday morning at Colin's flat. Roxy has made him a breakfast of Wall's sausages, fried egg, fried bread, unsmoked back bacon and button mushrooms, carefully washed and peeled, cut into two halves and fried in butter. The tea is Typhoo with two and one-third sugars.

She places the plate in front of Colin, who is working his way through the *Sunday Times* supplements, clattering a knife and fork down next to the unopened Business section.

That looks awesome.

You've got about ten minutes to eat it.

I won't need that long, he says, carefully cutting the rind from the bacon.

Don't give yourself heartburn.

Colin now has a mouthful of mushrooms.

Do you really want me to come? says Roxy. *As in, really really?*

You might like it more than you think.

You don't even believe in it anymore.

It's part of our culture, isn't it? Our heritage.

I haven't been to church since I was eight years old. And I was bored fuckless then. Also, I've got a rotten hangover.

You've always got a rotten hangover. Look, I'll never ask you to go again. Just this once. We are meant to be getting married there. Just do it for me.

Anything for a laugh, I suppose.

Thanks, doll.

She goes to their bedroom, throws off her towelling dressing gown and picks out a pink baby-doll dress and a giant black hat with a filigree of lace on it. Minutes later she reappears in the kitchen, applying lipstick the colour of pickled beetroot.

You're not really going to wear that, are you? says Colin, finishing the last of his fried bread with a contrived burp.

I've seen some of these black ladies, what they wear to church. The hat's a big thing.

Your dress is a bit short.

You don't tell me what to wear.

Colin turns his attention back to the paper. The headline reads: 'Countdown to War'.

So that big march we went on did a fat lot of good then, he says.

Saddam might still bottle it.

In the next three days?

Serves him right anyway. Gassing Kurds and that.

Ten minutes later, they leave the flat and make their way to the church. The bells chime for the start of service as they approach.

I knew we'd be late, says Colin. *Get a move on.*

It was you who wanted a fry-up. Anyway, what does it matter? God will forgive us.

How do you know?

That's his USP, isn't it? That's what he does.

Tottering in high heels, Roxy makes her way along the street, past the ancient graveyard and into the church ten minutes late. Colin is dressed in a sober grey suit. The church is around one half full. To Roxy's surprise, a good number of the congregants are young, well-dressed white couples with children. The remainder are largely older black men and women.

How come all the yuppies?

Good church school at the end of the road, mutters Colin. *Pay or pray.*

A few heads turn and nod at Colin, then eyes switch to Roxy. Roxy grins back cheerfully.

Ello. Morning. Ello, she mouths.

They find a pew and sit on it.

Christ, this is uncomfortable, she whispers to Colin.

It's not a boutique cinema.

Why have they got to make your arse hurt to be a Christian?

Yours is well enough insulated.

A loud '*shhhh*' comes from a ferocious-looking black woman standing behind them in a cerise hat with elaborate folds of lace, bows and crimps, topped with a riot of grey feathers.

Sorry love, says Roxy, adjusting her own hat, which keeps bumping against Colin's head.

The service starts with a hymn which Roxy does not know the tune of, but groans along with anyway. The sermon is something about living forever if you just put yourself into the arms of Jesus.

The vicar leads a prayer for peace in the Middle East. He is a tall scrawny man with thinning hair and stooped shoulders. He wears rectangular glasses behind which he is blinking furiously, giving the impression of two tiny, faulty televisions. The congregation dutifully mumbles along, reading from the hymn-and-prayer pamphlets that they have been handed at the entrance. Colin steals a glance at Roxy, who is signalling her boredom with shifts on the pew and frequent yawns. She has her mobile phone out and is checking it.

Put it away, will you, Rocks?

You're never going to make me do this again, right?

I'm never going to make you do this again. Now put it away. Please.

Sulkily, she puts her phone back in her bag and focuses on the vicar. The prayer finishes and the offertory is passed round, a dirty velvet plum-coloured bag with an elasticated collar. Inexorably, it makes its way towards them. Roxy fumbles in her purse.

Do they take plastic?

Don't be stupid.

I got no change. All I got is a Pavarotti.

When, a few seconds later, the collection bag arrives full of coins and a few buttons, she cheerfully drops the ten-pound note in. Colin is shocked.

Ten quid! What are you doing?

All for a good cause.

And now would you please share the peace, says the vicar.

A piece of what?

The peace. The peace, says Colin.

What's the piece? says Roxy

She sees everyone on the pews standing and beginning to break ranks and wander and start shaking hands with other members of the congregation.

You never told me nothing about this. It's a bit bloody weird.

A huge black man stuffed into a small powder-blue suit manifests behind Roxy. She turns and he holds out his hand.

Peace be with you, he says, in a small piping voice that surprises her.

Thanks, says Roxy, staring at the proffered hand.

No, like this, hisses Colin at Roxy. He turns to the man and takes his hand.

And peace be with you.

They shake hands. Now the man holds his hand out to Roxy. Roxy, awkwardly, takes it.

Peace be with you, pipes the man, smiling broadly.

Yeh, and with you then.

The man turns away and starts shaking the hands of a well-dressed, fashionable young couple who greet him slightly overenthusiastically.

That was easy, wasn't it? says Colin.

He tickled my palm with his finger when he was shaking my hand, the dirty old bastard.

But Colin has turned away, offering the peace to an elderly woman with starched hair. Roxy stubbornly sits back down on the pew.

Some minutes later, it is time for the Anglican Communion. Neither Colin nor Roxy choose to take it, instead watching the snaking queue of the well-dressed and overdressed. One man holds a mobile phone to his ear as he takes the communion wafer into his mouth. The vicar says nothing, blesses him, and merely passes on to the next congregant.

The body of Christ. The body of Christ. The body of Christ.

* * *

When they leave the church they shake hands with the vicar at the door, who greets them with enthusiasm and rhapsodizes over their forthcoming 'nuptials'. Then, instead of heading out directly through the gate and back to the car, Colin leads Roxy along the side of the church.

Where we going?

To say hello to Olive.

Who's Olive?

My old mum.

No. I've done my bit. I need to lie down now and think sinful thoughts for a while.

She takes a packet of sweets out of her pocket, then unwraps and starts to chew on a Black Jack. But Colin carries on walking and she follows. She accidentally drops the Black Jack wrapper and bends for a moment at a grass verge to pick it up while Colin pushes ahead.

He reaches a small grave in the corner of the churchyard, untended, with a black shiny marble headstone, an engraved gold crucifix and the inscription in gold lettering.

OLIVE BURDEN, BELOVED WIFE OF WILLIAM.
10 FEB, 1931 – 16 MARCH, 1999.
THE SUN SHINED BRIGHTER BECAUSE
SHE WAS HERE.

Hello, Mum, says Colin.
Colin stands rigid in front of the headstone, nodding slowly.
I'm getting married, he whispers to the ground.
He stands there still.
I think you'd like her.
Not that you ever liked anyone much.
You never thought I'd find anyone, did you?
Yes, Mum. But not like I did you.
She's pretty, yeh. Bit on the heavy side.
Who cares what Frankie thinks?
She's going to be my wife, not his.
He straightens up. He stares at the green carpet of grass with its hopeful, thrusting punctuation of stone. An exhausted leaf falls from a tree and lands on his shoe. He reaches down and wipes it off with his hand, leaving a smear of decay.

Out of nowhere, he remembers going to another

graveyard, one day twenty years ago with Nodge, Frankie and Tony. They were kids. It was the closest he'd come, really, to being happy, as a teenager. He even remembers the date. The fourteenth of August. For years, the four of them would celebrate that day together in honour of their indestructible friendship. So-called. Now Frankie was married and Nodge was gay and Tony had disappeared and he had been crazed with grief and Jesus fever and only half recovered his senses.

It wasn't until Roxy said yes to him that he'd felt that happy again.

Now Roxy totters through the grass after him, cursing. She comes to a halt, steadies herself and silently examines the inscription on the gravestone.

Did it? says Roxy.

Did what?

Did the sun shine brighter?

Not really.

So why put it on there?

Don't be stupid. Everything's lies. What do you think this . . . he gestures at the church *. . . is all about. Might as well join in.*

Roxy tries to take Colin's hand but sees that it is bunched into a fist.

Shouldn't it be 'the sun shone brighter'?

What?

Not 'shined'.

Colin ignores her and simply stares at the grave. There is a cheap glass vase there with the remains of a few empty flower stalks. Roxy studies the gravestone again, this time considering the dates.

Sixty-eight. Young, really. Oh. And she died on this day. This very day.

She stops chewing the Black Jack and swallows it.

That's why you wanted me to come today.

Colin still doesn't move.

Did you love her very much?

He says nothing.

I picked these flowers.

She holds out some wildflowers she has found on the verges.

Shall I put them in the vase? Freshen it up?

Colin looks at her. He shakes his head.

Look – I know they're fairly shit flowers, Col, but . . .

He looks at them again. He takes them from her, and casts them at the stone. The wind snatches at them and scatters them.

Let's go, he says, turning briskly on his heel, leaving a small, sharp indentation at the foot of the grave, a loamy full stop.

Back on the pavement Colin leaves a trail of mud behind him. He still has earth from the grave buried in the deep tread of his shoe. He stops and tries to scrape it off with a stick. It proves sticky and glutinous. He cannot get it all out, however hard he tries.

* * *

So, Veronica. What would your life look like if you did get what you want?

Veronica has not imagined that undergoing therapy would be so hard. She has never done it in the past, before her training started. She never thought that she needed it.

Elizabeth Pember, her supervisor, has eyes that are soft, hazy even, and yet which seem to be able to take her measure at a glance. She is not what Veronica expected a therapist to look like. She is too young, for a start, perhaps the same age as Veronica, and her clothes are colourful and flamboyant rather than the expected neutral. She is wearing a gipsy headscarf and a loud red print dress with huge purple flowers on it, and kitten heels. Above her is a clock that is making a loud ticking noise which annoys and distracts Veronica.

Do you mind if we turn the clock off? It has a very loud tick.

You get used to it. I can't switch it off actually. It's wired into the mains. So. As to what you want?

Veronica laughs awkwardly.

Is that a trick question?

Let me put it more concretely. If Frankie did cut back on his job hours. If he did come home and do the chores instead. Look after China alongside you.

That would be great.

Why would it be great?

It would make me feel loved.

And if the estate agency suffered as a result. Perhaps even failed. What would that make you feel?

I suppose it would make me feel even more loved. That he had made a sacrifice.

Don't you feel loved now?

Veronica takes a long draught from the glass of water on the table and checks the clock. Only ten minutes left. She'll be glad when it's over.

I don't think he knows how to love in that way. To that degree. It's all about him. The only reason he loves me is because it's a nice feeling for him.

Do you know that for a fact?

Veronica doesn't answer.

What about sexually? Doesn't he try to satisfy you?

It excites him to make a woman satisfied. It makes him feel like a man.

Some might see your attitude as cynical.

Frankie always says I'm a romantic.

Why does he say that?

Sometimes I believe in impossible things because I want to believe in them. Or so he says.

Meaning?

I used to be into crystals and feng shui and healing and horoscopes and all that new age stuff.

That surprises me. You don't seem the type.

Because I'm medically trained? Yes, I know. I suppose I just think there are different ways of knowing. Things science can't understand.

Do you still believe in the power of crystals?

Not so much. Not at all really.

But?

I don't know. I can't quite escape the idea that there's some . . . hidden order. Purpose. Pattern. I don't know what to call it.

Some secret you can't quite uncover.

I suppose.

Do these beliefs have any impact on your relationship with your husband?

I don't know.

Are you sure?

Perhaps.

It seems to me there's something you're not saying.

Well — it's embarrassing.

This is a safe space. Where—

208

Where no one will judge me. I get it.

So?

Okay. Here goes. I remember . . . I remember, just after Frankie and I got married, I went to see a . . . this is silly, I know . . . a clairvoyant. A friend of mine, a very good friend, said this man was amazing. So I was tempted. Even though I had promised I'd leave all that stuff behind. And I gave in. On a dare almost. And she was right. He was good. Very good. He gave me all the usual cushion filler. That I was special, loving, creative, all that sort of thing. But he also seemed to know things he couldn't know. Like the fact that my husband was 'marked'. Frankie has a birthmark on his forehead, see? And he knew that I had undergone a big change in my life and another big change was coming. I'd just got married. And soon after that, I got pregnant. Anyway, I don't know if this was me imagining it, but when I told him I had got married and was pregnant, instead of looking happy for me, his face went dark. Just for a moment. Then he tried to move the subject on. But I pressed him. I asked him if the marriage was going to last. Eventually he told me that he saw me with a dark man with a tattoo somewhere on his body. He was quite clear. A tattoo, not a birthmark. Or possibly it was a charm. On a necklace. He couldn't see it clearly. Said it might be an animal of some kind. Or a part of the body. Or a part of an animal. Or both. Anyway, whoever it was it didn't sound like Frankie.

Veronica stops and takes a drink from the glass of water in front of her.

So you think that you and your husband might not be 'destined' for one another.

Something like that.

Isn't it possible that your husband could get a tattoo?

He hates tattoos. Mainly because, like I say, he is already marked.

There is a long pause. Veronica is aware that Pember is waiting for her to talk, but she decides to sit it out. It becomes like a game in her mind that she is determined to win. Eventually, her supervisor breaks the silence.

What else did this clairvoyant tell you?

Not much. That I had a difficult relationship with another, older woman. A wealthy older woman.

Who might that be?

My mother, I expect.

Not that difficult to guess at, really.

No. I suppose it's silly that I took it at all seriously.

None of this would be difficult to guess. You were either wearing a brand-new wedding ring or the ring left a mark. If you had just got married, and you were the age you were, pregnancy was likely not going to be far off. And problems with their mother aren't unusual after people get married. Or before, for that matter.

All the same.

All the same, what?

I don't know why he came out with the stuff about that tattoo or charm or whatever it is. The tall dark man, etcetera. He was so . . . specific.

Perhaps he was simply mistaken. And it's part of their technique. To give details. Makes it seem much more plausible.

Perhaps. Probably. Yes.

You don't sound convinced.

I'm trying to be.

Pember pauses.

But he was right about you having difficulties with your mother?

My mother has difficulties with Frankie. That's for sure. She doesn't think Frankie's good enough for me. She never has. From the first time

210

I met him. She's always wanted me to marry a doctor or a lawyer. An estate agent is an embarrassment to her. She thinks they're vulgar. In fact, I can't think of another profession that would have irritated her more. Perhaps a bouncer.

Just sit with that thought for a moment.

Veronica looks puzzled and feels herself shifting uncomfortably in her chair.

What are you saying?

Is there any part of you that agrees with your mother?

Of course not!

Veronica is surprised at the anger in her voice. She breathes deeply to centre herself, as her mindfulness teacher has trained her to.

You once told me that you agreed to marry Frankie on what amounted to a whim.

That's not true.

Isn't it?

I did have some funny beliefs at the time, I suppose.

Unlike believing in clairvoyance.

Touché.

Tell the story again. Of the proposal. I can't quite remember. It was at a restaurant?

Do I have to? It's embarrassing. So stupid.

Humour me.

We were at this restaurant called Angel Eyes. We'd been seeing each other for six months or thereabouts. And quite out of the blue – I genuinely hadn't expected it – Frankie asked him to marry him. And I wasn't sure, I wasn't sure. I really wasn't.

Why weren't you sure?

I . . . I don't know. Something deep inside. Can't say. There was a hesitation. Isn't that how everybody feels? So then. Well, it sounds crazy. Looking back, it was crazy. I believed — see, I believed I had a guardian angel. Watching over me. I was very into all that new age stuff then. You grow out of it. At least I did. Anyway, when Frankie asked me I asked my guardian angel what to say, and it seemed like I was sent a sign.

Ah. Yes, now I remember. So you really had no choice, as it were. If your angel was telling you to do it.

I still had a choice.

But someone — something — was telling you to do it. And someone else was telling you not to do it.

My mother. Yes.

There is a long pause during which neither of them speaks.

Do you think your mother has your best interests at heart? Pember asks.

She has her best interests at heart.

Like your husband. Who has his own best interests at heart. Or so you believe. Who loves you because of how it will make him feel. Not for your sake. Who loves you but doesn't behave as if he loves you. Again, like your mother.

I'm not sure what I'm supposed to say to that. What are you driving at?

And you've got a child yourself now. What would you do for her?

Anything.

Another long pause.

Do you think that your mother felt differently?

Veronica struggles for an answer, but cannot dredge one from her depths.

Pember writes a short note, then looks up from her notebook as if it is a cue to change the subject.

How is your training coming along, do you think?

It's a long haul. But I'm loving it, actually. Although it's quite unsettling in some ways. Trying to go that deep.

Remind me. Why did you decide to embark on this course? You had a good career. Good salary and prospects.

I found the job was depressing.

Why did you go into clinical pathology in the first place?

To please my mother, of course. A sort of compromise, since I didn't want to become a GP. Not that she was satisfied. Not in the least.

Perhaps she never will be satisfied.

That's probably true.

So why do you keep trying to please her?

I don't. I married Frankie, after all.

There is another long silence. Again Veronica wins the exchange and Pember speaks first.

Have you considered the possibility that it might have also have been a reaction against your mother?

In what way?

Some kind of rebellion? Or revenge?

Veronica ignores the question.

I don't understand the way I am with him sometimes. With Frankie. He just makes me so angry.

How does that anger express itself?

The usual ways. Snapping. Nagging. Bitching.

Anything else?

Like what?

I don't know.

Veronica stares out of the window.

I sort of did something I shouldn't have done.

What?

I sort of threw an ashtray at him.

213

Sort of?

I did. I threw an ashtray at him. A heavy glass one. It could have done serious damage.

Anything else?

I slapped him once.

Pember says nothing. Veronica adjusts her legs but can't find a comfortable position.

Another time, I kicked him. That's not normal, is it?

They sit in silence.

You think I'm a terrible person, don't you?

Why would you think I think that?

I hate it when I behave that way. I feel so ashamed of myself.

Do you apologize?

No.

What do you do, then?

When he doesn't fight back, it makes me want to be even more horrible to him. That doesn't make sense, does it?

What is it that makes you so angry with him?

He's very frustrating.

He seems like he works hard. He's a loving father. He loves you.

Veronica says nothing.

Do you love him?

I married him, didn't I? I had a child with him.

Pember lets the question hang in the air. She looks up at the clock on the wall.

Stay with that thought. To be continued.

* * *

Afterwards, Veronica goes to visit Roxy. She always likes to see Roxy following a session with Elizabeth Pember. After all the soul-searching, she feels the urgent need for a dose of meaningless extroversion.

Roxy doesn't disappoint. She bursts into the café where they are meeting in a flurry of shopping bags and exclamations. She immediately orders a slice of chocolate cake and sits down opposite Veronica.

I heard a new one today.

Please don't.

A hot blonde walks into a bar and orders a double entendre. So the barman gave her one.

I'm looking old, says Veronica, examining herself in the mirrored wall behind Roxy.

How was therapy?

Disturbing, frankly.

All that thinking ages you, says Roxy. *I've got the answer.*

Bag over the head?

Therapy Roxanne Peacock style.

Not a foot massage and facial. Please.

Better. Botox and filler.

Veronica laughs despite herself and pours herself another cup of mint tea.

I'm not that desperate just yet.

I'm not joking.

That makes a change.

I've been invited to a Botox party next week. No, really. I was going to mention it to you. Why don't you come with me?

Because I don't want to end up with a face like a block of wood.

It's not like that, Vronks. It's got bad press. Look, why don't you come along anyway? Then you can decide. No commitment. It'll be a laugh.

Are you sure?

I'm certain. Two hundred per cent.

I don't know.

Keep me company at least.

If nothing else, I suppose I might pick up some clients for my therapy practice. Because anyone who does it must be a bit soft in the head.

Like me.

I didn't mean . . .

Oh don't worry. I'm as soft in the head as they come. Suits me down to the ground. If I was any smarter, I wouldn't be able to live with Colin.

I don't know why you always put on this dumb act. You're one of the smartest women I know.

Makes life easy. I'm no threat to men and women like it even better. Keep your weapon in the sheath. That's what my grandma always used to say to me. Just be ready to use it when you have to.

* * *

When Roxy and Veronica arrive at the nondescript terraced house, in South Acton, it is still light.

Roxy pushes the doorbell and a young woman, maybe in her early twenties, answers. She is wearing a white surgical coat – albeit tailored, nipped in at the waist, and very short on the leg – as well as blue surgical plastic gloves. She is made up thickly, like Roxy, pancaked, lipsticked and mascara-ed.

Hello! she trills, in a scented-candle bright voice. *You here for the Botox party?*

That's right, says Roxy.

She is, says Veronica. *Not me.*

You're both beautiful enough as it is.

216

I bet you say that to everyone who comes, says Roxy.

Course I do.

The woman's laugh is like a small dog's bark. She ushers them through the hallway into the house. Her voice drops an octave and takes on a note of serious purpose. She puts her hand above her heart.

My name's Coral. I'm in charge of the team.

Are you a nurse? asks Veronica

I'm a facial aesthetics technician.

They enter the living room, which is furnished with faux-antiques and white leather. On the wall, there are three framed impressionist posters – Degas, Monet and Toulouse-Lautrec – and as many large framed mirrors. Half a dozen young and not so young women, all with painted faces, plucked eyebrows and contoured cheeks, are standing around talking excitedly. It is as if they are airbrushed or Photoshopped. Several of them have unnaturally large and cantilevered breasts and most have shiny lips and fake eyebrows.

There are cupcakes arranged on a table and dozens of bottles of wine, mainly white. There are plates full of peanuts and salty snacks arranged around the room, along with vegetable crudités and dips.

An older woman with short black bobbed hair, very white teeth, outsize dangly earrings and a cruel beauty, all angles and planes, accentuated by her make-up, greets Roxy.

Roxy! Hello, doll. You're looking the business.

Roxy embraces her. They kiss the air, then part.

Who's this, then?

Veronica. Vronky. My newest bestie. Vronky, this is Ferne. We go ways back. To school days. We hadn't seen each for what? Fifteen years?

Found each other on Friends Reunited. Went out for a drink last month and it was like nothing had changed. So here we are.

Friends — reunited! says Ferne

She throws her arms around Veronica and Veronica feels herself stiffening. This isn't quite what she expected. She thought it would be quiet, clinical. This is more like a hen party with hypodermics. There are temporary posters erected on stands. One says, 'Wrinkled Is Not One of the Things I Wanted to Be When I Grew Up' and another, 'Botox — Because There Is No Gym for Your Wrinkles'.

A woman wearing jeans and a T-shirt who is sitting on a chair is receiving an injection in the forehead. There is blood trickling down the side of her face.

It's the alcohol, says Coral. *Thins the blood. Nothing to worry about.*

Next to the woman is a burly man, tanned, with black floppy hair, the only one in the room. He, too, has a needle hovering just between his eyebrows.

You get men here?

One or two. Haven't you heard of Brotox? giggles Ferne. *What you going to have done then?*

I'm just here to watch, says Veronica, lifting a glass of wine from a tray and taking a deep draught.

We'll see about that, says Roxy.

What about you? says Ferne.

You know me. I'll try anything for a laugh.

It looks painful, says Veronica, finishing her wine and reaching for another one.

A second woman, very young, is, at that moment, having an injection in her forehead. In her hand she holds an icepack,

ready to apply. Her eyes are open, she has not stopped talking, and seems entirely unintimidated by the needle piercing
her skin. An older woman stands beside her holding her
other hand.

Are you okay? says the older woman, puffing on a cigarette.

Yes, Mum. Stop fussing.

Veronica has always hated needles and the idea of one
going into her face turns her stomach. Ferne notices her
expression.

They put lidocaine on first, so it doesn't really hurt at all,
she says.

Things can go wrong, though, can't they? says Veronica.

It's completely safe, says Ferne. *Completely. I've had it done loads
of times. You can't tell, can you?*

Ferne offers up her face to be studied. Veronica seems to see
a plasticky quality around the eyes, and there is something of
the shiny effect of the back of a spoon to her face.

Not at all, says Veronica.

I'm going to get my lips done, says Roxy, *so I've got real blow-job
lips, hahaha.*

Here, take a look at these, says Coral.

She reaches for a plastic file, and brings out a handful
of eight-by-ten glossy photos of women before and after
treatment. Veronica cannot deny that they look better but
assumes they are Photoshopped. Covertly, she inspects herself
in one of the large mirrors in the room. There are faint lines
on her forehead, a tiny groove in between her eyes, emerging
crow's feet at the edges. Her mouth looks – to her – thin and
ungenerous.

You got what they call 'sad mouth', says Coral, brightly, who has noticed her inspecting herself. *It doesn't mean you're sad. It just means you've got a slight downturn at the corners. Easily fixed. It's enhancing what you got, not changing what you got.*

Best thing I ever did, says one woman, overweight in a vast pink floral dress, who is helping herself to the peanuts. *Feel so much better about myself.*

Veronica nods politely and turns away to scan the other women in the room. They are making a terrific noise – this and the empty glasses all over the room suggest that they have been drinking heavily. A large television, with the sound turned down, occupies one of the corners.

Are you sure you want to do this? she asks Roxy.

Why not? says Roxy. *It's like, you know, a new me.*

Coral hands her some papers, a legal waiver to sign. Roxy scrawls her name across the bottom without reading it.

What's wrong with the old you?

There's always something wrong, isn't there? And it isn't going to get better as the years tick by. Do you see what I'm getting at? I'm going to have some dermal fillers as well.

Dermal fillers?

It's like a gel. Same as you put in the lips. You inject it. I'm going to put some under my nose-to-mouth lines. That should do for them. Get the racehorse look. You know, big lips, big teeth.

Here's to racehorses, says the woman in the loud floral dress, raising a fluted glass of Prosecco.

One of the women in plastic gloves beckons to Veronica.

Hello there. I'm Jade. Let me know what you want done.

She hands a paper menu to Veronica. Veronica glances at it. *What are 'bunny lines'?*

Little wrinkles next to the nose, says Jade. *Funnily enough, some*

220

people get them from having Botox. But you can get rid of them with another injection.

Veronica holds her hands up.

Sorry, Jade. I'm just here for the free peanuts.

Come on, Vronky, give it a go, says Roxy, laughing. *Get your brows lifted a tiny, tiny bit. Make yourself look a bit more cheerful.*

Not my cup of tea. Veronica picks up another glass of wine. Her head is beginning to swim nicely. *Anyway, nothing wrong with my brows.*

She looks to one side where she can see a bedroom with a woman lying on a bed, being injected in the forehead by a white-coated nurse.

It's no more extreme than shaving your legs or dyeing your hair if it's done properly, says Jade.

Veronica hesitates, and pouts her lips in the mirror.

What about filler? How often would I have to have it done?

About four times a year. Expensive but worth it. Also, at your age, what are you, thirty . . . ?

Thirty-four!

Thirty-four then. It will have a preventative effect and stop wrinkles forming in the future.

Surely there are more important things to men than how good you look, says Veronica.

Ferne and Coral burst out laughing.

Yeh, right, says Ferne. *They're so deep!*

Listen. You do it for yourself, not for men, says Jade.

Veronica takes another deep swig of warm Pinot Grigio. And smiles.

* * *

What the fuck have you done to your face? says Frankie.

It is the following morning. Veronica hears Frankie though the mists of shallow sleep. She opens her eyes and sees him, still in his boxers, leaning over her, mouth partly open.

Veronica turns her face away.

Went to a Botox and filler party. With Roxy.

You did what?

I know it doesn't look great at the moment. I had a bit of an allergic reaction. It will settle down.

Plucking up courage, she turns again towards Frankie. Frankie stares at her lips, which are like distended inner tubes. The Botox injections for her crow's feet have made her look violently startled.

What did you go and do that for?

China walks into the room. She looks at Veronica and immediately starts to cry.

You're scaring her. In fact you're scaring me.

Veronica traces the lines of her face with the tips of her fingers.

I don't know why I did it. I had a few drinks. Roxy egged me on.

Frankie picks up China and tries to comfort her, but she just screams louder.

You're always trying to make yourself . . . I don't know. New.

I don't know what you mean.

A new job. A new house. A new kitchen. Now a new face.

Please, Frankie. I feel bad enough as it is.

Same lie that I'm always selling my clients. That if they get this view, that maisonette, this loft conversion — everything will be new.

What's wrong with that?

Now, by playing peek-a-boo with her, Frankie calms China down. She starts to giggle.

Nothing will ever be new. We're stuck with ourselves.

No, we're not.

Veronica tries to look fierce, but her face seems to only be able to manage one expression, that of seductive surprise.

I can't believe that. I just can't. If that's true all the work I've done learning about psychotherapy . . . it's a waste of time.

Psychotherapy is one thing. Making yourself look like a beached trout is another.

I made a mistake — all right?

Frankie shakes his head in disbelief.

Did Roxy have it done too?

Yes.

What did she look like?

Better than me. You'll be surprised. She loved what they did to her. She said it was 'empowering'.

Do you feel empowered?

China looks up at Veronica. And starts to cry again.

Not really.

* * *

Nodge and Fraser are watching the TV news together at Fraser's flat. The footage shows the appointment of Masoud Barzani as president of the Kurdish parliament in Northern Iraq. Celebrations throb through the streets, pulsing arteries of joy.

Looks like it might not be such a disaster after all, says Nodge. *I mean if you're a Kurd it might not be a disaster.*

223

You're joking, says Fraser. *How many suicide bombings last month? Four? How many killed? Two hundred? Three hundred? Just in May. And because some American puppet gets installed you think it's all hunky dory.*

It's as if you want it to go wrong. Just to spite the Americans and show that you were right. Just to get your precious revenge.

It's not a matter of whether I want it to go wrong or not. It is going wrong. It's a bloodbath.

You want it to fail because you hate Blair.

That's right. I do hate him.

And revenge.

Yes. And revenge.

So it's all about hate and revenge then. That's the spirit.

Fraser's voice modulates into a semi-snarl.

I don't know what I'm doing spending so much of my time with a New Labour neo-con sellout, yeh?

Nodge, stung, is nevertheless determined to appear aloof and says nothing.

Fraser, watching the pictures of Barzani being sworn in, is getting more and more agitated.

You can't just go waltzing into other people's countries and impose your version of so-called democracy, murdering people in their thousands.

These people seem quite pleased.

It's propaganda!

Fraser reaches for the television remote and switches off the TV. Then he slumps back on the sofa. He is dressed in his EasyJet pilot's uniform, a white shirt with yellow and black epaulettes and a black tie. He has a shift starting this afternoon. His bag is packed and by the door.

Christ. Another shift, says Fraser, dejectedly.

I thought you loved flying.

Being on EasyJet isn't flying.

What is it, then? asks Nodge.

Prostitution. Real flying is so different.

It's not so bad, is it? After all, we've got one another.

My life's been one big disappointment, says Fraser. *Bargain basement all the way. An EasyJet life. That's me.*

Nodge turns quickly and catches Fraser glaring at him.

That remark's aimed at me, isn't it?

You're not exactly a Piper Cub, are you? More like a bear cub.

I'm sorry I'm a disappointment.

It's not just disappointment.

What else is it?

Fraser takes a deep breath.

For a start, I think our politics are getting so far apart it feels like there's no bridge anymore.

Nodge stands up. He is now down to an almost ideal weight, but Fraser still isn't satisfied, constantly nagging him to work on his muscles.

I'm sick of you picking at me, Fraser. If you want a more streamlined model, go and get one. Just piss off down the gym and find somebody. You can discuss neo-Marxism with him while you're doing circle jerks over a picture of Jack Derrida.

Jacques, says Fraser, frostily. He gets up and opens his suitcase and starts to check his luggage. It is all perfectly neat and folded.

Do you even love me? says Nodge.

You're always asking me that.

But do you?

You're so needy.

You're not answering the question.

Alright then. Not really. I suppose, says Fraser, coldly, closing the bag again. His voice is completely flat. *I don't really. To be completely honest. Love you. No.*

Nodge sits down again on the sofa, winded.

Oh. Right.

Now Fraser comes over and looks down at Nodge. His face is hard and set.

I was going to have a talk with you after I came back from Spain. But since you've forced it onto the agenda.

Suddenly, Fraser softens. He sits next to Nodge on the sofa. He wafts Acqua di Parma. His elegantly lined face shines from scrubbing.

I'm sorry, Nodge. I didn't mean to be so brutal about it. But it's best to be honest. Things haven't been right between us for a long time. If they ever were.

He tries to take Nodge's hand, and Nodge lets him, but returns no pressure.

No worries.

Fraser narrows his eyes and looks sideways at Nodge.

You're taking this suspiciously well.

You know me. Stoic through and through.

Solid Nodge.

Solid. Yeh.

He pulls his hand away from Fraser's. Fraser sighs and stands up.

Should I take my stuff right away? says Nodge, staring at the carpet. His eyes are in danger of overflowing and he wipes them with the back of his sleeve.

No hurry. Sometime before I get back. Fraser is checking his bag again, locking it with a small key.

Every trace of me will have gone when you return. You'll never know I existed.

No need to be melodramatic. But thanks.

Nodge gets up from the sofa and turns to look at Fraser, who is picking up his neat Delsey Chatelet polycarbonate carry-on. Despite its bright whiteness there's not a speck of grime visible on it.

Fraser walks over and kisses him on the cheek.

I knew you'd understand.

Nodge wipes off the kiss with his hand.

You think you're better than me, don't you, Fraser?

It's not that.

But you're really the same as me in the end. A taxi driver. In the sky.

Don't be bitter, Jon. It's not a good look.

I'm not bitter.

Really?

Really.

Fraser seems to consider this for a moment.

Well, in that case — could you feed Harvey for me while I'm away?

Nodge almost spits out a laugh, but controls himself. Instead he nods casually.

Sure. No problem, Fraze.

Thanks. Really. You're being very grown up about this.

No point in crying over spilt milk, is there?

And don't give him any of the vegetarian stuff, will you?

Thank god you've got over that one. A vegetarian dog. Christ almighty.

I didn't mean that he's started eating meat. I would never let that happen.

What do you mean, then?

He's gone vegan.

It's good that you've still got a sense of humour, Fraser, at a time like this. Reminds me why I liked you in the first place.

No, I'm deadly serious. Harvey is vegan now. If you don't believe me, look in the larder. There are cans marked 'Benevo'. That's what you have to give him. The 'grain-free vegetable feast with mixed herbs'. Not the crunchy nuggets.

You're serious.

He won't even touch meat anymore. Took a long time to train him up. But he's there, I think.

Nodge considers this carefully.

Well then, Fraser. You should be proud.

I am. Thanks, Nodge. You're a mensch.

He leans over and tries to give Nodge a hug, but Nodge remains stiff in his arms.

No problem, says Nodge. *I hope everything goes well for you.*

Thank you.

Nodge nods. Fraser pulls up the handle of his bag and engages the wheels.

One more thing. Could you post your keys through the door before I get back?

Sure thing

No hard feelings?

No hard feelings.

Fraser takes one last backward look – at Harvey rather than Nodge – then leaves, closing the door softly behind him.

Nodge sits and begins to weep. He cries for maybe ten minutes.

He sees Harvey in the corner of the room. Harvey bares his teeth and drools. Nodge smiles mirthlessly at him.

Some minutes later, he dries his eyes, reaches for his phone and dials.

Hi. It's Nodge. Yeh, good. Yeh, long time no see.

Listen, do you fancy coming to the match at Loftus Road on Saturday?

No, Fraser won't mind.

* * *

Three days later Fraser returns home from his shuttling to Ibiza. As he pushes open the door he sees Nodge's keys on the floor by the doormat. He smiles. He will miss Nodge's reliability. Though not much else, to tell the truth.

He switches on the lights, and it is at that moment that a strange smell, pungent and nauseating, drills into his nostrils. He drops his bag and rushes through to the kitchen. Where he sees four empty cans of Pedigree Chum on the worktop, and an empty gold bowl on the floor with 'Harvey' inscribed in pale pink lettering.

Harvey looks up at him, ecstatic. There are still scraps of meat at the edges of his mouth. He jumps up at Fraser, but Fraser angrily pushes him away, wagging a finger at him. Then he picks up a rolled-up copy of *Gay Times* and starts to swipe him viciously round the head.

Bad dog! Bad dog! Stupid mutt!

Harvey whimpers piteously, looks sorrowful and slinks away. Coldly, Fraser picks up the cans between finger and thumb, rinses them, and drops them in the recycling bin. He tries to think of something else to do, but he is too angry.

Instead, Fraser stares out of the window for a very long time, while Harvey whimpers in the corner. Fraser clicks his fingers and Harvey pads over.

Fraser leans down and whispers into his ear.

We'll pay him back. Won't we, boy? Won't we? Yes, we will. Yes, we will.

2005: Sacrifice

Do we really have to go? says Colin without looking up from the screen of his iMac.

You're so boring, says Roxy, puffing testily on her cigarette. *If I'd known how boring you were, I'd never have married you.*

You knew exactly how boring I was. You just didn't care.

Colin still doesn't look up.

Can you stop playing that fucking computer game?

This fucking computer game is why we're now living in this fucking enormous house in fucking Harpenden.

I don't like it out here. It's dead. I'm a London girl. I should never have let you talk me into it. This is creepy. Old people all over the place grinning like they're happy.

Maybe they are happy.

How can they be? When they've got one foot in the grave. Anyway, there are no shops, nothing here. Just grass and trees, two pubs and a bowling green that's so perfectly cut it makes me want to die.

Grass and trees are nice. Everybody likes grass and trees.

I don't want nice. I want a bit of excitement.

You agreed to it. You don't have to work at that shop anymore. You're a lady of leisure. Stop complaining.

I thought it would be . . . I don't know. Different. Like on telly. All with a golden glow. Soft at the edges. And I miss work. I didn't think I would, but I do. At least I got to see people.

Go to the party then. There'll be plenty of people there. Frankie collects friends like football cards nowadays. I don't have to come, do I? It's just Frankie showing off his bling. You and me aren't joined at the hip. Anyway I went to that last party you made me go to, the School Disco. That was just embarrassing. Dancing to Human League records in a black tie and a pair of shorts.

It was fun!

Dressing up like teenagers? In uniforms? I'm a bit young for nostalgia. You and I have very different idea of what fun amounts to.

Roxy glares at him.

I'll go by myself.

Okay.

She reaches over and closes the lid on the laptop. Her voice softens.

I'll have sex with you tonight if you come.

Colin looks up from his computer.

You think I'm that easily bought?

Of course. So are you coming to the party?

Colin says nothing.

I'll sort you out some clothes then.

* * *

The first of the guests are yet to arrive at Frankie and Veronica's for their summer barbecue. Margaritas sit on multiple trays in the hall by the front door. Inside the main room Frankie finishes arranging the canapés on the new kitchen table. They bought it earlier that week on impulse from Skandium in Marylebone High Street. It was beautiful displayed in the shop, all curves and oak designed to resemble a falling teardrop, one flat oval plane connected by a stem into a smaller plane on which it stands. It seemed worth its £3,000 price tag.

Now, as he adds another plate of foie gras on bruschetta to the spread – there are quail's eggs, artisan cheese, rustic baguette, French butter, cornichons – Frankie considers ruefully how long it will take for the table to just become part of the background static of his life, a barely noticed element of the stage set. He considers how China will scratch it, and how all the money he spent on it has actually been spent on the idea of it. Reality itself decays more quickly than the organic fruit that is piled into a Heals's hand-turned ceramic bowl at the far end of the table.

But then – he reassures himself – he can afford it. The buy-to-let market is booming, there is no end to it. Since his first property in 2003 – a dilapidated bedsit – he's bought three flats and two houses and hopes to carefully grow the portfolio, caution always being Frankie's watchword in business.

The formula is simple. The banks are falling over themselves to lend. You get the loan on a phone call and a nod, do the paperwork, wait for the building to rise in value, borrow against it, rent it out, trouser the income, then either acquire a new building, or buy yourself a Merc. Or, as in this case, a new kitchen table.

But he is careful. He knows markets can get out of control, can fall as well as rise. He's been offered a big old detached house near Askew Road that's been broken down into tiny units for multiple occupation — always the most profitable way of squeezing the most income out of a place — but it's a risk. Anyway, even in this climate, the banks don't like to give mortgages to multi-occupancies.

Maybe he'll give it a pass this time. Keep his head down. No point in being reckless. He's been extravagant enough lately, spending heavily on the new basement for their house, a hundred K even using the cheap East European builders who have come in on a wave arriving at Victoria Coach Station over the last couple of years since the border restrictions were dropped. The Poles did a good job. It's a whole extra bedroom, although all they have in it at the moment is a camp bed. But it's extra space.

Suddenly, he has the heretical thought, *So what?* Sometimes he thinks space is like an addiction. You collect emptiness.

He dismisses it. After all, his big summer party is about to begin. No time for negative thinking. The karaoke machine he bought from Argos is plugged in and ready to go.

He yanks up his three-quarter length canvas trousers — he's lost weight since he started jogging to work — and checks the hall to make sure there is plenty of space to hang coats. The hooks are empty except for his Von Dutch trucker hat, which he removes and throws into the cupboard under the stairs, where it will stay, along with his Telecaster guitar and amp, also consigned to the under stair for the day. He was thinking of giving the guests a rendition of 'Knocking on Heaven's Door' but bottles it — three months of lessons have not been enough to bolster his confidence sufficiently. He takes one of the Margaritas and necks it. *Just right.*

His mountain bike hangs off the wall on a hook, so it's out of the way, but his micro scooter — and China's — are cluttering the space, so he takes them into the back garden, where Veronica is putting the finishing touches to a floral arrangement on a table while China plays with her plush Crazy Frog on the AstroTurf which covers the garden to save on the trouble of maintaining a lawn. China trips over a tent rope and falls, and although Frankie is sure she isn't hurt, she starts to cry and Veronica rushes to pick her up, although Frankie is closer. Veronica gives Frankie a reproving look. She puts China over her shoulder and rubs her back in a circular motion.

There there, she mutters, softly. *There there.*

China stops immediately. The front door bell rings.

It's all kicking off, says Frankie, and skips towards the door, leaving Veronica to return to the flowers, putting finishing touches to the stage set.

* * *

Colin rests his drink on the Stokke chair standing in the glass gazebo that adjoins the kitchen at the rear of the house. Nodge faces him, holding a glass of white wine. The whole ground floor is crammed with guests. Many others have spilled out into the garden. The increasingly drunken babble is deafening. 'Don't Phunk With My Heart' by the Black Eyed Peas is on the CD player.

Very homogenous, isn't it? says Nodge, sipping on the Chablis. *The guests, I mean.*

What do you want to do? says Colin, now on his fourth bottle of lager, having accepted two of the Margaritas Frankie pressed on him when he and Roxy arrived. *Bus in a load of Imams?*

Never really got on board with the multicultural society, have you, Colin? says Nodge, mildly.

Oh, you're very multicultural, says Colin.

Always nervous among crowds, Colin is taking refuge in the drink. He looks across at Roxy, who is talking animatedly to Veronica. Veronica laughs at something she says and Roxy joins in, bending double. They glance in his direction. Colin feels sure they are laughing at him. He sees Frankie approaching, so plainly this day overflowing with a sense of himself and his life.

Meaning what? says Nodge.

What? says Colin, wrenching himself away from his own vague, distant sense of resentment as Frankie joins them.

Alright? says Frankie.

You love it all, don't you? says Colin, ignoring Frankie and continuing his conversation with Nodge. *But you don't have to live among them.*

Neither do you. Not in Harpenden. Anyway, who's 'them'?

Remember the estate? The White City Estate.

He turns to Frankie now to include him in the conversation.

Where we all grew up? That estate was never white, but it was sort of white, because the blacks — we all wanted to be like them. Because they were cool and had great clothes and great music. Now it's half Islamics. They don't want to know anything about you.

We don't say 'blacks' anymore, Colin, says Nodge.

Don't we? says Frankie.

It's 'people of colour'.

But Colin, not hearing, simply continues.

I had to get out. First to Hammersmith. Now I've been chased out to Harpenden.

I wouldn't want to leave London myself, says Frankie.

I never wanted to leave. I'd have stayed in my mum's flat quite happily.

You're drinking too much, Colin, says Nodge.

They hate gays, you know. He looks at Nodge sullenly.

You can't generalize.

And women.

You should feel at home with them then, says Nodge.

Roxy joins them. She's had four of the Margaritas in quick succession.

What's the hap?

Colin was just telling me about his strong feminist convictions.

Oh yeh. Colin's a feminist all right. Isn't that right, Col? Tell them why you agreed to come tonight.

Colin looks at Roxy darkly, a plea radiating from his eyes.

Go on, Colinder! Tell them about our deal!

Colin pulls long and slow on his drink as if seeking to frame a suitable reply. Eventually he puts the glass down, and faces up to Roxy.

I never wanted to come in the first place. I hate parties. Especially parties like this.

What kind of party do you mean?

Parties that are just there to show off, says Colin, sullenly.

I think I need to make you a nice cup of coffee, says Frankie, regretting now that he has preloaded Colin.

Colin is rocking very slightly from side to side now, and slurring.

You've forgotten where you came from, mate. With your books on the wall and . . . wife . . . and that. And you, Nodge. Call yourself a socialist? That's a laugh. Where did you get that T-shirt from? Those jeans? Who do you think made them? Where were they made? How much for? And how much did they cost?

Colin, mate, you've had enough to drink, says Frankie.

You always know what's best for me, don't you? Frankie the big shot.

Colin woozily regards Frankie. He points a finger at him, as if to make an accusatory point. Then he lets the finger drop.

I'll go and get a glass of water.

Frankie watches as he walks unsteadily towards the kitchen, then makes an urgent diversion to the toilet, where he tries to exorcise his mounting bile, bitter in his throat.

What deal did you make with him then, Roxy? says Frankie.

It doesn't matter, says Roxy, suddenly repentant.

As if I can't guess.

Frankie spots Flossie, sitting alone in the corner with China sat on her knee. She is wearing Specsavers 2-for-1 glasses with a modern oval frame in beech brown. It makes her look younger, something that Frankie finds disconcerting. And she is tanned and has lost maybe ten pounds in weight.

She looks up from the book – *Hippos Go Berserk* – catches his eye and gives him a broad smile. It disappears in a fit of jagged coughing.

You alright, Mum?

Just got a Twiglet stuck in my throat.

The coughing continues, Flossie going red in the face. Frankie slaps her on the back.

She drinks from her glass and the coughing stops.

Thanks, son.

He turns to China.

What's the book about, China Girl?

Animals, says China, simply.

Well I can see that, silly. What about them?

When are we going to go the zoo, Daddy?

Soon. Anyway, you've already been with Mum.

I want to go with you, though.

I'm very busy.

You're never going to take me to the zoo. You've promised me about a thousand million gazillion times.

You're exaggerating.

And you're a meanie.

With that she springs off Flossie's knee, and runs to her mother.

Well, Mum, says Frankie, looking around the room, the gathering, the furniture, the walls, the pictures. *What do you think?*

Oh, I'm very proud of you, Frankie. You've done so well. This place is lovely. And so many friends!

You're looking well yourself. Cough or no cough. You been on holiday again?

Oh yes.

Where to this time?

Trinidad and Tobago. It was lovely. It's in the Caribbean.

I know, Mum.

Me and Gordon had such a nice time.

Gordon again, is it?

We're getting on like a house on fire.

Mum. I don't even believe Gordon exists.

Don't be silly.

Well, I've never met him. And you've been dropping hints about him for years.

That doesn't mean he doesn't exist! He just lives in Hemel Hempstead. So I don't see him all that much.

Except when you go on holiday.

Yes, it's nice to have company.

Who's paying for all these holidays?

None of your beeswax.

Gordon's got himself a sugar momma by the sound of it.

He's not got much money. I don't care. Money can't buy you love, you know.

You haven't got much money either.

Oh, it's easy to borrow now.

What do you do with yourselves all day anyway? I can't see you visiting ancient monuments.

You'd be surprised.

She looks arch. It makes Frankie feel uncomfortable.

Mum. You're shocking me.

Then you shouldn't ask.

She starts to cough again, less violently this time. She holds her hand up when Frankie reaches for her glass.

I'm alright. It'll pass in a moment.

Listen, Mum, I've got to make a speech. Don't go anywhere.

Where would I be going?

I don't know. The Maldives? Peru? Club 18-30?

Frankie leaves Flossie coughing gently now, stops the music and taps his wine glass with a spoon, until everyone falls silent. He feels he commands the room, and scans it affectionately, but also, perhaps, loftily.

Thanks, everyone, for coming. I just wanted to say a few words and thank a few people.

He turns towards Veronica, who is jigging China up and down on her lap.

Firstly, my wife, Veronica. Vronky. My support. My rock. Or at least, my Tree.

Light laughter. He turns to look at her. She can't quite

meet his eye, but smiles, seemingly embarrassed by the public flattery.

When she met me I was living on a diet of IKEA and tomato soup. Now look at what we have. This beautiful house.

He raises a glass to her.

You have given me a home. I want to thank you for that.

There is applause. Frankie turns again, this time towards the staircase.

I also want to thank Veronica's parents, Michael and Cordelia, who have very much welcomed me into their family. And helped me more than I can say.

He swaps a quick glance with Michael, which Michael returns, before readjusting his face to one of neutral humility. Michael and Cordelia smile politely at the light applause.

And Mum. My lovely mum, who gave me life. And appears to have a second lease on it herself, the amount of time she spends on cruises nowadays.

You're just jealous, calls Flossie.

She winks at him. Frankie can't help but feel obscurely disapproving. But now he takes a deep breath and takes in the scene around him, gesturing with an arm outstretched.

Feels like I've made it at last. The Poggenpohl kitchen and all that. The Eames chairs. Living it large. All the same. All this, you know, counts for nothing.

There are sceptical *ummhmms* and raised eyebrows.

No, not nothing. Not nothing. But . . . Family is what matters. Our beautiful China Doll . . .

He gestures towards China, who is indifferently sitting on the carpet by the light stand, eating from a bowl of low-salt Twiglets.

. . . who we made together the night of the Millennium. She is the one of the first children of the new millennium. Who knows, perhaps the first.

Shouts of 'wa-hay' and 'too much information'.

Frankie opens his arms as if to embrace the gathering.

I also want to thank you, all my friends, for coming today. And for being my friends and standing by me while I've been through the things I've been through. You all mean a lot to me.

Mutterings of approval.

I'd also like to thank absent friends. Not only friends who couldn't be here, but those we've fallen out with, or drifted apart from. Thanks to them for all we shared, while we could share it. Things get in the way sometimes. It's just the way it is. I miss them all. Absent friends!

He lifts up his glass until the reprise echoes round the room — *'Absent friends'*.

He pauses, takes stock of the space, which he still holds. China has now started wandering around the room, among their feet, with a giant My Little Pony which Frankie recognizes as Rainbow Dash. It was a present that day from her Aunty Rocks.

I look around at old friends and new. I look at myself, all Armani'd up. All the trappings. My amazing wife, my beautiful daughter, my lovely house, my wonderful friends. And I think, what did I do to deserve all this? I've been lucky. So, so lucky.

It's been a long road to here. A lot of hard work. As some of you know who grew up with me on the White City Estate, life was very different. No fancy cocktails then. All we could afford was lager. On draught. Because it was cheaper. Me and Colin and Nodge used to walk along the Goldhawk Road on the way to watching QPR and dream of the day when things would get better. Now they have. Not for QPR, though, sadly.

Laughter.

But for all of us, yes. Man, I'd never thought I'd say this. But we live in an amazing country, a country that's never been so full of promise and opportunity and pride.

Whoops of agreement.

And as for the Olympic bid, I've just got one thing to say. Fuck the French! You are going to be TOAST.

Even louder cheers.

So. Now. If I may just step away from the world stage for a moment. I want to raise a glass to my oldest friend. Nodge. And I want to raise my glass to Colin and Roxy, married earlier this year. I was proud to be his best man. Colin and I have known each other since we were at primary school together, and I have never seen him so happy as he is today.

All raise their glasses and cheer. Frankie looks for Colin but he is in the loo, throwing up again. Roxy holds his glass up for him in acknowledgement.

And to you. All of you — good luck and may your future be bright, says Frankie, feeling suddenly emotional, a tear welling up.

The future is Orange! shouts a wag.

No, it's Blue! shouts another.

Frankie waits for the laughter to die down then pats the air to quiet the gathering.

These are good times, people. Times of champagne and canapés. Times of children, times of wives and husbands and houses and holidays.

He pauses for dramatic effect.

It's our time. It's our generation. Let's celebrate it.

Roar of approval. He raises his glass once more.

To us. To our time.

They all raise their glasses, and repeat:

Our time!

Frankie and the crowd drain their glasses and cheer. Frankie shouts over the noise.

Enough talking bollocks. Let's karaoke!

Cheers and laughter. Frankie heads over to the karaoke machine, which is plugged into the TV, and switches it on.

I'll go first.

He hits the button and the first chords of 'You've Lost That Loving Feeling' by the Righteous Brothers fill the air. Frankie starts to sing in a deep, wavery voice, not entirely out of tune, but a fair way from pitch perfect.

He's not bad, is he? says Owen, who is drinking Diet Coke.

Not bad at all, says Nodge.

There's real feeling there.

Nodge and Owen begin close dancing, Nodge clumsily, Owen with his usual grace, but somehow leadenly. Nodge notices that he is pale and there is a frost of sweat on his brow. He stops dancing.

What's the matter with you, Owen?

I'm fine.

But Owen stumbles and almost falls.

Bullshit. I'm taking you home.

It's just getting started.

You're not well. You haven't been yourself all evening. We should go.

Nodge. Just a little longer. I'm fine, really.

I'm calling a cab.

Owen stares at him as if about to resist again. Then resignedly he nods.

Thanks, Nodge. Thank you.

A cab arrives in less than five minutes. After saying their goodbyes, Nodge and Owen climb into the back, where Owen nearly crumples and starts to shake.

How much have you had to drink? says Nodge as they are driven away.

Hardly anything.

Is there something you're not telling me?

Nodge, I don't know anything.

What exactly are the symptoms?

Tired. Pain in the stomach. My piss looks like coffee. My knees and elbows hurt like fuck. Itchy. Really itchy.

Let me see your eyes.

Nodge switches on the interior light of the cab, and stares into them. A coral island in a polluted sea.

They're yellow.

Probably the light.

Now he picks up Owen's hand and examines it.

Your skin looks yellow too.

I just need to sleep. Been working too hard.

In the curtain department at John Lewis? Pull the other one. You need to see the doctor.

There's no need to fuss. I'm fully grown.

You're going. End of.

* * *

Colin wakes and rubs his eyes. The hangover from the Saturday night at Frankie's took two days to wear off. But now, five days later, he's fresh, and brisk, even excited.

It's a big day for him — the day of the first presentation of his new game, *Clash of the Serpents* for Sony, the product of a year's solid work.

Roxy, already awake and nested in her waffle-weave bath-robe, sits on a chair at the end of the bedroom filing her toenails. She looks up at the sound of movement on the bed.

All right? says Colin, hauling himself out of the four-poster. It has semi-transparent drape lace curtains that stretch from vertice to vertice.

Cup of tea?

Let me make you one, Rocks.

He makes tea for them both, then takes a shower. He emerges ten minutes later, brushing his teeth. His gums leak blood, and he spits pink water into the sink. He dresses and walks to the kitchen where Roxy has made him a bacon sandwich.

Thanks, Rocks. What you going to do today then? He bites into the sandwich.

I might come with you, says Roxy. *Do a bit of shopping up town. I could use a new coat.*

You've already got about fifteen new coats.

So? Then I'll have sixteen. Anyway they're not new anymore. Might see if I can get Veronica to come with me.

Colin puts the three quarters of his sandwich down uneaten. He checks his watch.

I'd better get moving.

I'm not ready yet, says Roxy.

Come in later on the train.

Are you going to be there all day? We could have a celebration lunch. If it goes well.

It will, I'm sure. Clever Colin.

I'll give you a call later on, all right?

246

He bends down and plants a kiss too close to the edge of her open mouth. She recoils from the taste of his spit, and the hint of the blood from his gums.

Can you do me a favour before you go? says Roxy.

What is it? I'm really going to be late if I leave it much longer. But there is no irritation his voice, his mood is too bright.

I can't get my computer to boot up proper.

I'll sort it out when I get back.

Please, Colin. Have a quick look. There's some stuff I need to do online. It's important.

What stuff?

There's a twelve-hour sale of some shoes.

I thought you said it was important.

I'll drive you in to the station so you don't have to park. It'll only take you a sec.

He checks his watch again.

Anything for my Rocks.

Colin takes the laptop and switches it on, then goes through the safe startup mode. Two minutes later he hands it back.

There you go. Now let's get a move on.

You're a genius.

Let's just hope the big knobs at Sony think so too.

Roxy throws herself into a pair of white jeans, but can't find the right pair of shoes to match. Colin, anxiety finally wrung out of him, is now shouting at her from the bottom of the stairs.

Come on!

Just a minute! You'll be fine for time.

A minute later, she goes outside to find Colin sitting in the car, holding his briefcase on his lap.

We've still got ten minutes.

Colin says nothing and Roxy fires the engine. Five minutes later they hit traffic on the road to the station. There are roadworks ahead that weren't there yesterday. Colin checks his watch again.

I'm going to miss it.

There's another one in twenty minutes. You'll still make it in plenty of time for your meeting.

I don't want to wait at the station for twenty minutes.

You'll be fine. I bet you always sit in the same seat as well, don't you?

Colin says nothing.

You do, don't you?

If no one else is sitting in it. Why not? And the later train is more crowded. I like a bit of peace and quiet.

The lights finally change to green. When they arrive at the station car park, Colin sees his train on the platform.

I'm going to miss it.

Before he can even get out of the car, the train starts to pull out of the station.

Sorry, Colin. But it's not the end of the world, is it?

* * *

At King's Cross, he makes for the Piccadilly line southbound. He lets one train pass because it is just too full, commuters spilling out of the doors. Then there is an announcement. The Piccadilly Line is running late because of a fire at Caledonian Road. There is normally a train every minute or so, but now it is one every seven or eight minutes. Colin walks along the platform, trying to find a spot where there are fewer people. But the train, again, is too crowded. He manages finally to board the third, finds a seat and lowers himself into it, clasping his laptop with both hands, resting it on his lap in front of him.

Colin rarely feels excitement, but today he is jacked up and fizzing. This is the game that will finally cement his reputation. Probably land him a big promotion with Sony, certainly some shares.

As the train leaves the platform he idly reads an ad for life insurance, then one on how to send money back to Poland at a low price. He can smell the perfume of the woman next to him, something like apples, something like cloves.

He starts to think of what to get Roxy for a birthday present. It is three weeks away. Then he thinks of the leak in the roof, then the flowers that are blooming on the window-sill at the front of house, then Roxy's breasts last night in the moonlight, then he tries to focus back on *Clash of the Serpents* again and the presentation.

The train rocks him back and forth. He finds it soothing.

There is an ad in the carriage for retirement homes. It makes him think about his mother. What he did for her. What she did to him. What she didn't do for him.

The apple-and-cloves woman has a mirror out and is fixing her make-up. Three people are reading books. Colin thinks of getting his own out, Stephen King's *Song of Susannah*. But they will be at the station soon. It seems hardly worth it and anyway he has lost his place in the book.

His breakfast is repeating on him. He tastes burnt bacon on his tongue. His mind goes blank then drifts back into focus. Relieved that he won't be late, he tries to remember a joke

Roxy told him yesterday. He can tell it to his friends over a celebratory lunch.

A guy shows up for work. No, that's not it. *A guy shows up late for work.* That's it. *So the boss yells, 'You should've been here earlier . . .* no, the boss yells, *'you should have been here at eight-thirty' And the man replies . . .* what does the man reply?

It's a good one, he thinks, it will raise a laugh if he can remember it. Now he tastes a cornflake in his mouth. Which is odd because he didn't have any cornflakes that morning. Must have been from last night. Did he have a bowl? No, but he picked at some out of the container. That must be it then. Ten to nine. The noise of the train, now it is in a tunnel, is deafening, almost drowning his thoughts.

He glances at a sallow-skinned man sitting a few seats away from him. Barely a man at all, more a teenager. He looks very sad and very angry. He is bent forward almost double. His head is down but his eyes are looking up. He seems frightened and arrogant at the same time. His eyes keep scanning the carriage from the overhanging ledge of his black eyebrows. His knuckles are red as if he had recently hit someone.

Curious, Colin keeps his gaze on him and the man catches his eye. Colin smiles, involuntarily, out of embarrassment. The man briefly smiles back. Then the man straightens up and looks along the carriage. He closes his eyes.

Puzzlingly for Colin, there is a white flash, which he thinks at first is some kind of problem with his eyes, like spots before them. Then there is a sound that is so loud, he cannot hear it.

The carriage seems to expand and contract. He is thrown forwards and sideways. Then he observes with a calm detachment that he is miraculously outside the carriage.

There is a wall of noise like radio static. He feels he has been punched in both ears, or is deep underwater. There is an acrid smell of chemicals and burning rubber and singed hair.

Everything goes black and he thinks he has suddenly gone blind. When his vision returns he laughs in relief.

And the man replies, 'Why, what happened at eight-thirty?'

That's it.

Colin is beginning to understand that there is something wrong. The smell is overwhelming. Not apples and spice now. Cordite and overcooked meat. He looks down at his legs. One of them, strangely, is not there. The other is twisted backwards on itself.

There is a woman who appears to be an Asian since she is wearing a sari or something like that, he presumes she is an Asian, some kind of Asian, she is whimpering or something, he sees blood pumping out of her thigh.

He takes her hand. *It will be all right love, it will be all right.*

She looks at him with wide, wide eyes and something like love comes from them and he loves her too, loves everyone, loves life at that moment.

She starts to cry – softly, as if only mildly upset by a small inconvenience.

There there, he says. *There there.*

The blood is still pouring from her leg. He can hardly control his hands they are shaking so much, but he manages to get his tie off, it is the first time he has worn a tie to the office, it's a nice one, Roxy bought it for him, it is made of silk and it is green like China's eyes sometimes but not really there are no such things as green eyes Frankie told him Frankie told him.

He manages to get the tie round her naked, splattered leg,

and tries to tie it as tight as he can, using his pen, which is somehow still intact in his top pocket, to twist the tie. The woman's bleeding seems to be arrested.

Black again. When he comes round, someone is beside him and is tying something around his own legs, leg, legs.

Leg.

He remembers a moment long ago when Frankie was playing him at table football. For the first time ever, he beat Frankie.

One of the high points of his, of his, of his.

His ears seem to clear. Around him, the sound of screams. Shouts. A lump of pink and red in a blue summer dress. He glances back into what he thinks must have been the carriage. It looks like what was left of the tower after nine eleven nine eleven.

Then there is something in his field of vision so terrible, something like organs or offal, that he cannot help but look away, and cannot register what it is so he does not look again.

He gets out his phone to send a text to Roxy but cannot think what to say.

Something has happened.

He takes out his mobile phone but it is smashed to pieces.

The pain is now intense, more intense than he could ever think possible, it is like angel's wings on fire inside him. His mind is full only of pain now or rather his body has taken over his mind, he has no mind.

He drifts out of, then back into, consciousness. Eventually, ghostly uniforms manifest around him, smart and shining, holy heralds. Someone says he needs Colin's clothes for forensic purposes for forensic purposes, forensic porpoises, Roxy loves dolphins she wants to swim with the dolphins one day.

Colin asks if he can keep his clothes because he likes them and they're cutting them off with what, scissors, of course scissors. They put them what's left of them in a paper bag. His tie is ruined. The meeting is going to be postponed. Where is his laptop anyway? It doesn't matter it's all backed up on C . . . on C . . . on CommVault, EVault, NetMass, Acronic, Arkeia, CommVault, EVault, NetMass, Acronis, Arkeia, CommVault, EVault, NetMass, Acronic, Arkeia . . .

Someone making a joke in the darkness.

If my boss gives me grief about being late, I'll tell him where to get off.

The woman who speaks has a face covered in blood, but otherwise seems okay. Apart from that hole in head that hole in her head hole in her.

Someone else laughs, what's funny?

Why, what happened at eight-thirty?

The pain hits again, twice as bad, ten times as bad. He faints, faints deeper, deeper still and then the black suction of the ocean floor is pulling him to the dark opening which spreads wide to take him in as he tries to swim away, weakly, weakly. It seems too much trouble to swim; very gently, Colin allows himself to sink and then, with strange relief, to dissolve and merge with the border that he is now faintly, then sharply, aware of, the vague shimmering line which transforms the deepest and most hopeless iteration of midnight blue into a perfect, unremitting and indifferent black.

* * *

Frankie has taken the day off to visit London Zoo with China — at last. The summer heat has cooled the housing market that week, and there's not much on in the office. He has taken China out of school. When you're paying the fees they don't make such a fuss about it. He is determined to finally give her a day out with him, after promising so often for so long. Instructed by Veronica, he has dutifully switched his phone off, resolving not to check it until the two of them leave.

Frankie hasn't been to the zoo in twenty years and finds himself, to his own surprise, excited by the prospect. China holds his hand with a soft firm grip. Her shoulder-length brown hair, less curly than it was, is woven into two pigtails. A white smear of sunscreen daubs her forehead. Frankie reaches across and lovingly massages it until it disappears. China ignores him, concentrating instead on a Nobbly Bobbly ice lolly which is gradually disintegrating and rendering her hands and mouth sticky and red.

She finishes the ice lolly and carelessly drops the stick on the ground. Frankie shakes his head in disapproval, but says nothing, picks it up, puts it in a recycling bin, and finds a wet wipe in his pocket. He bends down and cleans China's face and hands. He is, as always, astonished by her effortless beauty, the smallness of her podgy hands, the wideness of her eyes, the reach of her eyelashes, the pink and white button of her nose. She is wearing a red gingham dress with a white collar, now stained with crimson, and red StartRite sandals stitched with white daisies. Frankie tries to wipe the dress, but only spreads the stain. He tuts and gives up.

There is barely any queue, it being a Thursday morning, and they pay and walk in through the barriers. China starts to skip and Frankie joins in next to her, feeling foolish, but enjoying himself all the same. China giggles and after a few seconds they come to a halt outside the entrance to the Reptile House.

What would you like to see first, China Girl?

I want to go to the gift shop.

There's plenty of time for that later.

I want to go to the gift shop now.

Don't pout.

I'm not.

China. There's lions here. Gorillas. Tigers. Penguins. Everything. What about the penguins?

Gift shop.

Frankie's eyes slide around the area past the entrance, fishing for something that will distract her from the five pounds in her pocket that Flossie gave her to spend. He sees a sign erected immediately beyond the Reptile House that reads 'Giants and Dragons – This Way'.

They have dragons over there, says Frankie, mock-excitedly. *And giants.*

Look at this house, Daddy. It's for reptiles. What a reptile?

Snakes and lizards and that. You wouldn't want to see them. What about the meerkats?

I want to see the snakes and lizards.

But it's a lovely day! Do you really want to go into the dark? It's creepy in there.

Can we go to the gift shop instead then?

Frankie gives up.

Okay. Reptiles it is.

They enter through the arched 1930s facade, with the green

lettering. Inside it the walls are dark green, the floor is stone. It is cool, almost cold. China lets go of Frankie's hand and rushes toward the first glass case in front of her.

Daddy! Look!

Inside there is a nine-foot black mamba, in a space marked with ropes and brushwood and old tin sheeting. Its head looks wet, as if oiled or moisturized, but its body unnaturally dry. Its tongue flicks out, forked and spindly. China takes a small step back.

Urrgh.

Frankie watches the slow coiling and uncoiling of the snake, mesmerized.

Is it dangerous? asks China.

Oh yes. It could kill you easily. It's poisonous.

It looks happy.

It's true — the expression on the face of the snake is of calm satisfaction. Frankie smiles mischievously.

It's just seen its dinner.

The snake is looking directly at China, who gives a shiver.

A delicious little China-snack. A Chinese takeaway.

China giggles and runs away beyond the glass case into the murk of the corridor beyond.

It won't catch me!

Frankie follows her. He catches up with her staring into what seems to be an empty glass box. Then he registers that it is festooned with empty snake skins.

What are these?

Frankie reads the information plaque.

The snakes shed their skins every year and then grow new ones.

Why? asks China.

Frankie rummages in the frayed satchel of his vaguely remembered school lessons for solutions.

They grow out of them. So they sort of burst out and then grow new ones.

Wouldn't it be funny if we did that too.

We sort of do. I read in the paper the other day that we get a whole new body every seven years.

Do we? For real?

Yes. Our cells are always dying and growing again. And after seven years there's not a single cell left that's the same.

So I'm going to get a new body soon?

Not for a few years.

And will it be exactly the same?

The same, only different. New.

Will you get one too?

Yes.

Good, coz you're all wrinkly.

She thinks for a moment.

How can you still be you, if there's nothing of you left?

Frankie considers this, trying to concoct a plausible answer, but China has run off again, this time to the anacondas and boas. She stops in front of an immense carpet python, body the thickness of a car tyre.

Daddy. It's so big.

Frankie, like China, is astonished at the terrifying size of the thing, a great coiled death-rope.

Is it poisonous too?

Frankie reads the caption.

It suffocates its prey and swallows it whole. Guess what, China? It can swallow a whole deer.

Stop joking me!

It really can.

Yuck, she says cheerfully. *That's horrible. It must get terrible ingidestion.*

Indigestion. Yes, I dare say.

Can we go to the gift shop now?

Don't you want to see the dragons?

There's no such thing as dragons.

But there are. They have some here. And giants.

China's eyes go wide, daring to believe it for a moment. Frankie picks her up, feels the warmth of her small body against the chill of the inside air. Hugs her just for gratitude and joy.

You're squeezing me too tight. I can't breathe.

I'm an anaconda!

Stop it! You're scaring me.

Sorry.

Frankie releases his grip.

Show me the dragons then, says China.

Okay.

They're not true, are they?

Come on. Let's have a look.

Still holding China in his arms – she is so light and smells of soap and cake and strawberry toothpaste – they head out into the bright sunlight. He sees to his left a symbol for gorillas and in front of him a sign for 'Dragons and Giants'.

Can we see the monkeys first? says Frankie.

That's because there's no such thing as dragons and you know it.

You'll see.

They walk over to the gorilla enclosure. China is walking

beside him now. They hold hands, hers tiny, nested in his palm. They walk past the mandrills, China giggling at their rainbow behinds, until they reach the gorilla cage. Frankie looks for the gorillas but can see nothing. China stands next to him. The cage appears to be empty.

Are they in there, Daddy?

Maybe not. They might be sleeping.

They are about to walk away and go to see the giants when suddenly there is an immense thud against the glass in front of them. China squeals and even Frankie takes a step back.

Shit! mutters Frankie.

An immense gorilla, maybe a hundred kilos, with sullen, intelligent, malicious eyes, gazes at them reproachfully. Frankie and China stare back. China holds Frankie's hand very tightly. Then the gorilla relaxes his gaze, bored, sits down and starts picking vaguely at his toes.

I don't like it.

It can't get out, says Frankie, nevertheless shaken at the force with which the gorilla had thrown itself at the barrier.

It might break the glass.

No, says Frankie, uncertain nonetheless. The thing is so huge.

I'm scared.

Don't be silly.

I'm not being silly! It's scary. And ugly.

Fine.

They make their way out of the gorilla enclosure. They have walked in a circle and the sign advertising dragons and giants appears again.

Right. Now I'm going to show you a dragon.

I bet you don't.

How much do you bet?

I bet you a kiss and a cuddle.

Done.

He puts his hand out and she shakes it solemnly.

They follow the signs that promise giants and dragons. A notice reads, 'Beware! A dragon may be watching you.'

Underneath is written 'These reptiles are intelligent. A dragon has sensed your presence.'

A few yards further on a sign announces the Dragon's Lair.

It's not true, is it Daddy? says China, hesitating slightly.

Don't you want to go in?

Not if there's real dragons.

Scaredy cat.

There aren't, are there?

Let's go and see.

He takes her hand and coaxes her through the doorway. To the left is a poster, explaining the behaviour of the Giant Komodo Dragon. Frankie stops and reads it.

It says here they have more than fifty kinds of bacteria in their spit. If they bite you, you die a week later.

Where is it? I can't see it.

Frankie turns and stares at the glass.

I don't know.

Can it breathe fire?

Maybe. I don't think so.

Suddenly loping from the back of the cage, eyes black and full of meaningless depth, comes the dragon. It pads silently towards them, then stops and fixes its gaze in their direction. It is about eight foot long, larger than Frankie had expected.

Are you scared, China?

That's not a real dragon!

Course it is. Read the sign.

It's too small. And it can't breathe fire. It's a rubbish dragon.

That's not very nice. You're hurting its feelings.

It can't hear me. Can we go to the gift shop now?

Don't you owe me something?

What?

A kiss and a cuddle.

They're not real dragons!

Frankie sighs, gives in and they start to make their way towards the shop by the Terrace Restaurant. China, waving her five-pound note in the air, a tiny flag of celebration, runs into the shop. Frankie waits outside, enjoying the sun on his face. He gives into temptation and switches on his phone.

To his surprise and consternation, it shows twenty-one messages, eight of them from Veronica.

When China emerges from the gift shop three minutes later, she finds her father sitting on a wooden bench, head down, staring at his feet, shaking softly.

Daddy? she says, holding a stuffed toy penguin in her hands. *Why are you crying?*

Frankie says nothing, does not move. China, stunned, stares at him, puts the down the toy, tries to calculate what to do.

Then she comes behind him, puts a small hand on his back and begins to rub in circular motions.

There, there Daddy, she says. *There there.*

* * *

Two weeks later

Nodge and Frankie are walking through Shepherd's Bush Market. The placc is fundamentally unchanged since they were children. Cheap fish, cheap meat, cheap toys for kids who can't afford the proper stuff, cheap perfume, knockdowns, past the sell-bys, counterfeits, back-of-a-lorry scatterlings. Dominating them all are fabric salesmen, great rolls of linen and wool and silk like upended tree trunks from a fantasy landscape. In fact the Goldhawk Road seems to be almost all fabric shops nowadays.

What the fuck do they do with all this cloth? says Frankie. *Got to be a front, doesn't it?*

It is tremendously hot, although there are thunderheads in the distance. Frankie takes off his jacket. The armpits of his shirt are stained with a marsh of perspiration. He walks up to the middle-aged West Indian man wearing a plastic red, green and gold apron stained with fish guts.

Alright, Carlton?

All right, Frankie. The fishmonger waves a haddock at him. *Want some fish?*

Not the shit you sell. I'd rather go down Tesco's.

Carlton laughs.

This is fresh, mate.

Fresh out the canal. Anyway. I don't like haddock. Yellow fish ain't natural.

Frankie the Fib! The butcher opposite is speaking now, a cigarette hanging out the side of his mouth, his body skinny, his face big and red. He has had his stall here since 1981, since Frankie was a teenager.

Couple of pork chops, please, Dave.

Dave, whistling to himself past the cigarette stub, tosses two chops aloft, lets them land, and starts to wrap them in greaseproof paper.

Not those ones. Too small.

Why's his meat okay and my fish ain't? shouts Carlton, mock-offended.

Don't take it personal, says Frankie. *It's just that your fish smells bad.*

Fish do smell bad, says Carlton.

How about these? says Dave, holding up a couple of larger chops, blood lining the crease between meat and fat.

They'll do.

On the house, says Dave.

No, you're all right, says Frankie, reaching for his wallet.

I heard about Colin. Take the chops. A little gesture.

He was Jewish though, says Frankie, reproachfully.

Dave blushes.

I'm sorry. I didn't . . .

Frankie laughs and points his finger at Dave like a pistol.

Colin was about as Jewish as those pork chops are Jewish.

Dave holds the chops up in salute and recognition of the wind-up.

Got me.

Frankie takes the chops and he and Nodge move on – through the battery stalls, the toy shops, the fruit and veg costers selling yams and plantains. He buys something for China – a Bratz doll – and orders a bacon sandwich. The woman selling, whose name Frankie can't remember, puts the HP on in the way she knows he likes it, thick like jam.

He checks his watch. Three minutes to twelve. He faces over the direction of the White City Estate where he, Tony, Colin and Nodge grew up together. The noise and bustle is immense. He bolts down his bacon sandwich to finish it in time.

You're in a hurry, says the woman serving him.

Twelve o'clock silence. Wouldn't be respectful to do it with half a rasher of streaky bacon hanging out my cakehole.

He finishes the sandwich, checks his watch again. The second hand climbs towards the twelve. He thinks again of Colin. They would come here sometimes together and buy sweets. Colin always bought Refreshers. Always.

Frankie takes the ceremonial Refresher he has bought earlier from the newsagent on the corner out of his pocket, unwraps it and places it solemnly in his mouth.

As twelve o'clock passes, a hush begins to take hold of the market. Like spreading mercury, it leaves gaps and spaces. Many people continue talking, oblivious to the dozens of people who, like Frankie, are standing stock still, staring at the ground or fixing their gaze on the sky.

Frankie feels tears begin to rush down his cheeks. Nodge puts a hand on his arm.

The silence is for two minutes, but thirty seconds on, the noise is still continuing – reduced but grating. Chatting, gossip, even laughter. He glares at a white teenage girl wearing a hoody who is laughing with her mate and puts his finger to his mouth to silence her. She holds up a finger and mouths at him to fuck off, then carries on giggling.

Frankie bites his lip and continues facing the White City Estate, chewing gravely on the Refresher. He can see Carlton, standing still by his fish, looking down at the ground. Hamid, one of the fabric salesmen, likewise. Two women in hijabs. One of them, like Frankie, is weeping. But Dave the butcher is still selling his chops and steaks, his raw meat, and chatting merrily to the customers.

He thinks of Colin, what was left of him.

Meat, it's all meat.

Meat dressed up and walking around.

It is like a semi-frozen tableau now, a paralysed version of the London he has always loved. The mixtures, the blaring noise, the colours, the sheer difference of one thing from the next. The cheerful rudeness, the mockery, the popping of bubbles of self-importance, always bringing down to earth, back to earth. Nothing too serious, no one too important.

Except this. Except this.

The two minutes ends and the scattered statues begin to move once more. The woman behind the breakfast counter, whose name Frankie still can't remember, begins again her endless round of frying eggs and bacon, the frying she has done for the last twenty years, more or less every day, the chips, the ketchup, the watery grey coffee.

Frankie walks back over to Dave.

Alright, Dave?

All right, Frankie.

He holds out the chops to Dave.

You can keep these.

He drops the bloody plastic bag on the display counter. Then he walks off towards the Uxbridge Road, leaving the butcher looking confused, a faint anger brewing. Frankie wipes his face with the back of his hand, leaving stains on his Paul Smith linen suit. The dark clouds in the sky do not release their burden. The sun hammers on, relentless and unyielding.

* * *

There are twenty-three people at Colin's funeral. Frankie counts them as the minister jabbers on, the same one who married Colin and Roxy, tall and stooping, insisting tediously on love and forgiveness. Frankie feels neither, only a swelling blackness that threatens to swallow him and spit out his bones.

He sits next to Veronica, who has been staring at the floor since taking her pew. Nodge is on his other side. China is at home with Cordelia and Michael. Roxy is on the far side of Nodge, dressed in black taffeta.

Did you see the reporters outside? whispers Frankie to Nodge. *Vultures.*

I can see the headlines now. '7/7 Hero Who Saved Imam's Wife Buried'.

Never figured Colin as a hero.

If you're dead you're always a hero, says Frankie. *He was probably just too dumb to use the tourniquet on himself.*

The droning of the organ fills the small space with a sound like sour treacle. Colin's coffin is up on a dais. It looks expensive, mahogany perhaps. Brass handles. Roxy chose it.

Nice casket, says Nodge.

She was never mean with Colin's money, says Frankie, lowering his voice further so Roxy won't hear.

Frankie can't stop staring at the coffin. Suddenly he has a scratchy film of Colin and himself as children flickering inside his head. Playing table football. Kicking cans in the park.

Colin's face, scaring Frankie with the openness of his love. With his worship. The love between them then, so long forgotten. But suddenly, here resurrected.

Now Colin in that fucking box.

Frankie begins to cry, for the lost child that became the lost adult, the scraps of whom are inside the casket. He suddenly sees himself in the box lying next to Colin then pushes the image urgently away. He feels Nodge's hand on his back, gently circling. His tears have started Roxy off.

Now Nodge turns to Roxy.

I know you loved him, says Nodge.

I didn't, says Roxy. *Well, that is to say, I did. But I only found out that I did after he got blown up. Anyway. That's not why I'm crying,* says Roxy, choking the words out between sobs.

Why?

I'm ashamed, Nodge, she says, between gobbets of tears.

Why on earth would you be ashamed?

Her weeping simply intensifies.

It doesn't matter now, I suppose, says Nodge.

Now Roxy brings her weeping under control, turns to Nodge and whispers in his ear.

I know you think I'm just a money-grubbing bitch and I was really, sort of. But in the end I loved him. He was just so helpless. You couldn't stop yourself.

So why are you ashamed?

Her voice drops to an almost inaudible level.

Because it was my fault.

Nodge is about to ask her to explain, but she turns away, as the vicar, monotoned, polished and insincere, reaches the end of the first part of the ceremony, leaving a flat silence. Frankie, meanwhile, hasn't really heard him, is lost in his thoughts. He then becomes conscious of the vicar inviting people up to the wooden podium, those who wish to make tributes. Frankie has a short speech prepared, but before he can stand, a bulky man pushes past the small congregation down the aisle and makes his way unsteadily up onto the dais and stands behind the lectern.

Frankie is bewildered. Then he recognizes the figure.

Tony Diamonte.

Tony is shaky on his feet. He sways and nearly falls, then steadies himself. He nods towards the coffin.

Lovely piece of timber there, he says. *Classy. You wouldn't think he would need a full-size one, would you? Given that he had no fucking legs at the end. Hold on, yes, come to think of it he did still have one. That explains it.*

He is theatrically drunk. The vicar stands up as if to usher him away from the podium, but Tony gives him a deadly look that makes him anxiously retreat further into the wings.

Frankie covers his face with the spread of his fingers. Veronica stares at the floor.

Who the fuck is that? says Roxy.

Déjà vu, says Frankie to Veronica.

Veronica says nothing. She has gone very pale.

Yeh, it really is a lovely box. Not really Colin, though. Not his style. Colin would be better off with one made out cornflake packets. Do you know, Colin, all his life, only ate cornflakes? Never muesli. Never granola. God forbid. Never Honey Nut Loops. Always cornflakes. Morning, noon and night. Kellogg's Cornflakes, no other brand would do. He could tell the difference, believe me. With exactly one spoon of sugar. Dessert spoon, I mean.

He casts his gaze blearily around the congregation.

He was the same with everything, was Colin. Would only drink Hofmeister lager. Broke his heart when they stopped doing it. Would only eat Walkers cheese and onion crisps. His underpants, they were always from Marks & Spencer. Even though Marks & Spencer have been shit for years, he would still buy his pants there. He really hated things to change.

He nods, then looks up and behind him at a portrait of Christ depicted in the stained-glass window.

Things have changed now, though, haven't they, Colin? Big time. Though they won't be changing any more. That should be right up your street.

Frankie, unable to stand the mortification any more, hisses at him.

Tony. Give it a rest. Have some respect.

Tony looks at him and points a shaky finger in his direction.

That's his friend, Frankie Blue, who's just having a pop at me there. For saying what I think. For being honest instead of the shit sandwich that's usually served up at these gaffs.

Tony looks threateningly in the direction of the vicar, who is standing ten foot to his right, alternately wringing his hands and adjusting and readjusting his spectacles.

Tony takes a handkerchief out of his pocket and blows his nose.

Colin used to worship Frankie. Didn't he, Frankie? Tony gives a grotesque pout. *He thought you were his bestest friend.*

Tony laughs bitterly.

You sold him out, though, didn't you? We all sold him out. Even his new best friend, Jesus, sold him out in the end.

He gestures towards the stained-glass window. There is absolute silence. A cloud passes over Tony's face, or perhaps a clearing of clouds, recognition of something within. Then he fixes the congregation with his blurry, red-eyed gaze again.

I used to bully Colin. Before he kicked it. I mean, obviously before he kicked it. Obviously. Wouldn't be much point now.

He begins to cry. Great heaving sobs. The vicar takes the opportunity to try and lead Tony away from the podium, but Tony roughly pushes him away. The sobs go on for what seem like minutes. Finally Tony speaks again. He turns to the coffin.

I just wanted to say, I'm sorry, Colin. I'm so, so sorry, mate. I never did anything but treat you like a muppet. But you were . . .

He stops, stares at the vaulted roof, as if searching for words there.

. . . You were Colin. *Weren't you? Colin Burden.*

The vicar is desperately consulting with some kind of church officer who has appeared stage left, no doubt wondering if it's worth causing a scene by trying to remove Tony forcibly from the lectern. But Tony is big. Making an even worse scene than the one that is going on now seems untenable.

Tony takes his eyes from the gabled roof and faces the congregation again.

I mean, let's face it, shall we? Colin was a boring little turd. But he never hurt anyone. Never. He was just struggling, like we're all struggling. To be someone. To matter. To have someone give a shit about you, one way or the other.

There is a glass of water on the lectern and Tony takes a long swig from it

That's better. I also want to say something about the people who blew him up. I mean, I know the vicar said we must forgive our enemies. But I just wanted to say this.

He takes a hip flask out of his pocket and swigs from that as well.

That's a load of shit.

Now he takes a grubby and crumpled piece of newspaper out of his pocket and reads from it.

Mohammad Sidique Khan, Edgware Road bomber. Shehzad Tanweer, Aldgate bomber. Hasib Mir Hussain, Tavistock Square bomber. Oh, hold on, here it is. This is the geezer. Germaine Lindsay. Nineteen years old. Russell Square bomber. We're all about forgiving him, is that right, Rev?

He looks over to the vicar, cowering at the end of the dais, who says nothing.

That's them alright. The fab four. They'll be in heaven now, shagging virgins and that. A hundred each they get. With wide lovely eyes. That's what it says in the Qu'ran. 'Wide lovely eyes'.

He takes another swig from the hip flask.

Anyway. I want to say this. I don't care what your religion is. I don't care what your faith is. I don't care who your god is, or if you feel you should wear a beard, or pray to Mecca or Barney the fucking dinosaur, I don't care, I really don't give a monkey's.

He screws up the piece of paper and flicks it at the stained-glass window. It bounces off Jesus's left foot, just below the stigma.

Because when it comes down to it, when all's said and done, they're just a bunch of cunts.

That's enough! says the vicar, finally marching across to the lectern. *This is a house of God!*

Tony, instead of resisting this time, meekly allows himself to be led away, mumbling distinctly enough for Frankie, Nodge and Roxy to hear him.

Thank you for your time. Sorry if I've embarrassed anyone. Sorry. Sorry.

Led by the church officer, he makes his way down from the lectern and is swiftly marched along the aisle and out of the church.

There is stillness for about five seconds, then the vicar comes and stands at front of the congregation again.

Well, he says.

He cannot quite look at the gathering. Instead, he goes straight into his speech.

Let us commend our brother, Colin Burden, to the mercy of God. I am the resurrection and the life, saith the Lord: he that believeth in me, though he were dead, yet shall he live: and whosoever liveth and believeth in me shall never die. We therefore commit his body to the ground; earth to earth, ashes to ashes, dust to dust; in the sure and certain hope of the Resurrection to eternal life.

The organ begins to sound. A purple curtain slowly closes around the coffin to conceal it from sight.

From the back, people slowly begin to file out of the chapel.

More entertaining than I expected, says Frankie to no one in particular.

* * *

There's a ring on Nodge's doorbell. He opens it to see Owen standing there huddled and lost in a coat two sizes too big for him.

Are you okay? says Nodge.

Can I come in?

Nodge has been watching *Top Gear*. He has always loved performance cars, though he has never owned one. In fact, apart from a second-hand Hillman Imp, his Hackney Cab is the only car he has ever paid for. He leads Owen into the living room, flicks off the volume and sits back down on the sofa. Owen, still in his coat, lowers himself into the space next to him.

So what's up, O?

Been to the doctor's.

Hmmm. And?

It's Hep B. It's sort of an STD.

Nodge takes his hand, which he feels is trembling.

Don't worry. We've been safe. And you'll be fine, O.

That's not what I'm worried about.

Owen squeezes Nodge's hand and sighs.

You didn't sign up for this, Nodge.

What is it that I didn't sign up for?

Could be bad. Liver damage. Apparently it's been in the blood for the last six months, so it's quite advanced. Or it could just go away. Sometimes it does that.

Nodge feels the words rush into his mouth, cannot censor them or choke them back.

Could you, you know. Die?

It's not impossible.

Now Owen begins to stroke the back of Nodge's hand in slow, tender sweeps.

How impossible is it? What are the stats?

Apparently there's a fifteen to twenty-five per cent chance.

Of what? Don't say survival.

The other way round. Seventy-five to eighty per cent chance of survival.

That's not so bad.

I'm scared, Jon.

Nodge puts his arms around Owen and holds him. They stay like that in silence for almost a minute. Then Owen suddenly pushes Nodge away.

This isn't your problem. We've been a proper couple — what? Six months? You hardly know me. I'm going to need a lot of looking after. And that's the best outcome. After that, who knows what? You'd be better out of it.

Nodge's face is now a stony mask, expressionless, flat.

I wish I could think of something comforting to say, he says.

'Fuck it'. *Try that.*

'Fuck it'. *How does that feel?*

Doesn't really help.

Another minute passes until the silence buckles.

Look, Jon. I'm going to go home now. I don't expect you to call me. I have lots of friends who can look after me. I have a mum and a dad who love me and still keep my old room empty. You have no responsibility for this. None. We'll see if I can go away and get better. Then if you still want me, I'll come back. Because, I sort of haven't told you this but I think you are terrific. I really do.

Thanks. That's nice of you.

That's why I'm not going to put you through this.

I see.

Owen stands up. Nodge can see the yellow tinge of his skin now, more clearly than ever. When Owen speaks again there is an imploring note in his voice.

It wasn't fair of me. Getting involved with you. At the back of my mind, I knew this was going to be a possibility. I've had suspicions for a long time. I was selfish. We should have stayed just friends. But I liked you so much. That's the only reason. I was weak. I'm sorry.

Nodge nods, turns his eyes back to the silent screen. Jeremy

Clarkson's mouth working up and down, his paunch hanging over his belt under a lilac shirt, his shock of curly hair greying and stretching wearily upwards.

So I'm going to go now. And not in a martyr-ish 'I'm going to go now' way. It's simply the best thing to do. I'll pick up my stuff later. Okay? I just need to get my toilet bag. And my Chanel Anteaus. I'm not letting you have that. It's still three-quarters full.

Right.

Owen goes into the bathroom, and comes out with the toilet bag and the bottle of cologne. He hands the cologne to Nodge, who takes it and stares at it.

A gift. When you wear it you can think about me.

Okay.

Bye then, Nodge.

Nodge continues to stare at the bottle.

Never really been my thing. I'm more a Lynx guy.

There's a pause.

Give me a hug, Nodge. I'll see you in a while. Probably.

Nodge violently throws the bottle of Anteaus at the fireplace. It shatters, emitting a cloud of scent and scatters shards of glass onto the coir carpet.

Sit down, he says.

Owen is stunned by this display of violence – he has never seen Nodge lose his temper. Nodge takes his wrist and pulls him down to the couch. Owen, astonished to find how strong Nodge is – and how feeble he himself has become – is powerless to resist.

Nodge holds him. The aroma of Anteaus from the fireplace gets stronger and stronger, scent molecules gathered into invisible fog drifting towards them.

That cost me a fortune, says Owen.

I hate the smell of it anyway, says Nodge.

Why didn't you tell me?

I don't always say what I think.

Can I go now? says Owen, weakly pulling away.

No, says Nodge, firmly, turning the TV back on with the remote. *I'm not watching this shit on my own.*

Clarkson pulls away in a GTR.

Owen tries to stand up again but Nodge pulls him back down.

It's for the best. You'll end up hating me. Let me go, Nodge.

But Nodge holds on to him, pulling him still closer. Jeremy Clarkson whoops with delight at the torque of his ride. Finally, resigned, Owen puts his head on Nodge's shoulder. Nodge turns up the volume with the remote. They watch the rest of the programme together, in calm quiet that, finally, to the surprise of both of them, becomes silently joyful.

* * *

Veronica sits on a tatty chair with a red vinyl seat scarred by deep, straight cuts at the drop-in centre in Hammersmith. To attend here is a necessary part of her training as a therapist. Some of the people in the room are, she feels, plainly crazy, muttering or waving their fists in the air at invisible enemies. She feels frightened, and ashamed of being frightened.

Good turnout today, says Peter Oakeshott – he is only ever known as Oakeshott – a middle-aged man with a riotously thick head of salt and pepper hair, looming above her and surveying his dowdy kingdom, a substantial Victorian house with damp spots on the ceiling, a carpet pocked with rips and bald patches and a few sticks of unstable chipboard furniture. Many of the chairs are, like Veronica's, distressed, stained or fraying as if they have been chosen to reflect the inner lives of those attending the centre.

There are about twenty-five 'clients' although 'client' sounds wrong, because Veronica doesn't get paid. That will come when she qualifies later in the year, with any luck. Towards the rear of the house is the small room, once a pantry, where she conducts her therapy sessions. Her first client for that day is a depressed Czech from Prague called Oleg, although everyone at the centre calls him Leggy, partly an ironic comment on his short fat legs which stretch against over-tight trousers.

She doesn't mind Oleg, although he is radioactively lonely. He is sitting on a green wing armchair staring at her mildly, waiting for the clock to erase the time between now and midday. Veronica offers him a noncommittal smile. His expression does not alter in response.

I sometimes wonder, says Veronica to Oakeshott, lowering her voice slightly, *and I know that I'm not meant to think this, but really, what is . . . ?*

The point? says Oakeshott, grimacing as he drinks from the coffee that one of his clients has made him, using barely fresh milk. There are small yellow flecks of sourish cream floating on the surface that make Veronica think of a Rorschach test.

You have to admit, she says, *the number of people who recover are vanishingly small. So far as I can see.*

I'm not even sure what recovery would look like. These are unhappy people. Just straightforward unhappy. Given how poor most of them are, I'm not surprised. I'm not even sure they are really ill. A lot of them just want to talk to someone. Anyone. The postman would do just as well.

She checks the clock. Oakeshott regards her steadily. His chin is punctuated with straws of long white stubble and he has deep-set, very melancholy eyes that can transform in a moment into sparkles of brilliant joy.

Sure. This is the high point of the week for some of them, says Oakeshott. *Just to be in a house where they know others are in the same boat as them. Just to be warm. Some soup. A little kindness.*

So this whole thing is just a kind of theatre? For appearances?

Oakeshott works his hair with his fingers, as if trying to braid it into knots.

On the contrary.

He leans forward, bringing his face within six inches of Veronica's. She can smell his toothpaste, cinnamon and liquorice.

Look, Veronica — what do you think therapy is? Do you think people wake up one day and they are all better? No. The tangles in their minds are like . . . like great fields of briar, and you are there with a tiny instrument, not necessarily the right shape — a teaspoon, say, or broken twig — trying to sort some of the tangles out. And if by some miracle you did sort some of the tangles out to the extent that they could find a path through the field — in other words, so they were only as tangled up and puzzled as the rest of us — then what would be there? On the other side? Do you think, golden fields? Do you think, blue skies? No. Not for them. Not for us either. You prune, you rearrange, you simplify, but then it all grows back again, sometimes even wilder, more out of control than before. There is simply — perhaps — a lessening of suffering. Temporarily. Or even a break from it. Or there is simply being heard. That's something.

So what am I? Just a signpost in a field? A broken twig?

If that. You are not so powerful as to offer a cure, Veronica. None of us are. And you are benefitting, are you not? You are learning?

Oakeshott leans back in his chair again, but keeps his eyes on her. Veronica notices Oleg take a dirty handkerchief out of his pocket and blow his nose. He is arranging his clothes as if in readiness for his session, pulling tight the piece of rope that holds his soiled trousers firmly around his swelling, vague midriff. His trousers are mildewed. His shoes, oddly enough, look expensive, and are polished to a high sheen.

It's hard to tell if I'm learning anything or not. This is what I have to do in order to get my qualification. So, I do it.

Is that all?

I've learned something, I suppose. I must have.

What have you learned?

Veronica considers this carefully, turning it around in her mind like a parcel that can be unwrapped, inside of which she fears there might be nothing at all.

That people don't know themselves. That they are self-destructive. That they will hurt others seriously in order to relieve a very small burden they are carrying. That they are narcissistic.

Is that what you've found from the people you've met here?

Veronica hesitates.

I'm not talking about the people I've met here. I'm talking about myself.

Ah, says Oakeshott, laughing. *Then you are beginning to learn something. So your supervision with Elizabeth Pember has been useful?*

It's in me that all the lessons are held. I understand that now. It's in me where all the answers are — if there are any answers. Looking inside myself — it's like the bramble fields you were talking about. It's as if I'm walking through the fields, blindfolded, crashing, tripping, then standing and believing that it all makes sense, then crashing and tripping again.

Doesn't sound like much fun.

Actually, it's exciting. But frightening. And it has side effects.

For instance?

It's having an effect on my marriage, for instance.

In what way?

Veronica doesn't answer.

Sorry. None of my business. Force of habit. We're a nosy bunch. I'll shut up.

I ask myself, really, what is love? she says, ignoring him. *Is it really only a form of . . . narcissism? The good feeling you get when someone else likes you? And when you like being liked? Why do we hitch ourselves to people, as if they were the answer to all our problems? As if they were the answer to even* one *problem. When maybe they* are *the problem.*

There is a retching sound. Oleg is bent over and, it seems, about to throw up in the waste paper bin.

Looks like you might have a postponement, says Oakeshott.

Oleg looks up and wipes his mouth with the back of his sleeve. It seems he has recovered himself.

We ready? he calls, cheerfully, as if nothing untoward has happened.

He gestures towards the therapy room. Veronica is just about to move in his direction when she glances across the room to check the clock, which hangs above the door to the outer hall. There, next to the door, standing in profile staring out of the grubby window into the street, is Tony Diamonte.

He looks just as handsome as before, but shabbier, much sadder than he did at the funeral.

Veronica thinks of trying to escape to the therapy room with Oleg, but at that exact moment Tony looks over in her direction. However, he doesn't seem to recognize her. He pauses as if he, too, is looking for escape. Then reluctantly, as if captured by her glance, he shuffles over towards Veronica. And it is a shuffle, the broken step of the defeated, not the confident stride that she remembers from years ago.

Hi, Vronky. That's what Frankie used to call you isn't it? Vronky?

Veronica stiffens and almost turns away, but in the end decides to stand her ground.

What are you doing here?

What's everybody doing here?

There's an embarrassed silence.

It's okay, Veronica. You don't have to talk to me. I know you never liked me. And I know I made a fool of myself at Colin's funeral. I was so . . . I was so angry. And so drunk. But it's no excuse.

Veronica looks him straight in the eyes. Which, she sees, are an extraordinary shade of deep chestnut.

No. I didn't like you.

I can't blame you.

She checks her watch. Even now it has gone past twelve and she has her excuse, she can't quite leave.

I've got an appointment.

Sure.

He turns to walk away. Something makes Veronica speak again.

How have you been?

Tony turns back. He scratches the back of his hand repeatedly with a dirty fingernail. Veronica notes red welts there.

Low. Very low. To be honest. I mean, after I stopped seeing Frankie and the boys. The gack got hold of me. I expect you know that. I didn't care about anything, really. Except the next score. The salon went down. I lost my flat.

I heard rumours. But — Jesus, Tony.

Found myself sleeping rough for a while. Then an old acquaintance of mine — not even a proper friend — gave me a part-time cutters job in his shop. Trusted me. Even though he knew I'd been hooked and was dossing on park benches. I won't forget what he did. Took me a long while to find my way back. After that I stopped. Was clean. Bumped into Nodge one day at a football match and I was feeling good, been steady for a good six months. I'd made enough contacts to go freelance. 'The Pirate Hairdresser'. But Colin — that knocked me back a bit again. Just for a few days. Well, a few weeks. A few non-stop weeks. Since then I've been trying to find my way out of the hole. It was that or lose all my clients. No. It was that or lose myself once and for all. I would be finished. So in the end I got the message. I have to take responsibility. That's what I'm doing. Haven't touched a drop since the funeral. Christ, I can't think of that day at the church without cringing. What sort of a mug am I anyway? Look, I'll just go away. I'm sorry if you've had to see me. I'll find a different drop-in centre. I don't want to embarrass you. Or myself. Any more than I already have done.

Veronica tries to work out if he is gaming her, glances at his eyes again. Sees momentarily in them a light that is guttering.

No need for that, she says.

This place keeps me on the straight and narrow. Oakeshott is a saint. He's a good man.

What you doing here anyway? You never stuck me as particularly nuts.

I'm training as a therapist.

Of course. Of course you are. That's good. Good for you then.

They fall into silence again.

Do me a favour, will you, Veronica? Don't tell Frankie that you saw me like this. I've got a little scrap of pride left. A little bit. Maybe one day it will be . . . you know. At a normal level. Whatever that is.

He starts to fidget with his gold necklace, with its charms, the horns and the hand. Veronica remembers that it was meant to fend off evil spirits, some kind of Calabrian folktale.

I won't say anything.

Thanks. Thank you.

Don't mention it.

Maybe I'll see you down here again.

You never know.

* * *

Nodge is sipping his cup of tea outside the London Taxi shelter in Notting Hill Gate. A little green pastoral hut, it looks like it was transported from the Tyrolean Mountains. Big Eddie Fox is leaning against the door eating a sausage sandwich. A black man, he is only five foot four but with enormous shoulders and a tiny head. Mickey the Wrench – so-called because he once attacked a drunken fare who wouldn't pay up with a wrench that he keeps in the front of the cab – is circling his cab restlessly, trying to keep warm. Nodge balances himself against the bonnet of his classic 1989 black Fairway. He is thinking about Owen who has a doctor's appointment today, he isn't sure where. Somewhere around this neck of the woods, he seems to remember.

Mickey wanders over. He's wearing a tweedy flat cap, which he's always compulsively fiddling with. His big, round, lugubrious face looms out from under the frayed, greasy peak.

All right, Nodge?

283

Mickey. How's the trade?

Shit.

You always say it's shit.

Because it always is shit. Minicabs are taking all the trade. Won't be any black cabs left in ten years. Mickey kicks a pebble across the tarmac.

They'll never see us off. They can't find their way around anywhere without spending half on hour with their nose in an A to Z. The Knowledge is still the gold standard.

They'll invent some kind of gadget for that, you wait and see. You seen these Garmins?

The Satnavs? Yeh, I seen them. Don't worry about it. No one's going to replace the London Cabbie. It'll take more than a few bits of hardware. We're a legend. You seem to be doing all right though. I heard you just got a place in Spain.

Marbella, yeh. Me and Judy going to retire there in a few years. Get away from this dump. How's things with you?

Not bad.

What about you and your missus? Fancy a place abroad? I know a bloke who does timeshares, kosher, not a con.

I haven't got one, says Nodge.

Haven't got one of what? says Eddie Fox, who has finished his sandwich and is edging closer.

Nodge says he hasn't got a missus, says Mickey the Wrench.

No, that's right. Never has had a missus so long as I've known him, says Eddie.

Probably a poof, says Mickey, mildly. *You a poof, Nodge?*

Yeh, says Nodge. *Course I am. Obviously. A nine bob note.*

Probably is at that, says Mickey. *Loves a Hampton up his jacks don't you, Nodge?*

I'm a giver more than a taker, says Nodge, checking his watch.
I'd better get back on shift.

He's just ugly, says Eddie. *Can't get a bird.*

Then, out of the corner of his eye, Nodge sees Owen
approaching along Kensington Park Road. He feels the urge to
duck behind the green awning of the cab shelter. But Owen spots
him, his face registering surprise and delight, and raises a hand.

Nodge shifts uncomfortably as Owen walks across the road
towards them. He thanks heaven that Owen is not and has
never been remotely camp. All the same, anxiety is pooling in
his stomach.

Hi, Nodge, says Owen. *Quelle surprise.*

Owen, says Nodge. *What you doing here?*

The doctor's, says Owen, looking puzzled. *I told you.
Portland Road.*

He waves his hand vaguely towards the west.

Eddie and Mickey, to Nodge's disappointment, do not
retreat. There is a brief silence.

This is Eddie, says Nodge. *And Mickey. This is Owen. A
mate of mine.*

Alright? says Eddie.

Alright? says Mickey, eyeballing him.

He's been to the doctors, says Nodge.

So he said, says Mickey. *You alright?*

I'm fine, says Owen, cheerfully. *Are you allowed to get a coffee
at the hut if you're not a cabbie?*

No, you're fucking not, says Eddie. *You got to show your badge and
answer three questions from the Knowledge.*

He's joking, says Mickey. *He thinks he's being amusing, don't you,
Eddie? What do you want? I'll get you one.*

Thanks, says Owen. *Have they got a flat white?*

They got white, says Mickey. *And it's flat.*

Sorry?

It's totally fucking flat. Flat as they come.

Oh, I'm being ridiculous. Sorry. I'll take whatever comes. Lovely.

Why, Nodge asks himself in frustration, is Owen suddenly choosing this moment to come over all Graham Norton?

Mickey heads towards the shelter, but Eddie holds his ground, lights a cigarette.

So, aren't you going to ask me? says Owen.

What?

About the doctor's.

Isn't it sort of private?

Yes, of course. Sorry.

Let's get in the back of the cab, shall we?

Mickey returns with the coffee which he hands to Owen.

Thanks a lot. He reaches in his pocket for change. *How much do I owe you?*

Don't be a cunt, says Mickey cheerfully.

Come on then, says Nodge. *Thanks, Mickey. See you, Eddie.*

See you.

Yeh.

Inside the back of the cab, Owen sits and sips at the coffee.

This is really horrible coffee.

The tea is better. Coffee's not really a thing here.

Owen sips the hot watery liquid thoughtfully.

They don't know, do they?

Who don't know what?

The other cabbies. They don't know that you're gay.

I don't have to tell the world. It's my business. What did the doctor say?
What are you ashamed of?

I'm not ashamed. It just makes life easier. If I worked at John Lewis it wouldn't be so much of a problem.

Owen shrugs.

It's your life. Hiding stuff doesn't really help in the long term, though.

You don't know London cabbies, mate. So to get back to the point. What did the doctor say?

Owen sighs.

It looks like there's fibrosis of the liver. Which could turn to cirrhosis. Or liver cancer.

Shit. And what then?

It probably won't come to that.

Nodge pauses to take this in. He had been more or less expecting it, but it still rocks him. There is sourness in his throat, fear. Nothing shows in his face.

What do you need to do in the meantime?

Take Lamivudine. It's a drug to help out. Might improve the symptoms. It can reduce the viral load. In the meantime it's business as usual.

Meaning?

Tiredness. Sleeplessness. Nausea. Weight loss.

I could use a bit of that.

Be my guest. Dizziness. Cramps in the lower abdomen. It's chronic rather than acute, I think. White tongue. It tastes like there's metal in my mouth.

You have all those old-fashioned fillings. That's probably the taste.

You should have an injection against the virus, Nodge.

Why? We're always careful.

All the same. Also, I've got to stop drinking alcohol. Eat more fruit. Spend a lot of time in bed probably. I can get fevers. Bad fevers. Feeling bloated and gaseous. I'm always cold. It's like having the flu.

What about your job?

I don't know. John Lewis has decent health care.

Just think. You'll get the chance to tell them that it might be curtains for you.

Almost makes it worth it.

They fall into silence.

I can't drink this, says Owen, eventually. He hands the coffee to Nodge, who pours it out of the open window.

Not flat enough for you?

In some cases, for no reason at all, the virus just goes away completely, says Owen.

Never know your luck.

Nodge nods, then clambers into the front of the cab and starts the engine.

Shall I sit up front with you?

It's fine. Make yourself comfortable.

They drive home to Nodge's flat. Owen can hardly make it up the stairs to Nodge's front door. Inside, he washes his face, then flops down on the sofa. Nodge stands over him.

Let me help you out of your clothes.

I'm not an invalid yet, Nodge. It will pass. Don't worry. I just need to rest for a few minutes. Then I'll get these off, put them in the laundry. Have a shower and go to bed with a book. I'm feeling much better, actually. Just knackered. Don't look so helpless.

But I am. I am helpless.

Welcome to the human race, then.

Owen manages a smile. Nodge smiles weakly back.

I'm going to the bedroom to meditate, says Nodge. *I'm stressing out.*

Since when did you meditate?

Veronica taught me to do it. Only she called it something else. 'Mindfulness'. It's quite good. Calms me down. Very good for road rage.

Five minutes after he has settled into his silence, he thinks he hears the latch go and breaks off his session. He gets up. Owen isn't in the living room. Further investigations reveal that Owen isn't in the flat at all.

Nodge rushes out into the corridor, where he catches Owen, bent double, waiting for the lift. He stares at Nodge despairingly. Nodge takes his arm and leads him back into the flat.

As he sits him down, he notices Owen reaching for a piece of paper he has left on the table. Nodge snatches it from his hand.

What's this?

Owen responds simply with a deep breath and a sigh. Nodge reads it.

> Nodge
> This is no good.
> I know you're trying hard, but you're just going to end up hating me.
> Don't come looking for me.
> I love you.
> O. x

You fucking twat, says Nodge, screwing up the piece of paper and throwing it at Owen's face.

It's for the best, says Owen, now in tears.

Stop being such a martyr. This is the second time you've pulled this shit on me. Don't pull it again. And don't say you're doing this for me. You're doing this because you want to be the noble hero.

What do you mean?

You've always loved those songs. Johnny Cash standing alone on the plain staring at the moon, strumming his guitar, nobly bemoaning his tragic fate.

It's no good, Nodge. It's not going to work.

What, because you love country and western?

It's not funny anymore.

Because you don't believe that I love you, says Nodge, furiously. *Not enough anyway. Not enough for this.*

* * *

Later that night, they lie curled in bed together. Owen is feeling better, almost normal. Nodge reaches for him. He wants to make love. Owen turns away, but Nodge persists, feeling obscurely insistent, and Owen begins to respond despite his weariness.

Owen reaches for the condoms by the side of the bed. Nodge takes them from him but tosses them aside.

What are you doing?

Owen starts to protest, but Nodge will not be halted. Eventually, Owen submits. The sex that follows is passionate, more than Owen can ever remember, tender, brutal, tender once more.

Afterwards, he stares at Nodge, eyes flickering with puzzlement.

Why did you do that?

What?

Go bareback. You could get infected. Did you get carried away? Are you just being reckless?

It won't happen again, says Nodge.

Why, then?

I wanted to prove something to you.

What did that prove?

That we're in this together.

Owen takes Nodge's hand. He does not try and leave again.

* * *

You need to get out of bed, Frankie, says Veronica. *And drag yourself out of the cellar. And have a shower, for god's sake. You reek of — I don't know what. Old underpants.*

Frankie is watching TV, stretched out on the camp bed in the basement, covered by a scratchy blanket. The sheets underneath the blanket are rumpled and stale. A DVD of *Pinocchio* is playing. Frankie has been watching it dully. China, who sits at his feet in a pile of crisps that Frankie has been eating and has since discarded, has grown bored with the film and is playing with her Furby.

Frankie has been in the basement since Colin's funeral. He says he can't sleep with another person in the room. Too many noises. Too much movement. Respiration. Stretches. Snores and coughs.

On the screen, Pinocchio, accompanied by Jiminy Cricket, is swimming down towards Monstro the Whale to save his father, Gepetto.

Propped against the wall is a framed poster of St George and the Dragon that Roxy took from Colin's workspace to give Frankie as a keepsake.

Have we got to keep that horrible BNP poster?

It's not a BNP poster. It was the dragon Colin was fascinated by, not St George. He always had this thing about dragons for some reason. He used the dragon as a template for his video game. He had dozens of pictures of the bloody things.

It's still hideous.

That one's from about a thousand years ago apparently. Not exactly a figure of fascism. They hadn't thought it up in those days. So it's not BNP. There isn't even a picture of a flag in it. Just a dragon.

And a virgin.

They usually come as a pair.

Gives me the creeps.

You don't have to like it, do you? Don't worry, I'll keep it down here hidden from all your Guardian-reading buddies.

I don't have any Guardian-reading buddies.

Veronica feels anger rise through her chest, imagines colour surging into her cheeks. Trying to draw on her professional training, she keeps her voice level, controlled.

I'm not saying that there's not a place for grieving, Frankie. I know you're a bit depressed. But you don't know how frustrating it is for me. It's months now since Colin passed.

That's all right then, says Frankie. *Months, is it? That should do the trick.*

And China needs supper. As she did yesterday. And the day before that. Always it's me that has to give it to her.

Supper, pipes China. She gets up and walks towards the stairs.

Daddy will come up in a moment, says Veronica. *You had three phone calls today from tenants who need work done. Have you got back to any of them?*

Tenants?

From your 'buy-to-let empire'.

His eyes, which are shark-like, without inner light, are stuck on the screen.

Veronica sits on the bed and holds Frankie's hand.

It's not even that you were that close to Colin anymore. Roxy is back at work, taking it in her stride.

I bet she is.

What's that mean?

She's a rich woman.

You shouldn't say that. She loved him.

If you say so.

Did you love him?

Frankie's hand is cold, like meat from the fridge.

Not really.

Frankie turns his eyes back to the screen, where Monstro, now breathing fire, is pursuing Gepetto and Pinocchio through mountainous waves.

Actually if I were an Islamic terrorist, I couldn't think of anyone I'd rather blow up.

That's a horrible thing to say, Frankie. Shame on you.

Truth hurts, isn't it? Frankie mumbles, thumb poised over the remote. Veronica grabs the control out of his hand and switches it off.

Frankie. Talk to me. I'm worried about you. What's wrong?

What's wrong? What's wrong?

Frankie looks like he's actually trying to work this out. His brow contracts with the effort.

It's obvious, isn't it?

Not to me it isn't.

Now he looks directly into her eyes. Veronica can see there no one that she recognizes. Only two black pools of sunken light. When Frankie speaks, he does so with an intensity that unnerves her.

Nobody's safe. Nothing makes any sense. That's what's wrong. It doesn't matter what you do. It's all completely random.

He slumps back, loses eye contact, reaches for the TV control again.

Not all of it, says Veronica, looking at China, who is still navigating the stairs. She has reached the top step.

Don't look at her, says Frankie. *She was random too. It's not like we sat down and made a decision or anything.*

Veronica unfurls her fingers from Frankie's, picks them off one by one.

It's not easy to be with someone so self-pitying.

Why don't you throw an ashtray at my head and see if that will perk me up.

Frankie, having retrieved the remote, switches the TV back on.

I can't take this much longer, Frankie.

I can't sleep. I can't stay awake. I can't do anything. I have bad dreams.

What do you dream about?

Snakes. Every night. Coming up under the floorboards.

Veronica nods, slipping into her professional mode.

Could mean anything. Snakes. Worms. Draw your own conclusions.

And you. I dream of you. Snakes coming out of your head. Like that monster woman in the old stories.

What did you do when you saw me with snakes coming out of my head?

I couldn't move. I was too scared.

Seems a natural enough reaction.

Thanks for the insight, says Frankie, closing his eyes. His body language, which was momentarily open, closes again. He pulls his knees up, and hugs himself. *So what next? Are you going to tell me to pull myself together?*

This isn't good for China. It isn't good for me. Are you taking the tablets?

Yes, I'm taking the tablets. Started two weeks ago. Makes no difference. We're all taking the tablets, aren't we? The whole fucking country. We're all rich and we're all taking the tablets. But they don't save us. They don't protect us. They don't make things better. There's nothing in the centre of us. Nothing behind us. Nothing underneath us. Just black. Black.

Veronica stands up, and begins to clear up the mess that China has made with the crisps.

Every week in my training, Frankie, I see people whose lives are destroyed. They have no family. No homes. They cannot go an hour without a drink. Or a fix. They are cold and tired. They are lost. But some of them have a lot more spirit than you do.

Frankie pulls the blanket up to his neck.

It's just how I feel. That's all that's important nowadays, isn't it? How you feel? And I don't feel good. In fact, I don't feel anything at all. At least your clients have got real problems to be miserable about. All I've got is a dead mate who wasn't even really my mate anymore. And that makes it worse. Because I haven't the right.

Frankie's face corrugates. It looks like he's about to cry. Veronica finds herself unable to move to comfort him.

I can smell urine, says Veronica. *Did China wet herself?*

It wasn't China, says Frankie, flatly. He wipes his eyes with the sleeve of his pyjamas and turns his eyes back to the television screen, where Pinocchio is lying in the surf, drowned.

* * *

Three days later Frankie appears at the breakfast table, shaved, showered and dressed in a clean and pressed suit.

Right, he says. *The bitch is back. Starting now. Mojo back, action stations.*

Veronica stares at him, bewildered.

What brought this on?

Victor rang me last night. There's a window on this deal. The six-bedder off the Askew Road.

You told me about that months ago. You said it was mad risky.

No avoiding risk, is there? I'm going to go for it. Life's too short. Look what happened to Colin. Cautious old Colin. I've got to move fast. I've wasted too much time for too long.

Where you going to get the money to buy a six-bedroom house? Even I know that no one is going to make a loan on a multi-occupancy.

There are ways and means. You clear the tenants out for the day the mortgage assessor comes round. Get some nice furniture in from one of your other properties. Bring in some nursery bits and pieces. Clear all the junk out from the individual rooms and bingo! It looks like one big happy family home. Anyway, I know a few friendly surveyors.

Isn't that dishonest?

That's just a way of a looking at it. It's the wheels of commerce. You have to keep them oiled.

Frankie starts to whistle as he helps himself to a cup of coffee from the cafetière. Veronica watches him carefully. He is clutching and unclutching one of his hands. His leg is tapping the floor furiously in an unceasing tattoo.

I hope you don't mind me saying this, Frankie.

Say whatever you like.

I'm pleased that you feel better. But you seem a little bit . . . I don't know. Hyper. A few nights ago you could barely get dressed.

Frankie knocks back the mug of coffee in one, smacks his lips in appreciation.

I'm absolutely fine. Please. Don't start on me with the Freudian analysis. We had a talk. It had an impact. Simple as. Thank you for that. Now I'm back in the saddle. Frankie the Fib is back.

Okay . . .

Another thing. Guess what?

I'm listening.

I'm going to get rid of my birthmark.

What?

You went and had your face fixed. I'm going to do the same.

This is hardly the time . . .

Don't try and talk me out of it. I've made the appointment.

He rushes across to Veronica, kisses her passionately and walks out of the room, whistling 'When You Wish Upon A Star'.

Veronica looks at China and whispers half to herself, half to China.

What on earth was that all about?

Daddy gone crazy, says China.

After she has finished her breakfast, Veronica heads down into the basement to make a dent in the chaos. The space, though, is immaculate. The bed has been stripped, the carpet hoovered. However, the litter bin is full. She goes and gets a black bin liner to clear it out. There are empty cigarette packets, a copy of *How to Win Friends and Influence People* by Dale

Carnegie, a takeaway Chinese food carton and, right at the bottom, the DVD of *Pinocchio*.

* * *

Roxy sits and stares at the enumerated and valued list of assets that she has inherited from Colin. She cannot believe the number of noughts at the bottom of the page. These noughts are now hers, to do with as she wishes. She had no idea.

The irony is that shopping, since Colin's death, has lost its appeal.

Veronica is there with her as she reads the financial statement. She has brought it to the house in North Kensington to try and make sense of it. Veronica stares over her shoulder.

I'm not sure what to do with it all, says Roxy. *It's not as if I earned it.*

Nice problem to have. Anyway, it's just irrational guilt. 'Survivors' guilt' they call it.

Have you learned a lot from your training then?

It's been an eye-opener, I'll say that much.

I'm going to give some of the money to charity. Colin would have wanted that.

Veronica bites her tongue, since Roxy's rosy view of Colin seems to be helping get her through the grief.

Also, I'm thinking of getting a lease on a little shop. I've got this idea for a business start-up.

What's the idea?

Promise you won't laugh?

I promise.

It came to me the other night when we were at the cinema watching, what was it?

'Mrs Henderson Presents'. Yes that's it. And we were sitting there munching on our popcorn.

Being bored half to death.

Yes, it was terrible. And the popcorn was terrible too. Nearly broke my tooth on one of the pieces.

That's exactly it! That's my idea!

What is?

Gourmet popcorn! Because at the moment it's just salt or sweet, right? But there are all sorts of possibilities. Imagine cherry popcorn. Chocolate popcorn. They have it in America. It's all about niche.

I don't know, Rocks. Is it wise to risk it all like that?

I'll put some money aside. Even if the popcorn idea is a flop, I'll be okay.

Well. If you're sure.

What should I do with it, though? The money I'm putting aside? Should I invest it?

Don't ask me. I'm hopeless with money. I was practically one of the only people in London in the last ten years to buy a flat that I lost money on. I thought the feng shui was more important than the survey. Frankie warned me against it, but I didn't listen.

What about gold? I'm feeling gold.

Frankie says it's waste of money. You got to buy some property at the moment or find a proper investment broker. So he says.

I don't trust those people with their stocks and shares. I still fancy gold.

You just like bling.

Yeh, no, yeh, I do like bling, so I'll get myself some nice pieces, I reckon. Put some more in a safe deposit box. I like the idea of money you can look at, do you see what I'm getting at? Hold in your hands.

Now Frankie walks through the door, eyes darting violently about the room. The slightly manic behaviour that appeared when he first emerged from the basement has, as far as Veronica is concerned, continued intermittently, although Frankie brushes it off as her imagination.

I heard what you said, Rocks. Money's not like that anymore. It's just digits on a screen.

That's my point, says Roxy. *Money is getting sort of spooky. Unreal. Gold, that's real.*

Gold is a mug's game, says Frankie, taking off his coat. *It just sits there for the most part. You should put it into property. I can give you a hand. Tell you what. Spain is a prime market at the moment. Villas going for a song. I've got contacts.*

I'm thinking of starting a gourmet popcorn shop. What do you think?

Long shot, says Frankie, tapping his foot frantically on the floor. *Long as you don't buy gold. Just because it's yellow and glitters.*

Who do you think you are? John Maynard Keynes?

Who's he when he's at home?

Come on, Veronica. Frankie must know what he's talking about. You just told me what happened when you didn't follow his advice. With the flat and that. I reckon Spanish property sounds like a good idea. You get an investment and a holiday gaff. Mini-breaks in the sun.

He's not infallible.

I am actually, says Frankie, not smiling.

The Spain thing sounds like it's worth looking into. Thanks, Frankie. Good move.

But what about the popcorn shop? I don't know anything about the popcorn. Or opening a shop, come to think of it.

Never stopped me when I was starting out, says Frankie, taking a coin out of his pocket and idly tossing it. Heads . . . tails . . . heads. *You go, girl.*

Okay, Frankie, I hear you. I hear and obey.

That's the spirit. No wonder Colin was nuts about you.

Anything for a laugh, isn't it?

* * *

Frankie is sitting spry and shaven in the office area of FLB Estates. His leg bounces up and down under the desk, as if sprung. There is a bandage on his head, where he has had surgery to remove his birthmark. In a few days' time he will take it off in order to properly assess the results. The surgeon warned him that the procedure could be unpredictable, but that the long-term outcome was reliable.

He's completed on the six-bedroom property off the Askew Road on a hundred per cent mortgage. He'll cover the repayment by renting out the rooms piecemeal on recurring six-month leases. That way, the repayments are easy. Even after the expenditure of keeping the places maintained, he has money to spare. The bricks are rising in value, every day. And the surveyor was an easy mark – he signed off the mortgage on inspection after Frankie had made it look very roughly like a family home and removed all the Yale locks from the inner doors. He replaced them the following day, once the surveyor was out of the picture.

Frankie feels good, purposeful, wonderfully and constantly agitated. No time to think about anything, and that's the way he likes it. He understands now why he was getting depressed. He simply wasn't working hard enough. He simply wasn't rich enough. He simply wasn't good enough.

Colin was unlucky, but then you make your own luck and Frankie's going to be one of the lucky ones, he'll make sure of it.

He is surprised about how much time buy to let takes up. Tenants who need a tap fixed, a piece of furniture replaced, a leaking roof repaired. He tries to be an adequate landlord — some of them around here, like Dirty Bob who sold Veronica her white elephant flat in Shepherd's Bush — are cowboys. But tenants, he learns, can be a giant pain as well. One couple, who rented a small house just off the Uxbridge Road, did a bunk in the middle of the night, leaving the place trashed. Shit on the floor. Literally human shit. Now he's spent the morning trying to organize workmen and cleaners to come in and sort the place out. He can't afford to lose the rent for more than a few weeks. He's stretched tight, but there's an excitement to it that he loves, that he needs. Without tension there's just entropy.

The work piles on the work. Twelve-hour days, sometimes seven days a week. Truth to tell, he hardly sees Veronica any more, but he expects that is a relief to her. They haven't had sex since Colin died. China doesn't need him, she's her mummy's little girl. Anyway, there will be time for that later. In the meantime the money is rolling in.

He does the maths in his head, over and over again, like an imagined pornographic tableau. Five properties in total. Combined rentals income £12,000 per month. Mortgage repayments on 100 per cent loans: £2,500 per month. Even taking into account refurbishments and missing weeks and repairs and legal fees, he is clearing £100,000 a year before his salary from the agency. Plus the capital is rising with every month. It's a licence to print money.

* * *

With hard work, application and much more capital than she had planned to use, Roxy has managed to set up the popcorn store in a tiny premises, no bigger than the kitchen of her house, near the Portobello Road in one of the less fashionable side streets. It is not far off Christmas now – she's determined to cash in on the seasonal market – and she has set up a number of gift packs ready for stocking fillers.

She is satisfied, at last, with the look of the shop, which has gone through a design, a redesign and then a refit. A flashing neon sign that reads 'PC GONE MAD' in yellow neon adorns the frontage, flanked by a flashing red-and-white striped vintage-style popcorn canister, with creamy fluorescent popcorn chunks spilling over the top.

The opening party starts in an hour, although they can only fit twenty people into the tiny space. There are popcorn-flavoured martinis made with popcorn water, butterscotch ripple, vodka and cream. Roxy is dressed as a carton of popcorn – all stripy red and white cardboard, crepe and foam rubber, with a crown of polystyrene popcorn resting gingerly on her head.

She is still in the back of the shop when Veronica arrives with China, followed almost immediately by Nodge and Owen. Owen looks ill and does not touch the popcorn. Frankie has rung to say he is going to be late because he is so busy. China wanders from table to table trying each of the popcorn flavours in turn and spitting them out in disapproval.

How much does it go for, then? says Nodge.

Four pounds a bag, says Veronica.

Steep, says Nodge.

Not like you to see the downside, Nodge. Where's Roxy?

Maybe the loo?

I don't know how she's going to manage a slash dressed up as a box of popcorn.

Veronica goes into the back of the shop to find Roxy. She tracks her to the toilet, where she is sitting on the lid of the bowl, crying.

What's the matter, Rocks?

Roxy looks up at Veronica through the neck frills of the popcorn outfit.

Colin would have hated the whole thing. Would have thought it typical of me. Frivolous. Impulsive. Childish.

Colin isn't here anymore, is he?

No. And that's how I get to open this frivolous and childish and impulsive popcorn shop. Using his money.

Why don't you come out of there?

I can't face it.

Veronica pulls up a packing case from the corridor and perches on it.

You asked me other day if I'd learned anything from my counseling training. If I've learned anything it's this. Guilt is a waste of time. It's even more a waste of time when the person is dead. You're still young and you've got lots of life in you. Use it. You're the one who's always saying that life's too short. You're seeing things all distorted.

But I'm not, though. Don't you see? I killed him in the first place. It was me.

Oh, come on, Rocks. How do you figure that one out?

That day I made him miss his usual train. Because I wanted him to fix my computer. If he had caught his train, he wouldn't have been caught up in the bombing. I didn't really need my computer fixed to be honest. But there was something I wanted to buy online. A pair of shoes. A pair of Jimmy Choos that I'd seen on Sex and the City. *That's what I killed Colin for. A pair of fucking spike heels. They arrived a week later. I put them on the fire. It's a disaster.*

You can always order another pair.

Roxy tries to laugh, but instead she breaks down into deeper sobs. Veronica tries to stand and put her arm around her, but the bulk of her outfit makes it impossible. She finds it hard to sound grave addressing a five-foot carton of popcorn.

Listen, Roxy. We're not gods. We can't see the future. I made a decision to come by public transport tonight because Frankie was so busy with work he couldn't pick me up. If I'd have been blown up on the bus, then Frankie would have blamed himself just like you did. But then let's say I was going to go on public transport and Frankie insisted he drive me and had a crash and I was killed, he would have blamed himself for that too.

What's your point?

We are all in the dark. We all have our heads in the same place — up our behinds. If things go well, we think we've been wise and clever. If things go badly, we think we have been stupid and foolish. Sometimes we have been wise and clever. Sometimes we have been stupid or foolish. But more often or not, it's just luck, good or bad. Things just happen and then other things happen and there's not much we can do about it.

Roxy dries her tears, and wipes her hands on her pink-and-white striped apron.

I don't care what clever things you say, says Roxy. *I still killed him. And it's not only that. At the same time as I'm beating myself up, every day, for killing him, at the very same time, I'm thinking how glad I* am that he isn't here anymore and that I've got all this money whereas before I didn't have any of my own and had to rely on him, ask him for everything. And then I feel guilty about that too.

It takes generosity to accept a gift. And to accept good fortune. There's no need to——

Don't tell me there's no need to feel guilty! Don't. Even though it's true. You seem to think in the end you can think everything through and, you know, make it make sense. Then it will be alright. Straight. But that's not true. Things are all twisted up. Don't they teach you that at shrink school? People are all bunched up and cross-wired inside and you can't untangle it. You can talk about it all you like. It don't make any difference. Some people they just got the skill, you know?

What skill?

Of ignoring it, of ignoring that it's all crossed wires in the end. They're like, the happy people. I thought I was one of those. But I'm not anymore. Not since Colin. I can't help it. Maybe one day it will go away, I don't know. But it's inside me, like a worm eating everything and I can't get away from it.

Come on, Roxy. It's the opening of your new shop. Dry your eyes and get out there. It's going to be fine. This should be a happy day.

Yeh, it's going to be fine. Lots of money. Lots of shoes. Everything's fine.

She dabs fiercely at her eyes with her apron.

I'm sorry, Vronky. I'm being a total fucking bitch and I know you're only trying to help.

I don't want to give you something else to feel guilty about.

Roxy finally manages a laugh.

Okay then, fair enough. I won't feel guilty. That's what you lot are all about, isn't it? Not feeling guilty about stuff. So right. Let's get out there.

The front of the shop is packed now with guests. The seventies record 'Popcorn' by Hot Butter is playing at full volume on a loop. Frankie has arrived and sees Roxy emerge from the back of the shop. He kisses her cheek.

Rocks. This looks great.

Thanks.

It's going to go gangbusters.

Hope so.

You put some money in the Spanish property too, right?

That sounds like a vote of confidence.

Better safe.

Yeh. I got a place lined up near Valencia.

That's the ticket.

Nodge pushes through the crowd, picking at a box of popcorn.

What do you think? says Roxy to Nodge.

First ever electro pop song. Beat Kraftwerk by years.

I mean the popcorn.

Yeh, alright, pretty good. Not sure about the Salt and Vinegar.

I know what you mean. Wasn't my greatest success.

Strawberries and Cream is nice, says Owen, nibbling at the edge of one.

That's my favourite, says Roxy. *I've also included a classic. Simple Sugar.*

She holds out a tub of popcorn to Nodge, then to Owen. They each take a piece and pop them into their mouths.

Nice, says Owen.

Hmmm, says Nodge. *Bit boring, though. For a gourmet popcorn shop.*

Give the girl a break, Nodge.

Nodge is right. It is boring. But it's what Colin would have chosen. He wouldn't have had anything to do with gin and tonic flavour or elderflower posset, I can tell you that. He was a traditionalist.

A square, says Veronica, who is wiping China's sticky hands with a screwed-up Kleenex.

A cube, says Nodge.

Roxy raises the cup of popcorn in the air.

This one's for Colin. To Colin!

Feeling slightly foolish, everyone else also picks up their cones and toasts Colin in popcorn.

To Colin. Wherever he's gone, I hope it's a boring paradise, where everything's always the same. Where he eats salt and vinegar crisps, where he drinks Hofmeister lager, where he watches QPR lose every Saturday. Or perhaps in heaven they actually win. Sometimes. And the rest of the time he watches video games. And has sex. In the missionary position. And can go to sleep as soon as he's finished. Which he always did anyway, to be honest.

To Colin!

* * *

At the drop-in centre, Veronica is sitting in the therapy room with Oleg. He is wearing a grey, shapeless T-shirt with the faded slogan, 'Every Time I Find the Meaning of Life They Change It' and a pair of thick brown corduroy trousers. He smells of something terrible, decay and bad food. He has been talking now for ten minutes, virtually without pause. Most of what he has said makes no sense whatsoever, although the general thrust seems to be towards the idea that nobody likes him and he finds it impossible to maintain any form of relationship. Veronica feels her attention wandering, and wonders how long is left of the session. Oleg at that moment looks up and catches her looking at her watch.

So why do you think that is? says Veronica. *That people have trouble relating to you?*

Oleg turns his fractured gaze onto her.

I saw you checking watch.

I'm sorry. I didn't mean to appear impatient.

You think you are better than me?

No, Oleg, I don't think I'm better than you.

His face is contorted into an expression Veronica has not seen before. It is partly anguished, partly furious.

You're sitting there. Judging me. People like me. We're just hobby. You sit in your chairs. Like you know what you're doing.

It's not that way.

You don't know what you do? Is right?

Oleg . . .

Which is it? You know what you do? Or you don't know what you do?

We're just trying to help people think about the world in a slightly different way is all. We haven't got any magic potions.

You sit there and say, 'I'm doctor, you the patient'. This is reason you do it. Someone more . . . fucked up than you.

Oleg, I've got my own problems. Believe me.

What are these problems?

I can't talk about them.

This is point.

I'm not sure how useful this line of conversation is.

Sorry if you don't have comfort.

Veronica is astonished. She had thought that Oleg was borderline deranged. Now he is speaking acutely, sharply. He leans forward.

You know what you are, do you?

I think it might be more useful to—

You are fucking stuck-up bitch.

Okay.

You're okay with that, yes? Me saying 'stuck-up bitch'.

I'm not sure that this session is getting us anywhere.

You want to go now, yes?

This session isn't about me, Oleg. It's about you. And I'm wondering why you're so angry?

You want to know why?

He looks down at his feet.

I don't know why I am so angry.

He suddenly seems ashamed, rueful.

I'm sorry I was rude, Doctor Tree.

I'm not a doctor, Oleg.

It gets too much. Other people. Successful people. Like you. People with houses. Jobs. Lives. I can't say it.

Tell me, Oleg.

I don't know. You will be angry.

You can trust me.

It makes me hate you.

Okay.

There you go. 'Okay'. This is alright, yes? To hate someone. Because they have more than you?

I'm not here to . . .

His voice increases in pitch again, drowning out her reply.

You're not here to this. You're not here to that. Why are you here? So you can play with minds. For your fun.

He looks down again.

Sorry. Sorry, doctor.

I think we may have reached the end of the session.

Oleg looks up suddenly.

There are four minutes left. You can't wait for to be away from me.

Now Oleg is leaning forward, baring his teeth. Veronica is suddenly afraid. She is unprotected. There is no security here.

Are you scared for me? says Oleg. *Of me.*

No, says Veronica.

Yes, you are. You have fear. Fear and hate.

No, says Veronica.

Oleg stands up very suddenly. He puts his face within two inches of hers. She tries not to flinch.

You are fucking tourist.

He leaves, slamming the door after him.

Veronica sits for some time alone on her chair, watching the clock tick off the minutes. She sits there for a long time, not moving. Eventually she reaches for her phone to call Frankie, but he doesn't answer. He never answers. He wouldn't be interested anyway.

He would pretend to be, but he wouldn't.

There is a soft knock on the door. She doesn't say anything but the door opens.

Tony Diamonte stands in the doorway.

Are you alright?

I'm fine.

Only Leggy seemed a bit unstable when he came out. Muttering to himself. Punching himself in the face. Then I noticed that you hadn't come out at all.

She looks up at Tony, aware that she is welling up, but unable to stop it. She takes a tissue from the box on the table and dabs at her eyes. Tony sits down in the chair opposite. He puts his hand on the back of her hand. She doesn't slide it away.

Looks to me like you could use a drink.

* * *

They go to the Duke of York round the corner, a tatty pub with four electronic fruit machines and three television screens all showing the same football match. Tony orders a Diet Coke, a large glass of Chardonnay for Veronica and a packet of peanuts. Every packet that comes off the display reveals another few square inches of a bikini-ed pin-up.

Only kind of coke I do nowadays, says Tony. Not as much fun as the other kind, but at least it won't empty my pockets and make me go insane in da membrane.

Veronica hazards a smile. She raises her glass.

Thanks, Tony. Who do you see at the centre? Oakeshott?

I don't really see anyone anymore. I go as a volunteer. Four times a week. Help clear up. Have a chat with the clients. They seem to guess I've been through what they're going through. They talk to me easily. I make myself useful. You know.

He sips at his Diet Coke. He is still, Veronica decides, sneaking a look, a beautiful-looking man, despite the lines, the dissipation, the receding hair, the rumpled clothes.

I sometimes wonder if I'm helping anyone at all. Oleg doesn't think so, says Veronica.

That's just Leggy. He's mental. Of course you're helping. You're helping people to be honest with themselves.

What use is that? One thing I'm beginning to learn from this job is that people thrive on their delusions. It's the only thing that stops them from going crazy. The people at the drop-in don't have very effective ones. Their delusions are a bit lurid and implausible and self-destructive. But that's the only difference. We're all making up stories about ourselves and believing in them. I'm making up a story about myself being a good person because I sit with lunatics like Oleg and let them abuse me.

Sounds to me like you're making up a story about you being a bad person. Why's being a good person so important, anyway?

It just is.

Maybe living your life without doing too much harm to anyone else is enough. If you had fucked up as many other people's lives as I have, you would know what I mean. From where I'm sitting, you're a saint.

Veronica sinks the wine in one go.

That's better.

You be careful. Believe me, that isn't the answer.

Veronica looks at Tony's face carefully for the first time. She sees pain and tenderness in his eyes.

You've changed, Tony.

Living in a park for three months will do that.

Did you learn anything from it all? Sleeping on the street?

Not really.

The sound of the slot machine penetrates the air. Tony seems unable or unwilling to say anything more.

How's Frankie, anyway?

He's doing well. I suppose. Making very good money. More and more and more money.

He always did want to be rich. Not as much as I did though. See where it got me.

What he wanted was people to think well of him. Money was just the way he was going to do it.

Do you think well of him?

Veronica opens the packet of peanuts.

He's so wrapped up in it all. To be honest, I don't think he gives me much of a thought. Me or China. He wasn't like that before. Or at least he tried not to be. Now it's like he's given up on us, ever since Colin died. He's changed.

I'm sure that's not true. I know Frankie. The day he met you was the best day of his life.

How would you know that?

Because he told me.

That was a long time ago. Nothing stays the same.

Did you tell Frankie about seeing me at the centre? Last time you were in?

Of course not. You told me not to.

I appreciate it. Really I do.

Veronica holds out her glass for a top up.

Are you sure? says Tony.

Nothing like a reformed addict to put the damper on things.

Tony returns with another glass of Chardonnay. She drinks it too quickly. Another ten minutes and she is feeling unsteady on her feet.

I think it's time you went home, says Tony. *I'll call you a cab.*

He takes out his phone and calls for a taxi.

They'll be here in five minutes.

Thanks.

You know, Veronica. I always liked Frankie.

I should hope so. You were his friend.

So were Nodge and Colin, but I didn't really like them so much. They were more like hangers-on. I did like Frankie, though. I couldn't believe it when he hooked up with you.

314

Why?

Out of his league, I would have said. But he was so thrilled. A proper posh bird. He couldn't believe his luck. He thought it would save him.

Save him from what?

From who he was. But no one can do that, can they? Save you from who you are.

That's sort of my job.

That doesn't mean it's possible.

You're depressing me now.

Veronica. You're a good person. Truly. And I know the difference. Because I'm not.

Tony's phone rings. He inspects the display.

That's your cab.

Veronica stands up, swaying slightly. He stands too, reaches out and roots her to the earth by holding her arm. She stays in that position a little longer than is necessary. Feeling his hand on her soft bicep.

Let's get you home.

Tony steers her out of the pub and onto the pavement outside where a minicab driver is waiting. It's then, as he leans over to help her into the back, that she notices the horns and the hands around his neck.

She'd forgotten all about them. Now they jangle something dark, distant, disturbing at the back of her mind.

He opens the door for her, kisses her on the cheek and guides her into the seat. She gives her address to the driver.

Bye, Veronica. See you at the centre soon maybe. One more thing about Leggy. It might make you feel better. He's a prize cunt. Everyone thinks so. Don't let him get you down. The last therapist he had punched him out. Even Oakeshott couldn't cope with him. So you're doing quite well really.

The door of the minicab closes, but Veronica keeps puzzling.

The horns and the hand, the horns and the hand.

Where has she seen them? Or spoken about them? Or imagined them?

Then it comes to her.

The clairvoyant.

What the clairvoyant told her.

A part of a body. Or a part of an animal.

Or both.

* * *

Nodge gazes at Owen, taking him in with his eyes like a drink of muddy, stagnant water for a desperately thirsty man. Owen is yellow-eyed, his skin the colour of flour paste, his hair matted with sweat and stuck to his skull. He is lying, sleeping with his mouth wide open, a scarlet and black cavern. Nodge remains unmoving as Owen's eyes flicker and open. He pauses, as if taking a moment to orient himself, then gives Nodge a wide, relieved smile as he recognizes him. Nodge does not smile in return. Instead he appears grave and concerned.

I think we should get married, says Nodge.

Owen's smile remains in place, but he says nothing.

I'm serious.

Owen still says nothing. Nodge begins to falter.

Half-serious, anyway.

We can't get married, says Owen, peremptorily, the smile disappearing, his raw throat ejecting the words like small, barely comprehensible coughs. *It's not legal.*

Civilly partnered, then.

I'm flattered. Thank you.

A flush rises in Nodge's cheeks.

That sounds like a no.

Can we wait until I'm better?

Before we get hitched? Or before you give me an answer.

Before I give you an answer.

Why?

With some difficulty, Owen raises himself up on one elbow.

Because a marriage — sorry, 'civil partnership' — can't be based on pity. It has to be between equals. I'm not your equal. I won't be your equal until I'm well.

That's ridiculous.

No, it isn't. I know you love me, Nodge. I love you too.

So? Then?

It's not enough. A relationship is as much about power as it is about love. The power between us — it's out of true. It's all right, Nodge. I am going to get better. I can feel it. It's going to be all right. Anyway I'm not walking down the aisle or the town hall corridor or whatever it is with parchment skin and eyes the colour of three-year-old eggs. My vanity won't stand it.

Owen starts to cough frantically again.

Thanks for asking, though.

There is suddenly a cacophony of bangs and screeches sounding outside the window.

What a racket. I suppose this is going to go on all night.

Four hundred years since the old left-footer tried to blow up Parliament, says Nodge. *That reminds me, I've got a present for you.*

He reaches behind the sofa and brings out a big holdall full to the brim with a jumble of fireworks

I was going to let them off after you said yes. Except that you didn't. It's not quite going to be Millennium night. All the same.

Nodge picks one out.

This one's called 'Flaming Balls'. I thought it might appeal to your puerile sense of humour.

Owen looks at the firework and smiles.

I've done some chipolatas on sticks as well. My mum always used to make them on fireworks night for some reason.

Help me up, then.

Slowly, painfully, Owen raises himself from the sofa, holding Nodge's hand. He puts his arm around Nodge and Nodge guides him out into the small back yard. He sits him in a wicker chair and brings him a blanket – a Welsh blanket, bought as a joke for his last birthday, but which turns out to be comforting, soft and warm – which he drapes over his lap. Then he brings out a can of Sprite, divides it into two wine glasses. Owen has been teetotal since his illness. Nodge has gone teetotal to support him. They toast one another in silence.

Nodge hands Owen a sparkler and ignites it with a disposable lighter. It sends out an aura of brilliant, shattered white light in an orb that disappears into night at the edges. Owen feebly sketches a luminescent heart in the frosty air with the glowing end. Nodge vigorously tries to sketch a cock and balls, but the balls disappear before the cock is finished.

After the sparklers have been exhausted, Nodge nails a Catherine wheel to the fence that supports a few tired and dusty vine creepers. He lights it and it screams and turns in accelerating circles on its pivot. Owen, the cordite expelled from the firework catching in his throat, begins to cough, and flaps his hand about. Nodge throws a glass of water over the Catherine wheel to douse it and the noise stops, but the smoke of the extinguished firework thickens.

Sorry, Owen. We should go inside.

He tries to help Owen up and out of the path of the still extant cloud of black smoke. But Owen waves him away and points to the enormous rocket that Nodge has bought, a Super Blaster Orion.

Set it off.

The cough continues.

I really should take you inside.

I'm not going till I've seen it.

Nodge sighs and puts the stalk of the rocket into an empty wine bottle and lights the touch paper, then steps back and kneels next to Owen. He takes his hand. The rocket takes, and launches itself into the mild night, mixing into the fading, scattered tapestries of other rockets and whizzers and starbursts.

Their rocket finally reaches its apex, with a resonating bang, then blooms of green, orange, yellow, white appear briefly over their patch of the Shepherd's Bush sky. Their rocket, their home, their own private light.

Nodge squeezes Owen's hand. Owen responds, feebly. Then he suddenly goes limp.

Owen?

Owen does not respond. Panicking, Nodge tries to rouse him and failing, drapes his limp arm over his shoulder and struggles with him back into the living room. He is so light, Nodge is amazed and frightened. It is easy to manoeuvre him onto the sofa, where Nodge lays him, ready to call an ambulance. He covers him with the blanket. Owen's eyes flicker open.

Thank god. Owen, are you alright?

Owen gives the faintest nod.

I'm going to dial 999.

Don't. I'm okay. It's just a spell.

Let me get you a glass of water.

Nodge hurries to the kitchen, feeling clumsy, drops a plastic glass on the floor before managing to find another one, a clean one, which he fills with Vichy water, Owen's favourite, he loves the soft soapy taste. He rushes back into the living room, where Owen has closed his eyes again.

Owen . . .

He holds out the water.

Owen does not open his eyes.

Panicking again, Nodge shakes his shoulders.

Owen.

Owen's head snaps upright.

Christ, Nodge, you're hurting me.

Owen takes the water in a long draught very slowly. Nodge watches his Adams apple bob up and down, feels faint and puzzled with concern.

I should call the ambulance now.

Stop fussing. I was just tired.

If something happened to you.

Nothing's going to happen to me. Come here.

Nodge sits on the end of the sofa.

No, I mean come here.

Owen holds out the blanket. Nodge lies down beside him and draws himself close. Owen covers him with the blanket

and pulls his arm around him. Nodge can feel the curve of his
raw bones under his shirt.

Thank you for tonight, Nodge. I can't tell you how much I
appreciate it.

Nearly choking you on cordite?

The rocket was spectacular.

Lot of money for something that lasted about fifteen seconds.

That's why it was so lovely, Nodge. Things that don't last are the
loveliest.

Is that some kind of, what? Some kind of secret message? Some
Christmas cracker prophecy of doom?

Just don't get too far ahead of me, Nodge.

I'm not ahead of you. I'm with you.

Owen closes his eyes, as if considering this closely. When
he opens them again, he finds Nodge, his eyes full of concern,
looking directly into them. Owen tries to breathe deeply, but
his lungs won't allow it.

Listen, Nodge. You proposed to me and you lit a firework for me and
you looked after me when I fainted. As you always do. You are everything
I want and hope for, Nodge. I hate to put this burden on you, but . . .

He hesitates. Nodge sees his eyes flicker back and forth in
his sockets. Then his face composes itself, and the eyes come
into focus.

Ask me again, Nodge.

Ask you what again?

You know.

Nodge's mind searches for the solution, finds it. Finally,
he smiles.

Owen. Will you marry me?

Sort yourself out, Nodge. I already told you. I can't marry you.

What?

God, give me strength.

Stop playing mind games!

Ask me if I will be your civil partner.

Oh. Right. Will you be . . .

Get down on one knee.

Nodge hastily pushes the blanket off himself and gets down on his knee. He takes Owen's shrivelled white left hand in both of his.

Owen Driscoll. Will you be my civil partner?

Owen pauses.

What are you waiting for now? demands Nodge.

Just to build the tension a bit, says Owen.

God, you're annoying.

Owen laughs, and, as firmly as he can manage, squeezes Nodge's hand.

Yes, Nodge. Jon. I will be your civil partner. Now you can get up. And I'm so happy that you asked me. Amazed, actually. So thank you. But just let me get better. I need to get better. You understand, don't you?

Nodge does not speak, but simply rises from his knees and burrows under the blanket again, his face close enough to Owen's to feel his breath. Owen plants a kiss on his stubbled cheek.

They fall asleep together, and do not wake until morning reveals a street strewn with used gunpowder, fallen sticks, charred paper.

* * *

It's eight o'clock in the evening and Frankie comes in from work. He's been at it since seven that morning. Veronica is in the living room reading *The Elephant and the Bad Baby* to China. He kisses them both, then goes silently upstairs to the bedroom to hang up his suit jacket. Inside the wardrobe, there is a teetering pile of presents blocking his way. He notices an immense, empty Christmas stocking draped over the bed. He knew that Veronica was going Christmas shopping with Roxy that day, but hadn't imagined they would produce such a haul. He tries to scratch his head out of puzzlement, but instead his fingers meet the bandage on his head from the operation to remove his birthmark. Neither he nor Veronica has seen the result yet.

Veronica appears in the doorway.

I've put China in the bath.

You've been busy, says Frankie.

Too much? says Veronica.

Frankie says nothing.

I know. It's sort of revolting, isn't it? says Veronica, ruefully regarding the pile of booty from Oxford Street.

Christmas is a time when excess is allowed.

But it's Christmas all the time. People just spending on mad things, 365 days a year. At Christmas it just gets sillier. It's like a magnifying window into how greedy we are the rest of the time. Ridiculous thing is, though, I can't stop myself. I feel like I would be being a bad mother, if I didn't get her everything I could. I want her so much to be happy.

Don't worry about it. She'll love it. And she's already happy. Children are, so long as you don't mess them up too much.

Frankie pulls at the base of the mountain of presents and they tumble out onto the carpet.

Look at this. A Tamagochi. A Spongebob action figure. A battery-operated hamster. What's not to like?

The word that keeps coming into my mind is decadent.

That's just your middle-class guilt. Bung some money to charity if you're feeling so down about it. I hear on the grapevine that donkeys are having a hard time of it.

If everyone bought hardly anything at Christmas like in the old days, she'd be sort of happier. We all would be.

Last year China had rushed through the berg of toys, discarding them one after another at a great speed, hardly any of them holding her attention, then spent the morning angry and tired, or playing with the boxes that the toys had come in.

Don't worry about it, Vronky. We're going to have a great Christmas. A good old old-fashioned avaricious, consumerist Christmas. With the artificial fire going and the artificial tree in the living room.

Veronica opens the windows to the cold night air and lights a joint that Roxy has slipped her earlier in the day to relax with.

Frankie looks anxiously towards the door.

Don't worry. China can't get out of the bath by herself. And I know she's all right because I can hear her.

China is chanting a line from the book: *rumpetarumpetaumptera.*

Veronica lights the joint and the sour smell of skunk fills the room. After taking a few puffs she holds it out to Frankie, who refuses it.

I don't know how anyone gets through a marriage without drugs, says Veronica.

Or a Christmas. Don't you think we should wrap up those presents?

Suddenly I can't be bothered. Veronica pulls deeply on the joint. *We're not getting an artificial tree, by the way. Not this year. Just too tacky.*

You were the one worrying about the extravagance. Okay, we'll get a proper one that will shit pines all over the carpet and which we won't be able to get out again.

Daddy said a bad word.

China has appeared at the doorway, naked, dripping with water, holding a Miffy towel in one hand.

What are all those toys for? she says, rondel-eyed.

They are both too stunned to respond.

You shouldn't get out of the bath by yourself, says Veronica who stares at China with the joint burning openly in her hand. *You could fall and hurt yourself.*

There's a horrid smell in here.

Veronica tries to cast the stub of the joint out of the window, but it misses the gap, and bounces back onto the carpet. Frankie rushes to retrieve it and throws the remnant out of the opening.

Daddy's been smoking.

Frankie throws Veronica a look.

Daddy! You mustn't smoke! It's bad for you! You promised.

Frankie scoops up China and tries to guide her eyes away from the pile of toys and the yawning Christmas stocking.

I'm sorry, darling, but it was just the one. It's herbal, so it's not really bad for you. I don't really smoke proper cigarettes.

Why are all these toys here?

We're going to give something for charity, for the poor children who Santa sometimes can't find. Now come on, let's get you into bed.

He wraps China in the towel and hustles her out of the room. Veronica hurriedly opens the rest of the windows to help fumigate it. She sets about putting all the presents and the stocking away. A few minutes after she has finished, Frankie returns.

Locking the stable door after the horse has bolted.

Shit, says Veronica. *Shit shit shit.*

It's not that bad.

It is that bad. It's totally that bad. I just fucking killed Santa. While I was blazed. It's not exactly Parent of the Year, is it?

Mummy said a bad word, says Frankie.

Frankie takes Veronica in his arms. She smells pungent.

She'll forget all about it. I'll tell her on Christmas Day it was all a dream. Or something. Children will believe pretty much anything you tell them when all's said and done.

I wish adults were like that.

They are, in my experience.

Frankie . . .

Yes?

Veronica takes a step closer to Frankie and kisses him on the lips. He tastes the acrid aftertaste of the roach.

Thank you for taking the rap for me.

Always, Vronky. Always.

* * *

At 7 a.m. on Christmas day, China bursts into their bedroom.

Mummy. Santa came!

They haul themselves out of bed and make their way to China's room, the walls hung with pony pictures, posters of Charlie and Lola and Fifi and the Flowertots. Frankie has donned his red Santa cap.

It takes a full half an hour to unwrap all the presents. In truth, China is tired after the first five minutes and is tossing aside gifts to get on to the next one like a heavy smoker, lighting their next cigarette before the previous one has finished, just like the year before. Exhausted, they stand by a pile of torn, tumbled Christmas wrapping.

Daddy? Is Santa Claus real? Like, really real?

Of course he's real.

How does he get down the chimney?

He's magic.

Is Jesus real too?

Yes, he's real too. Probably.

Where does Santa buy his presents?

He doesn't. His elves make them.

She seems satisfied with this answer and begins to play with a set of Sylvanian Families, but grows quickly bored.

Can I watch telly downstairs?

Don't you want to play with your presents? says Frankie, barely concealing his irritation.

It's okay, poppet, interrupts Veronica. *It's Christmas.*

Can I eat these? asks China.

She holds up a packet of six mini chocolate elves that were in her stocking.

I suppose so. But don't eat them all. There'll be a lot of food today. You can have three. Okay?

Okay.

Promise?

I promise.

Clutching the chocolate elves, she leaves the whole pile of detritus, paper and all, on her floor and heads down to the living room. Veronica begins to put the paper into a plastic bin liner. Frankie in the meantime tries to stack the presents into some sort of pile. It takes them fifteen minutes to finish tidying the room. They go back to their bedroom to exchange cards.

Hold on, before we start. I want to show you something. You get first look.

Veronica stares at him in puzzlement. Then she sees his hand move up to the bandage on his forehead.

Is it ready?

The surgeon said it should be fully healed by today. Ready? It's my Christmas present to you. A beautiful, unblemished husband.

You never told me how much it cost you. I hope you went to one of the best.

Best I could afford. They're all much of a muchness.

What should I expect?

Like I said. Fully healed. It should look perfect.

Okay.

Very slowly, Frankie peels the bandage from his head. Veronica is very aware of how her face should look. All the same she can't stop recoiling slightly when the bandage is removed.

What do you think? says Frankie.

Great, says Veronica. *It's really a great job. You look . . .*

She runs out of words. Frankie seizes a mirror and examines himself. The wound is, apparently, and as promised, fully healed. But a not-so-faint blemish remains, from the surgery, almost as purple and distinct as the original.

That will fade in time, I suppose, says Frankie, squinting at the mark, palpably disappointed.

Of course it will, says Veronica, half-heartedly.

Anyway, I love it! I feel like a new man.

Let's open our cards, shall we?

Anxious to move on, Veronica tears open the envelope of her card from Frankie. It depicts Father Christmas coming down the stairs into a warmly coloured sitting room with a blazing fire. At the bottom of the stairs is a small wide-eyed boy, looking up at him, standing next to the Christmas tree which awaits its presents.

Santa Claus is saying, *I'm sorry you've seen me, Timmy. Now I'm going to have to kill you.*

Veronica laughs.

That's a good one.

Yeh, Roxy found it for me. She's good on jokes.

Now Frankie, leaving the incessant exploration of his new scar with his fingertips, opens the card from Veronica. Hers is always much the same – minimal. A little heart, or a drawing of something, an 'I love you' or 'I love you very much' – always the same three to five words – and an indeterminate number of kisses.

The card from Veronica shows a dead robin on its back with 'May Yours Be a Joyful Christmas'.

What this? says Frankie

It's Victorian, says Veronica. *A curiosity. Ironic. You know.*

Funny.

He opens the card. Inside, written in Veronica's copperplate are the words, *With Love to You.* Frankie tosses it to one side, registering it, incorrectly, as the standard offering. He gives Veronica a peck on the cheek and a hug.

Thanks, darling.

Already from downstairs they can hear the sound of *Peppa Pig* blaring from the TV.

'Everybody loves jumping in muddy puddles . . .'

Why is Daddy Pig such a useless twat? says Frankie.

Is he? says Veronica, still stuffing glossy paper into the bin bag, and picking up hers and Frankie's cards.

He's well-meaning enough, says Frankie, *but he's stupid. Even for a pig. He doesn't get anything, does he.*

Did you take a few bites of the carrots and the cookies we left for Santa in the living room? And drink the milk?

You told me you had already done that.

No, I didn't.

Are you sure?

Frankie remembers now that he told Veronica that he had already done it because he was meant to have done it and hadn't, so he'd decided to avoid mentioning his incompetence and go and do it later. And then he forgot.

Right.

But you told me you'd done it.

China probably won't notice.

Frankie exchanges glances with Veronica and sees anger sparking in her eyes. He starts towards the door.

You should probably put the bandage back on. China might, you know . . . be surprised.

Right.

Frankie goes to the bathroom and applies a new plaster, then makes his way downstairs to the living room. In front of the fireplace is the plate with cookies, milk and a carrot, which are all entirely untouched.

China seems oblivious. Her face and hands are covered in chocolate. She is watching *Peppa Pig* with her usual addict's intensity. Convinced that she is suitably absorbed, Frankie with a swift movement picks up the milk, cookies and carrot, and heads out of the room again to the kitchen, disposes of the evidence, than goes back up to the bedroom.

I think we got away with it, he says.

One thing I ask you to do, says Veronica. *One thing.*

Sorry.

I wrapped all the presents.

Sorry.

I went out and got them all.

I was busy.

You're always busy.

Don't start on me. You fucked up by not hiding the presents.

There is a silence, while Veronica hopes that Frankie isn't then going to say what she thinks he's going to say.

And on top of that, I paid for them all.

She nods, as if finally acknowledging something she has known for a long time.

You know something, Frankie?

What, Vronky?

She hesitates. It is, after all, Christmas Day.

Nothing.

Fifi and the Flowertots can be heard from the living room in place of *Peppa Pig.*

I'll go and see if she wants some breakfast, says Frankie.

Veronica doesn't reply.

When he reaches the living room, the chocolate has spread from China's mouth and hands to the sofa.

Did you eat just three of the chocolate elves?

Yes.

Do you promise?

Yes.

She does not take her eyes off the TV.

Frankie searches around on the floor until he locates the

empty cellophane packet that the elves had been factory shrink-wrapped in.

He holds up the empty packet in front of China.

You've eaten all of them. Haven't you?

No.

Don't lie to me.

Not lying.

Where are the rest of them then?

Don't know.

Frankie kneels down on the floor.

You know that it's very, very bad to lie, don't you?

Her voice starts to quaver.

Why?

He thinks of telling her the story of the 'boy who cried wolf' for the umpteenth time, but decides that it will be a waste of time.

Uncle Nodge told me that you used to be called 'Frankie the Fib'. Fibbing is the same as lying.

Uncle Nodge told you that?

Yes.

Fibbing isn't the same as lying, says Frankie, sternly, trying in his mind to work out the distinction.

What's the difference?

Fibbing is tiny little . . . sort of . . . white lies. You don't mean any harm by them, see. Not like bad lies.

China nods as if she understands.

So. Did you eat all the chocolate elves?

Now, to Frankie's horror, China bursts into floods of desperate tears. Her whole body shakes. Her eyes become rimmed red and she gasps for breath.

Moments later, Veronica appears at the door.

What did you say to her? says Veronica.

He holds up the pack of empty chocolate elves. She picks up China and holds her over her shoulder but she will not stop crying. It simply becomes more intense. Shamed, Frankie retreats to the kitchen.

China, her back to the wall, through scrunched up and blurred eyes stares, stares at the empty fireplace and thinks only, desperately, of the uneaten carrots, the intact cookies, the full glass of milk. The empty, yawning red stocking.

2007: The Grail

Frankie sits up in bed, staring hard into the darkness as if it might reveal something through its thick night vacuum.

It is at this time that the shadow thoughts always come. He dismisses them as Night Demons – frightening premonitions that disappear with the morning light. But somehow, tonight, they seem more substantial than ever.

He is doing well. FLB Estates has been growing. But the growth is stalling lately. He himself is always stretched, the piece of elastic growing thinner and thinner. What if someone lets go of one of the ends? Or something snaps?

He has ten properties in the buy-to-let market now, all leveraged to the limit. Yet instability seems to threaten. Property prices are looking shaky for the first time in years. Earlier in August, a huge French bank Frankie has never heard of – BNP Paribas – has stopped trading in some fund or other that they had created, which apparently is important and dangerous in some distant way, although Frankie has never really understood economics, he only understands money.

Meanwhile, Bank of England interest rates have been creeping up – a point and a quarter since this time last year, mortgage rates always a few points ahead, so he's coughing up more than seven points on most of his properties now, two more than a year or so back. They show no sign of dropping again.

The elastic is stretching and stretching. Frankie can barely make the monthly repayments any longer. Two of his properties are already on the market to help ease the repayment pressure on him, but they won't sell even at the price he bought them for. He's been drifting into negative equity with more properties than he likes to think about, but if he can just hold on, he can see out the storm, he's sure of it. It will all blow over. It always does.

Night thoughts, he thinks. Only night thoughts. After all, there is capital in most of the properties, so long as the prices remain stable. They have been rising pretty much for as long as he can remember. This stalling is just a blip.

He turns to looks at Veronica asleep behind him, snoring softly. Her therapy business is working well now. She is tired much of the time. Making good money. Loves the work. Offices near Harley Street, a stone's throw from Oxford Circus. But she seems more and more distanced, somehow. They are pulling in two different directions. Sometimes it seems like only the cord of China keeps them together. But the cord is also a wall.

The great wall of China, Frankie thinks to himself and laughs out loud, then just as suddenly, stops, hearing himself laughing into the night.

Sometimes he thinks nothing in his head has been right

since Colin died. He's been working so hard. He can't stop, he can't pause.

Otherwise the night thoughts start to come in the day.

He makes a promise to himself to pay more attention to China and Veronica, ignoring, for the moment, that he is a liar, most particularly to himself. This he often forgets. Or denies. The line between the two is confused.

His mind turns firmly back to business, back to money, away from the night. He will speak to Victor in the morning, see if he can pull down some more credit to help with the repayments. Victor has always been helpful.

He still can't sleep. He gets up, goes downstairs and fetches himself a glass of water, being careful not to wake Veronica – she is a light sleeper. He walks around in the shadows of the big North Kensington house. Bigger than ever, soon. They are having a kitchen extension, another two hundred K to rustle up out of the air. But the air is always generous and reliably conjures more and more credit. There are two BMWs outside – his and hers. Everything is spotless thanks to the Filipino cleaner they have visiting every day.

Returning upstairs, he looks in at China's bedroom. She is asleep, her uniform from Francis Holland School laid up neatly on her chair. It's one of the best – or at least the most expensive – in West London. She has been down on the list since birth and Veronica wangled her in somehow. She didn't allow Frankie to come to any of the interview sessions. Frankie thought she was embarrassed by him. Veronica said she was just being practical. Which amounted, in his mind, to the same thing.

He looks at the Farrow & Ball paint on the walls, the original art, chosen by Veronica. The blurry orange blob next to the bathroom is worth about twenty K. He begins to calculate how much he might be able to sell it for if things go tits up, which they won't.

They can't.

He goes back upstairs to the bedroom.

Veronica has not moved, but has stopped snoring. Everything is normal.

Everything is normal, he tells himself.

Night thoughts.

* * *

In the morning Veronica wakes him with a cup of cappuccino, made with their home Gaggia. He also has a slice of Hovis with Marmite. He still prefers Hovis to the fancy sourdoughs and ryes that Veronica insists on buying. Perhaps there's more of Colin in him than he likes to admit.

He looks at Veronica. As usual nowadays her eyes are stuck on her Sony Vaio laptop, with the fiddly Windows Vista software. Frankie hates PCs, swears by his MacBook Pro.

You're obsessed with The Facebook. You spend more time on that computer than you do with me.

It's not 'The Facebook'. It's 'Facebook'. And I'm on Twitter, not Facebook.

What's Twitter?

She sighs.

Get with the programme, Frankie.

You got any clients today?

Finally she looks up, gazes fuzzily at him, the bright screen of the computer still reflected onto her eyes.

One or two. Will you be able to make China's assembly today?

No. Yes. I think so. Probably.

Can you pick up some cereal for her on your way home?

What brand?

The same brand she always has.

I . . . I can't . . . what?

Jordans. The reduced sugar one.

Sorry.

And she's got a play date tonight. Pick her up, can you? About seven.

Who with?

It's on the wall chart.

I haven't had time to look at the wall chart, says Frankie.

How long does it take?

I'm not going to get dragged into an argument.

That's right. Just walk away. That's what you do.

Her eyes swivel back to the computer and her expression takes on a serene, slightly torpid aspect.

So often now, thinks Frankie, they talk to each other like colleagues or rivals rather than lovers. The discussions are practical and formal.

But Frankie is grateful. He has surprised himself by remaining loyal to her, despite a number of opportunities that have presented themselves. He convinces himself, through these voluntary abstinences, that he has finally grown up. He is, after all, married with a child. A respectable businessman. A pillar of the community, he has even joined the local chamber of commerce.

Sometimes he looks in Veronica's eyes for what he once saw there – passion, love, interest? – but it is hiding, always hiding nowadays. Behind the reflection in her eyes of her computer screen and her brand-new iPhone. The first person in the street to own one, it already owns her.

* * *

When Frankie arrives at FLB Estates he pulls his Beemer up outside on the yellow line, where, to his consternation and puzzlement, a group of people, maybe twenty in all, are chanting, *Yuppies out!*

Some of them hold placards. 'Reclaim the Bush'. 'Gentrification Displaces Low Income Residents'. 'Die Yuppie Scum'.

Frankie is sure it is much the same bunch – or at least the same breed – he saw at the anti-war march nearly five years ago, wearing their silly fucking Peruvian woolly hats over artfully dreadlocked hair. Two policemen are attending, looking respectively bored and amused.

As he approaches the door a chorus of boos begins. Frankie, made irritable by the night's lack of sleep, rounds on the crowd.

Who the fuck are you?

No one says anything. The bored policeman perks up.

Frankie picks out one of the women – the one with the Peruvian hat on. Young, scoured pinkish skin.

Where do you come from? What do your parents do?

Leave her alone! shouts another woman, with an anorak and a placard that reads 'Eat the Rich'.

You then. He turns to the placard waver. *Where you from?*

It's you that needs to answer the questions. People like you – you're ruining it for the local community, declares Anorak.

A third person, a man this time, well dressed in expensive jeans, conventional in a pressed white shirt, chimes in.

My kids can't afford to live in places like this. It's about a million quid for a broom cupboard.

Where do you live, then? Frankie says, swivelling again to catch him in his gaze.

Stoke Newington, says the man. *So what?*

I'll tell you so what. I grew up over there . . .

He points to the grim outline of the White City Estate.

My mum worked as a dinner lady. My dad Joe worked at the brewery in Fulham. I went to that shit school over there. That one with all the asbestos in the roof, which you can't see under the concrete cladding. That one that looks like Stalag Luft 17. So don't talk to me about local this and local that. This is my manor.

Check your privilege, shouts Peruvian Hat.

You check your fucking privilege.

One of the policemen – the formerly bored one – steps up, holding his palm out.

No need for bad language, sir.

Frankie turns to him in desperation.

Who are these people? What do they want?

A diminutive Asian woman steps forward. She is tiny, old and looks scared. She is holding a plastic bag with something in it. When she speaks, her accent is thick, Bangladeshi, Frankie would guess.

I grew up around here too. My children — I don't know where they're going to live.

How many children you got then?

What's that got to do with it? calls Peruvian Hat.

How many?

I got six children, says the woman.

Check my privilege? says Frankie, turning to Peruvian Hat.

She should check hers. What you doing have six kids when you've got nowhere to put them?.

Birth is a birthright, says Peruvian Hat.

I built up this place, says Frankie. *This place from nothing. From a slum house. And now you're telling me I'm a yuppie. Go and do something useful. Go and get a job.*

He turns his back on the crowd to walk into the office. He feels the slap of something wet on his back. The crowd cheers feebly, as if unsure that they haven't gone too far.

He takes his suit jacket off to examine it. The tiny Asian woman has thrown an egg at him and it has broken on his Armani suit. One of the policemen is closing in on her. She cowers back.

Leave her alone, for fuck's sake, says Frankie, wearily. *I can get it cleaned.*

He walks into the office. The others have been watching him.

Losers, mutters Frankie.

He looks behind him to the outside. To his astonishment, the policeman is wrestling with the old Asian woman. Several of the other protestors are shouting and taking pictures with their mobile phones.

Frankie rushes out.

Leave her alone.

One of the policemen, the amused one, no longer amused, steps forward.

Sir, I don't think . . .

She's about bloody eighty, for Christ's sake. Leave her alone!

Now the crowd turns and starts uncertainly cheering Frankie.

She's guilty of causing an affray, says the policeman, clearly losing confidence.

You're guilty of making a fuss about nothing. Just let it go.

The policeman looks at his colleague, who gives him some kind of signal.

We'll let you off with a warning this time, he says.

That's better, says Frankie.

No, you. We'll let you off with a warning, says the other policeman. *For Obstruction of Justice. Unless you go back inside right now and let us do our job.*

Frankie squares up to the copper. The policeman is loving it, he sees. He wants to arrest someone. Frankie will do as well as the Asian woman.

A voice screeches from the radio of the policeman who is holding the old lady. As if it is a cue, he loosens his grip on the woman, and answers the call.

Just leave it, says Frankie.

The policeman backs off. There is a moment's silence. Then Frankie silently walks back in to the office. This time, a rattle of applause from the street follows him. Mixed with catcalls. The policemen consult with one another. Then with straightened backs and sheathed notebooks, they head to their patrol car.

You must have generated some good karma, says Victor.

Huh?

Instant results. We just got a message through. Some good news.

Victor stands up and the rest of the office stand up with him.

What's going on?

Frankie, says Jane. *We've been nominated for Estate Agent of the Year.*

The whole office breaks out in cheers, clapping and

whooping. Victor pulls out a bottle of champagne he's been concealing under the desk and pops the cork. Foam flies everywhere.

Oh, my bloody god, says Frankie. *Oh, my lord.*

Ceremony's in a few weeks, sputters Victor. *Fancy hotel. Up West.*

Frankie grabs the champagne bottle, does a little dance as he swigs from it.

Old Ratchett's going to bust a gut! Fucking hilarious. Awesome!

Now the noise of the clapping and whooping dies down.

Possibly not, says Victor, taking the champagne bottle from Frankie and pouring it into a plastic cup.

What do you mean? says Frankie, still grinning idiotically.

Farley and Ratchett have been shortlisted too.

* * *

Nodge and Owen are walking down the aisle or, to be exact, the central corridor of the Purple Room at Marylebone Register Office. It is an elegant space with art-deco style pendant lamps hanging from the ceilings, purple ruched curtains on high sash windows, a paler purple carpet and lilac walls. There are eighty chairs arranged in two groups of forty either side of a central aisle.

The room is practically full, primarily of men in their thirties. Slightly out of place are two burly men in ill-fitting suits, sitting next to one another, one black and one white – Mickey the Wrench and Big Eddie Fox. Each of them wears a red carnation in his lapel.

Frankie and Veronica are in the second row back with China between them. Roxy is next to Veronica, wearing an outrageously frou-frou dress with a giant ruff of feathers round the neckline and clouds of sky-blue taffeta emerging from the shoulders.

In front of them are Owen's family, his mother and father – a milkman and a school dinner lady – both beaming with pride. Nodge's sister is on the other side of the aisle, with her daughters Flossie and Dilly. His mother and father are to the right. A gas fitter and a shop assistant, staunchly conservative, they look severe rather than delighted, having long struggled to reconcile themselves to Nodge's sexuality. But they are here, which as far as Nodge is concerned, is what counts. Nodge smiles at them. Wearily, they smile back.

They don't look exactly ecstatic, whispers Owen, from the back of the room, where they wait for the ceremony to begin. Owen is fully recovered, blooming. The weight he has lost from his illness suits him, now that he is tanned, clear-skinned and straight-backed once more.

They're getting there, says Nodge. *They're good people. Just a bit old-fashioned.*

Nodge is wearing a canary yellow suit, Owen more formal in charcoal grey.

The music starts – 'You Make Me Feel Mighty Real' by Sylvester – and the registrar beckons. The couple approach the front of the room with slow steps, turning towards the left then the right, greeting all with smiles and waves.

When they reach the lectern where the registrar stands, Nodge holds Owen's hand. He can feel himself beginning to tear up. The registrar is a smartly dressed black woman with cropped short hair, in a dark blue formal suit and fashionable oversized spectacles. She seems genuinely happy. She nods to each of the couple as if seeking permission to begin. In sync, they return her nod. The assembly fall silent.

This place in which we are now met has been duly sanctioned according to law for the celebration of marriages.

You are here today to witness the joining in civil partnership of Jonathan Percival Drysdale and Owen Emrys Driscoll.

Owen and Nodge gaze at one another, astonished that such a tremendous event can be happening to them.

If any person here present knows of any lawful impediment to this civil partnership they should declare it now.

There is the conventional staged silence. It is suddenly split by a familiar, acidic voice, somewhere at the back of the room.

Romantic, isn't it? I think I'm going to cry.

Nodge turns to see, in the back row, Fraser Pike standing with a swarthy-looking man whom he does not recognize.

I know of a lawful impediment all right. Yeh? says Fraser, grinning like a crocodile. There are mutterings from the congregation, some angry, mostly puzzled.

It is Owen's face that frightens Nodge now, not Fraser's, because it has turned bone white.

You look worried, love, says Fraser, speaking to Owen now. He is making no secret of the fact that he is enjoying himself, a coyote smile plastered across his moisturized, tanned and carefully plucked face.

Owen does not speak but looks at the floor.

May I ask what is going on here? says the registrar.

Then the swarthy-looking man speaks up. His voice is reedy and high with a strong Spanish accent.

I obhect, says the man. *Because this man he is already marry-ed.*

I beg your pardon? says the registrar.

He is marry-ed. Esta casado conmigo. *To me. To me.*

Nodge looks at Owen who, although it is barely possible, has turned paler still. Finally he turns to Nodge and speaks, in a hoarse whisper.

It wasn't a marriage. It was a bit of fun. That's all. We were out of our skulls.

Who is he? says Nodge, pushing the words out of a cauterized throat.

Now the man steps out into the aisle. He is tall and attractive, but his shoes are scuffed and the sole is curling at the front.

My name is Jesus Lopez. He pronounces it 'Haysus'. *We are marry-ed in Madrid. In two thousand hand fife.*

He reaches into his pocket and holds up a limp scrap of paper. Owen shakes his head.

Why would you do this? says Nodge to the Spanish man, his voice loud but shaky. *Why are you telling these lies?*

Hwhy? He holds up two fingers. *Hwhy? Two reasons. Hwone. You dump me and disappear without word. Two. This man he left me with enfermedad infecciosa.*

Nodge looks at Owen who seems to have shrunk inside his suit. The congregation is dead silent.

I didn't know, says Owen, desperately, raising his head slightly in the direction of Jesus. *I didn't know then that I was ill. And when I found out, I didn't know how to get in touch with you, Jesus. I'm sorry, but there was nothing I could do.*

Jesus is stony, unimpressed. His face is lined with pride, but also, somehow, what appears to Nodge grained with poverty. He walks up to the registrar and hands her the certificate. She inspects it and nods.

This seems authentic. I will have to check.

Jesus smiles without pleasure. He is no more than a foot away from Owen now.

I have thought of revenge often. Of-ten. And you know? Muy bien. *It feels good. When Mr Pike here got in touch with me — well, you understand I know. It was a nice little holiday. With this . . . show at the end of it. This . . . what is word? Panty. Panta.*

Pantomime, says Fraser, relishing each syllable.

Jesus pauses. Nobody seems to know what to do next. The registrar is on her phone, apparently trying to find information.

Vale, okay. Now I have done what I have come here to do. You can have the registration certificate. I don't want it any more. Use it for papel higienico.

Jesus bows his head slightly towards Nodge.

I am sorry, Mr Drysdale. 'Nodge'. Lo siento. You have done me no harm. But I thought you should know what this man is. Of what he is capable.

And he turns on his tired shoes, with some style, and walks out of the wedding chamber. Fraser, smirking, blows Nodge a kiss and follows him.

Owen is in tears. The assembly still do not react. Many are staring at the floor or inspecting their fingernails.

It's Nodge's tall, overweight gas fitter father who finally steps forward. His voice is grave and rough, but tender.

Just marry him, Nodge, for Christ's sake. Get on with it!

Nodge stares at him astonished. Owen is shaking his head. Nodge feels as if the invisible strings which hold him together have been severed.

Can he? says Nodge to the registrar.

The registrar is still checking her phone.

Just a minute.

Do it, Nodge! shouts Frankie. Then Roxy. *Do it!*

Then the congregation, one by one, takes up the chant in unison.

Do it! Do it! Do it!

Finally the registrar has finished checking her phone. She holds a hand up and the crowd falls silent. Her head high, her voice sharp and officious, she makes her announcement.

This office does not recognize a Spanish civil registration. There is absolutely no reason not to go ahead.

Nodge is shaking, Owen is crying.

Jesus has left the building, says Frankie. *Let's get on with it. Also the place I got your wedding present from doesn't take returns.*

Nodge suddenly laughs. Owen looks at him in astonishment, not quite ready to believe it.

Nodge becomes serious again, seems to gather himself. Owen cannot tear his gaze away from the floor, but Nodge stares at him, then slowly takes his hand. Now Owen looks up at him.

Nodge takes the Spanish registration certificate that the registrar is holding and tears it into small shreds. He holds it over his head and drops the pieces so they land on both him and Owen.

Confetti, says Nodge.

Let's get on with it, he says to the registrar.

Do you mean it? says Owen.

Think I care less about Jesus? He could have come with his twelve disciples as far as I'm concerned, and it wouldn't have made any difference.

Owen throws his arms around Nodge's neck then kisses him full on the lips.

Nodge, after the briefest of pauses, kisses him back.

The registrar smiles and, on cue, everyone in the congregation breaks out in fervid, relieved applause.

* * *

The coffee bar on Marylebone High Street is one of a small chain in London, 'Patisserie Valerie'. The original one, which Veronica prefers, is in Soho, but Soho is too oppressive for Cordelia. She can just about bear the quiet gentility that lies north of Oxford Street and east of Marble Arch. She is flying to France that evening on one of her frequent luxury retirement breaks and has invited Veronica for tea before she heads off to a villa in Nice for the rest of the month.

There is a gold chandelier on the ceiling and frescos on the walls of classical balconies with trailing vines and seascapes disappearing into mist. Behind a glass counter there are rows of patisserie. They have been sitting at the table now for ten minutes, and little real information has been exchanged, only pleasantries about Michael, and generalities about the new work that is being done to restore the old stables next to the house in Buckinghamshire. Veronica is having difficulty hiding her impatience. Cordelia has the knack of infuriating her without doing anything specific that she can put her finger on. The generation of Veronica's pique customarily marks a victory for Cordelia as well as a staging post; after she has asserted her control of the dialogue in this fashion, she will permit herself to get to the main point of the conversation. Veronica assumes this thrust will be revealed shortly, since Veronica has, despite herself, taken to biting her fingernails and tapping her spoon on the saucer, long-established tells that reveal all too plainly her frustration. That Cordelia does have an agenda is not in doubt – she never voluntarily meets Veronica one-to-one without some secret purpose.

Cordelia sips at her cappuccino, and wipes her lips with a paper napkin. The remains of an outsize strawberry millefeuille are in front of her, which she has somehow consumed without getting a crumb on herself or the table. Veronica has stuck to lemon tea, no sugar or milk.

Veronica listens to Cordelia, talking now about the architectural challenges of converting the old stable into a guest room, and the unreliability and surliness of the labourers. Her crow's feet contract and expand as she talks, and her turkey neck wobbles in time. Her make up is professionally applied, but cannot conceal the fading of herself as the beauty she once thought herself to be.

Finally, Veronica can take it no longer.

So. What is it you want to talk about?

Why the hurry?

I'm not the one that's in a hurry. You are. I thought you had a plane to catch.

Plenty of time. It doesn't leave until seven.

Won't Daddy be getting worried? You know how neurotic he is about plane departures.

Cordelia pauses, a pause that Veronica recognizes as being for effect.

Michael isn't coming.

What?

In all their marriage, so far as Veronica knows, Michael and Cordelia have never been on holiday without one another.

Why not?

I'm too angry with him.

Oh my god, Mummy. What has he done?

Cordelia says nothing.

He's hasn't had an affair, has he?

Worse than that.

What could be worse than that?

He betrayed me.

How?

Veronica is beginning to feel worried. Her mother knows each of the tender spots of her psyche and takes a casual pleasure in prodding them. Cordelia looks up through her half-moon spectacles, secured around her neck by a silver cord. Another pause for effect, but Veronica is too anxious now to feel irritated.

He betrayed you as well, Veronica.

Mummy, what on earth are you talking about?

I thought long and hard about telling you. I only found out this afternoon, and I wasn't going to cancel my holiday because of him. But I'm not going with him. No chance of that.

You didn't think that long and hard about it if it was only a few hours ago.

Now Veronica registers something odd in Cordelia's responses. She sees controlled fury there, certainly. And upset, and disappointment. But there's something else, something that makes her wary, makes her want to get up and leave before she hears what she has to say.

I didn't really have time to spend days chewing it over.

Get to the point, then.

Cordelia takes a sip of the cappuccino and wipes her lips again, this time firmly, as if her mind is finally made up.

I got some old boxes out of the stable before they came in to work on it. They've been waiting in the hall cupboard for a while. I couldn't find my passport, so I decided to start going through them to see if it was there for any reason. Not that it was very likely but I was running out of places to look. Anyway.

She fumbles in her bag, and brings out a buff A4 envelope. She holds it out to Veronica.

I found this.

Veronica stares. She cannot bring herself to reach out and take it.

What is it?

It's something you need to know.

Is this what made you refuse to go on holiday with Daddy?

Yes.

So what's it got to do with me?

You'll see.

Cordelia puts her hand over Veronica's. Veronica withdraws it, but takes the envelope.

I'm sorry, darling. I did try to warn you.

Veronica sees, immediately and with agonizing clarity, that she isn't sorry at all.

The feeling she couldn't identify before is now plain on that leathery face, barely disguised.

Triumph.

* * *

Veronica meets Tony at the business hotel near Hammersmith Broadway in the afternoon and they make love in a third-floor room that is neither pleasant nor unpleasant, simply anonymous. Plate-glass windows reflect their bodies on the bed in the falling light.

Tony does not treat her with the gentle, firm respect that Frankie does. He throws her around like a rag doll, seems to want to destroy her with every thrust. From the front, from the back, in the mouth and in places she has never allowed Frankie to trespass. She is horrified, puzzled and above all, excited at her eagerness. Nothing in her therapy training has prepared her for this. She is disgusted by herself, and yet stimulated by her own self-disgust. She is appalled by her submission and yet fascinated by it.

When Veronica has screamed herself to a conclusion, and Tony has lifted himself off, he turns to her as she lies, as if broken, on the left side of the bed, gazing blankly at the ceiling.

Why do you stay with him? says Tony, carelessly wiping the end of his cock on the bed sheets.

He's my husband, says Veronica, without looking at him.

What do you get out of it?

He tries to understand me.

Okay.

You don't.

It's impossible for anyone to understand anyone.

Now she does take her eyes away from the ceiling and look at him.

Yet somehow without thinking about it at all, you do. You do understand me. At one level. Some level that I can't understand myself.

Don't come over all Sigmund on me.

Now Tony is out of the bed. Veronica leans back, feeling the stretch marks by her belly. Tony leans over and kisses them.

Do you feel guilty? he asks.

I don't. Because he deserves it. This.

Why? What did he do? Is this a revenge fuck? Not that I particularly care.

Veronica skirts the question.

It's a strange thing, guilt. It's there where it has no place to be. And nowhere where it should be. I've seen it in my clients over and again. It's like some kind of random virus that can generate out of nothing.

I don't suffer from it, says Tony. *I just don't.*

So why do you spend all this time looking after drug addicts and alcoholics at the centre? For no money? When you don't have any money yourself.

Not because I feel guilty. It just makes me feel useful. I don't know why. I like doing it. Do I need more of a reason than that?

Do you never get, you know, depressed?

Don't understand the word. I know drinking and taking coke were meant to be filling some 'deep hole' in me.

He makes speech marks with his hands around the words 'deep hole'.

Thing is, I didn't see it that way. I just enjoyed them. Now I don't enjoy them. I don't because I can't. But not because they were ever covering up anything.

What about betraying Frankie? You don't feel bad about that?

Frankie blanked me after the golf game. He didn't even invite me to your wedding.

The famous golf game.

He blanked me when I needed him. I never heard from him when I was in rehab. So, frankly, you know what? Fuck Frankie.

Is that what you're doing when you're fucking me? Fucking Frankie?

You mean that this is a double revenge fuck? Me and you both?

He glances over at her with sly, lizard eyes.

I don't want to fuck Frankie. I want to fuck you.

355

Come on then, says Veronica, feeling the wetness between her legs, the pulse inside her, again, insisting, longing.

Tony looks at his watch.

Sorry, babes. I've got to be at the centre in fifteen. You'd better clean yourself up or Frankie might notice something.

Veronica, disappointed, idly starts to play with herself. Her back arches slightly, her chin stretches back.

Frankie never notices anything. He's happy so long as he gets a smile and an occasional ride.

Sounds fair enough.

Doesn't that bother you?

What?

That Frankie and I are having sex.

Tony appears puzzled as he pulls on his Margaret Howell trousers. Somehow, despite his modest income, working part-time at a run-down Greek barber's in Acton, he still manages to dress expensively.

Should I? It would hardly be fair of me. Anyway, I don't believe you.

Uh?

You don't have the taste of a woman who's been having sex. See you later, Vronky.

Veronica takes her hand away from between her legs and sits up.

Don't go, you bastard.

Tony pulls on his sweater, pecks her on the cheek.

I have to. Responsibilities. By the way. Your office is near Oxford Street, right?

What? Why?

You're going to think I'm vain.

You are vain.

I know. But there's a flash sale at one of the department stores for fashion. I need a new suit, for a job interview, and I can't afford one. But I'm going to get one anyway. Have to, the other one the moths have been at. Only I can't afford to get one that fits wrong, and you're good at that sort of thing.

Am I?

Women are as a rule.

What's the job interview for?

You'll laugh. Chauffeur. Part time.

Veronica laughs.

Better than begging for change on a park bench, says Tony, a slight curdle in his tone suggesting he is genuinely piqued.

Of course it is. Sorry.

I'm not bothered. Take the piss all you want.

So what do you want from me then?

Will you come and give me a second opinion? It's a big investment.

It's just an excuse to see me again, isn't it?

Don't flatter yourself.

When?

Can you do tomorrow?

He says it as if he knows perfectly well she will accept. Her hackles rise. But all that comes out of her mouth is, *What time? Where?*

I'll let you know.

I've got other things to do. Appointments with clients.

Like I said. I'll let you know.

He walks towards the door, still the slight swagger in him that she remembers from before he split from Frankie. She watches him go, astonished and partly repelled. Even his closing of the door seems to gesture towards an indestructible indifference.

357

She wonders once again if it is purely sex that makes her return to Tony, but she knows that it isn't. And yet she cannot work out why it is. He seems half-bored and unsolicitous. He is not the father of her child. She is not even particularly attracted to him at a physical level. She doesn't like his smell, musk and cigarettes and earth.

She supposes it is to do with Tony being so unremittingly – Tony. There is no apology in him, no remorse. He is not concerned what she, or anyone else, thinks of him. He is invulnerable. It's as if his short time on the streets has toughened him rather than softened him.

And Frankie is weak. With all his love. With all his tenderness. With all his concealed vanity. With all his money, trying to buy himself strength.

With all his lies. With all his unavoidable, unforgivable lies.

She arches her back again and with her finger, tries to make herself forget.

* * *

The next evening, Owen returns home from John Lewis to find Nodge cooking dinner.

That smells good.

Thank you.

Sit down, it's nearly ready.

Owen takes off his coat and sits at the table which is already laid for two with a bottle of wine in the middle. He brings the casserole pot and removes the lid.

It looks good, too.

Appearances can be deceptive.

You can say that again, says Owen, archly.

Nodge, looking puzzled, starts to ladle out the food, chicken with chorizo and rioja.

What does that mean?

I saw something this afternoon that I would rather not have seen.

The new Laura Ashley curtain designs?

I've been debating with myself ever since whether to tell you about it.

Obviously, you're going to. Hold on, I forgot the garlic bread.

Nodge goes to the oven and takes out a Tesco baguette smeared with garlic butter. He tears a lump off for himself and bites into it with pleasure, unsullied by a fear of gaining weight since he knows what a matter of indifference the shape of his body is to Owen.

I decided I've got to. Although to be honest, I don't want to.

Why?

Because it's going to put you on the spot.

Can I open the wine before you tell me?

He pours out a glass for himself and a glass for Owen.

Get on with it, then.

Nodge takes a large swig of the wine.

So. This is the thing. I was taking my lunch break and going out the back way because there's a little coffee bar that way. I don't know if you know, but to get out the back way from the curtain department, you have to go through menswear.

Is all this scene setting strictly necessary?

Nodge still seems to be concentrating more on the food than on Owen. He is already halfway through his plateful.

Probably not. I was making my way out and it wasn't too crowded or anything, but I noticed quite a few people staring over by the Ralph Lauren counter. Then I saw there was this couple, snogging like billy-o. It was really embarrassing. But they didn't care, they were so carried away. Tongues down the throat, everything. Someone shouted 'get a room', but they didn't take any notice. Anyway, I had to walk past them to get out. I walked right past them. They both had their eyes closed, they were so lost in it.

I hope this is going somewhere. This chicken's a bit pink in the middle.

I think you'll find it interesting.

It's not even mildly diverting so far.

What if I was to tell you that the woman was Veronica?

Nodge stops poking at the chicken with his fork, puts his cutlery carefully down on the table.

Fuck.

He stares in bewilderment at Owen.

It gets worse.

How could it get worse? Did they rip each other's clothes off and shag next to the gloves and accessories?

The other person was Tony.

Tony who?

Tony. Your old friend Tony. Frankie's old friend. Tony Diamonte?

Now Nodge falls silent, and stares straight ahead of him, past Owen, at the wall with the framed Frida Kahlo print on it.

I told you it puts you in a difficult position.

I can't believe it. Tony? With Veronica? She always hated Tony.

Hate is a very powerful emotion.

What did you have to tell me for?

Because you had a right to know.

Thanks a lot. What should I do now?

That's got to be up to you.

Now that you've told me, I'm complicit. I'm party to it.

That's exactly what I felt. Complicit. Which is why I had to tell you.

But before you make any decision. It's different with Frankie. I made a decision that puts you in a difficult position. The decision you make could destroy his marriage.

Yes, I know that, O.

So you don't necessarily feel you have to do what I did.

I'd never forgive myself if I didn't say, I don't know, something.

I expect you'll find a way. I always thought you were the pragmatist. It's probably just some brief fling that will blow over. Look, why don't you have a quiet chat with Veronica about it? That should at least make her think twice.

You know how that goes down, Owen. Her guilt will make her hate me. She'll say I've been snooping. Or that it's none of my business. Or something along those lines. And then she'll set about turning Frankie against me. Just in case.

You have a pretty negative view of women for someone with your politics.

It's nothing to do with her being a woman. It's just the way people are. What do you think I should do?

I don't think you should go and blurt it all to Frankie. I imagine he's got enough on his plate as it is. Haven't you noticed? The property market is going down the toilet. If you're any sort of friend, you won't add to his troubles. Remember how he was after Colin died? Went down like a stone.

He got up again, didn't he? In the end.

Yeh, but he's . . .

'He's never been quite the same'. I know. Or perhaps too much the same. Only brittle. Manic. I don't know. Like he's been running so fast he's afraid to stop.

This could push him over the edge.

I don't know what to do, Owen. My conscience . . .

There's more important things than your conscience, dear.

I could have said the same to you! You didn't have to tell me what you saw.

I didn't ruin your life. Like I said, it's different.

I'm not so sure about that. A principle is a principle.

Look, you're a good man, Nodge. A wonderful man. You don't have to go and prove it to everybody by smashing Frankie's marriage.

He trusts me. Probably the only person he does trust really. Or should trust.

He trusts you to act in his best interest. And his best interest in this case is very much keeping absolutely schtum.

I don't know, Owen. I just don't know.

Nodge stares at his plate of unfinished stew. He sits, unmoving.

Do you want that? says Owen.

Lost my appetite.

* * *

Hello, Mum.

Hello, Frankie. You come and have a seat. How's everything with you and Veronica?

Couldn't be better.

The old house. Unchanged since forever. Thank god he still has some security in the world. Whatever happens to him, the house will always be there. Sooner or later, it will be his. Every few months Flossie invites the family over for Sunday lunch. This time Veronica can't make it, she has accompanied China on yet another one of the endless, extra-curricular and very expensive 'educational' trips her school is continually arranging. This time it's a sculpture park in the Cotswolds.

I've done the roast well done like you like it. I know you pretend you like it with all the blood running out of it but you don't really, do you?

Frankie feels the weight of the chair under him, looks at the net curtains.

Do you want a glass of plonk or somethink?

I'll take whatever you've got, Mum. How's the mysterious Gordon?

You'll find out. He's joining us.

You what? Really? What prompted this?

Oh, nothing much. Thought it was about time.

I don't know why I haven't been introduced to him sooner.

Tell you the truth, I don't know either. One of those things I suppose.

I must say I'm honoured.

The table, he now registers, is set for three. Flossie retreats to the kitchen. He hears a brief fit of coughing, then she brings out the lamb on a plate, then the vegetables and roast potatoes.

No one makes a roast like his mum.

You still got that cough, Mum?

I went to the doctor. He said it was asthmatic or something. Gave me an inhaler.

Are you using it regularly?

When I remember.

You've never had asthma before.

Well, I have now, says Flossie, as if that settles the matter. Frankie takes the hint and drops the subject.

So you said you had something to tell me then, Mum.

Can't it wait until you've had your dinner?

She starts to put out the vegetables, overcooked, and the roast potatoes, done perfectly in beef dripping.

Why, will it ruin my appetite?

Nothing like that.

Don't tell me. You're getting married. Is that it? He laughs.

Gawd, what on earth gave you that idea? I'm not marrying no one.

Frankie breathes a sigh of relief. Although he doesn't understand why and although he knows he should wish his mother every happiness, he doesn't like the idea of her getting married again. She is, after all, his. His mother. And his father's wife.

Frankie applies a liberal spoonful of Colman's mint sauce on the lamb and shakes salt out of the cruet.

Oh yes, Mum. This looks good. The business.

Gordon rang to say he'll be a bit late. Problems with the bus. I'm sure you'll enjoy meeting him. He's a very nice man. But he said we shouldn't wait.

Frankie starts chewing on his lamb determinedly. It is almost grey, it is so overdone.

Flossie, he notices, looks nervous and will not meet his eye. She fiddles with the food in front of her absently. Eventually she says:

I suppose I'd better spit it out.

Oh Mum, it's not that bad. Bit overdone perhaps.

Shut up you!

She puts her hand on his, her liver spots like water marks on tissue paper.

Look, Frankie. This is it. I know you love this old house. But. Well, I'll come to the point. I'm selling it.

What?

In fact, I've sold it.

Frankie's food stops halfway to his mouth. A wave of panic unexpectedly hits him. The house has always been here. Solid, stable, immovable, like his mother.

You've sold it?

Yes. I got half a million quid. Just fancy that.

Frankie has put his fork back down again.

Right.

You look upset, Frankie.

Do I?

I expect you're upset that I didn't ask you to sell it for me, aren't you? But just for once, you know, I wanted to do something on my own. You do so much for me.

Frankie is surprised to find himself fighting back tears. But his countenance gives nothing away.

Do I?

Oh, you know me too well, don't you, Frankie. Too well. Truth is, I thought you'd try and talk me out of it. You would have tried, wouldn't you? You love this old house. And I couldn't sort of deal with it. I'd cave in. That's what Gordon said anyway. He said it was best not to say anything.

Well, that's brilliant, Mum, says Frankie. *But what on earth are you going to do with half a million quid?*

She cackles cheerfully.

Oh, I won't end up with anything like half a million quid. It's all remortgaged up to the hilt, isn't it? How do you think I paid for all those cruises? No, probably there's one hundred and fifty thousand left in it. I can't keep paying the mortgage. I always think — well I have thought since your father died — that you can't keep thinking about tomorrow. But it does come in the end, doesn't it? Now Gordon has a nice clean place in Hemel Hempstead. Or it will be clean when I've had a go at it. He'll let me stay there and we'll still have that money in the bank. We might even get a few more cruises out of it. I mean I'm sixty-five years old now, Frankie, and I'm not getting any younger. I don't want to let it all slip through my fingers. I never got the opportunities that you got when I was younger. Spent my life doing nothing much really. Tootling around the house and that. I want to live, see. And you're doing all right, you're all sorted out. I know we won't see so much of each other anymore, but you don't come round that much anyway nowadays, which I don't blame you for, honest I don't, you've family responsibilities.

The sound of the doorbell interrupts this lengthy soliloquy.

I'll get that, love. Probably Davina from next door after a cup of milk or something. She's always on the cadge. Why have you stopped eating? Isn't it very nice?

No, Mum, of course it's nice. Tell you what, why don't I get the door? You rest your legs. You've gone to all the trouble of cooking.

Are you sure?

Frankie is already on his feet.

That's very nice of you. Thank you, Frankie. I do feel a bit frazzled.

Frankie, in a daze, makes his way to the front door. When he opens it, an enormous black man, maybe six foot three, with dreadlocks, dirty to the point of turning green, is standing there. He looks to be about forty years old, but it's hard to tell. He is shabbily dressed, in jogging trousers, a chunky grey sweater and what looks like an ex-military overcoat. His trainers are old and dirty and one of the shoelaces is undone.

Yes. Can I help you? says Frankie, reaching in his pocket for change.

The man stares at him. Frankie starts to feel irritated.

What do you want, mate? I'm in the middle of my Sunday dinner.
I'm Gordon.

His voice is soft and quiet with a slight West Indian accent.
You're Gordon.
Gordon Lucas. Yes.

He puts his hand out.

Frankie automatically takes it and allows his to be shaken. Gordon smiles, showing rows of large, yellowing teeth. The two lower front ones are missing.

She didn't tell you, did she?

What?

She didn't tell you I was black. She's a bit of a racist, old Flossie, he says cheerfully. *Probably ashamed.*

Now he pushes past Frankie and calls out. Frankie catches the reek of skunk.

Floss! It's me, darling.

Lucozade!

She runs up to him and throws her arms round his neck. They kiss. Passionately. And Frankie looks away.

Gordon takes his coat off and comes and sits down heavily at the table. His eyes are bloodshot, but he seems entirely content and at home. Frankie sits opposite him, unable to stop staring.

So. Frankie. Flossie tells me you're an estate agent, says Gordon and smiles as if he is performing a job interview.

Yeh.

Nice business to be in.

Right.

Frankie's not happy being in the interviewee's seat and he tries to turn the tables.

You got kids, Gordon?

Oh yes.

How many?

Seven.

Five different mothers, says Flossie almost proudly.

Don't see much of them nowadays, says Gordon cheerfully,

picking a roast potato off Flossie's plate with his nicotine-stained fingers.

That's a lot of kids. And a lot of mothers, says Frankie.

That's the way we did things in the old days. Stupid, innit? But I was a young man. Wanted to be a babyfather. Didn't know any better. They're good kids. I still see some of them.

What do they do?

Oh, you know. This and that.

Got any pictures of them?

Not on me, no, I don't. Too many of 'em, they don't fit in the wallet.

He laughs, a sparkling, deep chuckle.

Frankie, refusing to be put off, continues the interview.

So you have a house in Hemel Hempstead?

Not mine exactly. It's a council house. Well, flat. It's a nice one, though. Well, it will be, when Flossie has finished with it. I was never that house-proud, you hear what I'm saying?

Ooh, he's a filthy pig, says Flossie, grinning broadly. Her face is flushed. There is blood suffusing her lips. *Don't you worry, Lucozade. I'll make it lovely for you. He used to live in the Bush, didn't you, Gordon?*

I did indeed, says Gordon, helping himself now to a parsnip. *Twenty-five years. Plumbing was my trade.*

Amazing we never met before. I mean before we really met. When you came round to fix my washer.

Frankie's meal has gone cold now and he cannot even bother to pick at it anymore.

You've been quite a mystery to me, Gordon.

Gordon chuckles again, a sound of stewing fruit.

I bet I have. I bet I have.

We're out of wine, says Flossie.

Gordon leaps with surprising speed to his feet.

I'll go and get some. I could use the walk, tell you the truth. There's a handy Gandhi by the bus stop, isn't there, Floss?

Are you sure? says Frankie. Gordon, who up until now has moved with an arrested, slow loping motion, looks sprightly and urgent.

Yeh, course.

He reaches in his pocket.

Only . . .

He takes out a cheap plastic wallet and opens it to inspect it.

Frankie reaches into his pocket, hands him a twenty-pound note. He smiles.

He's a fine boy, Flossie. You should be proud. I'm embarrassed, Francis.

Oh, he don't mind, says Flossie. *My Frankie's got money coming out his jacksie.*

I'll get some beer for myself as well, if you don't mind, Frankie.

Be my guest.

With that he is gone.

Well, Mum, says Frankie, staring at the space that Gordon has left. *It's nice to see you've become a liberal in your old age.*

He's not like a lot of them other blacks. He's a lovely feller. Heart of gold. You like him, don't you?

Course I like him, Mum. When's the house sale going through?

End of the month.

That soon!

You'll come and see me in Hemel, won't you?

Wouldn't miss it for the world. Mum . . . ?

Yes, dear?

Why didn't you tell me he was Jamaican?

Oh, I don't know. Tell the truth, I always thought you was a little bit racially prejudiced about coloured people. Anyway, he's from Guyana.

Her eyes glitter, knowingly.

Mum, I'm not a racialist. Racist. Anyway, does he know what 'Lucozade' is rhyming slang for?

Don't know what you're talking about, she simpers.

And we don't call them coloured people anymore.

Well what are we meant to call them, then?

People of colour.

Well, what's the bleeding difference?

She coughs again into her handkerchief. This time, Frankie notices, there are small spots of blood on the handkerchief, imprints of a tiny, invisible cloud.

* * *

Veronica has come round to Roxy's rented flat because Roxy has told her that she has important news.

They sit at the kitchen table, sipping cups of builder's tea. Roxy shovels another cup of sugar into hers.

So what's the big news?

The big news? I'm closing the popcorn shop, announces Roxy, almost as if with pride.

You're not! says Veronica.

It's closed already, actually. Two days ago.

Veronica takes a deep draught of the tea.

I'm sorry, Rocks. Tell you the truth, though, I'm not surprised. You've been worried about it for months, I know you have.

Not anymore.

I hope you don't mind me asking but — how much did you lose?

Altogether? I don't know. A lot. To be honest? All the money I put into it.

So why are you so cheerful?

I'm just a cheerful character.

No one's that cheerful.

Roxy reaches across the table and takes a Choco Leibniz from the plate.

Maybe there is a reason.

Don't be mysterious. It doesn't suit you.

I know you must think I'm a complete idiot. The popcorn. But I'm not. Not completely.

I hate to ask this, Roxy, but didn't you buy that house in Spain? Because I read that the property market there has gone into meltdown.

No. I never got that.

But you told Frankie . . .

I didn't want to upset him. You know how fragile his ego is. I wasn't going to touch no gaff in the Med, though.

You're still being mysterious.

I want to show you something, says Roxy.

She gets to her feet.

Where are we going?

It's a secret. Follow me.

Veronica, puzzled, follows her up the steps to her bedroom. It is bare, minimalist, just a framed poster of Kate Moss on the wall.

I know this is a cliché, but that's me, ain't it? A cliché.

She takes the picture off the wall. Behind there is a safe. Veronica can't help laughing.

Like in the movies.

Great, innit?

Roxy is fumbling with the combination. Seems to have found it. Then stops.

I can never quite remember the bloody thing. Hold on a sec.

She gets her phone out and checks.

That's it. Last four digits of Colin's old phone number.

She goes back to the safe and swivels the dial again. This time the door swings open.

Go on then. Have a look inside.

Veronica takes a step forward. The inside of the safe is not lit and it is set surprisingly deep into the wall. It is hard to see at first what she's looking at. There appear to be several large lumps at the back, or something wrapped in tissue paper.

Go on, take them out.

Veronica reaches for them and is surprised by how heavy they are. She peels the tissue paper off.

Inside are thirty ten-ounce bars of gold.

I bought them in the summer of '05, says Roxy. *With what was left after I'd sold the house and invested in the shop. Bottom of the market. They're worth a quarter again what I paid for them.*

Oh, my fucking god.

Told you I liked bling.

The gold bars are exposed now. They are stamped with 'Credit Suisse. 10 oz. Fine Gold. 999.9.' And a serial number.

I didn't want to take all risks, did I? Whatever Frankie said, I didn't feel gold could be a risk. Every one of those babies is worth about five thousand pounds. Cost me about three and a half K to buy each one. That should see me all right for a little while. Get me a few nice little black dresses.

Veronica bursts out laughing.

Not so thick, am I?

You were never thick, says Veronica. *That was what I always liked about you. Smart as a whippet.*

And fit as a butcher's dog, as Colin always liked to say. One thousand per cent.

One thousand and ten per cent.

Veronica strokes a gold bar. It feels soft under her touch.

Shall I put it back?

Shall we just look at it for a little while? It's pure money, that. Not just some digits on a screen. Not just something someone's made up.

You're well and truly middle class now, says Veronica.

No, I'm not. Never wanted to be neither. But I've got a few bob. That's all I ever wanted. A bit of cock and some dosh. I suppose I'm all right for the dosh anyway. But my god, I could do with a shag. I mean, I know sex without love is meaningless. But as Woody Woodpecker said, as meaningless experiences go, it's one of the best.

Woody Allen.

Whatever. Now I'd just like to have some totally irresponsible sex with a gorgeous bloke who doesn't give a shit and doesn't want any ties.

Veronica pauses.

I might be able to help you with that, says Veronica.

Really? says Roxy.

Actually. Perhaps not.

* * *

The phone rings in the office. Frankie picks up to hear an unfamiliar, but unusually officious voice on the other end of the line.

Are you Francis Loftus Blue?

Yeh.

You're the proprietor of 221 Wendell Road?

Who is this?

You're the proprietor?

My name is on the deeds, yes.

I've got some bad news, I'm afraid.

That's nothing new. Who is this?

I'm from the London Fire Service. There's been a conflagration at the property.

A conflagurwhat?

A fire, Mr Blue.

Frankie feels a cold churning in his stomach.

What kind of fire?

There's only one kind of fire. We don't know how it started. But a fairly extensive one.

What's the damage? Has anyone been hurt?

I'm pleased to say that the property was safely evacuated. Quite a rabbit warren in there. Quite a crowd living there.

How extensive is 'extensive'?

It might be best if you came and took a look for yourself.

* * *

When he arrives at the property, he feels panic, then his emotions numbing, a self-protective device he recognizes of old. There are four fire trucks outside and an ambulance. A crowd of maybe fifty people is watching. Some of them he recognizes as his tenants. They include a few of the Polish workmen who dug out his basement, as well as some students and some local authority placements. One Polish workman is holding a few scraps of clothes tightly across his chest like a comfort blanket.

The building is a burned-out shell. There is nothing left of it. The front of the building has gone entirely, revealing the rotten warren inside. A sad little charred television set sits in the corner of one room in front of a blackened IKEA rug. There is rubble strewn everywhere, shards of timber, piles of plaster. Smoke is still rising from the ashes.

Could you stand back, please, sir? It's not safe.

Frankie barely registers the fireman who is standing in front of him. He blinks and finally the man comes into focus.

It's my property, says Frankie robotically.

I see. Could I just have a word, sir? Over here.

Frankie steps over to a quiet space by the fire truck.

He has noticed that one of the tenants is staring at him, the Pole Radowicz who helped dig out his basement. Frankie turns away, but it is too late.

Mr Blue! Mr Blue. Where I live now? You must help me.

Alerted by this, several of the other people, whom Frankie recognizes as tenants, start to join the chorus.

Mr Blue! Everything is lost, says the foreign student. Was he from Iraq or Iran? Or Syria? Frankie can't quite remember, only that he always paid cash on the nail, in full, no arguments.

I have nowhere to liff. It is the Somalian cleaner. Her face is streaked with grey and blood and tears.

Mr Blue. I need to talk to you. About some of the fire regulations. Were you up to date with your safety certificates? says the fireman.

What?

You are insured, yes? says the Iraqi/Syrian/Iranian. Or was he Egyptian? Frankie struggles again to remember.

Of course I'm insured, says Frankie, almost in anger.

Mr Blue, says the fireman, sternly. *You need to contact the police. They have been wanting to talk to you.*

Right, says Frankie, automatically. Then he notices the police car parked beyond the fire trucks, a sergeant looking over at him with a questioning gaze.

As Frankie speaks, he moves away from the scene slowly at first, then fast, faster, as fast as he can. Runs for his car.

Mr Blue! shouts Radowiz.

Mr Blue! shouts the fireman

The policeman narrows his eyes and reaches for his radio.

But Frankie is gone around the corner, springing into the seat of his car, accelerating away and driving nowhere in particular.

He circles the streets of Shepherd's Bush, up the Askew Road, along Uxbridge Road, down Shepherd's Bush Road to Hammersmith Broadway and back again. He drives without purpose and without direction.

Eventually, an hour later, he decides he has no option but to go home.

* * *

When he gets there Veronica is waiting for him.

What's that grey stuff all over you?

Ash, says Frankie, in a voice that sounds like it's been through a wringer.

Ash?

From the fire, he says irritably, as if it makes no sense that Veronica cannot know what he is talking about. Then he registers her bewildered expression and collapses, with a deep sigh, into a chair.

The house. The buy to let in Wendell Road. There was a fire.

Oh my god, Frankie.

I know.

Was anyone hurt?

No.

Thank god for that. That's the main thing. How badly damaged is it?

Nothing left.

There's nothing left of the house?

Nothing left. A shell.

He shakes his head.

Veronica does not understand why, but she cannot bring herself to comfort him. She stands rooted to the spot.

When she speaks again, the tone of her voice shifts from vaporous concern to hardnosed pragmatism. This is a manoeuvre Frankie has witnessed many times, but it still unnerves him.

It was insured — right?

Frankie rears up, standing and waving his arms around wildly, as if batting away the doubts in his own mind.

Of course it was insured. I'm not an idiot. Apart from anything else, it had to be insured. Otherwise you can't get a loan on it.

Well, that's something. It could have been a disaster. I mean, it is a disaster, but at least it's not going to ruin us.

Now his voice falls to something softer.

I suppose.

Veronica immediately picks up on the shadow of uncertainty in the tone.

What do you mean, you suppose?

Frankie looks up at her with eyes still red and watering from the toxic fumes escaping from the house. He is tired. He can't trouble himself to lie anymore.

You know. These insurance companies can be difficult.

Difficult how?

I don't know. You remember when we had a break-in? And they said that we hadn't got the window locks fitted properly? And they used that as an excuse to stiff us?

Yes, but something like this! You must have had it nailed down.

No one nails everything down, says Frankie, feebly.

What if they don't pay out?

They'll pay out.

What if they don't?

Frankie despite himself finds himself looking around at the house. Veronica notices it immediately.

The house is safe, right? This house, I mean.

Of course we're safe! They're not going to put us out on the street.

But the house . . . our house . . . it's not at risk, right?

No!

But the way his eyes dart to one side leaves her with a stab of doubt.

Frankie. Look at me.

She forces him to hold her gaze. What's left of his birthmark — and a shadow still remains after the scar has faded to its full extent — is a shade darker than usual. This, she knows, is usually his only giveaway sign of mendacity.

Is. Our. House. At. Risk?

Frankie summons up what is left of his strength.

It might be I suppose, purely theoretically, but . . .

He can't finish because she hits him across the mouth. Once and then again.

Fuck! Veronica!

This is where we live! With our daughter!

Frankie holds his face with his hand. Then his head droops towards the floor. He does not raise it to look at her again when he starts speaking.

There's no need to start panicking. The insurance company will pay out. But on a sum the size of this we're probably going to have to go to litigation. I mean, I shouldn't be surprised.

He gradually raises his head, but his eyes do not meet Veronica's.

How did this house get mixed up in it all, Frankie?

You have to speculate to accumulate. That's the truth. Right at the beginning of all this. When I started doing the buy to let. Back in 2003. I got a loan against the house.

Why didn't you tell me?

I didn't want to concern you.

You didn't want to concern me. Well that's nice of you. Not to tell me about a loan against our house. How big?

Quite big.

How big?

I don't know. Two hundred K?

Veronica looks relieved. The house, she knows, is worth at least £1 million.

That's not so bad.

There is a long silence, enough space for anxiety to breed and the gap to become unbearable.

Then Frankie finally says, in a very quiet voice:

At first, I mean. I topped up. Had to.

Veronica snaps to attention.

How big is the loan now? Just tell me and tell me straight.

Veronica . . .

Just tell me.

Nine hundred.

What? Nine hundred what?

Nine hundred thousand.

Veronica looks out of the window as if a plane had just crash-landed there.

They won't put us out of the house, Veronica. It's too bad for their PR. And that's all a long way down the line.

She turns.

My mother was right. She was right all along about you. God, I've been such an idiot!

Frankie feels a wave of defiance and hurt pride gather inside him like a slow electrical thrum.

Don't start with the holier than thou crap. You're not exactly spotless in all this. You saw your chance and took it.

What's that supposed to mean?

Pathologist on a crummy NHS salary. Nice little wide boy on the make. Nice house in Kensington. Nice house for nice kid. Get yourself up the duff.

I'm going to pretend I didn't hear that. Any of it.

Want some more?

I don't think so. Now we're on the subject though. You've done quite well out of me too.

Have I? How's that? Because I can't work out what you've done for me except sucked money out of my pocket.

Okay. Let's talk about money. Good call. Where did you get the money to fund FLB Estates in the first place?

What?

You heard me. I said, 'Where did you get the money to fund FLB estates in the first place?' When you were sacked — sorry, quit, without asking me — your job at Farley Ratchett and Gwynne.

That was . . . seven years ago! Why are we even talking about it?

Because this other loan. This secret loan. For the buy to let. It's a repeat offence. Isn't it?

I don't see what you're getting at.

Answer me this. Exactly how did you manage it? Because you were struggling to make even the basics. To cover the bills. I was pregnant. You lost your salary after you quit the agency. The new house was already mortgaged up to the hilt. I was about to lose my salary too. How on earth did you manage to start a new estate agency?

I don't see why it matters.

I should have asked that question of myself a long time ago. But I didn't. Because I believed in you Frankie. I trusted you.

Bullshit. You didn't ask me because you didn't want to know.

So where did you get the money then? Who lent it to you?

Frankie pulls a cigarette packet out of a drawer and takes one.

You told me you'd given up.

I have, more or less.

He lights up and inhales furiously.

So where did you get the money?

Here and there. You know. Why do you keep going on about it?

Any particular here? Or any particular there?

Personal contacts.

Would you like to be any more specific?

Not really. I can't remember the details.

Personal contacts? Or a personal contact?

Why does it make any difference? Water under the bridge.

Personal contacts? Or a personal contact, Frankie?

A personal contact. Not that it makes any difference.

Now Veronica looks him in the eyes, full on.

Look at me, Frankie. Look right at me.

Frankie reluctantly complies, but blows smoke in between them as if it might mask him.

Where did you get the money? Tell me the truth.

Frankie stares at her. His eyes dart from side to side, once. He scratches at the shadow of his birthmark.

I told you.

No one I know.

No one you know.

Okay.

Now Veronica relaxes.

Let's play a guessing game. You know that clairvoyant I went to see? He taught me a few mind-reading tricks. Are you up for it?

What?

This personal contact. Was his name . . . Mmm . . . Mmm . . .

Why are you playing games at this moment?

. . . It's coming to me . . .

Veronica. For Christ's sake, be serious.

Mmmm . . . Michael?

Frankie feels the black point of light at the heart of him coldly expanding.

Michael?

Michael. Michael Tree? My father, Michael Tree?

Frankie runs dry of words.

That's right, Frankie. Cordelia told me. In fact, she told me with the greatest of pleasure. I've never seen her look so pleased with herself.

When Frankie speaks again his voice is low, and burning with both shame and defiance.

If you know that I borrowed money from Michael, then you know I paid him back years ago. With interest. A lot of interest. He was hardly making an act of charity.

That's not the point! The point is, you promised me that you'd never borrow anything from my family. Never, never, never.

But I paid him back! And if I hadn't taken the loan, we wouldn't be living here. I couldn't let you down and pull out of the house!

In this house we're about to lose, you mean? Christ, Frankie. My mother always said that you would come to them cap in hand for money sooner or later. And she was right. She was right, Frankie. You did. But you swore on the grave of your dead father that you wouldn't.

It's all just words. Reality has to be dealt with. No harm was done. The fire was just bad luck.

My mother was right all along. You're a chancer. And a liar. And not good enough for me.

Michael made a packet.

You sold me out.

Frankie searches around in his mind but can find nowhere else to go.

Anyway, at least . . .

At least what, Frankie?

Veronica stands with her arms crossed in a gesture of fury, righteous fury.

Frankie can hold himself back no longer.

At least I haven't been shagging someone.

What?

Yeh, you're so moral, aren't you? Right there on your high ground, hovering above the atmosphere in your oxygen mask.

What are you talking about?

Don't waste your breath. Nodge told me all about it.

Nodge? What the hell does Nodge know about anything?

Owen saw you with someone. Some . . . man. At John Lewis. Between hats and socks.

It is the thought of the socks that somehow breaks Frankie and he starts to cry.

And I didn't say anything, Vronky. I didn't say anything to you about it.

Why? How could you not say anything? How could you cover up something like that?

How could you? How could you not say anything about what you were up to?

Frankie . . .

I could stay quiet, though. I could, because I didn't want to lose you. I thought it would pass.

Oh.

Has it? Did it pass?

Veronica nods. Her eyes are dry.

Yes. It's passed.

Who was it?

Nodge didn't . . . ? I mean . . .

What? Who was it? Nodge said Owen didn't recognize the man.

It was . . . no one. No one you know.

Who, then?

Someone from the drop-in centre.

One of the loonies?

We don't say that anymore, Frankie.

Fuck I care what we say or don't say. Who?

No. Not one of the clients. Someone who worked there. Temporarily.

What was his name?

Oleg . . . Oakeshott.

Oleg? You had an affair with someone called Oleg?

No one calls him Oleg. He's just Oakeshott.

I'm going to . . . I don't know what I'm going to do. But I'm going to give him something to go properly mental about. When he's picked up his teeth from the floor.

You can't. He's left. He was only there for a few weeks. He's gone back to Prague. That's where he's from. Prague.

You're lying.

No. I swear.

On China's life.

Don't be so melodramatic.

On. China's. Life.

I swear on . . . her life. That he doesn't work there anymore.

And he's gone back to Prague.

And he's gone back, yes, to Prague.

How long were you seeing him for?

A month.

How often?

A few times. That's all.

Now Frankie looks up, a pleading look in his eyes.

So we're equal.

Equal failures.

Why did you do it, Veronica?

Why does anyone do anything, Frankie? Because we'll all be dead sooner or later and the opportunity came up. And I was angry that you had gone behind my back to Michael. And you never asked me. And you never told me.

So, says Frankie, lost entirely for what else to say.

So I presume you're going to leave me now, says Veronica, with a matter of factness that Frankie finds unnerving.

Frankie looks around wildly.

What? No!

You have to.

Why?

Because if you don't, I won't respect you.

But . . . I love you. You're my wife.

It doesn't matter. You have to leave me. You have to leave me and China.

I won't. No. I won't. I forgive you, Veronica. Maybe you don't forgive me, but I forgive you.

You'll never forgive me. You'll just try and find ways to punish me that I won't know about.

No. No, Veronica. I want us to stay together. Forever.

Frankie. Be a man. Just for once.

I won't leave you.

Please.

I won't. Never. No.

Why not?

Because you're all I've got left. You're everything. You and China.

Then I'll have to leave you.

But you're the one who's been unfaithful!

And you're the one who's lied through your teeth.

I didn't lie!

No. You just didn't say anything.

Like you didn't say anything about . . . Oleg.

It's not the same.

Look. At least think it over. At least give me until after the awards. I can't go through that on my own. I want you there. For my big night. It's only a few more days.

Veronica considers this. Her face is a mask. Frankie cannot read it.

A few more days, then.

And then?

And then I'll make up my mind. Since you won't.

* * *

The Estate Agent of the Year Ceremony is at the Camelot Hotel in Charing Cross Road. It is held in the Long Room, one of three function rooms. It is a rectangular room more suited towards sales conferences, with plain cream walls and giant banks of recessed lights in the ceiling that emit a steady, abrasive glare. The tables are laid with a mix of studied pretension and slack planning. The sprays of flowers at the centerpiece are slightly too large and block most of the view of the other side of the table. The bread rolls at the side of the main plates still have the chill of recent defrosting. The Prosecco is sugary.

Only ten of the twenty eight-person tables are full. Five are unoccupied. The ten full tables are closest to the front of the room, facing a podium. A very minor celebrity is on the stage, an occasional female presenter from a popular TV property programme. She has streaked blonde hair and an indestructible smile, and seems delighted beyond belief with everything anybody says or does. The publisher of *Estate Agency Today* is also on the stage, a vast man with a head the size of a bowling ball, sweating in his dinner jacket, looking uncomfortable and flushed. The presenter, whose name is Phoebe Witter, is doing her best to inject some enthusiasm and excitement into the proceedings, which increasingly have taken on the atmosphere of a drunken stag party. About eighty per cent of the attendees are men, all pressed into rented dinner jackets.

At one table on the far side of the room sits the contingent from Farley and Ratchett. Ratchett has been looking daggers at the FLB table all night. Frankie, meanwhile, has been assiduously keeping the F&R table out of his field of vision. He can't bear to contemplate the idea that they will take the prize, although he has heard from several insider sources that they are the favourites, because Ratchett has been spreading a few bungs to make sure of victory. Frankie wouldn't put it past him.

Frankie smiles at his guests. Victor and Jane are there, all that is left of the original team, along with three other salesmen and the PA, a graduate who is biding her time before 'finding her true vocation'. Veronica is there as his guest, as is Nodge. Frankie couldn't swing any more tickets so Owen is at home watching *Ugly Betty*.

Frankie's smile is at odds with the slick of acid in his gut. Earlier that day, unknown to the rest of the table, he received a letter from the insurance company confirming that they would not pay out as the property was multi-occupancy and not single occupancy as declared on the application form. Frankie cannot deny it. He also cannot possibly bear the rebuilding cost. He is finished. He will lose his other properties. He will lose the house. He will lose his home.

Their home.

But there is still this one last night in which joy and triumph and affirmation are a possibility, just within his reach, only a few metres away, the distance between his table and the podium.

How are you feeling, Frankie? says Veronica.

Bit nervous, to tell you the truth. Never thought we would get this far. It's very exciting, isn't it?

I'm proud of you whatever happens, she says. *And whatever happens afterwards.*

The words fly out of her throat, loosened by champagne and guilt.

Frankie, startled, is set to challenge her on it – what is the implication? – but the presenter has finished her patter and jokes and is about to announce the next set of winners.

Now, says Phoebe Witter. *It's time to announce the winner of the Small Estate Agent of the Year, London West!*

Her hand stretches out to the outsize silver cup on the table in front of her, almost the dimensions of a soup tureen, in pure nickel silver.

To receive the Holy Grail of the estate agency world.

She nods towards the tureen. There is scattered applause.

Behind her is an illuminated screen, still showing information about the last winners, Small Estate Agent of the Year, London East. Now the letters dissolve, and a new shortlist appears on the screen.

She reads out the shortlist from an autocue. Frankie translates in his mind. A bunch of mugs in Chiswick. Another bunch of mugs in Kensal Green. Then a posh Kensington bunch and some out in a London satellite town. Farley and Ratchett. And Frankie.

The publisher of *Estate Agency Today* hands her a navy blue envelope. She tears it open and pauses for some ten seconds for effect. The room is duly hushed.

And the winner is – FIB Estates! FIB is this year's winner!

Instead of sounding the initials – F L B – Phoebe Witter misreads the letters and pronounces the word *'fib'*. And on a giant illuminated board behind them the pulsing letters 'F I B' appear illuminated in neon.

FLB! declares Frankie. *It's FLB!*

But it is too late. The noise swallows his desperate correction, the table of Ratchett and Co. are laughing loudly, and the laughter is beginning to spread. The presenter does not correct her mistake.

F.I.B. Scott, calls out Ratchett in a convincing impersonation of *Thunderbirds'* Jeff Tracy. *Thunderbird 2 is GO.*

Victor and Jane and Frankie and the rest of the employees all jump to their feet, ignoring the ruckus, while scatterings of polite applause break out in the room to drown out the laughter.

Frankie the Fib! Frankie the Fib! chants Ratchett, on fire with his own disappointment.

Frankie leans over and kisses Veronica, then he and the rest of his staff make their way in a snaking crocodile towards the stage. Farley and Ratchett's table keep their hands firmly on their knees as the applause gathers. Frankie glances over to Ratchett and tips him a wink and a finger. Ratchett picks his nose in response.

A camera somewhere is flashing, turning the event, for Frankie, into a silvery dream. On the podium the group of them gather round and Phoebe Witter hands Frankie the immense trophy. Frankie sees his name on it – Frankie Blue. Once again the inscription reads, 'FIB Estates'.

And yet, in the beating heart of this moment, despite everything, he has never felt so happy.

Supporting the cup in one hand – it is much lighter than he expects so he manages it easily – he waves towards Veronica, but cannot find her in the glare of the lights.

At the table Veronica is crying behind a red paper serviette. Nodge leans over.

This is about Tony. Am I right?

Veronica snaps her head up, rubs her eyes with the back of her sleeve.

So Owen did know who it was.

Of course.

You knew all along.

Yes.

I didn't think Owen even knew Tony.

He remembered him from the funeral.

On stage there is a huddle as the group gather for the official photographs. Frankie's face is the moon, glowing with temporary reflected light from the flashes.

Tony and I . . . all that stopped months ago. For god's sake, Nodge. You can't tell Frankie it was Tony. It will kill him.

Nodge fidgets with his wine glass.

Why did you do it?

Veronica looks away, hardly able to meet Nodge's eye. Frankie on the stage, beaming, flushed, trying to find her again in the darkness.

He's been ignoring me for a long time. Trying to make money. Trying to be this thing that he's always wanted to be. The top . . . the top . . . estate agent.

The way you say it. 'Estate agent'. It's like you're saying 'dogshit agent'. Hasn't he been doing it all for you? For you and China?

He's been doing it for him. He's always been doing it for him.

Because you think he's only interested in money? You're wrong about that.

I know. That's the irony. He's actually not interested in money. He just wants me to admire him. And he wants himself to admire him. And he wants the world to admire him. But he doesn't care about money. Not really.

Frankie takes the microphone from the presenter and starts to make his speech, the speech he has delivered so many times inside his head over the years.

. . . I want to thank all the team . . . the late, great Ralphy Gwynne who started me off in this game . . . my old friend Colin who can't be here tonight . . . Jane and Victor . . .

You're hardly in a position to judge him, hisses Nodge. *How can you possibly know that? How can you possibly know why anyone does anything? You're a therapist, for god's sake. You should know that.*

You're right, Nodge. Of course you're right. Not that it matters who's right.

Frankie is holding the cup aloft. He approaches the microphone to speak again.

The truth is, says Veronica, *I've never really made any proper decisions. Leaving him seems like the first one I've made since . . . well, forever.*

You're leaving him because you feel it's time you made a decision of some kind about something or other?

Frankie's eyes now glitter, starstruck in the spotlight.

We started with nothing. A single room on the Askew Road and central heating that didn't work, says Frankie, his voice almost cracking with emotion. *We had to wear thermal underwear beneath our fancy suits the first two months. And now somehow, from that frail beginning, all my dreams have come true.*

At the table, Veronica turns on Nodge, angry, not with Nodge, not with Frankie, but with the way everything is and the invisible forces that make it so.

Do you know why I married Frankie? Well, that's a long story. But I thought it was fate. Do you know why we had a baby together? Because we were too pissed to go and get some condoms. I even slept with Tony because a clairvoyant told me about the horns and hand round his neck.

What?

It doesn't matter now. You wouldn't understand. Do you know why else I married Frankie? Because I wanted to upset my mother. Or so it turns out. That's what I've learned from therapy. My mother was right all along. And I just couldn't face that. I couldn't face her being right. But I'm ready now. At last. I'm ready to admit defeat. I'm finally making a decision. Because Frankie won't. He's too scared. And I'll stand by the consequences. Frankie will have to do the same.

Frankie continues on the stage, holding the mike stand in two hands, caressing it like a cabaret crooner.

But most of all I'd like to thank my beautiful wife Veronica, without whom none of this would mean anything. And our beautiful daughter . . .

He seems okay, says Nodge. *He's enjoying himself.*

He's in trouble Nodge. Big, big trouble. Financial trouble.

I didn't think it was that bad.

Oh, it's bad all right.

. . . China, who means the world to me, but who can't be with us tonight because, well, because she's in bed asleep! . . .

Onstage, a smile has spread across Frankie's face such as Veronica has never seen before.

He stands there, tall on the stage, and she does, in truth, feel proud of him.

Whatever happens he will have this. He will have this night and this silver-plated trophy. This outsize, shining, empty cup.

2008: Fall and Epiphany

Frankie is in the back of the cab with Nodge at the wheel. They are on their way to the opening of Westfield Shopping Centre in White City, which will be the biggest shopping centre in Europe. The figures have been blared out in continuous advertising streams, on radio, on vast billboards. Two hundred and sixty-five stores. Ninety-six escalators. 1.6 million square feet. Fifty restaurants. £1.7 billon investment.

How is it going to survive in the middle of this economic shitstorm? says Frankie. *No chance.*

They reckon it's going to pull in twenty million shoppers in the first year.

Chances are there won't even be money. They nearly closed down the cashpoints.

Scaremongering. I think it will do all right, myself, says Nodge.

It'll be bust in six months. You'll see.

Hmmm.

At least it should help keep property prices in the Bush stable for a while, because they are tanking everywhere else. Have you seen the figures? Fifteen per cent down in a year!

Yeh, should give the agency a bit of a boost. Very desirable to live round here now.

For a while maybe.

How is business, anyway?

Flat. Very flat. Trade hasn't seen anything like it since '89.

FLB Estates are still managing to stay solvent – Frankie's buy-to-let business was a purely personal affair – and are still somehow getting by, especially as they now have a 'London Small Estate Agent of the Year (London West)' plaque displayed prominently on their wall.

Frankie himself, however, is a bankrupt. Most of the salary he awards himself from the agency gets creamed off by the mortgage company who owned the burned-out house. All his other properties have been sold off, at the bottom of the market. It's nowhere near enough to cover his debt.

Around his neck he fingers a golden key on a chain. Veronica left it on the bedside table when she moved out of the house with China. It is itching at his neck, irritating his skin, causing blemishes. He undoes the catch, takes it off to try and relieve the itching, then morosely examines it.

There's a spot of rust on this. It's meant to be gold.

Where did you get it? You told me you got it from Tiffany's.

Well, yeh. Not that Tiffany's.

Frankie ruefully puts the key into his pocket.

How do you make love work? he says, still fingering the key in his pocket.

Why ask me?

You and Owen seem solid as a rock.

Unconditional acceptance on one side. Recognition of the unconditionality on the other side. Gratitude for it on both sides. That's all there is to it.

But Frankie doesn't appear to be listening.

I've lost everything.

You haven't, says Nodge. *You've still got China.*

Every other weekend.

And the agency.

The part of it that doesn't belong to the bank.

I thought I was meant to be the pessimist.

At least nothing much else can go wrong.

Don't count on it.

That's the depressing bastard I know and love. Thanks.

You're welcome.

Nodge. Do you think Veronica ever loved me?

Don't be stupid.

If she did, then why did she stop?

Because you lied to her.

Frankie stares out of the cab window at the dull October day.

My life doesn't amount to much.

Course it does, says Nodge.

At least Veronica's given something to the world. She was in medicine. Now she's helping people with counselling. What do I do? Sell space. Empty space. I thought if I just got enough, made enough . . .

Frankie's voice trails off.

See. I was never sure she loved me. Not really. How could she? I thought I had to be really successful, or she would dump me.

After you have a kid it's not about success anymore. It's just about being there.

She was better than me.

She slept with another man. She threw ashtrays at your head when she was angry.

Frankie is in a dark, sullen reverie now, lapsing into silence. Nodge keeps his concentration on the road.

How much longer till we get there?

Ten minutes if the traffic is okay.

They exit the M4 at Hammersmith, go round the roundabout and head along the Shepherd's Bush Road.

Can you stop for a moment, please, Nodge? Just pull into this side road.

What? Why?

I'll only be a sec.

Hold on. Isn't this where Veronica works? The drop-in centre?

That's right.

Frankie!

Just pull over, Nodge. I want to see if she's there.

What for?

I've got some papers for her to sign. To do with the divorce.

Is it so urgent?

The decree nisi came through today.

Oh, I see. I'm sorry. That must be hard.

Nodge turns the corner, double parks just past the large Victorian house.

I don't see why you need to do this. You can put the papers in the post.

Better to be sure with something like this.

Hmmm.

Don't hmmm me.

Hmmmm. You're still hoping to get her back. She's not coming back. You don't have a crystal ball.

Veronica does, apparently. She's looked into it. And guess what? No Frankie.

I'll only be a moment.

Outside a patch of rain, a surprise in an otherwise blue sky, is getting heavier.

Take this, says Nodge, passing over an outsize umbrella. *You'll be soaked.*

A huge articulated lorry pulls up behind Nodge and starts honking.

Shit. I'll just go round the block. Get out. I'll be back in a moment.

Frankie gets out of the cab to be faced with a penetrating sheet of rain. Standing under the umbrella, he waits a few minutes for Nodge to return, but he doesn't appear. He can wait no longer, he is getting cold and makes his way into the drop-in centre. Once inside he closes the umbrella, and noticing a stand, puts the brolly into it.

Maybe twenty lost souls are arrayed around the room. Nobody seems to be in charge. Frankie stands there, confused. Veronica is nowhere to be seen.

He starts to cast around for someone to give him information. Eventually, by the fire doors, he finds a man in a polo neck jumper with a riot of salt-and-pepper hair who is wearing a lanyard with a local authority insignia on it.

Excuse me. I'm looking for Veronica Tree. She works here. Sometimes.

May I ask who wants to know?

I'm her husband.

The man looks sad and severe and regretful all at once.

Ah yes. Frankie is it? A pleasure to meet you. Veronica's not here in the mornings on Thursdays anymore, I'm afraid. She'll be in late afternoon, I think.

Frankie doesn't try to hide his disappointment.

Ah. Okay.

He looks the man up and down. He is old but attractive.

Can I ask your name?

My name is Oakeshott.

Oakeshott? Oleg Oakeshott?

Oleg? No, my name isn't Oleg. It's Peter. Peter Oakeshott.

He holds out his lanyard to Frankie, which reads *Dr P. Oakeshott.*

We do have someone called Oleg here, though. That's him.

He nods to a dissolute man sitting in a crummy armchair, sullenly smoking.

He was one of Veronica's clients. Between you and me, probably the most difficult one.

Frankie looks puzzled.

So there's no one here called Oleg Oakeshott? Who went to Prague?

Oakeshott responds slowly, as if explaining something simple to a child.

There's someone called Oleg. Who is from Prague. And I'm called Oakeshott. But there is no one called Oleg Oakeshott. Who's gone to Prague.

Has anyone gone to Prague? Anyone at all?

Not so far as I'm aware.

Frankie considers this, and can only find partial sense in it. Why would Veronica lie about which stranger she slept with? He packs the thought away before he can be troubled by any possible answer.

Look, would you do me a favour? I've got to give Veronica some papers. Very important. Can I trust you to give them to her?

No problem.

Frankie hands the envelope to Oakeshott, then, his head spinning, he turns in a daze and returns to the street where

Nodge's cab can be seen at the kerb through a curtain of rain. He reaches the cab, pulls open the door and climbs in.

Was she there? says Nodge.

No. You want to know something funny?

What?

She told me she had an affair with a man called 'Oleg Oakeshott' at the centre. But there is no Oleg Oakeshott. Why would she lie like that? I mean it wouldn't matter one way or the other. I don't know the guy, after all. She told me he'd gone to Prague. Swore to it.

Beats me, says Nodge, urgently starting the cab. Because he has seen, in his rear-view mirror, Tony Diamonte approaching the door of the drop-in centre.

At least the rain has eased off a bit.

Shit! I forgot your umbrella.

Leave it. Really. I'll drop back later.

But Frankie is gone, before Nodge can protest further.

Nodge watches in the rear-view mirror as he sees Frankie and Tony nearly collide. They both stop and stare at one another. He watches as they exchange words. A silent soundtrack plays out. Nodge thinks of going to intervene, but it is clearly too late to save the situation.

Moments later, Frankie starts waving his arms wildly. Tony is laughing. Frankie goes to punch him, but Tony dodges him, traps him and sends him flying. Frankie falls to the wet pavement, the slabs cracked by the swelling earth underneath, open to the rain. He lies there, like a crab upended, as Tony walks away and unhurriedly enters the drop-in centre.

Nodge sighs and gets out of the cab. When he reaches Frankie, he has not moved from his prone position.

You need to get up, Frankie.

Frankie says nothing.

It's wet. You can't stay there all day.

Frankie looks up at Nodge. It's as if he doesn't recognize him at all.

Come on, Frankie. Let's go to the opening, says Nodge, softly.

I saw Tony.

I know.

We had a fight.

I know.

Nodge hauls him onto his feet. He notices there is a smear of blood on Frankie's forehead.

Come on. Back to the cab. You'll catch your death otherwise.

Frankie says nothing. He lets Nodge lead him back to the cab and throws himself into a slump in the back seat. Nodge takes up his position behind the steering wheel.

You okay, Frankie?

Do you know what he told me?

Nodge turns round and looks at Frankie, who is sitting shivering in his mud-smeared suit.

I think I can guess.

Now Frankie looks up at him, blinking at twice the normal rate.

What do you mean — you think you can guess? He told me he was the one Veronica had an affair with. Him! Tony Diamonte. That can't be true, can it? I mean that's not possible, is it? Tony doesn't work at the drop-in centre. Does he? Veronica would have told me.

Nodge says nothing because he can think of nothing to say.

Frankie feels dark, suffocating vapour of understanding rising.

Did you know?

Frankie . . .

All this time. You knew. *Didn't you?*

How could I tell you, Frankie? You were in a bad enough way as it was.

Right. Okay. No. Right. You kept it from me.

Frankie says nothing for a long time.

Do you still want to go to the shopping centre opening? says Nodge.

Doesn't matter, he mumbles, looking out of the window at nothing at all.

* * *

The crowd inside the shopping centre is immense. There are balloons, posters and most strikingly, a procession from the McDonald's franchise, dressed up in foam-rubber glory. Hamburglar, masked and bucktoothed, Ronald McDonald, psychotically happy. Mayor McCheese looks to be the most uncomfortable – a heavy man wearing a huge foam rubber bun on his head, a tiny top hat on top of that, then a slice of yellow foam cheese and brown foam patty sandwiched between the slices of the bun. Underneath this arrangement there are a pair of concealed eyeholes to enable the unfortunate occupant of the costume to navigate. He wears a sash emblazoned with the word 'Mayor' and carries a pair of large round plastic spectacles. McCheese is a character who looks sinister, frightened and depressed, the most disturbed member of the McDonald's family, nervous of Hamburglar and Ronald, almost certainly bullied by them, at least in Nodge's imagination.

Nodge and Frankie make their way up to the first tier of the shopping centre. Frankie slopes behind Nodge, each step appearing to be an enormous effort. Nodge tries to get him to talk but he remains stubbornly silent.

The opening ceremony is about to begin. The presenter walks on to a crescendo of anticipatory strings. She is wearing an op-art dress, Bridget Riley inspired, black and white.

Good morning Westfiellllllld, shouts the presenter. *How exciting is this? Are you ready to shop?*

There is a muted cheer.

Who's she? says Nodge.

Frankie doesn't answer.

I said, are you ready to SHOP?

The second cheer is rather more enthusiastic but still somewhat muted. There are a few whistles and cheers mixed into the gruel of the reception.

I'm delighted to welcome you to this fantastic, amazing new shopping destination. Or 'experience', as I'd like to call it.

Frankie has fished the gold key out of his pocket and is fumbling with it.

I'd like to introduce you to the founder of Westfield London, the man who had the vision fifty years ago . . . Mr Frank Lowie.

An elderly man in a suit and white shirt and tie comes onto the stage amid uninterested applause and starts making a dull speech.

The incredible mix of retailers . . . quality . . . service . . . provide for shoppers . . . more than fifty years of Westfield experience . . . London . . . very special city.

He keeps the speech short, to the obvious relief of the shoppers who are largely ignoring him and crowding in and out of the stores. Then Boris Johnson, mayor of London, wearing a suit with a blue tie and a poppy in the lapel, appears on the podium to cheers and some scattered boos.

Good morning, ladies and gentlemen. My fellow consumers. What a fantastic event. Absolutely amazing!

I was asked on my way in by a reporter whether this was the right time, in these dark days of austerity, to be opening a shopping mall the size of thirty football pitches, as big as Buckingham Palace and its gardens combined. With free champagne and chocolates. And white marble floors. And I have to tell you, my fellow consumers, in a hotly contested field, it was one of the silliest questions I have ever been asked.

Are you in favour of it?

Weak cheers float up across from the balconies. Johnson, unfazed by the lack of response, continues.

Some eight minutes later, the great tousled windbag finally concludes his speech and announces with as much gravitas as he can manage:

It is my privilege to declare this great shopping centre – open.

He cuts the red ribbon. On cue, a fifteen-piece gospel group headed by Leona Lewis turns out to sing 'Feeling Good'.

It's a new dawn . . .

The violins crash in.

Overkill, says Nodge. But when he turns to look, Frankie isn't there.

He scans the balcony. To his right, he immediately spots Frankie. He is sitting on the edge of the glass wall that stands at the edge of the balcony above the main space, with his back to the drop. His feet swing, searching the air for support.

Frankie cranes his neck to stare down at the marble floors below, showing muscles bulging beneath the chin.

Nodge starts to shout his name, tries to make his way there, but the crowd is too dense.

Frankie's mind is fully focused on what he can see of the floor beneath and behind him. The tiny, pointless, milling people below. The huge looming shops. The brutal, reflecting glass above his head. The processed air in front of his face, the air he breathes day in day out, pointlessly, without ceasing. Until the meaningless cessation. Whether it comes now or in fifty years no longer seems to matter.

Nodge fights his way forward. A security guard is gesticulating for Frankie to come down from the glass partition.

Frankie!

Nodge is edging closer, but the churning crowd blocks his path.

Frankie feels the pull, the magnet of black. To fall from the cinema level – the fantasy level – to the lifestyle level beneath. On 9/11, there was this one man who simply just flew, you could see his poise, the falling man, it was beautiful, he had made his peace.

Frankie.

The security guard is nearly there too, they can both just about reach Frankie. Nodge makes a grab at his jacket and catches a corner of material.

Frankie turns his gaze to Nodge, then to his sleeve where Nodge has touched it.

His face is completely blank.

He lets himself slide backwards over the sharp polished glass edge, and lets himself fall.

Fall.

* * *

Nodge has never moved so fast, down the stairs down another set of stairs, elbowing people aside to yells of protest.

At the bottom he pushes through the crowd distracted momentarily by Frankie's descent. He is greeted not with the mess of blood and organs he had expected. Frankie is straddled across a fallen Mayor McCheese, the foam rubber distended by his splayed body.

Frankie is not moving. He is completely still. Bystanders seem scared to touch him. Nodge pushes everyone out of the way. He can see that Frankie isn't marked, but he remains unmoving, silent. The huge man in the Mayor McCheese outfit is bellowing in pain and outrage.

Nodge reaches Frankie, pushing through the knot of rubberneckers, and whispers in his ear.

Frankie.

Someone in the crowd mumbles. Somehow Nodge hears this through the screams and commotion.

He's a goner.

Nodge puts himself directly into Frankie's eye line, takes him by his shoulders and shakes him gently.

Frankie.

Frankie's eyes open, eyelids flickering, curtains on a stage. There is a pause, then he starts to gabble.

Sorry, mate. Really sorry, mate. Sorry. Sorry. I don't know.

Frankie! Are you alright, Frankie?

Uh.

Are you hurt? Do you feel okay?

I think so.

I'm fucking not, interrupts Mayor McCheese, ripping his foam rubber costume off to see if any permanent damage has been done. But the rubber has protected him, there is barely a bruise.

As Frankie sits up and checks his limbs, all of which appear to be undamaged, the onlookers start to drift away. It was, after all, just another part of the entertainment, with an anti-climactic ending.

Now, without warning, Frankie rolls over, suddenly enough to shock the remaining bystanders looming over him. He stands and looks behind him, takes in, for the first time, the squirming mass that is Mayor McCheese, a moaning flurry of yellow foam rubber and outraged occupant. The joke spectacles he was wearing lie shattered, and his sash, emblazoned with the McDonald's logo, is soiled and torn. Hamburglar is standing in front of Mayor McCheese helplessly holding out a tissue. Ronald McDonald is wringing his hands furiously, his painted-on smiling face undermined by the rictus of fury evident now beneath his orange fright wig. His accent is Liverpudlian.

Are you messin'? Are you feckin messin'?

Suddenly, taking himself by surprise, Frankie starts to laugh, prompting a matching fury in the man wearing the McCheese costume, whose tiny top hat has collapsed.

What's so fucking funny?

Nodge, despite himself, cannot help but join in with Frankie, while the rest of the crowd stand around in confusion. Minutes later, when the ambulance and the police arrive, Nodge and Frankie are still laughing helplessly as the lights play from the ceiling and the pop music, the big hit of the year, blares indifferently, penetratingly, inescapably from the invisible, arc-lit heavens.

Hallelujah
Hallelujah
Halleluuum
jah.

Epilogue: The Phoenix and the Crocodile

Mum. I want you to listen to me.

I know you have to go, but just try and listen this once.

Don't go. Listen.

Please.

You're not listening!

You're not even looking at me.

Do you remember when I was, maybe, six years old?

Yeh, I know. You're right. I was a funny kid.

That's what you used to say, anyway. I believed you too.

Even apart from the birthmark, I was a funny kid.

I had a bit of a stutter as well for a little while.

Do you remember that?

Course you do.

Shall I tell you a secret about that stutter?

I sort of did it deliberately.

No, I did though. I did it on purpose.

I knew you wouldn't believe me. But it's true. Cross fingers and hope to die.

Why? That's obvious.

So you would take notice of me.

I wanted you to notice me, Mum.

And Dad, too, but he was always so busy.

And then he wasn't there any more.

But you were there. Most of the time. When I went to school. When I came home. You were there. With my meals and my clothes and everything else I needed.

But you couldn't look at me. Not quite. Not right full on.

You learned to. I know you did.

But the mark on my face. You struggled with that. Didn't you?

Don't pretend you didn't.

Don't, Mum.

It's too late now to pretend.

It's our last chance.

You wanted a beautiful baby and you got me.

Frankie Blue.

With a scarlet map on my forehead.

Which all the other mothers pretended not to see.

But they saw it alright.

I saw their eyes.

You saw it too, didn't you?

Mum.

Mum?

The thing is, I understand.

That's what I want to say.

I forgive you, Mum.

It doesn't matter anymore.

Can you hear me?

I think she's gone, son. Frankie? I think she's gone.

Frankie looks up at Gordon, who has a big, sombre, drooping tear balancing at the corner of his eye.

I think she's been gone a while.

Yes, says Frankie. *I expect so.*

He is still holding his mother's hand.

It was good that you could say goodbye, son. It mustn't have been easy.

Frankie looks at Gordon, shabby, grey-haired, lines mapped like graphite on his kind, weathered face. For Frankie sees, now, that it *is* kind – kind and sad and lost.

He lets go of his mother's hand. Still warm.

I'm glad. This time. That I did. Say goodbye.

Yes.

I never did with my dad.

That's a shame.

Or Colin. Or Ralph.

Who's they?

She saw me, didn't she, Gordon? She heard me. She heard what I said.

I know she did, bwoy.

I looked into her eyes. It was only a few minutes ago. I could see her there. Way deep in there. Still there.

She's not there no more, Frankie bwoy. Gone far away.

She was my mum, Gordon.

I know she was, son.

My mum.

Yes.

My mummy.

He begins to weep, silently. Gordon rests his hand lightly on Frankie's back.

She was a good woman, Frankie.

Frankie shakes himself out, straightens up, drags a sleeve across his face.

She was about average. But you made her happy these last few years, Gordon.

Did I?

You did.

I hope so.

You know when I first met you, I thought you were a bit of a hustler. Something of a rogue.

Gordon gives a deep gravelled chuckle.

Oh yes. I know that.

Well. You probably were.

He shrugs helplessly.

Always have been, I suppose. Just the way I am. Eye for the main chance. And for the ladies. Ha.

Yes.

But we had some good times, me and Floss. Some lovely times together, we had.

Spending my fucking inheritance.

That's right, son.

Gordon laughs again, more emphatically this time.

Spending your fucking inheritance, bwoy.

Frankie manages to laugh too.

Thank you, Gordon.

My pleasure, son.

It's time to say goodbye, says the nurse who has appeared from her ward round. She is beginning to draw the curtain around the bed.

Yes, says Frankie.

Okay, says Gordon.

Frankie and Gordon step back, and the nurse closes the curtain, making a soft squeal like air escaping or a rush of wind.

She had a good innings, says Gordon.

She did. In the end, says Frankie, turning away.

Gordon turns away too. They make their way in silence to the door of the ward.

Drink? says Gordon. *I need a stiff one.*

Sorry, Gordon. I've got to go and tell my daughter. Flossie's granddaughter. She's waiting for me downstairs.

Little China. Not so little now, isn't it?

Not so little. Eight years old.

I'll go and have one by myself then. Raise a glass to old Flossie.

You do that, Gordon.

Only I'm a bit . . .

Gordon looks at Frankie, a faint smile on his face that Frankie recognizes all too well.

Frankie sighs, reaches in his pocket, pulls out his wallet and then a five-pound note.

Maybe buy a round, says Gordon, not taking the note.

You never stop do you, you bloody villain.

For Flossie.

For Mum then, says Frankie, smiling and handing Gordon a twenty.

* * *

Veronica is standing there with China in the café by the entrance.

It's over, says Frankie to Veronica.

Oh, Frankie, says Veronica.

Is Grandma dead? says China, cheerfully.

Yes, China. Grandma's passed on.

Has she gone to heaven?

Yes, says Frankie.

Yes, says Veronica.

The three of them stand in silence.

I thought I'd take her over to the park.

She's meant to be getting back with me, Frankie. That was the arrangement.

Frankie looks at her pleadingly.

We don't have to follow the court ruling to the letter. Do we? Not today.

Okay then. Yes, for a little while.

Thanks, Vronky. I'll have her back with you in an hour.

See you back here then. Don't be late. She's got school tomorrow.

Frankie pauses.

I love you, Veronica.

Veronica looks back at him, her eyes giving nothing away.

I know you do, Frankie.

Frankie picks up takes his daughter's hand and leads her out towards his car. It is only then that China starts crying.

* * *

Frankie drives to Kensington Gardens. He buys China a Mr Softee cone from an ice cream van with Flake bunnies' ears, while he treats himself to a banana cream lolly, his favourite since he was a boy. Flossie would always treat him in the summer. It comforts him.

They make their way into the Princess Diana memorial playground. China has never been here before. It seems that with the ice cream and the prospect of a new play space, she has forgotten about her grandmother already. The tears will return, Frankie knows. But he is thankful for China's blessed forgetfulness, the miraculous quick oblivion of being a child.

What is this place, Daddy?

Neverland.

There are tipis here and swings, and totem poles carved with ancient faces. There are treasure chests and a sea-serpent. China finishes the rest of her ice cream, and rushes to the wooden pirate ship that is the centerpiece of the playground. She disappears into the hull and reappears moments later, clambering up the mast.

Frankie checks his phone, always waiting for a message that will somehow change his life. He does not know what it will be, it has never come before, but he somehow still believes that it will pop up. Perhaps a job, or a woman, an unknown woman who will redeem him, change him, save him. He cannot take his eyes off the phone. Waiting.

. . . and it's like a big green brush that someone has put there, like a giant has put there . . .

He realizes that China has climbed down from the mast, left the wooden ship and has been talking to him for some time. He has not heard any of it.

What?

Daddy, why don't you listen to me?

What did you say, darling?

That tree. Look how pretty it is.

She points to an old tree that stands outside the perimeter fence shading part of the playground.

The sun is catching all the leaves. They're trembling like they're scared.

Frankie puts the phone away and looks up at the tree. He sees, immediately and vividly, that it is beautiful and glowing, rooted and real, gnarled with imperfection and yet somehow at the same time perfect.

Yes, says Frankie. *It is beautiful.*

They stand together like this for some time, staring. Frankie feels a pinch at his heart, a tug, of something lost, or something promised and never delivered.

Now China's gaze has shifted.

Look, there's another daddy with his little girl. She's wearing the same dress as I've got.

Frankie adjusts his gaze. A melancholy-looking man is pushing his daughter up and down on the swings, the hinges creaking on each flying ellipse. He catches Frankie's eye and gives a weak smile, one that seems to carry a strange recognition. The solitary father's club. The man's daughter is indeed wearing exactly the same dress as China once had, from Petit Bateau, eighty pounds, Frankie now remembers. He argued with Veronica about it, she thought it was worth it. She won of course. China grew out of it in six weeks.

He leads China over towards the swings.

That's a co inkydink, says China.

A what?

A co inkydink.

He concentrates. He can never quite remember all China's idiosyncratic phrases.

Oh. Yes. It is a coincidence.

I wish Mummy was here too. Don't you love Mummy anymore? China asks, suddenly. There is a mess of dried ice cream around her mouth. Frankie leans down and wipes it away with a tissue that he has surreptitiously licked.

Yes, I love Mummy, says Frankie.

He has been expecting a question like this. He also knows, agonizingly in the moment, that his answer is true.

Does Mummy still love you?

I think you need to ask her that question. But the thing to remember is, we both love you, very very much.

China appears to consider this carefully.

Can love stop?

Not with mummies and daddies and their children. No.

Do you want to love someone else?

Not really. Look! The swing is free now. Let's go on the swing.

But I don't want to . . .

Frankie, ignoring her, picks up China and places her on the swing. She protests, but Frankie pushes her anyway. Pushes her and catches her. The swing rises and falls, brings her protests far away, then closer. Like a vibration or an incantation.

Eventually her complaints are overcome by laughter. Frankie keeps pushing, pushing for all his life. She flies higher and higher, so high he almost thinks that she is going to circum-navigate the horizontal pole and go round in an entire circle

Whee! says China.

That's right, China. Up and down. Up and down. Over and over again.

Whee! Whee! Whee!

Frankie keeps pushing, harder and harder. Then he stops, goes round to the other side, so he can push China from the front. Her cheeks are flushed, her teeth white and tiny, her feet splayed. She is laughing now, then squealing with every push, as if not altogether sure whether she is enjoying it or not. Frankie keeps pushing her, until he is almost exhausted.

Stop now, she says, sternly.

Frankie stops pushing and China slows the swing with her feet, scraping her shoes into the dust, until she rocks to a halt.

I want to go the sandpit.

Without waiting for a reply, she runs to the sandpit and starts throwing sand about. There are boulders and rocks among the sand. He reaches the play area and sits down on an adjacent bench.

See the crocodile, Daddy?

Where?

He can see nothing but an apparently random array of small, smooth boulders.

There!

Frankie leans back and squints. He sees now that the rocks are in fact arranged to mimic the shape of a crocodile.

Yes. I see it.

China puts her ear to the largest rock in the centre of the formation.

I can hear it, she says.

What can you hear?

The ticking from the clock.

What clock?

The alarm clock that he swallowed.

Frankie smiles. He looks at her, seeming to see momentarily the infant he once held in his arms.

Come here, Daddy. Listen.

Frankie gets up from the bench gets on his knees and puts his ear to the stone.

Can you hear it?

Sure enough, it seems to him, as he pretends to strain to hear, that a slight rhythm is in the rock.

I can hear it, says Frankie.

It's scary, says China, who is now standing at the edge of an arrangement of water fountains that spout from the ground adjacent to the sandpit. Toddlers immersing themselves squeal in delight at the shock.

No, says Frankie, softly. *It's nothing to be afraid of. It's nothing at all.*

Without warning, he crawls past China, on all fours and immerses himself in the icy drizzle. Several of the young children in the fountain point at him and laugh.

Daddy! What are you doing?

He stays under the water until his hair and clothes are soaked through. He finds he is shivering and then crying under the water jets. China stares at him, puzzled. Frankie beckons China in, and, after a moment's hesitation, she joins him, screaming delightedly as the water engulfs her too. Frankie smiles and takes China's hands and starts to sing what he can remember of 'Never Smile at a Crocodile' from *Peter Pan*. They jig slowly together around in a ragged circle, until he forgets the rest of the words. They finally separate and fall to the ground at the same time, laughing.

We're drowned! says China.

Not drowned, says Frankie.

What then? says China, shivering.

Baptized.

China looks puzzled, but she comes across to Frankie and sits on his lap, and hugs him to keep herself warm. Frankie feels the warmth of her body, and brings her closer. They rock back and forward, as the late afternoon light, too slowly to detect, stretches their shadows unstoppably towards the east.

Acknowledgements

Hospitality: Christina Ostrem and all at the Hotel Portixol, Palma de Mallorca, Kit and Penny Noble at Nonsuch House in Dartmouth.

Publishing: My editor Suzanne Baboneau and my agents Clare Alexander and Lesley Thorne, both of to whom I am deeply grateful for their loyalty, faith, hard work and imagination. Charlotte Knight, just for being so upstanding. And everyone at Simon & Schuster who has given their efforts, time and talent. Thank you.

Video games: David and Caroline Miller, Sean Brennan, Steven Poole, Graeme Struthers, Dan Pearson.

The London scene: Paul Gould, Michael McGrath and Peter Gordon.

Labour Party politics: Neil Nerva.

Therapy training: Cordelia Bradby.

Kyle Clark at Daniels Estate Agents, Kensal Rise, for helping me to understand the property market and proving to me once again that estate agents are much nicer than everybody thinks.

My children, Ruby, Cissy, Lydia and Esme, for living so patiently with my Johnny-head-in-the-air distractedness.

Also the several people I have inevitably forgotten. Thank you and forgive me.